WASTELANDS
STORIES OF THE APOCALYPSE

Also available from John Joseph Adams
and Titan Books

Dead Man's Hand: An Anthology of the Weird West
Wastelands 2: More Stories of the Apocalypse
(February 2015)

WASTELANDS

STORIES OF THE APOCALYPSE

EDITED BY
JOHN JOSEPH ADAMS

TITAN BOOKS

Wastelands: Stories of the Apocalypse
ISBN: 9781783291489

Published by Titan Books
A division of Titan Publishing Group Ltd
144 Southwark St, London SE1 0UP

First Titan Books edition: January 2015
6 8 10 9 7 5

This is a work of fiction. Names, places and incidents are either
products of the author's imagination or used fictitiously.
Any resemblance to actual persons, living or dead (except for
satirical purposes), is entirely coincidental.

"Introduction" © 2008 by John Joseph Adams. Appears for the first time
in this volume.
"The End of the Whole Mess" © 1986 by Stephen King. Originally
published in Omni, October 1986. Reprinted by permission of the
author.
"Salvage" © 1986 by Orson Scott Card. Originally published in
Isaac Asimov's Science Fiction Magazine, February 1986. Reprinted by
permission of the author.
"The People of Sand and Slag" © 2004 by Paolo Bacigalupi. Originally
published in The Magazine of Fantasy & Science Fiction, February 2004.
Reprinted by permission of the author.
"Bread and Bombs" © 2003 by Mary Rickert. Originally published in
The Magazine of Fantasy & Science Fiction, April 2003. Reprinted by
permission of the author.
"How We Got In Town and Out Again" © 1996 by Jonathan Lethem.
Originally published in Asimov's Science Fiction, September 1996.
Reprinted by permission of the author.
"Dark, Dark Were the Tunnels" © 1973 by George R. R. Martin.
Originally published in Vertex, December 1973. Reprinted by
permission of the author.
"Waiting for the Zephyr" © 2002 by Tobias S. Buckell. Originally
published in Land/Space, 2002. Reprinted by permission of the author.
"Never Despair" by Jack McDevitt © 1997 by Cryptic, Inc. Originally
published in Asimov's Science Fiction, April 1997. Reprinted by
permission of the author.
"When Sysadmins Ruled the Earth" © 2006 by Cory Doctorow.
Originally published in Jim Baen's Universe, August 2006. Reprinted by
permission of the author.
"The Last of the O-Forms" © 2002 by James Van Pelt. Originally
published in Asimov's Science Fiction, September 2002. Reprinted by
permission of the author.

"Still Life with Apocalypse" © 2002 by Richard Kadrey. Originally published in *The Infinite Matrix*, May 29, 2002. Reprinted by permission of the author.

"Artie's Angels" © 2001 by Catherine Wells Dimenstein. Originally published in *Realms of Fantasy*, December 2001. Reprinted by permission of the author.

"Judgment Passed" © 2008 by Jerry Oltion. Appears for the first time in this volume.

"Mute" © 2002 by Gene Wolfe. Originally published in *2002 World Horror Convention Program Book*. Reprinted by permission of the author and the author's agents, the Virginia Kidd Agency.

"Inertia" © 1990 by Nancy Kress. Originally published in *Analog Science Fiction & Fact*, January 1990. Reprinted by permission of the author.

"And the Deep Blue Sea" © 2005 by Elizabeth Bear. Originally published in *SCI FICTION*, May 4, 2005. Reprinted by permission of the author.

"Speech Sounds" © 1983 by Octavia E. Butler. Originally published in *Asimov's Science Fiction*, Mid-December 1983. Reprinted by permission of the estate of Octavia E. Butler.

"Killers" © 2006 by Carol Emshwiller. Originally published in *The Magazine of Fantasy & Science Fiction*, October/November 2006. Reprinted by permission of the author.

"Ginny Sweethips' Flying Circus" ©1988 by Neal Barrett, Jr. Originally published in *Asimov's Science Fiction*, February 1988. Reprinted by permission of the author.

"The End of the World as We Know It" © 2004 by Dale Bailey. Originally published in *The Magazine of Fantasy & Science Fiction*, October/November 2004. Reprinted by permission of the author.

"A Song Before Sunset" © 1976 by David Rowland Grigg. Originally published in *Beyond Tomorrow*, 1976. Reprinted by permission of the author.

"Episode Seven: Last Stand Against the Pack in the Kingdom of the Purple Flowers" © 2007 by John Langan. Originally published in *The Magazine of Fantasy & Science Fiction*, September 2007. Reprinted by permission of the author.

Visit our website:
www.titanbooks.com

No part of this publication may be reproduced, stored in a retrieval system, or transmitted, in any form or by any means without the prior written permission of the publisher, nor be otherwise circulated in any form of binding or cover other than that in which it is published and without a similar condition being imposed on the subsequent purchaser.

A CIP catalogue record for this title is available from the British Library.

Printed and bound in the USA.

CONTENTS

INTRODUCTION
BY JOHN JOSEPH ADAMS

Famine. Death. War. Pestilence. These are said to be the harbingers of the biblical apocalypse—Armageddon, The End of The World. In science fiction, the end of the world is usually triggered by more specific means: nuclear warfare, biological disaster (or warfare), ecological/geological disaster, or cosmological disaster. But in the wake of any great cataclysm, there are survivors—and post-apocalyptic science fiction speculates what life would be like for them.

The first significant post-apocalyptic work is *The Last Man* (1826), by the mother of science fiction—*Frankenstein* author Mary Shelley—so the sub-genre is in essence as old as science fiction itself. Although its origins are firmly rooted in science fiction, post-apocalyptic fiction has always been able to escape traditional genre boundaries. Several classic novels of the genre, such as *Alas, Babylon* by Pat Frank, *On the Beach* by Nevil Shute, and *Earth Abides* by George R. Stewart, were published as mainstream novels. That trend is seeing a resurgence, with authors like Cormac McCarthy venturing into post-apocalyptic territory with his bleak new novel *The Road*—which was not only a best-selling book and an Oprah Book Club pick, but a winner of the Pulitzer Prize as well.

But SF has produced its share of novel-length classics as well, including the undisputed king of the sub-genre, Walter Miller's *A Canticle for Leibowitz*. Not to mention Leigh Brackett's *The Long Tomorrow*, John Christopher's *No Blade of Grass*, or Wilson Tucker's criminally underappreciated *The Long Loud Silence*.

Post-apocalyptic SF first rose to prominence in the aftermath of World War II—no doubt due in large part to the world having witnessed the devastating destructive power of the atomic bomb—and reached the height of its popularity during the Cold War, when the threat of worldwide nuclear annihilation seemed a very real possibility.

But when the Berlin Wall fell, so did the popularity of post-apocalyptic fiction. If you examine the copyright page of this anthology, you'll note that just two of the stories in this volume were written in the '90s. On the other hand, more than half of these stories were originally published since the turn of the millennium. So why the resurgence? Is it because the political climate now is reminiscent of the climate during the Cold War? During times of war and global unease, is it that much easier to imagine a depopulated world, a world destroyed by humanity's own hand?

Is that all there is to it, or is there something more? What is it that draws us to those bleak landscapes—the wastelands of post-apocalyptic literature? To me, the appeal is obvious: it fulfills our taste for adventure, the thrill of discovery, the desire for a new frontier. It also allows us to start over from scratch, to wipe the slate clean and see what the world may have been like if we had known then what we know now.

Perhaps the appeal of the sub-genre is best described by this quote from "The Manhattan Phone Book (Abridged)" by John Varley:

> We all love after-the-bomb stories. If we didn't, why would there be so many of them? There's something attractive about all those people being gone, about wandering in a depopulated world, scrounging cans of Campbell's pork and beans, defending one's family from marauders. Sure it's horrible, sure we weep for all those dead people. But some secret part of us thinks it would be good to survive, to start over. Secretly, we know we'll survive. All those other folks will die. That's what after-the-bomb stories are all about.

Or is that just the beginning of the conversation? Read the stories, and you decide.

The stories in this volume go beyond the "wandering," "scrounging," and "defending" that Varley describes above. What you will find here are tales of survival and of life in the aftermath that explore what scientific, psychological, sociological, and physiological changes will take place in the wake of the apocalypse.

What you will *not* find here are tales depicting the

aftermath of aliens conquering the Earth, or the terror induced by a zombie uprising; both scenarios are suitably apocalyptic, but are subjects for another time (or other anthologies, as it were).

In the stories that follow, you will find twenty-two different science fictional apocalyptic scenarios. Some of them are far-fetched and unlikely, while others are plausible and all-too-easy to imagine. Some of the stories flirt with the fantastic. Many venture into horrific territory. All of them explore one question:

What would life be like after the end of the world as we know it?

THE END OF THE WHOLE MESS

BY STEPHEN KING

Stephen King needs no introduction. He is the award-winning, best-selling author of novels such as *Carrie* and the post-apocalyptic masterpiece *The Stand*. Although he is most well-known for his novels and the movies they've inspired, he is a prolific author of short fiction as well, having written enough of it to warrant several collections including: *Everything's Eventual*, *Night Shift*, *Skeleton Crew*, and *Nightmares & Dreamscapes*. "The End of the Whole Mess" appeared in the latter volume, but was originally published in *Omni* magazine in 1986. It was nominated for the World Fantasy Award, and was later adapted into a one-hour movie as part of a TNT *Nightmares & Dreamscapes* miniseries.

There are several factors that go into deciding which story to lead off an anthology with. You might pick a story that's by a high-profile contributor, one that's uncommonly good and packs a strong emotional punch, or one that will set the tone for the rest of the book; this story is all three.

I want to tell you about the end of war, the degeneration of mankind, and the death of the Messiah—an epic story, deserving thousands of pages and a whole shelf of volumes, but you (if there are any "you" later on to read this) will have to settle for the freeze-dried version. The direct injection works very fast. I figure I've got somewhere between forty-five minutes and two hours, depending on my blood-type. I think it's A, which should give me a little more time, but I'll be goddamned if I can remember for sure. If it turns out to be O, you could be in for a lot of blank pages, my hypothetical friend.

In any event, I think maybe I'd better assume the worst and go as fast as I can.

I'm using the electric typewriter—Bobby's word-processor is faster, but the genny's cycle is too irregular to be trusted, even with the line suppressor. I've only got one shot at this; I can't risk getting most of the way home and then seeing the whole thing go to data heaven because of an ohm drop, or a surge too great for the suppressor to cope with. My name is Howard Fornoy. I was a freelance writer. My brother, Robert Fornoy, was the Messiah. I killed him by shooting him up with his own discovery four hours ago. *He* called it The Calmative. A Very Serious Mistake might have been a better name, but what's done is done and can't be undone, as the Irish have been saying for centuries…which *proves* what assholes they are.

Shit, I can't afford these digressions.

After Bobby died I covered him with a quilt and sat

at the cabin's single living-room window for some three hours, looking out at the woods. Used to be you could see the orange glow of the hi-intensity arc-sodiums from North Conway, but no more. Now there's just the White Mountains, looking like dark triangles of crepe paper cut out by a child, and the pointless stars.

I turned on the radio, dialed through four bands, found one crazy guy, and shut it off. I sat there thinking of ways to tell this story. My mind kept sliding away toward all those miles of dark pinewoods, all that nothing. Finally I realized I needed to get myself off the dime and shoot myself up. Shit. I never *could* work without a deadline.

And I've sure-to-God got one now.

Our parents had no reason to expect anything other than what they got: bright children. Dad was a history major who had become a full professor at Hofstra when he was thirty. Ten years later he was one of six vice-administrators of the National Archives in Washington, D.C., and in line for the top spot. He was a helluva good guy, too—had every record Chuck Berry ever cut and played a pretty mean blues guitar himself. My dad filed by day and rocked by night.

Mom graduated magna cum laude from Drew. Got a Phi Beta Kappa key she sometimes wore on this funky fedora she had. She became a successful CPA in D.C., met my dad, married him, and took in her shingle when she became pregnant with yours truly. I came along in 1980. By '84 she was doing taxes for some of my dad's associates—she called this her "little hobby." By the time Bobby was born in 1987, she was handling taxes, investment portfolios, and estate-planning for a dozen powerful men. I could name them, but who gives a wad? They're either dead or driveling idiots by now.

I think she probably made more out of "her little hobby" each year than my dad made at his job, but that never mattered—they were happy with what they were to themselves and to each other. I saw them squabble lots of times, but I never saw them fight. When I was growing up, the only difference I saw between my mom and my playmates' moms was that their moms used to read or iron or sew or talk on the phone while the soaps played on the tube, and my mom used to run a pocket calculator and write down numbers on big green sheets of paper while the soaps played on the tube.

I was no disappointment to a couple of people with Mensa Gold Cards in their wallets. I maintained A's and B's through my public-school career (the idea that either I or my brother might go to a private school was never even discussed so far as I know). I also wrote well early, with no effort at all. I sold my first magazine piece when I was twenty—it was on how the Continental Army wintered at Valley Forge. I sold it to an airline magazine for four hundred fifty dollars. My dad, whom I loved deeply, asked me if he could buy that check from me. He gave me his own personal check and had the check from the airline magazine framed and hung it over his desk. A romantic genius, if you will. A romantic *blues-playing* genius, if you will. Take it from me, a kid could do a lot worse. Of course he and my mother both died raving and pissing in their pants late last year, like almost everyone else on this big round world of ours, but I never stopped loving either of them.

I was the sort of child they had every reason to

expect—a good boy with a bright mind, a talented boy whose talent grew to early maturity in an atmosphere of love and confidence, a faithful boy who loved and respected his mom and dad.

Bobby was different. *Nobody,* not even Mensa types like our folks, *ever* expects a kid like Bobby. Not *ever.*

I potty-trained two full years earlier than Bob, and that was the only thing in which I ever beat him. But I never felt jealous of him; that would have been like a fairly good American Legion League pitcher feeling jealous of Nolan Ryan or Roger Clemens. After a certain point the comparisons that cause feelings of jealousy simply cease to exist. I've been there, and I can tell you: after a certain point you just stand back and shield your eyes from the flashburns.

Bobby read at two and began writing short essays ("Our Dog," "A Trip to Boston with Mother") at three. His printing was the straggling, struggling galvanic constructions of a six-year-old, and that was startling enough in itself, but there was more: if transcribed so that his still-developing motor control no longer became an evaluative factor, you would have thought you were reading the work of a bright, if extremely naive, fifth-grader. He progressed from simple sentences to compound sentences to complex ones with dizzying rapidity, grasping clauses, sub-clauses, and modifying clauses with an intuitiveness that was eerie. Sometimes his syntax was garbled and his modifiers misplaced, but he had such flaws—which plague most writers all their lives—pretty well under control by the age of five.

He developed headaches. My parents were afraid he had

some sort of physical problem—a brain-tumor, perhaps—and took him to a doctor who examined him carefully, listened to him even more carefully, and then told my parents there was nothing wrong with Bobby except stress: he was in a state of extreme frustration because his writing-hand would not work as well as his brain.

"You got a kid trying to pass a mental kidney stone," the doctor said. "I could prescribe something for his headaches, but I think the drug he really needs is a typewriter." So Mom and Dad gave Bobby an IBM. A year later they gave him a Commodore 64 with WordStar for Christmas and Bobby's headaches stopped. Before going on to other matters, I only want to add that he believed for the next three years or so that it was Santa Claus who had left that word-cruncher under our tree. Now that I think of it, that was another place where I beat Bobby: I Santa-trained earlier, too.

There's so much I could tell you about those early days, and I suppose I'll have to tell you a little, but I'll have to go fast and make it brief. The deadline. Ah, the deadline. I once read a very funny piece called "The Essential *Gone with the Wind*" that went something like this:

"'A war?' laughed Scarlett. 'Oh, fiddle-de-dee!'

"Boom! Ashley went to war! Atlanta burned! Rhett walked in and then walked out!

"'Fiddle-de-dee,' said Scarlett through her tears, 'I will think about it tomorrow, for tomorrow is another day.'"

I laughed heartily over that when I read it; now that I'm faced with doing something similar, it doesn't seem quite so funny. But here goes:

"A child with an IQ immeasurable by any existing test?"

smiled India Fornoy to her devoted husband, Richard. "Fiddle-de-dee! We'll provide an atmosphere where his intellect—not to mention that of his not-exactly-stupid older brother—can grow. And we'll raise them as the normal all-American boys they by gosh are!"

Boom! The Fornoy boys grew up! Howard went to the University of Virginia, graduated cum laude, and settled down to a freelance writing career! Made a comfortable living! Stepped out with a lot of women and went to bed with quite a few of them! Managed to avoid social diseases both sexual and pharmacological! Bought a Mitsubishi stereo system! Wrote home at least once a week! Published two novels that did pretty well! "Fiddle-de-dee," said Howard, "this is the life for me!"

And so it was, at least until the day Bobby showed up unexpectedly (in the best mad-scientist tradition) with his two glass boxes, a bees' nest in one and a wasps' nest in the other, Bobby wearing a Mumford Phys Ed tee-shirt inside-out, on the verge of destroying human intellect and just as happy as a clam at high tide.

Guys like my brother Bobby come along only once every two or three generations, I think—guys like Leonardo da Vinci, Newton, Einstein, maybe Edison. They all seem to have one thing in common: they are like huge compasses which swing aimlessly for a long time, searching for some true north and then homing on it with fearful force. Before that happens such guys are apt to get up to some weird shit, and Bobby was no exception.

When he was eight and I was fifteen, he came to me and said he had invented an airplane. By then I knew Bobby too well to just say "Bullshit" and kick him out of my room. I went out to the garage, where there was this weird plywood contraption sitting on his American Flyer red wagon. It looked a little like a fighter plane, but the wings were raked forward instead of back. He had mounted the saddle from his rocking horse on the middle of it with bolts. There was a lever on the side. There was no motor. He said it was a glider. He wanted me to push him down Carrigan's Hill, which was the steepest grade in D.C.'s Grant Park—there was a cement path down the middle of it for old folks. That, Bobby said, would be his runway.

"Bobby," I said, "you got this puppy's wings on backward."

"No," he said. "This is the way they're supposed to be. I saw something on *Wild Kingdom* about hawks. They dive down on their prey and then reverse their wings coming up. They're double-jointed, see? You get better lift this way."

"Then why isn't the Air Force building them this way?" I asked, blissfully unaware that both the American and the Russian air forces had plans for such forward-wing fighter planes on their drawing boards.

Bobby just shrugged. He didn't know and didn't care.

We went over to Carrigan's Hill and he climbed into the rocking-horse saddle and gripped the lever. "Push me *hard*," he said. His eyes were dancing with that crazed light I knew so well—Christ, his eyes used to light up that way in his cradle sometimes. But I swear to God I never would have pushed him down the cement path as hard as I did if I thought the thing would actually work.

But I *didn't* know, and I gave him one hell of a shove. He went freewheeling down the hill, whooping like a cowboy just off a traildrive and headed into town for a few cold beers. An old lady had to jump out of his way, and he just missed an old geezer leaning over a walker. Halfway down he pulled the handle and I watched, wide-eyed and bullshit with fear and amazement, as his splintery plywood plane separated from the wagon. At first it only hovered inches above it, and for a second it looked like it was going to settle back. Then there was a gust of wind and Bobby's plane took off like someone had it on an invisible cable. The American Flyer wagon ran off the concrete path and into some bushes. All of a sudden Bobby was ten feet in the air, then twenty, then fifty. He went gliding over Grant Park on a steepening upward plane, whooping cheerily.

I went running after him, screaming for him to come down, visions of his body tumbling off that stupid rocking-horse saddle and impaling itself on a tree, or one of the park's many statues, standing out with hideous clarity in my head. I did not just imagine my brother's funeral; I tell you I *attended* it.

"*BOBBY!*" I shrieked. "*COME DOWN!*"

"*WHEEEEEEEE!*" Bobby screamed back, his voice faint but clearly ecstatic. Startled chess-players, Frisbee-throwers, book-readers, lovers, and joggers stopped whatever they were doing to watch.

"*BOBBY THERE'S NO SEATBELT ON THAT FUCKING THING.*'" I screamed. It was the first time I ever used that particular word, so far as I can remember.

"*Iyyyy'll beeee all riyyyyht…*" He was screaming at the top of his lungs, but I appalled to realize I could barely hear him. I went running down Carrigan's Hill, shrieking all the way. I don't have the slightest memory of just what I was yelling, but the next day I could not speak above a whisper. I *do* remember passing a young fellow in a neat three-piece suit standing by the statue of Eleanor Roosevelt at the foot of the hill. He looked at me and said conversationally, "Tell you what, my friend, I'm having one *hell* of an acid flashback."

I remember that odd misshapen shadow gliding across the green floor of the park, rising and rippling as it crossed park benches, litter baskets, and the upturned faces of the watching people. I remember chasing it. I remember how my mother's face crumpled and how she started to cry when I told her that Bobby's plane, which had no business flying in the first place, turned upside down in a sudden eddy of wind and Bobby finished his short but brilliant career splattered all over D Street.

The way things turned out, it might have been better for everyone if things had actually turned out that way, but they didn't.

Instead, Bobby banked back toward Carrigan's Hill, holding nonchalantly onto the tail of his own plane to keep from falling off the damned thing, and brought it down toward the little pond at the center of Grant Park. He went air-sliding five feet over it, then four…and then he was skiing his sneakers along the surface of the water, sending back twin white wakes, scaring the usually complacent (and overfed) ducks up in honking indignant flurries before him, laughing his cheerful laugh. He came down on the far side, exactly between two park benches that snapped off the wings of his plane. He flew out of the saddle, thumped his head, and started to bawl.

That was life with Bobby.

* * *

Not everything was that spectacular—in fact, I don't think *anything* was…at least until The Calmative. But I told you the story because I think, this time at least, the extreme case best illustrates the norm: life with Bobby was a constant mind-fuck. By the age of nine he was attending quantum physics and advanced algebra classes at Georgetown University. There was the day he blanked out every radio and TV on our street—and the surrounding four blocks—with his own voice; he had found an old portable TV in the attic and turned it into a wide-band radio broadcasting station. One old black-and-white Zenith, twelve feet of hi-fi flex, a coathanger mounted on the roofpeak of our house, and presto! For about two hours four blocks of Georgetown could receive only WBOB…which happened to be my brother, reading some of my short stories, telling moron jokes, and explaining that the high sulfur content in baked beans was the reason our dad farted so much in church every Sunday morning. "But he gets most of 'em off pretty quiet," Bobby told his listening audience of roughly three thousand, "or sometimes he holds the real bangers until it's time for the hymns."

My dad, who was less than happy about all this, ended up paying a seventy-five-dollar FCC fine and taking it out of Bobby's allowance for the next year.

Life with Bobby, oh yeah…and look here, I'm crying. Is it honest sentiment, I wonder, or the onset? The former, I think—Christ knows how much I loved him—but I think I better try to hurry up a little just the same.

Bobby had graduated high school, for all practical purposes, by the age of ten, but he never got a B.A. or B.S., let alone any advanced degree. It was that big powerful compass in his head, swinging around and around, looking for some true north to point at.

He went through a physics period, and a shorter period when he was nutty for chemistry...but in the end, Bobby was too impatient with mathematics for either of those fields to hold him. He could do it, but it—and ultimately all so-called hard science—bored him.

By the time he was fifteen, it was archaeology—he combed the White Mountain foothills around our summer place in North Conway, building a history of the Indians who had lived there from arrowheads, flints, even the charcoal patterns of long-dead campfires in the Mesolithic caves in the mid-New Hampshire regions.

But that passed, too, and he began to read history and anthropology. When he was sixteen my father and my mother gave their reluctant approval when Bobby requested that he be allowed to accompany a party of New England anthropologists on an expedition to South America.

He came back five months later with the first real tan of his life; he was also an inch taller, fifteen pounds lighter, and much quieter. He was still cheerful enough, or could be, but his little-boy exuberance, sometimes infectious, sometimes wearisome, but always there, was gone. He had grown up. And for the first time I remember him talking about the news...how bad it was, I mean. That was 2003, the year a PLO splinter group called the Sons of the Jihad (a name that always sounded to me hideously like a Catholic community service group somewhere in western Pennsylvania) set off a Squirt Bomb in London, polluting sixty per cent of it and making the rest of it extremely unhealthy for people who ever planned to have children (or to live past the age of fifty, for that matter). The year we tried to blockade the Philippines after the Cedeno administration accepted a "small group" of Red Chinese advisors (fifteen thousand or so, according to our spy satellites), and only backed down when it became clear that (a) the Chinese weren't kidding about emptying the holes if we didn't pull back, and (b) the American people weren't all that crazy about committing mass suicide over the Philippine Islands. That was also the year some other group of crazy motherfuckers—Albanians, I think—tried to air-spray the AIDS virus over Berlin.

This sort of stuff depressed everybody, but it depressed the *shit* out of Bobby.

"Why are people so goddam mean?" he asked me one day. We were at the summer place in New Hampshire, it was late August, and most of our stuff was already in boxes and suitcases. The cabin had that sad, deserted look it always got just before we all went our separate ways. For me it meant back to New York, and for Bobby it meant Waco, Texas, of all places…he had spent the summer reading sociology and geology texts—how's that for a crazy salad?—and said he wanted to run a couple of experiments down there. He said it in a casual, offhand way, but I had seen my mother looking at him with a peculiar thoughtful scrutiny in the last couple of weeks we were all together. Neither Dad nor I suspected, but I think my mom knew that Bobby's compass needle had finally stopped swinging and had started pointing.

"Why are they so mean?" I asked. "I'm supposed to answer that?"

"*Someone* better," he said. "Pretty soon, too, the way things are going."

"They're going the way they always went," I said, "and I guess they're doing it because people were built to be mean. If you want to lay blame, blame God."

"That's bullshit. I don't believe it. Even that double-X-chromosome stuff turned out to be bullshit in the end. And don't tell me it's just economic pressures, the conflict between the haves and have-nots, because that doesn't explain all of it, either."

"Original sin," I said. "It works for me—it's got a good beat and you can dance to it."

"Well," Bobby said, "maybe it *is* original sin. But what's the instrument, big brother? Have you ever asked yourself that?"

"Instrument? What instrument? I'm not following you."

"I think it's the water," Bobby said moodily.

"Say *what?*"

"The water. Something in the water."

He looked at me.

"Or something that *isn't*."

The next day Bobby went off to Waco. I didn't see him again until he showed up at my apartment wearing the inside-out Mumford shirt and carrying the two glass boxes. That was three years later.

"Howdy, Howie," he said, stepping in and giving me a nonchalant swat on the back as if it had been only three days.

"Bobby!" I yelled, and threw both arms around him in a bear-hug. Hard angles bit into my chest, and I heard an angry hive-hum.

"I'm glad to see you too," Bobby said, "but you better go easy. You're upsetting the natives."

I stepped back in a hurry. Bobby set down the big paper bag he was carrying and unslung his shoulder-bag. Then he carefully brought the glass boxes out of the bag. There was a beehive in one, a wasps' nest in the other. The bees were already settling down and going back to whatever business bees have, but the wasps were clearly unhappy about the whole thing.

"Okay, Bobby," I said. I looked at him and grinned. I couldn't seem to stop grinning. "What are you up to this time?"

He unzipped the tote-bag and brought out a mayonnaise jar which was half-filled with a clear liquid.

"See this?" he said.

"Yeah. Looks like either water or white lightning."

"It's actually both, if you can believe that. It came from an artesian well in La Plata, a little town forty miles east of Waco, and before I turned it into this concentrated form, there were five gallons of it. I've got a regular little distillery running down there, Howie, but I don't think the government will ever bust me for it." He was grinning, and now the grin broadened. "Water's all it is, but it's still the goddamndist popskull the human race has ever seen."

"I don't have the slightest idea what you're talking about."

"I know you don't. But you will. You know what, Howie?"

"What?"

"If the idiotic human race can manage to hold itself together for another six months, I'm betting it'll hold itself together for all time."

He lifted the mayonnaise jar, and one magnified Bobby-eye stared at me through it with huge solemnity. "This is the big one," he said. "The cure for the worst disease to which *Homo sapiens* falls prey."

"Cancer?"

"Nope," Bobby said. "War. Barroom brawls. Drive-by shootings. The whole mess. Where's your bathroom, Howie? My back teeth are floating."

When he came back he had not only turned the Mumford tee-shirt right-side out, he had combed his hair—nor had his method of doing this changed, I saw. Bobby just held his head under the faucet for awhile then raked everything back with his fingers.

He looked at the two glass boxes and pronounced the bees and wasps back to normal. "Not that a wasps' nest ever approaches anything even closely resembling 'normal,' Howie. Wasps are social insects, like bees and ants, but unlike bees, which are almost always sane, and ants, which have occasional schizoid lapses, wasps are total full-bore lunatics." He smiled. "Just like us good old *Homo saps*." He took the top off the glass box containing the beehive.

"Tell you what, Bobby," I said. I was smiling, but the smile felt much too wide. "Put the top back on and just *tell me* about it, what do you say? Save the demonstration for later. I mean, my landlord's a real pussycat, but the super's this big bull dyke who smokes Odie Perode cigars and has thirty pounds on me. She—"

"You'll like this," Bobby said, as if I hadn't spoken at all—a habit as familiar to me as his Ten Fingers Method of Hair Grooming. He was never impolite but often totally absorbed. And could I stop him? Aw shit, no. It was too good to have him back. I mean I think I knew even then that something was going to go totally wrong, but when I was with Bobby for more than five minutes, he just hypnotized me. He was Lucy holding the football and promising me this time *for sure,* and I was Charlie Brown, rushing down the field to kick it. "In fact, you've probably seen it done before—they show pictures of it in magazines from time to time, or in TV wildlife documentaries. It's nothing very special, but it *looks* like a big deal because people have got these totally irrational prejudices about bees."

And the weird thing was, he was right—I *had* seen it before.

He stuck his hand into the box between the hive and the glass. In less than fifteen seconds his hand had acquired a living black-and-yellow glove. It brought back an instant of total recall: sitting in front of the TV, wearing footie pajamas and clutching my Paddington Bear, maybe half an hour before bedtime (and surely years before Bobby was born), watching with mingled horror, disgust, and fascination as some beekeeper allowed bees to cover his entire face. They had formed a sort of executioner's hood at first, and then he had brushed them into a grotesque living beard.

Bobby winced suddenly, sharply, then grinned.

"One of 'em stung me," he said. "They're still a little upset from the trip. I hooked a ride with the local insurance lady from La Plata to Waco—she's got an old Piper Cub—and flew some little commuter airline, Air Asshole, I think it was, up to New Orleans from there. Made about forty connections, but I swear to God it was the cab ride from LaGarbage that got 'em crazy. Second Avenue's still got more potholes than the Bergenstrasse after the Germans surrendered."

"You know, I think you really ought to get your hand out of there, Bobs," I said. I kept waiting for some of them to fly out—I could imagine chasing them around with a rolled-up magazine for hours, bringing them down one by one, as if they were escapees in some old prison movie. But none of them had escaped…at least so far.

"Relax, Howie. You ever see a bee sting a flower? Or even hear of it, for that matter?"

"You don't look like a flower."

He laughed. "Shit, you think *bees* know what a flower looks like? Un-uh! No way, man! They don't know what a flower looks like any more than you or I know what a cloud sounds like. They know I'm sweet because I excrete sucrose dioxin in my sweat…along with thirty-seven other dioxins, and those're just the ones we know about."

He paused thoughtfully.

"Although I must confess I *was* careful to, uh, sweeten myself up a little tonight. Ate a box of chocolate-covered cherries on the plane—"

"Oh Bobby, Jesus!"

"—and had a couple of MallowCremes in the taxi coming here."

He reached in with his other hand and carefully began to brush the bees away. I saw him wince once more just before he got the last of them off, and then he eased my mind considerably by replacing the lid on the glass box. I saw a red swelling on each of his hands: one in the cup of the left palm, another high up on the right, near what the palmists call the Bracelets of Fortune. He'd been stung, but I saw well enough what he'd set out to show me: what looked like at least four hundred bees had investigated him. Only two had stung.

He took a pair of tweezers out of his jeans watch-pocket, and went over to my desk. He moved the pile of manuscript beside the Wang Micro I was using in those days and trained my Tensor lamp on the place where the pages had been—fiddling with it until it formed a tiny hard spotlight on the cherrywood.

"Writin' anything good, Bow-Wow?" he asked casually, and I felt the hair stiffen on the back of my neck. When was the last time he'd called me Bow-Wow? When he was four? Six? Shit, man, I don't know. He was working carefully on his left hand with the tweezers. I saw him extract a tiny something that looked like a nostril hair and place it in my ashtray.

"Piece on art forgery for *Vanity Fair*," I said. "Bobby, what in hell are you up to this time?"

"You want to pull the other one for me?" he asked, offering me the tweezers, his right hand, and an apologetic smile. "I keep thinking if I'm so goddam smart I ought to be ambidextrous, but my left hand has still got an IQ of about six."

Same old Bobby.

I sat down beside him, took the tweezers, and pulled the bee stinger out of the red swelling near what in his case should have been the Bracelets of Doom, and while I did it he told me about the differences between bees and wasps, the difference between the water in La Plata and the water in New York, and how, goddam! everything was going to be all right with his water and a little help from me.

And oh shit, I ended up running at the football while my laughing, wildly intelligent brother held it, one last time.

* * *

"Bees don't sting unless they have to, because it kills them," Bobby said matter-of-factly. "You remember that time in North Conway, when you said we kept killing each other because of original sin?"

"Yes. Hold still."

"Well, if there *is* such a thing, if there's a God who could simultaneously love us enough to serve us His own Son on a cross and send us all on a rocket-sled to hell just because one stupid bitch bit a bad apple, then the curse was just this: He made us like wasps instead of bees. *Shit,* Howie, what are you doing?"

"Hold still," I said, "and I'll get it out. If you want to make a lot of big gestures, I'll wait."

"Okay," he said, and after that he held relatively still while I extracted the stinger. "Bees are nature's kamikaze pilots, Bow-Wow. Look in that glass box, you'll see the two who stung me lying dead at the bottom. Their stingers are barbed, like fishhooks. They slide in easy. When they pull out, they disembowel themselves."

"Gross," I said, dropping the second stinger in the ashtray. I couldn't see the barbs, but I didn't have a microscope.

"It makes them particular, though," he said.

"I bet."

"Wasps, on the other hand, have smooth stingers. They can shoot you up as many times as they like. They use up the poison by the third or fourth shot, but they can go right on making holes if they like...and usually they do. Especially wall-wasps. The kind I've got over there. You gotta sedate 'em. Stuff called Noxon. It must give 'em a hell of a hangover, because they wake up madder than ever."

He looked at me somberly, and for the first time I saw the dark brown wheels of weariness under his eyes and realized my kid brother was more tired than I had ever seen him.

"*That's* why people go on fighting, Bow-Wow. On and on and on. We got smooth stingers. Now watch this."

He got up, went over to his tote-bag, rummaged in it, and came up with an eye-dropper. He opened the mayonnaise jar, put the dropper in, and drew up a tiny bubble of his distilled Texas water.

When he took it over to the glass box with the wasps' nest inside, I saw the top on this one was different—there was a tiny plastic slide-piece set into it. I didn't need him to draw me a picture: with the bees, he was perfectly willing to remove the whole top. With the wasps, he was taking no chances.

He squeezed the black bulb. Two drops of water fell onto the nest, making a momentary dark spot that disappeared almost at once. "Give it about three minutes," he said.

"What—"

"No questions," he said. "You'll see. Three minutes."

In that period, he read my piece on art forgery... although it was already twenty pages long.

"Okay," he said, putting the pages down. "That's pretty good, man. You ought to read up a little on how Jay Gould furnished the parlor-car of his private train with fake Manets, though—that's a hoot." He was removing the cover of the glass box containing the wasps' nest as he spoke.

"Jesus, Bobby, cut the comedy!" I yelled.

"Same old wimp," Bobby laughed, and pulled the nest, which was dull gray and about the size of a bowling ball, out of the box. He held it in his hands. Wasps flew out and lit on his arms, his cheeks, his forehead. One flew across to me and landed on my forearm. I slapped it and it fell dead to the carpet. I was scared—I mean really scared. My body was wired with adrenaline and I could feel my eyes trying to push their way out of their sockets.

"Don't kill 'em," Bobby said. "You might as well be killing babies, for all the harm they can do you. That's the whole *point*." He tossed the nest from hand to hand as if it were an overgrown softball. He lobbed it in the air. I watched, horrified, as wasps cruised the living room of my apartment like fighter planes on patrol.

Bobby lowered the nest carefully back into the box and sat down on my couch. He patted the place next to him and I went over, nearly hypnotized. They were everywhere: on the rug, the ceiling, the drapes. Half a dozen of them were crawling across the front of my big-screen TV.

Before I could sit down, he brushed away a couple that were on the sofa cushion where my ass was aimed. They flew away quickly. They were *all* flying easily, crawling easily, moving fast. There was nothing drugged about their behavior. As Bobby talked, they gradually found their way back to their spit-paper home, crawled over it, and eventually disappeared inside again through the hole in the top.

"I wasn't the first one to get interested in Waco," he said. "It just happens to be the biggest town in the funny little nonviolent section of what is, per capita, the most violent state in the union. Texans *love* to shoot each other, Howie—I mean, it's like a state hobby. Half the male population goes around armed. Saturday night in the Fort Worth bars is like a shooting gallery where you get to plonk away at drunks instead of clay ducks. There are more NRA card-carriers than there are Methodists. Not that Texas is the only place where people shoot each other, or carve each other up with straight-razors, or stick their kids in the oven if they cry too long, you understand, but they sure do like their firearms."

"Except in Waco," I said.

"Oh, they like 'em there, too," he said. "It's just that they use 'em on each other a hell of a lot less often."

Jesus. I just looked up at the clock and saw the time. It feels like I've been writing for fifteen minutes or so, but it's actually been over an hour. That happens to me sometimes when I'm running at white-hot speed, but I can't allow myself to be seduced into these specifics. I feel as well as ever—no noticeable drying of the membranes in the throat, no groping for words, and as I glance back over what I've done I see only the normal typos and strike-overs. But I can't kid myself. I've got to hurry up. "Fiddle-de-dee," said Scarlett, and all of that.

The nonviolent atmosphere of the Waco area had been noticed and investigated before, mostly by sociologists. Bobby said that when you fed enough statistical data on Waco and similar areas into a computer—population density, mean age, mean economic level, mean educational level, and dozens of other factors—what you got back was a whopper of an anomaly. Scholarly papers are rarely jocular, but even so, several of the better than fifty Bobby had read on the subject suggested ironically that maybe it was "something in the water."

"I decided maybe it was time to take the joke seriously," Bobby said. "After all, there's something in the water of a lot of places that prevents tooth decay. It's called fluoride."

He went to Waco accompanied by a trio of research assistants: two sociology grad-students and a full professor of geology who happened to be on sabbatical and ready for adventure. Within six months, Bobby and the sociology guys had constructed a computer program which illustrated what my brother called the world's only calmquake. He had a slightly rumpled printout in his tote. He gave it to me. I was looking at a series of forty concentric rings. Waco was in the eighth, ninth, and tenth as you moved in toward the center.

"Now look at this," he said, and put a transparent overlay on the printout. More rings; but in each one there was a number. Fortieth ring: 471. Thirty-ninth: 420. Thirty-eighth: 418. And so on. In a couple of places the numbers went up instead of down, but only in a couple (and only by a little).

"What are they?"

"Each number represents the incidence of violent crime in that particular circle," Bobby said. "Murder, rape, assault and battery, even acts of vandalism. The computer assigns a number by a formula that takes population density into account." He tapped the twenty-seventh circle, which held the number 204, with his finger. "There's less than nine hundred people in this whole area, for instance. The number represents three or four cases of spouse abuse, a couple of barroom brawls, an act of animal cruelty—some senile farmer got pissed at a pig and shot a load of rock-salt into it, as I recall—and one involuntary manslaughter."

I saw that the numbers in the central circles dropped off radically: 85, 81, 70, 63, 40, 21, 5. At the epicenter of

Bobby's calmquake was the town of La Plata. To call it a sleepy little town seems more than fair.

The numeric value assigned to La Plata was zero.

"So here it is, Bow-Wow," Bobby said, leaning forward and rubbing his long hands together nervously, "my nominee for the Garden of Eden. Here's a community of fifteen thousand, twenty-four per cent of which are people of mixed blood, commonly called Indios. There's a moccasin factory, a couple of little motor courts, a couple of scrub farms. That's it for work. For play there's four bars, a couple of dance-halls where you can hear any kind of music you want as long as it sounds like George Jones, two drive-ins, and a bowling alley." He paused and added, "There's also a still. I didn't know anybody made whiskey that good outside of Tennessee."

In short (and it is now too late to be anything else), La Plata should have been a fertile breeding-ground for the sort of casual violence you can read about in the Police Blotter section of the local newspaper every day. Should have been but wasn't. There had been only one murder in La Plata during the five years previous to my brother's arrival, two cases of assault, no rapes, no reported incidents of child abuse. There had been four armed robberies, but all four turned out to have been committed by transients...as the murder and one of the assaults had been. The local Sheriff was a fat old Republican who did a pretty fair Rodney Dangerfield imitation. He had been known, in fact, to spend whole days in the local coffee shop, tugging the knot in his tie and telling people to take his wife, please. My brother said he thought it was a little more than lame humor; he was pretty sure the poor guy was suffering first-stage

Alzheimer's Disease. His only deputy was his nephew. Bobby told me the nephew looked quite a lot like Junior Samples on the old *Hee-Haw* show.

"Put those two guys in a Pennsylvania town similar to La Plata in every way but the geographical," Bobby said, "and they would have been out on their asses fifteen years ago. But in La Plata, they're gonna go on until they die… which they'll probably do in their sleep."

"What did you do?" I asked. "How did you proceed?"

"Well, for the first week or so after we got our statistical shit together, we just sort of sat around and stared at each other," Bobby said. "I mean, we were prepared for *something*, but nothing quite like this. Even Waco doesn't prepare you for La Plata." Bobby shifted restlessly and cracked his knuckles.

"Jesus, I hate it when you do that," I said.

He smiled. "Sorry, Bow-Wow. Anyway, we started geological tests, then microscopic analysis of the water. I didn't expect a hell of a lot; everyone in the area has got a well, usually a deep one, and they get their water tested regularly to make sure they're not drinking borax, or something. If there had been something obvious, it would have turned up a long time ago. So we went on to submicroscopy, and that was when we started to turn up some pretty weird stuff."

"What kind of weird stuff?"

"Breaks in chains of atoms, subdynamic electrical fluctuations, and some sort of unidentified protein. Water ain't really H_2O, you know—not when you add in the sulfides, irons, God knows what else happens to be in the aquifer of a given region. And La Plata water—you'd have to give it a string of letters like the ones after a professor emeritus's name." His eyes gleamed. "But the protein was the most interesting thing, Bow-Wow. So far as we know, it's only found in one other place: the human brain."

Uh-oh.

It just arrived, between one swallow and the next: the throat-dryness. Not much as yet, but enough for me to break away and get a glass of ice-water. I've got maybe forty minutes left. And oh Jesus, there's so much I want to tell! About the wasps' nests they found with wasps that wouldn't sting, about the fender-bender Bobby and one of his assistants saw where the two drivers, both male, both drunk, and both about twenty-four (sociological bull moose, in other words), got out, shook hands, and exchanged insurance information amicably before going into the nearest bar for another drink.

Bobby talked for hours—more hours than I have. But the upshot was simple: the stuff in the mayonnaise jar.

"We've got our own still in La Plata now," he said. "This is the stuff we're brewing, Howie; pacifist white lightning. The aquifer under that area of Texas is deep but amazingly large; it's like this incredible Lake Victoria driven into the porous sediment which overlays the Moho. The water is potent, but we've been able to make the stuff I squirted on the wasps even more potent. We've got damn near six thousand gallons now, in these big steel tanks. By the end of the year, we'll have fourteen thousand. By next June we'll have thirty thousand. But it's not enough. We need more, we need it faster...and then we need to transport it."

"Transport it where?" I asked him.

"Borneo, to start with."

I thought I'd either lost my mind or misheard him. I really did.

"Look, Bow-Wow…sorry. Howie." He was scrumming through his tote-bag again. He brought out a number of aerial photographs and handed them over to me. "You see?" he asked as I looked through them. "You see how fucking perfect it is? It's as if God Himself suddenly busted through our business-as-usual transmissions with something like 'And now we bring you a special bulletin! This is your last chance, assholes! And now we return you to *Days of Our Lives.*'"

"I don't get you," I said. "And I have no idea what I'm looking at." Of course I knew; it was an island—not Borneo itself but an island lying to the west of Borneo identified as Gulandio—with a mountain in the middle and a lot of muddy little villages lying on its lower slopes. It was hard to see the mountain because of the cloud cover. What I meant was that I didn't know what I was looking *for.*

"The mountain has the same name as the island," he said. "Gulandio. In the local patois it means *grace,* or *fate,* or *destiny,* or take your pick. But Duke Rogers says it's really the biggest time-bomb on earth…and it's wired to go off by October of next year. Probably earlier."

The crazy thing's this: the story's only crazy if you try to tell it in a speed-rap, which is what I'm trying to do now. Bobby wanted me to help him raise somewhere between six hundred thousand and a million and a half dollars to do the following: first, to synthesize fifty to seventy thousand gallons of what he called "the high-test"; second, to airlift all of this water to Borneo, which had landing facilities (you could land a hang-glider on Gulandio, but that was about all); third, to ship it over to this island named Fate, or Destiny, or Grace; fourth, to truck it up the slope of the volcano, which had been dormant (save for a few puffs in 1938) since 1804, and then to drop it down the muddy tube of the volcano's caldera. Duke Rogers was actually John Paul Rogers, the geology professor. He claimed that Gulandio was going to do more than just erupt; he claimed that it was going to explode, as Krakatoa had done in the nineteenth century, creating a bang that would make the Squirt Bomb that poisoned London look like a kid's firecracker.

The debris from the Krakatoa blow-up, Bobby told me, had literally encircled the globe; the observed results had formed an important part of the Sagan Group's nuclear winter theory. For three months afterward sunsets and sunrises half a world away had been grotesquely colorful as a result of the ash whirling around in both the jet stream and the Van Allen Currents, which lie forty miles below the Van Allen Belt. There had been global changes in climate which lasted five years, and nipa palms, which previously had grown only in eastern Africa and Micronesia, suddenly showed up in both South and North America.

"The North American nipas all died before 1900," Bobby said, "but they're alive and well below the equator. Krakatoa seeded them there, Howie…the way I want to seed La Plata water all over the earth. I want people to go out in La Plata water when it rains—and it's going to rain a lot after Gulandio goes bang. I want them to drink the La Plata water that falls in their reservoirs, I want them to wash their hair in it, bathe in it, soak their contact lenses in it. I want whores to *douche* in it."

"Bobby," I said, knowing he was not, "you're crazy."

He gave me a crooked, tired grin. "I ain't crazy," he said. "You want to see crazy? Turn on CNN, Bow...Howie. You'll see crazy in living color."

But I didn't need to turn on Cable News (what a friend of mine had taken to calling The Organ-Grinder of Doom) to know what Bobby was talking about. The Indians and the Pakistanis were poised on the brink. The Chinese and the Afghans, ditto. Half of Africa was starving, the other half on fire with AIDS. There had been border skirmishes along the entire Tex-Mex border in the last five years, since Mexico went Communist, and people had started calling the Tijuana crossing point in California Little Berlin because of the wall. The saber-rattling had become a din. On the last day of the old year the Scientists for Nuclear Responsibility had set their black clock to fifteen seconds before midnight.

"Bobby, let's suppose it could be done and everything went according to schedule," I said. "It probably couldn't and wouldn't, but let's suppose. You don't have the slightest idea what the long-term effects might be."

He started to say something and I waved it away.

"Don't even suggest that you do, because you don't! You've had time to find this calmquake of yours and isolate the cause, I'll give you that. But did you ever hear about thalidomide? That nifty little acne-stopper and sleeping pill that caused cancer and heart attacks in thirty-year-olds? Don't you remember the AIDS vaccine in 1997?"

"Howie?"

"*That* one stopped the disease, except it turned the test

subjects into incurable epileptics who all died within eighteen months."

"Howie?"

"Then there was—"

"Howie?"

I stopped and looked at him.

"The world," Bobby said, and then stopped. His throat worked. I saw he was struggling with tears. "The world needs heroic measures, man. I don't know about long-term effects, and there's no time to study them, because there's no long-term prospect. Maybe we can cure the whole mess. Or maybe—"

He shrugged, tried to smile, and looked at me with shining eyes from which two single tears slowly tracked.

"Or maybe we're giving heroin to a patient with terminal cancer. Either way, it'll stop what's happening now. It'll end the world's pain." He spread out his hands, palms up, so I could see the stings on them. "Help me, Bow-Wow. Please help me."

So I helped him.

And we fucked up. In fact I think you could say we fucked up big-time. And do you want the truth? I don't give a shit. We killed all the plants, but at least we saved the greenhouse. Something will grow here again, someday. I hope.

Are you reading this?

My gears are starting to get a little sticky. For the first time in years I'm having to think about what I'm doing. The motor-movements of writing. Should have hurried more at the start.

Never mind. Too late to change things now.

We did it, of course: distilled the water, flew it in, transported it to Gulandio, built a primitive lifting system—half motor-winch and half cog railway—up the side of the volcano, and dropped over twelve thousand five-gallon containers of La Plata water—the brain-buster version—into the murky misty depths of the volcano's caldera. We did all of this in just eight months. It didn't cost six hundred thousand dollars, or a million and a half; it cost over four million, still less than a sixteenth of one per cent of what America spent on defense that year. You want to know how we razed it? I'd tell you if I had more thyme, but my head's falling apart so never mend. I raised most of it myself if it matters to you. Some by hoof and some by croof. Tell you the truth, I din't know I could do it muself until I did. But we did it and somehow the world held together and that volcano—whatever its name wuz, I can't exactly remember now and there izzunt time to go back over the manuscript—it blue just when it was spo

Wait

Okay. A little better. Digitalin. Bobby had it. Heart's beating like crazy but I can think again.

The volcano—Mount Grace, we called it—blue just when Dook Rogers said it would. Everything when skihi and for awhile everyone's attention turned away from whatever and toward the skys. And bimmel-dee-dee, said Strapless!

It happened pretty fast like sex and checks and special effex and everybody got healthy again. I mean

wait

* * *

Jesus please let me finish this.

I mean that everybody stood down. Everybody started to get a little purstective on the situation. The wurld started to get like the wasps in Bobbys nest the one he showed me where they didn't stink too much. There was three yerz like an Indian sumer. People getting together like in that old Youngbloods song that went cmon everybody get together rite now, like what all the hippeez wanted, you no, peets and luv and

wt

Big blast. Feel like my heart is coming out thru my ears. But if I concentrate every bit of my force, my *concentration—*

It was like an Indian summer, that's what I meant to say, like three years of Indian summer. Bobby went on with his resurch. La Plata. Sociological background etc. You remember the local Sheriff? Fat old Republican with a good Rodney Youngblood imitashun? How Bobby said he had the preliminary simptoms of Rodney's Disease?

concentrate asshole

Wasn't just him; turned out like there was a lot of that going around in that part of Texas. All's Hallows Disease is what I meen. For three yerz me and Bobby were down there. Created a new program. New graff of circkles. I saw what was happen and came back here. Bobby and his to asistants stayed on. One shot hisself Boby said when he showed up here. Wait one more blas

All right. Last time. Heart beating so fast I can hardly

breeve. The new graph, the *last* graph, really only whammed you when it was laid over the calmquake graft. The calmquake graff showed ax of vilence going down as you approached La Plata in the muddle; the Alzheimer's graff showed incidence of premature seenullity going *up* as you approached La Plata. People there were getting very silly very yung.

Me and Bobo were careful as we could be for next three years, drink only Parrier Water and wor big long sleekers in the ran. so no war and when everybobby started to get seely we din and I came back here because he my brother I cant remember what his name

Bobby

Bobby when he came here tonight cryeen and I sed Bobby I luv you Bobby sed Ime sorry Bowwow Ime sorry I made the hole world ful of foals and dumbbels and I sed better fouls and bells than a big black sinder in spaz and he cryed and I cryed Bobby I luv you and he sed will you give me a shot of the spacial wadder and I sed yez and he said wil you ride it down and I sed yez an I think I did but I cant reely remember I see wurds but dont no what they mean

I have a Bobby his nayme is bruther and I theen I an dun riding and I have a bocks to put this into thats Bobby sd full of quiyet air to last a milyun yrz so gudboy gudboy every-brother, Im goin to stob gudboy bobby i love you it wuz not yor falt i love you

forgivyu

love yu

sinned (for the wurld),

BOWWOW FORNOY

SALVAGE

BY ORSON SCOTT CARD

Orson Scott Card is the best-selling author of *Ender's Game*, which was a winner of both the Hugo and Nebula Awards. The sequel to *Ender's Game*, *Speaker for the Dead*, also won both awards, making Card the only author to have captured the field's two most coveted prizes in consecutive years. Card is also the winner of the World Fantasy Award, eight Locus Awards, and a slew of other honors.

In addition to *Ender's Game* and the other books in the Enderverse, Card is the author of dozens of other novels, including the books in the *Tales of Alvin Maker* saga and the *Homecoming* series. He has also published more than eighty short stories, which have been collected in several volumes, most notably in *Maps in a Mirror* and *Keeper of Dreams*.

"Salvage" was one of the first stories in which Card openly

explored his religion, and was among his first forays into post-apocalyptic SF. This tale, one of Card's "Mormon Sea" stories, originally appeared in *Isaac Asimov's Science Fiction Magazine* and was later included in *Folk of the Fringe*, a collection of stories set in the post-apocalyptic state of Deseret. There, on the shores of a flooded Great Salt Lake, the remnants of a ruined civilization rely on their faith—and each other—to carry on and rebuild...

The road began to climb steeply right from the ferry, so the truck couldn't build up any speed. Deaver just kept shifting down, wincing as he listened to the grinding of the gears. Sounded like the transmission was chewing itself to gravel. He'd been nursing it all the way across Nevada, and if the Wendover ferry hadn't carried him these last miles over the Mormon Sea, he would have had a nice long hike. Lucky. It was a good sign. Things were going to go Deaver's way for a while.

The mechanic frowned at him when he rattled in to the loading dock. "You been ridin the clutch, boy?"

Deaver got down from the cab. "Clutch? What's a clutch?"

The mechanic didn't smile. "Couldn't you hear the transmission was shot?"

"I had mechanics all the way across Nevada askin to fix it for me, but I told em I was savin it for you."

The mechanic looked at him like he was crazy. "There ain't no mechanics in Nevada."

If you wasn't dumb as your thumb, thought Deaver, you'd know I was joking. These old Mormons were so straight they couldn't sit down, some of them. But Deaver didn't say anything. Just smiled.

"This truck's gonna stay here a few days," said the mechanic.

Fine with me, thought Deaver. I got plans. "How many days you figure?"

"Take three for now, I'll sign you off."

"My name's Deaver Teague."

"Tell the foreman, he'll write it up." The mechanic lifted the hood to begin the routine checks while the dockboys loaded off the old washing machines and refrigerators and other stuff Deaver had picked up on this trip. Deaver took his mileage reading to the window and the foreman paid him off.

Seven dollars for five days of driving and loading, sleeping in the cab and eating whatever the farmers could spare. It was better than a lot of people lived on, but there wasn't any future in it. Salvage wouldn't go on forever. Someday he'd pick up the last broken-down dishwasher left from the old days, and then he'd be out of a job.

Well, Deaver Teague wasn't going to wait around for that. He knew where the gold was, he'd been planning how to get it for weeks, and if Lehi had got the diving equipment like he promised then tomorrow morning they'd do a little freelance salvage work. If they were lucky they'd come home rich.

Deaver's legs were stiff but he loosened them up pretty quick and broke into an easy, loping run down the corridors of the Salvage Center. He took a flight of stairs two or three steps at a time, bounded down a hall, and when he reached a sign that said SMALL COMPUTER SALVAGE, he pushed off the doorframe and rebounded into the room. "Hey Lehi!" he said. "Hey it's quittin time!"

Lehi McKay paid no attention. He was sitting in front

of a TV screen, jerking at a black box he held on his lap.

"You do that and you'll go blind," said Deaver.

"Shut up, carpface." Lehi never took his eyes off the screen. He jabbed at a button on the black box and twisted on the stick that jutted up from it. A colored blob on the screen blew up and split into four smaller blobs.

"I got three days off while they do the transmission on the truck," said Deaver. "So tomorrow's the temple expedition."

Lehi got the last blob off the screen. More blobs appeared.

"That's real fun," said Deaver, "like sweepin the street and then they bring along another troop of horses."

"It's an Atari. From the sixties or seventies or something. Eighties. Old. Can't do much with the pieces, it's only eight-bit stuff. All these years in somebody's attic in Logan, and the sucker still runs."

"Old guys probably didn't even know they had it."

"Probably."

Deaver watched the game. Same thing over and over again. "How much a thing like this use to cost?"

"A lot. Maybe fifteen, twenty bucks."

"Makes you want to barf. And here sits Lehi McKay, toodling his noodle like the old guys use to. All it ever got *them* was a sore noodle, Lehi. And slag for brains."

"Drown it. I'm trying to concentrate."

The game finally ended. Lehi set the black box up on the workbench, turned off the machine, and stood up.

"You got everything ready to go underwater tomorrow?" asked Deaver.

"That was a good game. Having fun must've took up a lot of their time in the old days. Mom says the kids used to not even be able to get jobs till they was sixteen. It was the law."

"Don't you wish," said Deaver.

"It's true."

"You don't know your tongue from dung, Lehi. You don't know your heart from a fart."

"You want to get us both kicked out of here, talkin like that?"

"I don't have to follow school rules now, I graduated sixth grade, I'm nineteen years old, I been on my own for five years." He pulled his seven dollars out of his pocket, waved them once, stuffed them back in carelessly. "I do OK, and I talk like I want to talk. Think I'm afraid of the Bishop?"

"Bishop don't scare me. I don't even go to church except to make Mom happy. It's a bunch of bunny turds."

Lehi laughed, but Deaver could see that he was a little scared to talk like that. Sixteen years old, thought Deaver, he's big and he's smart but he's such a little kid. He don't understand how it's like to be a man. "Rain's comin."

"Rain's always comin. What the hell do you think filled up the lake?" Lehi smirked as he unplugged everything on the workbench.

"I meant *Lor*raine Wilson."

"I know what you meant. She's got her boat?"

"And she's got a mean set of fenders." Deaver cupped his hands. "Just need a little polishing."

"Why do you always talk dirty? Ever since you started driving salvage, Deaver, you got a gutter mouth. Besides, she's built like a sack."

"She's near fifty, what do you expect?" It occurred to Deaver that Lehi seemed to be stalling. Which probably meant he botched up again as usual. "Can you get the diving stuff?"

"I already got it. You thought I'd screw up." Lehi smirked again.

"You? Screw up? You can be trusted with *anything*." Deaver started for the door. He could hear Lehi behind him, still shutting a few things off. They got to use a lot of electricity in here. Of course they had to, because they needed computers all the time, and salvage was the only way to get them. But when Deaver saw all that electricity getting used up at once, to him it looked like his own future. All the machines he could ever want, new ones, and all the power they needed. Clothes that nobody else ever wore, his own horse and wagon or even a car. Maybe he'd be the guy who started *making* cars again. He didn't need stupid blob-smashing games from the past. "That stuff's dead and gone, duck lips, dead and gone."

"What're you talking about?" asked Lehi.

"Dead and gone. All your computer things."

It was enough to set Lehi off, as it always did. Deaver grinned and felt wicked and strong as Lehi babbled along behind him. About how we use the computers more than they ever did in the old days, the computers kept everything going, on and on and on, it was cute, Deaver liked him, the boy was so *intense*. Like everything was the end of the world. Deaver knew better. The world was dead, it had already ended, so none of it mattered, you could sink all this stuff in the lake.

They came out of the Center and walked along the retaining wall. Far below them was the harbor, a little circle of water in the bottom of a bowl, with Bingham City perched on the lip. They used to have an open-pit copper mine here, but when the water rose they cut a channel to it and now they had a nice harbor on Oquirrh Island in the middle of the Mormon Sea, where the factories could stink up the whole sky and no neighbors ever complained about it.

A lot of other people joined them on the steep dirt road that led down to the harbor. Nobody lived right in Bingham City itself, because it was just a working place, day and night. Shifts in, shifts out. Lehi was a shift boy, lived with his family across the Jordan Strait on Point-of-the-Mountain, which was as rotten a place to live as anybody ever devised, rode the ferry in every day at five in the morning and rode it back every afternoon at four. He was supposed to go to school after that for a couple of hours but Deaver thought that was stupid, he told Lehi that all the time, told him again now. School is too much time and too little of everything, a waste of time.

"I gotta go to school," said Lehi.

"Tell me two plus two, you haven't got two plus two yet?"

"*You* finished, didn't you?"

"Nobody needs anything after fourth grade." He shoved Lehi a little. Usually Lehi shoved back, but this time no.

"Just try getting a real job without a sixth-grade diploma, OK? And I'm pretty close now." They were at the ferry ship. Lehi got out his pass.

"You with me tomorrow or not?"

Lehi made a face. "I don't know, Deaver. You can get arrested for going around there. It's a dumb thing to do. They say there's real weird things in the old skyscrapers."

"We aren't going *in* the skyscrapers."

"Even worse in *there*, Deaver. I don't want to go there."

"Yeah, the Angel Moroni's probably waiting to jump out and say booga-booga-booga."

"Don't talk about it, Deaver." Deaver was tickling him; Lehi laughed and tried to shy away. "Cut it out, chigger-head. Come on. Besides, the Moroni statue was moved to the Salt Lake Monument up on the mountain. And that has a guard all the time."

"The statue's just gold plate anyway. I'm tellin you those old Mormons hid tons of stuff down in the Temple, just waitin for somebody who isn't scared of the ghost of Bigamy Young to—"

"Shut *up*, snotsucker, OK? People can hear! Look around, we're not alone!"

It was true, of course. Some of the other people were glaring at them. But then, Deaver noticed that older people liked to glare at younger ones. It made the old farts feel better about kicking off. It was like they were saying, OK, I'm dying, but at least you're stupid. So Deaver looked right at a woman who was staring at him and murmured, "OK, I'm stupid, but at least I won't die."

"Deaver, do you always have to say that where they can hear you?"

"It's true."

"In the first place, Deaver, they aren't dying. And in the second place, you're definitely stupid. And in the third place, the ferry's here." Lehi punched Deaver lightly in the stomach.

Deaver bent over in mock agony. "Ay, the laddie's ungrateful, he is, I give him me last croost of bread and this be the thanks I gets."

"*Nobody* has an accent like that, Deaver!" shouted Lehi. The boat began to pull away.

"Tomorrow at five-thirty!" shouted Deaver.

"You'll never get up at four-thirty, don't give me that, you never get up..." But the ferry and the noise of the factories and machine and trucks swallowed up the rest of his insults. Deaver knew them all, anyway. Lehi might be only sixteen, but he was OK. Someday Deaver'd get married but his wife would like Lehi, too. And Lehi'd even get married, and his wife would like Deaver. She'd better, or she'd have to swim home.

He took the trolley home to Fort Douglas and walked to the ancient barracks building where Rain let him stay. It was supposed to be a storage room, but she kept the mops and soap stuff in her place so that there'd be room for a cot.

Not much else, but it was on Oquirrh Island without being right there in the stink and the smoke and the noise. He could sleep and that was enough, since most of the time he was out on the truck.

Truth was, his room wasn't home anyway. Home was pretty much Rain's place, a drafty room at the end of the barracks with a dumpy frowzy lady who served him good food and plenty of it. That's where he went now, walked right in and surprised her in the kitchen. She yelled at him for surprising her, yelled at him for being filthy and tracking all over her floor, and let him get a slice of apple before she yelled at him for snitching before supper.

He went around and changed light bulbs in five rooms before supper. The families there were all crammed into two rooms each at the most, and most of them had to share kitchens and eat in shifts. Some of the rooms were nasty places, family warfare held off only as long as it took him to change the light, and sometimes even that truce wasn't observed. Others were doing fine, the place was small but they liked each other. Deaver was pretty sure his family must have been one of the nice ones, because if there'd been any yelling he would have remembered.

Rain and Deaver ate and then turned off all the lights while she played the old record player Deaver had wangled away from Lehi. They really weren't supposed to have it, but they figured as long as they didn't burn any lights it wasn't wasting electricity, and they'd turn it in as soon as anybody asked for it.

In the meantime, Rain had some of the old records from when she was a girl. The songs had strong rhythms, and tonight, like she sometimes did, Rain got up and moved to the music, strange little dances that Deaver didn't understand unless he imagined her as a lithe young girl, pictured her body as it must have been then. It wasn't hard to imagine, it was there in her eyes and her smile all the time, and her movements gave away secrets that years of starchy eating and lack of exercise had disguised.

Then, as always, his thoughts went off to some of the girls he saw from his truck window, driving by the fields where they bent over, hard at work, until they heard the truck and then they stood and waved. Everybody waved at the salvage truck, sometimes it was the only thing with a motor that ever came by, their only contact with the old machines. All the tractors, all the electricity were reserved for the New Soil Lands; the old places were dying. And they turned and waved at the last memories. It made Deaver sad and he hated to be sad, all these people clinging to a past that never existed.

"It never existed," he said aloud.

"Yes it did," Rain whispered. "Girls just wanna have fu-un," she murmured along with the record. "I hated this song when I was a girl. Or maybe it was my mama who hated it."

"You live here then?"

"Indiana," she said. "One of the states, way east."

"Were you a refugee, too?"

"No. We moved here when I was sixteen, seventeen, can't remember. Whenever things got scary in the world, a lot of Mormons moved home. This was always home, no matter what."

The record ended. She turned it off, turned on the lights.

"Got the boat all gassed up?" asked Deaver.

"You don't want to go there," she said.

"If there's gold down there, I want it."

"If there was gold there, Deaver, they would've taken it out before the water covered it. It's not as if nobody got a warning, you know. The Mormon Sea wasn't a flash flood."

"If it isn't down there, what's all the hush-hush about? How come the Lake Patrol keeps people from going there?"

"I don't know, Deaver. Maybe because a lot of people feel like it's a holy place."

Deaver was used to this. Rain never went to church, but she still talked like a Mormon. Most people did, though, when you scratched them the wrong place. Deaver didn't like it when they got religious. "Angels need police protection, is that it?"

"It used to be real important to the Mormons in the old days, Deaver." She sat down on the floor, leaning against the wall under the window.

"Well it's nothin now. They got their other temples,

don't they? And they're building the new one in Zarahemla, right?"

"I don't know, Deaver. The one here, it was always the real one. The center." She bent sideways, leaned on her hand, looked down at the floor. "It still is."

Deaver saw she was getting really somber now, really sad. It happened to a lot of people who remembered the old days. Like a disease that never got cured. But Deaver knew the cure. For Rain, anyway. "Is it true they used to kill people in there?"

It worked. She glared at him and the languor left her body. "Is that what you truckers talk about all day?"

Deaver grinned. "There's stories. Cuttin people up if they told where the gold was hid."

"You know Mormons all over the place, now, Deaver, do you really think we'd go cuttin people up for tellin secrets?"

"I don't know. Depends on the secrets, don't it?" He was sitting on his hands, kind of bouncing a little on the couch.

He could see that she was a little mad for real, but didn't want to be. So she'd pretend to be mad for play. She sat up, reached for a pillow to throw at him.

"No! No!" he cried. "Don't cut me up! Don't feed me to the carp!"

The pillow hit him and he pretended elaborately to die.

"Just don't joke about things like that," she said.

"Things like what? You don't believe in the old stuff anymore. Nobody does."

"Maybe not."

"Jesus was supposed to come again, right? There was atom bombs dropped here and there, and he was supposed to come."

"Prophet said we was too wicked. He wouldn't come cause we loved the things of the world too much."

"Come on, if he was comin he would've come, right?"

"Might still," she said.

"Nobody believes that," said Deaver. "Mormons are just the government, that's all. The Bishop gets elected judge in every town, right? The president of the elders is always mayor, it's just the government, just politics, nobody believes it now. Zarahemla's the capital, not the holy city."

He couldn't see her because he was lying flat on his back on the couch. When she didn't answer, he got up and looked for her. She was over by the sink, leaning on the counter. He snuck up behind her to tickle her, but something in her posture changed his mind. When he got close, he saw tears down her cheeks. It was crazy. All these people from the old days got crazy a lot.

"I was just teasin," he said.

She nodded.

"It's just part of the old days. You know how I am about that. Maybe if I remembered, it'd be different. Sometimes I wish I remembered." But it was a lie. He never wished he remembered. He didn't like remembering. Most stuff he couldn't remember even if he wanted to. The earliest thing he could bring to mind was riding on the back of a horse, behind some man who sweated a lot, just riding and riding and riding. And then it was all recent stuff, going to school, getting passed around in people's homes, finally getting busy one year and finishing school and getting a job. He didn't get misty-eyed thinking about any of it, any of those places. Just passing through, that's all he was ever doing, never belonged anywhere until maybe now. He belonged here. "I'm sorry," he said.

"It's fine," she said.

"You still gonna take me there?"

"I said I would, didn't I?"

She sounded just annoyed enough that he knew it was OK to tease her again. "You don't think they'll have the Second Coming while we're there, do you? If you think so, I'll wear my tie."

She smiled, then turned to face him and pushed him away. "Deaver, go to bed."

"I'm gettin up at four-thirty, Rain, and then you're one girl who's gonna have fun."

"I don't think the song was about early morning boat trips."

She was doing the dishes when he left for his little room.

Lehi was waiting at five-thirty, right on schedule. "I can't believe it," he said. "I thought you'd be late."

"Good thing you were ready on time," said Deaver, "cause if you didn't come with us you wouldn't get a cut."

"We aren't going to find any gold, Deaver Teague."

"Then why're you comin with me? Don't give me that stuff, Lehi, you know the future's with Deaver Teague, and you don't want to be left behind. Where's the diving stuff?"

"I didn't bring it *home*, Deaver. You don't think my mom'd ask questions then?"

"She's always askin questions," said Deaver.

"It's her job," said Rain.

"I don't want anybody askin about everything I do," said Deaver.

"Nobody has to ask," said Rain. "You always tell us whether we want to hear or not."

"If you don't want to hear, you don't have to," said Deaver.

"Don't get touchy," said Rain.

"You guys are both gettin wet-headed on me, all of a sudden. Does the temple make you crazy, is that how it works?"

"I don't mind my mom askin me stuff. It's OK."

The ferries ran from Point to Bingham day and night, so they had to go north a ways before cutting west to Oquirrh Island. The smelter and the foundries put orange-bellied smoke clouds into the night sky, and the coal barges were getting offloaded just like in daytime. The coal-dust cloud that was so grimy and black in the day looked like white fog under the floodlights.

"My dad died right there, about this time of day," said Lehi.

"He loaded coal?"

"Yeah. He used to be a car salesmen. His job kind of disappeared on him."

"You weren't there, were you?"

"I heard the crash. I was asleep, but it woke me up. And then a lot of shouting and running. We lived on the island back then, always heard stuff from the harbor. He got buried under a ton of coal that fell from fifty feet up."

Deaver didn't know what to say about that.

"You never talk about your folks," said Lehi. "I always remember my dad, but you never talk about your folks."

Deaver shrugged.

"He doesn't remember em," Rain said quietly. "They found him out on the plains somewhere. The mobbers got his family, however many there was, he must've hid or something, that's all they can figure."

"Well what was it?" asked Lehi. "Did you hide?"

Deaver didn't feel comfortable talking about it, since he didn't remember anything except what people told him. He knew that other people remembered their childhood, and he didn't like how they always acted so surprised that he didn't. But Lehi was asking, and Deaver knew that you don't keep stuff back from friends. "I guess I did. Or maybe I looked too dumb to kill or somethin." He laughed. "I must've been a real dumb little kid, I didn't even remember my own name. They figure I was five or six years old, most kids know their names, but not me. So the two guys that found me, their names were Teague and Deaver."

"You gotta remember somethin."

"Lehi, I didn't even know how to talk. They tell me I didn't even say a word till I was nine years old. We're talkin about a slow learner here."

"Wow." Lehi was silent for a while. "How come you didn't say anything?"

"Doesn't matter," said Rain. "He makes up for it now, Deaver the talker. Champion talker."

They coasted the island till they got past Magna. Lehi led them to a storage shed that Underwater Salvage had put up at the north end of Oquirrh Island. It was unlocked and full of diving equipment. Lehi's friends had filled some tanks with air. They got two diving outfits and underwater flashlights. Rain wasn't going underwater, so she didn't need anything.

They pulled away from the island, out into the regular shipping lane from Wendover. In that direction, at least, people had sense enough not to travel at night, so there wasn't much traffic. After a little while they were out into open water. That was when Rain stopped the little outboard motor Deaver had scrounged for her and Lehi had fixed. "Time to sweat and slave," said Rain.

Deaver sat on the middle bench, settled the oars into the locks, and began to row.

"Not too fast," Rain said. "You'll give yourself blisters."

A boat that might have been Lake Patrol went by once, but otherwise nobody came near them as they crossed the open stretch. Then the skyscrapers rose up and blocked off large sections of the starry night.

"They say there's people who was never rescued still livin in there," Lehi whispered.

Rain was disdainful. "You think there's anything left in there to keep anybody alive? And the water's still too salty to drink for long."

"Who says they're alive?" whispered Deaver in his most mysterious voice. A couple of years ago, he could have spooked Lehi and made his eyes go wide. Now Lehi just looked disgusted.

"Come on, Deaver, I'm not a kid."

It was Deaver who got spooked a little. The big holes where pieces of glass and plastic had fallen off looked like mouths, waiting to suck him in and carry him down under the water, into the city of the drowned. He sometimes dreamed about thousands and thousands of people living under water. Still driving their cars around, going about their business, shopping in stores, going to movies. In his dreams they never did anything bad, just went about their business. But he always woke up sweating and frightened. No reason. Just spooked him. "I think they should blow up these things before they fall down and hurt somebody," said Deaver.

"Maybe it's better to leave em standing," said Rain. "Maybe there's a lot of folks like to remember how tall we once stood."

"What's to remember? They built tall buildings and then they let em take a bath, what's to brag for?"

Deaver was trying to get her not to talk about the old days, but Lehi seemed to like wallowing in it. "You ever here before the water came?"

Rain nodded. "Saw a parade go right down this street. I can't remember if it was Third South or Fourth South. Third I guess. I saw twenty-five horses all riding together. I remember that I thought that was really something. You didn't see many horses in those days."

"I seen too many myself," said Lehi.

"It's the ones I don't see that I hate," said Deaver. "They ought to make em wear diapers."

They rounded a building and looked up a north-south passage between towers. Rain was sitting in the stern and saw it first. "There it is. You can see it. Just the tall spires now."

Deaver rowed them up the passage. There were six spires sticking up out of the water, but the four short ones were under so far that only the pointed roofs were dry. The two tall ones had windows in them, not covered at all. Deaver was disappointed. Wide open like that meant that anybody might have come here. It was all so much less dangerous than he had expected. Maybe Rain was right, and there was nothing there.

They tied the boat to the north side and waited for daylight. "If I knew it'd be so easy," said Deaver, "I could've slept another hour."

"Sleep now," said Rain.

"Maybe I will," said Deaver.

He slid off his bench and sprawled in the bottom of the boat.

He didn't sleep, though. The open window of the steeple was only a few yards away, a deep black surrounded by the starlit grey of the temple granite. It was down there, waiting for him; the future, a chance to get something better for himself and his two friends. Maybe a plot of ground in the south where it was warmer and the snow didn't pile up five feet deep every winter, where it wasn't rain in the sky and lake everywhere else you looked. A place where he could live for a very long time and look back and remember good times with his friends, that was all waiting down under the water.

Of course they hadn't *told* him about the gold. It was on the road, a little place in Parowan where truckers knew they could stop in because the iron mine kept such crazy shifts that the diners never closed. They even had some coffee there, hot and bitter, because there weren't so many Mormons there and the miners didn't let the Bishop push them around. In fact they even called him Judge there instead of Bishop. The other drivers didn't talk to Deaver, of course, they were talking to each other when the one fellow told the story about how the Mormons back in the gold rush days hoarded up all the gold they could get and hid it in the upper rooms of the temple where nobody but the prophet and the twelve apostles could ever go. At first Deaver didn't believe him, except that Bill Horne nodded like he knew it was true, and Cal Silber said you'd never catch him messin with the Mormon temple, that's a good way to get yourself dead. The way they were talking, scared and quiet, told Deaver that they believed it, that it was true, and he knew something else, too: if anyone was going to get that gold, it was him.

Even if it *was* easy to get here, that didn't mean anything. He knew how Mormons were about the temple. He'd asked around a little, but nobody'd talk about it. And nobody ever went there, either, he asked a lot of people if they ever sailed on out and looked at it, and they all got quiet and shook their heads no or changed the subject. Why should the Lake Patrol guard it, then, if everybody was too scared to go? Everybody but Deaver Teague and his two friends.

"Real pretty," said Rain.

Deaver woke up. The sun was just topping the mountains; it must've been light for some time. He looked where Rain was looking. It was the Moroni tower on top of the mountain above the old capitol, where they'd put the temple statue a few years back. It was bright and shiny, the old guy and his trumpet. But when the Mormons wanted that trumpet to blow, it had just stayed silent and their faith got drowned. Now Deaver knew they only hung on to it for old times' sake. Well, Deaver lived for new times.

Lehi showed him how to use the underwater gear, and they practiced going over the side into the water a couple of times, once without the weight belts and once with. Deaver and Lehi swam like fish, of course—swimming was the main recreation that everybody could do for free. It was different with the mask and the air hose, though.

"Hose tastes like a horse's hoof," Deaver said between dives.

Lehi made sure Deaver's weight belt was on tight. "You're the only guy on Oquirrh Island who knows." Then he tumbled forward off the boat. Deaver went down too straight and the air tank bumped the back of his head a little, but it didn't hurt too much and he didn't drop his light, either.

He swam along the outside of the temple, shining his light on the stones. Lots of underwater plants were rising up the sides of the temple, but it wasn't covered much yet. There was a big metal plaque right in the front of the building, about a third of the way down. THE HOUSE OF THE LORD it said. Deaver pointed it out to Lehi.

When they got up to the boat again, Deaver asked about it. "It looked kind of goldish," he said.

"Used to be another sign there," said Rain. "It was a little different. That one might have been gold. This one's plastic. They made it so the temple would still have a sign, I guess."

"You sure about that?"

"I remember when they did it."

Finally Deaver felt confident enough to go down into the temple. They had to take off their flippers to climb into the steeple window; Rain tossed them up after. In the sunlight there was nothing spooking about the window. They sat there on the sill, water lapping at their feet, and put their fins and tanks on.

Halfway through getting dressed, Lehi stopped. Just sat there.

"I can't do it," he said.

"Nothin to be scared of," said Deaver. "Come on, there's no ghosts or nothin down there."

"I can't," said Lehi.

"Good for you," called Rain from the boat.

Deaver turned to look at her. "What're you talkin about!"

"I don't think you should."

"Then why'd you bring me here?"

"Because you wanted to."

Made no sense.

"It's holy ground, Deaver," said Rain. "Lehi feels it, too. That's why he isn't going down."

Deaver looked at Lehi.

"It just don't feel right," said Lehi.

"It's just stones," said Deaver.

Lehi said nothing. Deaver put on his goggles, took a light, put the breather in his mouth, and jumped.

Turned out the floor was only a foot and a half down. It took him completely by surprise, so he fell over and sat on his butt in eighteen inches of water. Lehi was just as surprised as he was, but then he started laughing, and Deaver laughed, too. Deaver got to his feet and started flapping around, looking for the stairway. He could hardly take a step, his flippers slowed him down so much.

"Walk backward," said Lehi.

"Then how am I supposed to see where I'm going?"

"Stick your face under the water and look, chigger-head."

Deaver stuck his face in the water. Without the reflection of daylight on the surface, he could see fine. There was the stairway.

He got up, looked toward Lehi. Lehi shook his head. He still wasn't going.

"Suit yourself," said Deaver. He backed through the water to the top step. Then he put in his breathing tube and went down.

It wasn't easy to get down the stairs. They're fine when you aren't floating, thought Deaver, but they're a pain when you keep scraping your tanks on the ceiling. Finally he figured out he could grab the railing and pull himself down. The stairs wound around and around. When they ended, a whole bunch of garbage had filled up the bottom of the stairwell, partly blocking the doorway. He swam above the garbage, which looked like scrap metal and chips of wood, and came out into a large room.

His light didn't shine very far through the murky water, so he swam the walls, around and around, high and low. Down here the water was cold, and he swam faster to keep warm. There were rows of arched windows on both sides, with rows of circular windows above them, but they had been covered over with wood on the outside; the only light was from Deaver's flashlight. Finally, though, after a couple of times around the room and across the ceiling, he figured it was just one big room. And except for the garbage all over the floor, it was empty.

Already he felt the deep pain of disappointment. He forced himself to ignore it. After all, it wouldn't be right out here in a big room like this, would it? There had to be a secret treasury.

There were a couple of doors. The small one in the middle of the wall at one end was wide open. Once there must have been stairs leading up to it. Deaver swam over there and shone his light in. Just another room, smaller this time. He found a couple more rooms, but they had all been stripped, right down to the stone. Nothing at all.

He tried examining some of the stones to look for secret doors, but he gave up pretty soon—he couldn't see well enough from the flashlight to find a thin crack even if it was there. Now the disappointment was real. As he swam along, he began to wonder if maybe the truckers hadn't known he was listening. Maybe they made it all up just so someday he'd do this. Some joke, where they wouldn't even see him make a fool of himself.

But no, no, that couldn't be it. They believed it, all right. But he knew now what they didn't know. Whatever the Mormons did here in the old days, there wasn't any gold in the upper rooms now. So much for the future. But what the hell, he told himself, I got here, I saw it, and I'll find something else. No reason not to be cheerful about it.

He didn't fool himself, and there was nobody else down here to fool. It was bitter. He'd spent a lot of years thinking about bars of gold or bags of it. He'd always pictured it hidden behind a curtain. He'd pull on the curtain and it would billow out in the water, and here would be the bags of gold, and he'd just take them out and that would be it. But there weren't any curtains, weren't any hideyholes, there was nothing at all, and if he had a future, he'd have to find it somewhere else.

He swam back to the door leading to the stairway. Now he could see the pile of garbage better, and it occurred to him to wonder how it got there. Every other room was completely empty. The garbage couldn't have been carried in by the water, because the only windows that were open were in the steeple, and they were above the water line. He swam close and picked up a piece. It was metal. They were all metal, except a few stones, and it occurred to him that this might be it after all. If you're hiding a treasure, you don't put it in bags or ingots, you leave it around looking like garbage and people leave it alone.

He gathered up as many of the thin metal pieces as he could carry in one hand and swam carefully up the stairwell. Lehi would have to come down now and help him carry it up; they could make bags out of their shirts to carry lots of it at a time.

He splashed out into the air and then walked backward up the last few steps and across the submerged floor. Lehi was still sitting on the sill, and now Rain was there beside him, her bare feet dangling in the water. When he got there he turned around and held out the metal in his hands. He couldn't see their faces well, because the outside of the facemask was blurry with water and kept catching sunlight.

"You scraped your knee," said Rain.

Deaver handed her his flashlight and now that his hand was free, he could pull his mask off and look at them. They were very serious. He held out the metal pieces toward them. "Look what I found down there."

Lehi took a couple of metal pieces from him. Rain never took her eyes from Deaver's face.

"It's old cans, Deaver," Lehi said quietly.

"No it isn't," said Deaver. But he looked at his fistful of metal sheets and realized it was true. They had been cut down the side and pressed flat, but they were sure enough cans.

"There's writing on it," said Lehi. "It says, Dear Lord heal my girl Jenny please I pray."

Deaver set down his handful on the sill. Then he took one, turned it over, found the writing. "Forgive my adultery I will sin no more."

Lehi read another. "Bring my boy safe from the plains O Lord God."

Each message was scratched with a nail or a piece of glass, the letters crudely formed.

"They used to say prayers all day in the temple, and

people would bring in names and they'd say the temple prayers for them," said Rain. "Nobody prays here now, but they still bring the names. On metal so they'll last."

"We shouldn't read these," said Lehi. "We should put them back."

There were hundreds, maybe thousand of those metal prayers down there. People must come here all the time, Deaver realized. The Mormons must have a regular traffic coming here and leaving these things behind. But nobody told me.

"Did you know about this?"

Rain nodded.

"You brought them here, didn't you."

"Some of them. Over the years."

"You knew what was down there."

She didn't answer.

"She told you not to come," said Lehi.

"You knew about this too?"

"I knew people came, I didn't know what they did."

And suddenly the magnitude of it struck him. Lehi and Rain had both known. All the Mormons knew, then. They all knew, and he had asked again and again, and no one had told him. Not even his friends.

"Why'd you let me come out here?"

"Tried to stop you," said Rain.

"Why didn't you tell me this?"

She looked him in the eye. "Deaver, you would've thought I was givin you the runaround. And you would have laughed at this, if I told you. I thought it was better if you saw it. Then maybe you wouldn't go tellin people how dumb the Mormons are."

"You think I would?" He held up another metal prayer

and read it aloud. "Come quickly, Lord Jesus, before I die." He shook it at her. "You think I'd laugh at these people?"

"You laugh at everything, Deaver."

Deaver looked at Lehi. This was something Lehi had never said before. Deaver would never laugh at something that was really important. And this was really important to them, to them both.

"This is yours," Deaver said. "All this stuff is yours."

"I never left a prayer here," said Lehi.

But when he said *yours* he didn't mean just them, just Lehi and Rain. He meant all of them, all the people of the Mormon Sea, all the ones who had known about it but never told him even though he asked again and again. All the people who belonged here. "I came to find something here for *me,* and you knew all the time it was only *your* stuff down there."

Lehi and Rain looked at each other, then back at Deaver.

"It isn't ours," said Rain.

"I never been here before," said Lehi.

"It's your stuff." He sat down in the water and began taking off the underwater gear.

"Don't be mad," said Lehi. "I didn't know."

You knew more than you told me. All the time I thought we were friends, but it wasn't true. You two had this place in common with all the other people, but not with me. Everybody but me.

Lehi carefully took the metal sheets to the stairway and dropped them. They sank once, to drift down and take their place on the pile of supplications.

Lehi rowed them through the skyscrapers to the east of the old city, and then Rain started the motor and they skimmed along the surface of the lake. The Lake Patrol didn't see them, but Deaver knew now that it didn't matter much if they did. The Lake Patrol was mostly Mormons. They undoubtedly knew about the traffic here, and let it happen as long as it was discreet. Probably the only people they stopped were the people who weren't in on it.

All the way back to Magna to return the underwater gear, Deaver sat in the front of the boat, not talking to the others. Where Deaver sat, the bow of the boat seemed to curve under him. The faster they went, the less the boat seemed to touch the water. Just skimming over the surface, never really touching deep; making a few waves, but the water always smoothed out again.

Those two people in the back of the boat, he felt kind of sorry for them. They still lived in the drowned city, they belonged down there, and the fact they couldn't go there broke their hearts. But not Deaver. His city wasn't even built yet. His city was tomorrow.

He'd driven a salvage truck and lived in a closet long enough. Maybe he'd go south into the New Soil Lands. Maybe qualify on a piece of land. Own something, plant in the soil, maybe he'd come to belong there. As for this place, well, he never had belonged here, just like all the foster homes and schools along the way, just one more stop for a year or two or three, he knew that all along. Never did make any friends here, but that's how he wanted it. Wouldn't be right to make friends, cause he'd just move on and disappoint them. Didn't see no good in doing that to people.

THE PEOPLE OF SAND AND SLAG
BY PAOLO BACIGALUPI

Paolo Bacigalupi is the bestselling author of the novels *The Windup Girl*, *Ship Breaker*, *The Drowned Cities*, *Zombie Baseball Beatdown*, and the collection *Pump Six and Other Stories*. He is a winner of the Michael L. Printz, Hugo, Nebula, Locus, Compton Crook, and John W. Campbell Memorial awards, and was a National Book Award finalist. A new novel for young adults, *The Doubt Factory*, came out in 2014, and a new science fiction novel, *The Water Knife*, is due out in May 2015.

Bacigalupi says that this story was inspired by a feral animal that lived in the Atlantic Richfield Company's Berkeley Pit, a toxic waste site outside of Butte, Montana. It was too wild to catch, but it would accept food that was set out for it, and it somehow managed to survive despite the sulfuric-acid and heavy metals that were poisoning its surroundings.

* * *

Set in the far-future, featuring characters barely recognizable as human, "The People of Sand and Slag" considers and comments on humanity, technological progress, and our love for the simple solution to the complex problem.

"Hostile movement! Well inside the perimeter! Well inside!"

I stripped off my Immersive Response goggles as adrenaline surged through me. The virtual cityscape I'd been about to raze disappeared, replaced by our monitoring room's many views of SesCo's mining operations. On one screen, the red phosphorescent tracery of an intruder skated across a terrain map, a hot blip like blood spattering its way toward Pit 8.

Jaak was already out of the monitoring room. I ran for my gear.

I caught up with Jaak in the equipment room as he grabbed a TS-101 and slashbangs and dragged his impact exoskeleton over his tattooed body. He draped bandoleers of surgepacks over his massive shoulders and ran for the outer locks. I strapped on my own exoskeleton, pulled my 101 from its rack, checked its charge, and followed.

Lisa was already in the HEV, its turbofans screaming like banshees when the hatch dilated. Sentry centaurs leveled their 101's at me, then relaxed as friend/foe data spilled into their heads-up displays. I bolted across the tarmac, my skin pricking under blasts of icy Montana wind and the jet wash of Hentasa Mark V engines. Overhead, the clouds glowed orange with light from SesCo's mining bots.

"Come on, Chen! Move! Move! Move!"

I dove into the hunter. The ship leaped into the sky. It banked, throwing me against a bulkhead, then the Hentasas cycled wide and the hunter punched forward. The HEV's hatch slid shut. The wind howl muted.

I struggled forward to the flight cocoon and peered over Jaak's and Lisa's shoulders to the landscape beyond.

"Have a good game?" Lisa asked.

I scowled. "I was about to win. I made it to Paris."

We cut through the mists over the catchment lakes, skimming inches above the water, and then we hit the far shore. The hunter lurched as its anti-collision software jerked us away from the roughening terrain. Lisa overrode the computers and forced the ship back down against the soil, driving us so low I could have reached out and dragged my hands through the broken scree as we screamed over it.

Alarms yowled. Jaak shut them off as Lisa pushed the hunter lower. Ahead, a tailings ridge loomed. We ripped up its face and dropped sickeningly into the next valley. The Hentasas shuddered as Lisa forced them to the edge of their design buffer. We hurtled up and over another ridge. Ahead, the ragged cutscape of mined mountains stretched to the horizon. We dipped again into mist and skimmed low over another catchment lake, leaving choppy wake in the thick golden waters.

Jaak studied the hunter's scanners. "I've got it." He grinned. "It's moving, but slow."

"Contact in one minute," Lisa said. "He hasn't launched any countermeasures."

I watched the intruder on the tracking screens as they displayed real-time data fed to us from SesCo's satellites.

"It's not even a masked target. We could have dropped a mini on it from base if we'd known he wasn't going to play hide-and-seek."

"Could have finished your game," Lisa said.

"We could still nuke him," Jaak suggested.

I shook my head. "No, let's take a look. Vaporizing him won't leave us anything and Bunbaum will want to know what we used the hunter for."

"Thirty seconds."

"He wouldn't care, if someone hadn't taken the hunter on a joyride to Cancun."

Lisa shrugged. "I wanted to swim. It was either that, or rip off your kneecaps."

The hunter lunged over another series of ridges.

Jaak studied his monitor. "Target's moving away. He's still slow. We'll get him."

"Fifteen seconds to drop," Lisa said. She unstrapped and switched the hunter to software. We all ran for the hatch as the HEV yanked itself skyward, its auto pilot desperate to tear away from the screaming hazard of the rocks beneath its belly.

We plunged out the hatch, one, two, three, falling like Icarus. We slammed into the ground at hundreds of kilometers per hour. Our exoskeletons shattered like glass, flinging leaves into the sky. The shards fluttered down around us, black metallic petals absorbing our enemy's radar and heat detection while we rolled to jarred vulnerable stops in muddy scree.

The hunter blew over the ridge, Hentasas shrieking, a blazing target. I dragged myself upright and ran for the ridge, my feet churning through yellow tailings mud and rags of jaundiced snow. Behind me, Jaak was down with smashed arms. The leaves of his exoskeleton marked his roll path, a long trail of black shimmering metal. Lisa lay a hundred yards away, her femur rammed through her thigh like a bright white exclamation mark.

I reached the top of the ridge and stared down into the valley.

Nothing.

I dialed up the magnification of my helmet. The monotonous slopes of more tailings rubble spread out below me. Boulders, some as large as our HEV, some cracked and shattered by high explosives, shared the slopes with the unstable yellow shale and fine grit of waste materials from SesCo's operations.

Jaak slipped up beside me, followed a moment later by Lisa, her flight suit's leg torn and bloodied. She wiped yellow mud off her face and ate it as she studied the valley below. "Anything?"

I shook my head. "Nothing yet. You okay?"

"Clean break."

Jaak pointed. "There!"

Down in the valley, something was running, flushed by the hunter. It slipped along a shallow creek, viscous with tailings acid. The ship herded it toward us. Nothing. No missile fire. No slag. Just the running creature. A mass of tangled hair. Quadrupedal. Splattered with mud.

"Some kind of bio-job?" I wondered.

"It doesn't have any hands," Lisa murmured.

"No equipment either."

Jaak muttered. "What kind of sick bastard makes a bio-job without hands?"

I searched the nearby ridgelines. "Decoy, maybe?"

Jaak checked his scanner data, piped in from the

hunter's more aggressive instruments. "I don't think so. Can we put the hunter up higher? I want to look around."

At Lisa's command, the hunter rose, allowing its sensors a fuller reach. The howl of its turbofans became muted as it gained altitude.

Jaak waited as more data spat into his heads-up display. "Nope, nothing. And no new alerts from any of the perimeter stations, either. We're alone."

Lisa shook her head. "We should have just dropped a mini on it from base."

Down in the valley, the bio-job's headlong run slowed to a trot. It seemed unaware of us. Closer now, we could make out its shape: A shaggy quadruped with a tail. Dreadlocked hair dangled from its shanks like ornaments, tagged with tailings mud clods. It was stained around its legs from the acids of the catchment ponds, as though it had forded streams of urine.

"That's one ugly bio-job," I said.

Lisa shouldered her 101. "Bio-melt when I'm done with it."

"Wait!" Jaak said. "Don't slag it!"

Lisa glanced over at him, irritated. "What now?"

"That's not a bio-job at all." Jaak whispered. "That's a dog."

He stood suddenly and jumped over the hillside, running headlong down the scree toward the animal.

"Wait!" Lisa called, but Jaak was already fully exposed and blurring to his top speed.

The animal took one look at Jaak, whooping and hollering as he came roaring down the slope, then turned and ran. It was no match for Jaak. Half a minute later he overtook the animal.

Lisa and I exchanged glances. "Well," she said, "it's

awfully slow if it's a bio-job. I've seen centaurs walk faster."

By the time we caught up with Jaak and the animal, Jaak had it cornered in a dull gully. The animal stood in the center of a trickling ditch of sludgy water, shaking and growling and baring its teeth at us as we surrounded it. It tried to break around us, but Jaak kept it corralled easily.

Up close, the animal seemed even more pathetic than from a distance, a good thirty kilos of snarling mange. Its paws were slashed and bloody and patches of fur were torn away, revealing festering chemical burns underneath.

"I'll be damned," I breathed, staring at the animal. "It really looks like a dog."

Jaak grinned. "It's like finding a goddamn dinosaur."

"How could it live out here?" Lisa's arm swept the horizon. "There's nothing to live on. It's got to be modified." She studied it closely, then glanced at Jaak. "Are you sure nothing's coming in on the perimeter? This isn't some kind of decoy?"

Jaak shook his head. "Nothing. Not even a peep."

I leaned in toward the creature. It bared its teeth in a rictus of hatred. "It's pretty beat up. Maybe it's the real thing."

Jaak said, "Oh yeah, it's the real thing all right. I saw a dog in a zoo once. I'm telling you, this is a dog."

Lisa shook her head. "It can't be. It would be dead, if it were a real dog."

Jaak just grinned and shook his head. "No way. Look at it." He reached out to push the hair out of the animal's face so that we could see its muzzle.

The animal lunged and its teeth sank into Jaak's arm. It shook his arm violently, growling as Jaak stared down at the creature latched onto his flesh. It yanked its head back and forth, trying to tear Jaak's arm off. Blood spurted around its muzzle as its teeth found Jaak's arteries.

Jaak laughed. His bleeding stopped. "Damn. Check that out." He lifted his arm until the animal dangled fully out of the stream, dripping. "I got me a pet."

The dog swung from the thick bough of Jaak's arm. It tried to shake his arm once again, but its movements were ineffectual now that it hung off the ground. Even Lisa smiled.

"Must be a bummer to wake up and find out you're at the end of your evolutionary curve."

The dog growled, determined to hang on.

Jaak laughed and drew his monomol knife. "Here you go, doggy." He sliced his arm off, leaving it in the bewildered animal's mouth.

Lisa cocked her head. "You think we could make some kind of money on it?"

Jaak watched as the dog devoured his severed arm. "I read somewhere that they used to eat dogs. I wonder what they taste like."

I checked the time in my heads-up display. We'd already killed an hour on an exercise that wasn't giving any bonuses. "Get your dog, Jaak, and get it on the hunter. We aren't going to eat it before we call Bunbaum."

"He'll probably call it company property," Jaak groused.

"Yeah, that's the way it always goes. But we still have to report. Might as well keep the evidence, since we didn't nuke it."

We ate sand for dinner. Outside the security bunker, the mining robots rumbled back and forth, ripping deeper into the earth, turning it into a mush of tailings and rock acid that they left in exposed ponds when they hit the water table, or piled into thousand-foot mountainscapes of waste soil. It was comforting to hear those machines cruising back and forth all day. Just you and the bots and the profits, and if nothing got bombed while you were on duty, there was always a nice bonus.

After dinner we sat around and sharpened Lisa's skin, implanting blades along her limbs so that she was like a razor from all directions. She'd considered monomol blades, but it was too easy to take a limb off accidentally, and we lost enough body parts as it was without adding to the mayhem. That kind of garbage was for people who didn't have to work: aesthetes from New York City and California.

Lisa had a DermDecora kit for the sharpening. She'd bought it last time we'd gone on vacation and spent extra to get it, instead of getting one of the cheap knock-offs that were cropping up. We worked on cutting her skin down to the bone and setting the blades. A friend of ours in L.A said that he just held DermDecora parties so everyone could do their modifications and help out with the hard-to-reach places.

Lisa had done my glowspine, a sweet tracery of lime landing lights that ran from my tailbone to the base of my skull, so I didn't mind helping her out, but Jaak, who did all of his modification with an old-time scar and tattoo shop in Hawaii, wasn't so pleased. It was a little frustrating because her flesh kept trying to close before we had the blades set, but eventually we got the hang of it, and an hour later, she started looking good.

Once we finished with Lisa's front settings, we sat around and fed her. I had a bowl of tailings mud that I drizzled into her mouth to speed her integration process. When we weren't feeding her, we watched the dog. Jaak had shoved it into a makeshift cage in one corner of our common room. It lay there like it was dead.

Lisa said, "I ran its DNA. It really is a dog."

"Bunbaum believe you?"

She gave me a dirty look. "What do you think?"

I laughed. At SesCo, tactical defense responders were expected to be fast, flexible, and deadly, but the reality was our SOP was always the same: drop nukes on intruders, slag the leftovers to melt so they couldn't regrow, hit the beaches for vacation. We were independent and trusted as far as tactical decisions went, but there was no way SesCo was going to believe its slag soldiers had found a dog in their tailings mountains.

Lisa nodded. "He wanted to know how the hell a dog could live out here. Then he wanted to know why we didn't catch it sooner. Wanted to know what he pays us for." She pushed her short blond hair off her face and eyed the animal. "I should have slagged it."

"What's he want us to do?"

"It's not in the manual. He's calling back."

I studied the limp animal. "I want to know how it was surviving. Dogs are meat eaters, right?"

"Maybe some of the engineers were giving it meat. Like Jaak did."

Jaak shook his head. "I don't think so. The sucker threw up my arm almost right after he ate it." He wiggled his new stump where it was rapidly regrowing. "I don't think we're compatible for it."

I asked, "But we could eat it, right?"

Lisa laughed and took a spoonful of tailings. "We can

eat anything. We're the top of the food chain."

"Weird how it can't eat us."

"You've probably got more mercury and lead running through your blood than any pre-weeviltech animal ever could have had."

"That's bad?"

"Used to be poison."

"Weird."

Jaak said, "I think I might have broken it when I put it in the cage." He studied it seriously. "It's not moving like it was before. And I heard something snap when I stuffed it in."

"So?"

Jaak shrugged. "I don't think it's healing."

The dog did look kind of beat up. It just lay there, its sides going up and down like a bellows. Its eyes were half-open, but didn't seem to be focused on any of us. When Jaak made a sudden movement, it twitched for a second, but it didn't get up. It didn't even growl.

Jaak said, "I never thought an animal could be so fragile."

"You're fragile, too. That's not such a big surprise."

"Yeah, but I only broke a couple bones on it, and now look at it. It just lies there and pants."

Lisa frowned thoughtfully. "It doesn't heal." She climbed awkwardly to her feet and went to peer into the cage. Her voice was excited. "It really is a dog. Just like we used to be. It could take weeks for it to heal. One broken bone, and it's done for."

She reached a razored hand into the cage and sliced a thin wound into its shank. Blood oozed out, and kept oozing. It took minutes for it to begin clotting. The dog lay still and panted, clearly wasted.

She laughed. "It's hard to believe we ever lived long enough to evolve out of that. If you chop off its legs, they won't regrow." She cocked her head, fascinated. "It's as delicate as rock. You break it, and it never comes back together." She reached out to stroke the matted fur of the animal. "It's as easy to kill as the hunter."

The comm buzzed. Jaak went to answer.

Lisa and I stared at the dog, our own little window into pre-history.

Jaak came back into the room. "Bunbaum's flying out a biologist to take a look at it."

"You mean a bio-engineer," I corrected him.

"Nope. Biologist. Bunbaum said they study animals."

Lisa sat down. I checked her blades to see if she'd knocked anything loose. "There's a dead-end job."

"I guess they grow them out of DNA. Study what they do. Behavior, shit like that."

"Who hires them?"

Jaak shrugged. "Pau Foundation has three of them on staff. Origin of life guys. That's who's sending out this one. Mushi-something. Didn't get his name."

"Origin of life?"

"Sure, you know, what makes us tick. What makes us alive. Stuff like that."

I poured a handful of tailings mud into Lisa's mouth. She gobbled it gratefully. "Mud makes us tick," I said.

Jaak nodded at the dog. "It doesn't make that dog tick."

We all looked at the dog. "It's hard to tell what makes it tick."

* * *

Lin Musharraf was a short guy with black hair and a hooked nose that dominated his face. He had carved his skin with swirling patterns of glow implants, so he stood out as cobalt spirals in the darkness as he jumped down from his chartered HEV.

The centaurs went wild about the unauthorized visitor and corralled him right up against his ship. They were all over him and his DNA kit, sniffing him, running their scanners over his case, pointing their 101's into his glowing face and snarling at him.

I let him sweat for a minute before calling them away. The centaurs backed off, swearing and circling, but didn't slag him. Musharraf looked shaken. I couldn't blame him. They're scary monsters: bigger and faster than a man. Their behavior patches make them vicious, their sentience upgrades give them the intelligence to operate military equipment, and their basic fight/flight response is so impaired that they only know how to attack when they're threatened. I've seen a half-slagged centaur tear a man to pieces barehanded and then join an assault on enemy ridge fortifications, dragging its whole melted carcass forward with just its arms. They're great critters to have at your back when the slag starts flying.

I guided Musharraf out of the scrum. He had a whole pack of memory addendums blinking off the back of his skull: a fat pipe of data retrieval, channeled direct to the brain, and no smash protection. The centaurs could have shut him down with one hard tap to the back of the head. His cortex might have grown back, but he wouldn't have been the same. Looking at those blinking triple fins of intelligence draping down the back of his head, you could tell he was a typical lab rat. All brains, no survival instincts. I wouldn't have stuck mem-adds into my head even for a triple bonus.

"You've got a dog?" Musharraf asked when we were out of reach of the centaurs.

"We think so." I led him down into the bunker, past our weapons racks and weight rooms to the common room where we'd stored the dog. The dog looked up at us as we came in, the most movement it had made since Jaak put it in the cage.

Musharraf stopped short and stared. "Remarkable."

He knelt in front of the animal's cage and unlocked the door. He held out a handful of pellets. The dog dragged itself upright. Musharraf backed away, giving it room, and the dog followed stiff and wary, snuffling after the pellets. It buried its muzzle in his brown hand, snorting and gobbling at the pellets.

Musharraf looked up. "And you found it in your tailings pits?"

"That's right."

"Remarkable."

The dog finished the pellets and snuffled his palm for more. Musharraf laughed and stood. "No more for you. Not right now." He opened his DNA kit, pulled out a sampler needle and stuck the dog. The sampler's chamber filled with blood.

Lisa watched. "You talk to it?"

Musharraf shrugged. "It's a habit."

"But it's not sentient."

"Well, no, but it likes to hear voices." The chamber finished filling. He withdrew the needle, disconnected the collection chamber and fitted it into the kit. The analysis software blinked alive and the blood disappeared into the heart of the kit with a soft vacuum hiss.

"How do you know?"

Musharraf shrugged. "It's a dog. Dogs are that way."

We all frowned. Musharraf started running tests on the blood, humming tunelessly to himself as he worked. His DNA kit peeped and squawked. Lisa watched him run his tests, clearly pissed off that SesCo had sent out a lab rat to retest what she had already done. It was easy to understand her irritation. A centaur could have run those DNA tests.

"I'm astounded that you found a dog in your pits," Musharraf muttered.

Lisa said, "We were going to slag it, but Bunbaum wouldn't let us."

Musharraf eyed her. "How restrained of you."

Lisa shrugged. "Orders."

"Still, I'm sure your thermal surge weapon presented a powerful temptation. How good of you not to slag a starving animal."

Lisa frowned suspiciously. I started to worry that she might take Musharraf apart. She was crazy enough without people talking down to her. The memory addendums on the back of his head were an awfully tempting target: one slap, down goes the lab rat. I wondered if we sank him in a catchment lake if anyone would notice him missing. A biologist, for Christ's sake.

Musharraf turned back to his DNA kit, apparently unaware of his hazard. "Did you know that in the past, people believed that we should have compassion for all things on Earth? Not just for ourselves, but for all living things?"

"So?"

"I would hope you will have compassion for one foolish scientist and not dismember me today."

Lisa laughed. I relaxed. Encouraged, Musharraf said, "It truly is remarkable that you found such a specimen amongst your mining operations. I haven't heard of a living specimen in ten or fifteen years."

"I saw one in a zoo, once," Jaak said.

"Yes, well, a zoo is the only place for them. And laboratories, of course. They still provide useful genetic data." He was studying the results of the tests, nodding to himself as information scrolled across the kit's screen.

Jaak grinned. "Who needs animals if you can eat stone?"

Musharraf began packing up his DNA kit. "Weeviltech. Precisely. We transcended the animal kingdom." He latched his kit closed and nodded to us all. "Well, it's been quite enlightening. Thank you for letting me see your specimen."

"You're not going to take it with you?"

Musharraf paused, surprised. "Oh no. I don't think so."

"It's not a dog, then?"

"Oh no, it's quite certainly a real dog. But what on Earth would I do with it?" He held up a vial of blood. "We have the DNA. A live one is hardly worth keeping around. Very expensive to maintain, you know. Manufacturing a basic organism's food is quite complex. Clean rooms, air filters, special lights. Re-creating the web of life isn't easy. Far more simple to release oneself from it completely than to attempt to re-create it." He glanced at the dog. "Unfortunately, our furry friend over there would never survive weeviltech. The worms would eat him as quickly as they eat everything else. No, you would have to manufacture the animal from scratch. And really, what would be the point of that? A bio-job without hands?" He laughed and headed for his HEV.

We all looked at each other. I jogged after the doctor and caught up with him at the hatch to the tarmac. He had paused on the verge of opening it. "Your centaurs know me now?" he asked.

"Yeah, you're fine."

"Good." He dilated the hatch and strode out into the cold. I trailed after him. "Wait! What are we supposed to do with it?"

"The dog?" The doctor climbed into the HEV and began strapping in. Wind whipped around us, carrying stinging grit from the tailings piles. "Turn it back to your pits. Or you could eat it, I suppose. I understand that it was a real delicacy. There are recipes for cooking animals. They take time, but they can give quite extraordinary results."

Musharraf's pilot started cycling up his turbofans.

"Are you kidding?"

Musharraf shrugged, and shouted over the increasing scream of the engines. "You should try it! Just another part of our heritage that's atrophied since weeviltech!"

He yanked down the flight cocoon's door, sealing himself inside. The turbofans cycled higher and the pilot motioned me back from their wash as the HEV slowly lifted into the air.

Lisa and Jaak couldn't agree on what we should do with the dog. We had protocols for working out conflict. As a tribe of killers, we needed them. Normally, consensus worked for us, but every once in a while, we just got tangled up and stuck to our positions, and after that, not much could get done without someone getting slaughtered. Lisa and Jaak dug in, and after a couple days of wrangling, with Lisa threatening to cook the thing in the middle of the night while Jaak wasn't watching, and Jaak threatening to cook her if she did, we finally went with a majority vote. I got to be the tie-breaker.

"I say we eat it," Lisa said.

We were sitting in the monitoring room, watching satellite shots of the tailings mountains and the infrared blobs of the mining bots while they ripped around in the earth. In one corner, the object of our discussion lay in its cage, dragged there by Jaak in an attempt to sway the result. He spun his observation chair, turning his attention away from the theater maps. "I think we should keep it. It's cool. Old-timey, you know? I mean, who the hell do you know who has a real dog?"

"Who the hell wants the hassle?" Lisa responded. "I say we try real meat." She cut a line in her forearm with her razors. She ran her finger along the resulting blood beads and tasted them as the wound sealed.

They both looked at me. I looked at the ceiling. "Are you sure you can't decide this without me?"

Lisa grinned. "Come on, Chen, you decide. It was a group find. Jaak won't pout, will you?"

Jaak gave her a dirty look.

I looked at Jaak. "I don't want its food costs to come out of group bonuses. We agreed we'd use part of it for the new Immersive Response. I'm sick of the old one."

Jaak shrugged. "Fine with me. I can pay for it out of my own. I just won't get any more tats."

I leaned back in my chair, surprised, then looked at Lisa. "Well, if Jaak wants to pay for it, I think we should keep it."

Lisa stared at me, incredulous. "But we could cook it!"

I glanced at the dog where it lay panting in its cage. "It's like having a zoo of our own. I kind of like it."

Musharraf and the Pau Foundation hooked us up with a supply of food pellets for the dog and Jaak looked up an old database on how to splint its busted bones. He bought water filtration so that it could drink.

I thought I'd made a good decision, putting the costs on Jaak, but I didn't really foresee the complications that came with having an unmodified organism in the bunker. The thing shit all over the floor, and sometimes it wouldn't eat, and it would get sick for no reason, and it was slow to heal so we all ended up playing nursemaid to the thing while it lay in its cage. I kept expecting Lisa to break its neck in the middle of the night, but even though she grumbled, she didn't assassinate it.

Jaak tried to act like Musharraf. He talked to the dog. He logged onto the libraries and read all about old-time dogs. How they ran in packs. How people used to breed them.

We tried to figure out what kind of dog it was, but we couldn't narrow it down much, and then Jaak discovered that all the dogs could interbreed, so all you could do was guess that it was some kind of big sheep dog, with maybe a head from a Rottweiler, along with maybe some other kind of dog, like a wolf or coyote or something.

Jaak thought it had coyote in it because they were supposed to have been big adapters, and whatever our dog was, it must have been a big adapter to hang out in the tailings pits. It didn't have the boosters we had, and it had still lived in the rock acids. Even Lisa was impressed by that.

* * *

I was carpet bombing Antarctic Recessionists, swooping low, driving the suckers further and further along the ice floe. If I got lucky, I'd drive the whole village out onto a vestigial shelf and sink them all before they knew what was happening. I dove again, strafing and then spinning away from their return slag.

It was fun, but mostly just a way to kill time between real bombing runs. The new IR was supposed to be as good as the arcades, full immersion and feedback, and portable to boot. People got so lost they had to take intravenous feedings or they withered away while they were inside.

I was about to sink a whole load of refugees when Jaak shouted. "Get out here! You've got to see this!"

I stripped off my goggles and ran for the monitoring room, adrenaline amping up. When I got there, Jaak was just standing in the center of the room with the dog, grinning.

Lisa came tearing in a second later. "What? What is it?" Her eyes scanned the theater maps, ready for bloodshed.

Jaak grinned. "Look at this." He turned to the dog and held out his hand. "Shake."

The dog sat back on its haunches and gravely offered him its paw. Jaak grinned and shook the paw, then tossed it a food pellet. He turned to us and bowed.

Lisa frowned. "Do it again."

Jaak shrugged, and went through the performance a second time.

"It thinks?" she asked.

Jaak shrugged. "Got me. You can get it to do things. The libraries are full of stuff on them. They're trainable.

Not like a centaur or anything, but you can make them do little tricks, and if they're certain breeds, they can learn special stuff, too."

"Like what?"

"Some of them were trained to attack. Or to find explosives."

Lisa looked impressed. "Like nukes and stuff?"

Jaak shrugged. "I guess."

"Can I try?" I asked.

Jaak nodded. "Go for it."

I went over to the dog and stuck out my hand. "Shake." It stuck out its paw. My hackles went up. It was like sending signals to aliens. I mean, you expect a bio-job or a robot to do what you want it to. Centaur, go get blown up. Find the op-force. Call reinforcements. The HEV was like that, too. It would do anything. But it was designed.

"Feed it," Jaak said, handing me a food pellet. "You have to feed it when it does it right."

I held out the food pellet. The dog's long pink tongue swabbed my palm.

I held out my hand again. "Shake." I said. It held out its paw. We shook hands. Its amber eyes stared up at me, solemn.

"That's some weird shit," Lisa said. I shivered, nodding and backed away. The dog watched me go.

That night in my bunk, I lay awake, reading. I'd turned out the lights and only the book's surface glowed, illuminating the bunkroom in a soft green aura. Some of Lisa's art buys glimmered dimly from the walls: a bronze hanging of a phoenix breaking into flight, stylized flames glowing around it; a Japanese woodblock print of Mount Fuji and another of a village weighed down under thick snows; a photo of the three of us in Siberia after the Peninsula campaign, grinning and alive amongst the slag.

Lisa came into the room. Her razors glinted in my book's dim light, flashes of green sparks that outlined her limbs as she moved.

"What are you reading?" She stripped and squeezed into bed with me.

I held up the book and read out loud.

> Cut me I won't bleed. Gas me I won't breathe.
> Stab me, shoot me, slash me, smash me
> I have swallowed science
> I am God.
> Alone.

I closed the book and its glow died. In the darkness, Lisa rustled under the covers.

My eyes adjusted. She was staring at me. "'Dead Man,' right?"

"Because of the dog," I said.

"Dark reading." She touched my shoulder, her hand warm, the blades embedded, biting lightly into my skin.

"We used to be like that dog," I said.

"Pathetic."

"Scary."

We were quiet for a little while. Finally I asked, "Do you ever wonder what would happen to us if we didn't have our science? If we didn't have our big brains and our weeviltech and our cellstims and—"

"And everything that makes our life good?" She laughed. "No." She rubbed my stomach. "I like all those little worms that live in your belly." She started to tickle me.

Wormy, squirmy in your belly,
wormy squirmy feeds you Nelly.
Microweevils eat the bad,
and give you something good instead.

I fought her off, laughing. "That's no Yearly."

"Third Grade. Basic bio-logic. Mrs. Alvarez. She was really big on weeviltech."

She tried to tickle me again but I fought her off. "Yeah, well Yearly only wrote about immortality. He wouldn't take it."

Lisa gave up on the tickling and flopped down beside me again. "Blah, blah, blah. He wouldn't take any gene modifications. No c-cell inhibitors. He was dying of cancer and he wouldn't take the drugs that would have saved him. Our last mortal poet. Cry me a river. So what?"

"You ever think about why he wouldn't?"

"Yeah. He wanted to be famous. Suicide's good for attention."

"Seriously, though. He thought being human meant having animals. The whole web of life thing. I've been reading about him. It's weird shit. He didn't want to live without them."

"Mrs. Alvarez hated him. She had some rhymes about him, too. Anyway, what were we supposed to do? Work out weeviltech and DNA patches for every stupid species? Do you know what that would have cost?" She nuzzled close to me. "If you want animals around you, go to a zoo. Or get some building blocks and make something, if it makes you happy. Something with hands, for god's sake, not like that dog." She stared at the underside of the bunk above. "I'd cook that dog in a second."

I shook my head. "I don't know. That dog's different from a bio-job. It looks at us, and there's something there, and it's not us. I mean, take any bio-job out there, and it's basically us, poured into another shape, but not that dog...." I trailed off, thinking.

Lisa laughed. "It shook hands with you, Chen. You don't worry about a centaur when it salutes." She climbed on top of me. "Forget the dog. Concentrate on something that matters." Her smile and her razor blades glinted in the dimness.

I woke up to something licking my face. At first I thought it was Lisa, but she'd climbed into her own bunk. I opened my eyes and found the dog.

It was a funny thing to have this animal licking me, like it wanted to talk, or say hello or something. It licked me again, and I thought that it had come a long way from when it had tried to take off Jaak's arm. It put its paws up on my bed, and then in a single heavy movement, it was up on the bunk with me, its bulk curled against me.

It slept there all night. It was weird having something other than Lisa lying next to me, but it was warm and there was something friendly about it. I couldn't help smiling as I drifted back to sleep.

We flew to Hawaii for a swimming vacation and we brought the dog with us. It was good to get out of the northern cold and into the gentle Pacific. Good to stand on the beach, and look out to a limitless horizon. Good to walk along the beach holding hands while black waves crashed on the sand.

Lisa was a good swimmer. She flashed through the ocean's metallic sheen like an eel out of history and when she surfaced, her naked body glistened with hundreds of iridescent petroleum jewels.

When the Sun started to set, Jaak lit the ocean on fire with his 101. We all sat and watched as the Sun's great red ball sank through veils of smoke, its light shading deeper crimson with every minute. Waves rushed flaming onto the beach. Jaak got out his harmonica and played while Lisa and I made love on the sand.

We'd intended to amputate her for the weekend, to let her try what she had done to me the vacation before. It was a new thing in L.A., an experiment in vulnerability.

She was beautiful, lying there on the beach, slick and excited with all of our play in the water. I licked oil opals off her skin as I sliced off her limbs, leaving her more dependent than a baby. Jaak played his harmonica and watched the Sun set, and watched as I rendered Lisa down to her core.

After our sex, we lay on the sand. The last of the Sun was dropping below the water. Its rays glinted redly across the smoldering waves. The sky, thick with particulates and smoke, shaded darker.

Lisa sighed contentedly. "We should vacation here more often."

I tugged on a length of barbed wire buried in the sand. It tore free and I wrapped it around my upper arm, a tight band that bit into my skin. I showed it to Lisa. "I used to do this all the time when I was a kid." I smiled. "I thought I was so bad-ass."

Lisa smiled. "You are."

"Thanks to science." I glanced over at the dog. It

was lying on the sand a short distance away. It seemed sullen and unsure in its new environment, torn away from the safety of the acid pits and tailings mountains of its homeland. Jaak sat beside the dog and played. Its ears twitched to the music. He was a good player. The mournful sound of the harmonica carried easily over the beach to where we lay.

Lisa turned her head, trying to see the dog. "Roll me."

I did what she asked. Already, her limbs were regrowing. Small stumps, which would build into larger limbs. By morning, she would be whole, and ravenous. She studied the dog. "This is as close as I'll ever get to it," she said.

"Sorry?"

"It's vulnerable to everything. It can't swim in the ocean. It can't eat anything. We have to fly its food to it. We have to scrub its water. Dead end of an evolutionary chain. Without science, we'd be as vulnerable as it." She looked up at me. "As vulnerable as I am now." She grinned. "This is as close to death as I've ever been. At least, not in combat."

"Wild, isn't it?"

"For a day. I liked it better when I did it to you. I'm already starving."

I fed her a handful of oily sand and watched the dog, standing uncertainly on the beach, sniffing suspiciously at some rusting scrap iron that stuck out of the beach like a giant memory fin. It pawed up a chunk of red plastic rubbed shiny by the ocean and chewed on it briefly, before dropping it. It started licking around its mouth. I wondered if it had poisoned itself again.

"It sure can make you think," I muttered. I fed Lisa

another handful of sand. "If someone came from the past, to meet us here and now, what do you think they'd say about us? Would they even call us human?"

Lisa looked at me seriously. "No, they'd call us gods."

Jaak got up and wandered into the surf, standing knee-deep in the black smoldering waters. The dog, driven by some unknown instinct, followed him, gingerly picking its way across the sand and rubble.

The dog got tangled in a cluster of wire our last day on the beach. Really ripped the hell out of it: slashes through its fur, broken legs, practically strangled. It had gnawed one of its own paws half off trying to get free. By the time we found it, it was a bloody mess of ragged fur and exposed meat.

Lisa stared down at the dog. "Christ, Jaak, you were supposed to be watching it."

"I went swimming. You can't keep an eye on the thing all the time."

"It's going to take forever to fix this," she fumed.

"We should warm up the hunter," I said. "It'll be easier to work on it back home." Lisa and I knelt down to start cutting the dog free. It whimpered and its tail wagged feebly as we started to work.

Jaak was silent.

Lisa slapped him on his leg. "Come on, Jaak, get down here. It'll bleed out if you don't hurry up. You know how fragile it is."

Jaak said, "I think we should eat it."

Lisa glanced up, surprised. "You do?"

He shrugged. "Sure."

I looked up from where I was tearing away tangled

wires from around the dog's torso. "I thought you wanted it to be your pet. Like in the zoo."

Jaak shook his head. "Those food pellets are expensive. I'm spending half my salary on food and water filtration, and now this bullshit." He waved his hand at the tangled dog. "You have to watch the sucker all the time. It's not worth it."

"But still, it's your friend. It shook hands with you."

Jaak laughed. "You're my friend." He looked down at the dog, his face wrinkled with thought. "It's, it's…an animal."

Even though we had all idly discussed what it would be like to eat the dog, it was a surprise to hear him so determined to kill it. "Maybe you should sleep on it." I said. "We can get it back to the bunker, fix it up, and then you can decide when you aren't so pissed off about it."

"No." He pulled out his harmonica and played a few notes, a quick jazzy scale. He took the harmonica out of his mouth. "If you want to put up the money for his feed, I'll keep it, I guess, but otherwise.…" He shrugged.

"I don't think you should cook it."

"You don't?" Lisa glanced at me. "We could roast it, right here, on the beach."

I looked down at the dog, a mass of panting, trusting animal. "I still don't think we should do it."

Jaak looked at me seriously. "You want to pay for the feed?"

I sighed. "I'm saving for the new Immersive Response."

"Yeah, well, I've got things I want to buy too, you know." He flexed his muscles, showing off his tattoos. "I mean, what the fuck good does it do?"

"It makes you smile."

"Immersive Response makes you smile. And you don't have to clean up after its crap. Come on, Chen. Admit it. You don't want to take care of it either. It's a pain in the ass."

We all looked at each other, then down at the dog.

Lisa roasted the dog on a spit, over burning plastics and petroleum skimmed from the ocean. It tasted okay, but in the end it was hard to understand the big deal. I've eaten slagged centaur that tasted better.

Afterward, we walked along the shoreline. Opalescent waves crashed and roared up the sand, leaving jewel slicks as they receded and the Sun sank red in the distance.

Without the dog, we could really enjoy the beach. We didn't have to worry about whether it was going to step in acid, or tangle in barbwire half-buried in the sand, or eat something that would keep it up vomiting half the night.

Still, I remember when the dog licked my face and hauled its shaggy bulk onto my bed, and I remember its warm breathing beside me, and sometimes, I miss it.

BREAD AND BOMBS
BY MARY RICKERT

Mary Rickert's short fiction has appeared in many magazines, such as The *Magazine of Fantasy & Science Fiction*, *SCI FICTION*, Tor.com, and *Lightspeed*, as well as in many anthologies, including *Under My Hat*, *Brave New Worlds*, and numerous best-of-the-year annuals. Her work has been nominated for the Nebula Award, she is the winner of two World Fantasy Awards, and her collection, *Map of Dreams*, won the William L. Crawford Award for best first book-length work of fantasy. Her first novel, *The Memory Garden*, was published in 2014.

Rickert says that she wrote this story in response to news reports concerning food packages being dropped in Afghanistan which were wrapped in the same color packaging as bombs—which detonated when picked up by hungry children. Many authors have been moved to write 9/11 stories; this is Rickert's.

* * *

The strange children of the Manmensvitzender family did not go to school so we only knew they had moved into the old house on the hill because Bobby had watched them move in with their strange assortment of rocking chairs and goats. We couldn't imagine how anyone would live there, where the windows were all broken and the yard was thorny with brambles. For a while we expected to see the children, two daughters who, Bobby said, had hair like smoke and eyes like black olives, at school. But they never came.

We were in the fourth grade, that age that seems like waking from a long slumber into the world the adults imposed, streets we weren't allowed to cross, things we weren't allowed to say, and crossing them, and saying them. The mysterious Manmensvitzender children were just another in a series of revelations that year, including the much more exciting (and sometimes disturbing) evolution of our bodies. Our parents, without exception, had raised us with this subject so thoroughly explored that Lisa Bitten knew how to say vagina before she knew her address and Ralph Linster delivered his little brother, Petey, when his mother went into labor one night when it suddenly started snowing before his father could get home. But the real significance of this information didn't start to sink in until that year. We were waking to the wonders of the world and the body; the strange realizations that a friend was cute, or stinky, or picked her nose, or was fat, or wore dirty underpants, or had eyes that didn't blink when he looked at you real close and all of a sudden you felt like blushing.

When the crab apple tree blossomed a brilliant

pink, buzzing with honey bees, and our teacher, Mrs. Graymoore, looked out the window and sighed, we passed notes across the rows and made wild plans for the school picnic, how we would ambush her with water balloons and throw pies at the principal. Of course none of this happened. Only Trina Needles was disappointed because she really believed it would but she still wore bows in her hair and secretly sucked her thumb and was nothing but a big baby.

Released into summer we ran home or biked home shouting for joy and escape and then began doing everything we could think of, all those things we'd imagined doing while Mrs. Graymoore sighed at the crab apple tree which had already lost its brilliance and once again looked ordinary. We threw balls, rode bikes, rolled skateboards down the driveway, picked flowers, fought, made up, and it was still hours before dinner. We watched TV, and didn't think about being bored, but after a while we hung upside down and watched it that way, or switched the channels back and forth or found reasons to fight with anyone in the house. (I was alone, however and could not indulge in this.) That's when we heard the strange noise of goats and bells. In the mothy gray of TV rooms, we pulled back the drapes, and peered out windows into a yellowed sunlight.

The two Manmensvitzender girls in bright clothes the color of a circus, and gauzy scarves, one purple, the other red, glittering with sequins, came rolling down the street in a wooden wagon pulled by two goats with bells around their necks. That is how the trouble began. The news accounts never mention any of this; the flame of crab apple blossoms, our innocence, the sound of bells.

Instead they focus on the unhappy results. They say we were wild. Uncared for. Strange. They say we were dangerous. As if life was amber and we were formed and suspended in that form, not evolved into that ungainly shape of horror, and evolved out of it, as we are, into a teacher, a dancer, a welder, a lawyer, several soldiers, two doctors, and me, a writer.

Everybody promises during times like those days immediately following the tragedy that lives have been ruined, futures shattered but only Trina Needles fell for that and eventually committed suicide. The rest of us suffered various forms of censure and then went on with our lives. Yes, it is true, with a dark past but, you may be surprised to learn, that can be lived with. The hand that holds the pen (or chalk, or the stethoscope, or the gun, or lover's skin) is so different from the hand that lit the match, and so incapable of such an act that it is not even a matter of forgiveness, or healing. It's strange to look back and believe that any of that was me or us. Are you who you were then? Eleven years old and watching the dust motes spin lazily down a beam of sunlight that ruins the picture on the TV and there is a sound of bells and goats and a laugh so pure we all come running to watch the girls in their bright colored scarves, sitting in the goat cart which stops in a stutter of goat-hoofed steps and clatter of wooden wheels when we surround it to observe those dark eyes and pretty faces. The younger girl, if size is any indication, smiling, and the other, younger than us, but at least eight or nine, with huge tears rolling down her brown cheeks.

We stand there for a while, staring, and then Bobby says, "What's a matter with her?"

The younger girl looks at her sister who seems to be

trying to smile in spite of the tears. "She just cries all the time."

Bobby nods and squints at the girl who continues to cry though she manages to ask, "Where have you kids come from?"

He looks around the group with an are-you-kidding kind of look but anyone can tell he likes the weeping girl, whose dark eyes and lashes glisten with tears that glitter in the sun. "It's summer vacation."

Trina, who has been furtively sucking her thumb, says, "Can I have a ride?" The girls say sure. She pushes her way through the little crowd and climbs into the cart. The younger girl smiles at her. The other seems to try but cries especially loud. Trina looks like she might start crying too until the younger one says, "Don't worry. It's just how she is." The crying girl shakes the reigns and the little bells ring and the goats and cart go clattering down the hill. We listen to Trina's shrill scream but we know she's all right. When they come back we take turns until our parents call us home with whistles and shouts and screen doors slam. We go home for dinner, and the girls head home themselves, the one still crying, the other singing to the accompaniment of bells.

"I see you were playing with the refugees," my mother says. "You be careful around those girls. I don't want you going to their house."

"I didn't go to their house. We just played with the goats and the wagon."

"Well all right then, but stay away from there. What are they like?"

"One laughs a lot. The other cries all the time."

"Don't eat anything they offer you."

"Why not?"

"Just don't."

"Can't you just explain to me why not?"

"I don't have to explain to you, young lady, I'm your mother."

We didn't see the girls the next day or the day after that. On the third day Bobby, who had begun to carry a comb in his back pocket and part his hair on the side, said, "Well hell, let's just go there." He started up the hill but none of us followed.

When he came back that evening we rushed him for information about his visit, shouting questions at him like reporters. "Did you eat anything?" I asked. "My mother says not to eat anything there."

He turned and fixed me with such a look that for a moment I forgot he was my age, just a kid like me, in spite of the new way he was combing his hair and the steady gaze of his blue eyes. "Your mother is prejudiced," he said. He turned his back to me and reached into his pocket, pulling out a fist that he opened to reveal a handful of small, brightly wrapped candies. Trina reached her pudgy fingers into Bobby's palm and plucked out one bright orange one. This was followed by a flurry of hands until there was only Bobby's empty palm.

Parents started calling kids home. My mother stood in the doorway but she was too far away to see what we were doing. Candy wrappers floated down the sidewalk in swirls of blue, green, red, yellow, and orange.

My mother and I usually ate separately. When I was at my dad's we ate together in front of the TV, which she said was barbaric.

"Was he drinking?" she'd ask. Mother was convinced

my father was an alcoholic and thought I did not remember those years when he had to leave work early because I'd called and told him how she was asleep on the couch, still in her pajamas, the coffee table littered with cans and bottles, which he threw in the trash with a grim expression and few words.

My mother stands, leaning against the counter, and watches me. "Did you play with those girls today?"

"No. Bobby did though."

"Well, that figures, nobody really watches out for that boy. I remember when his daddy was in high school with me. Did I ever tell you that?"

"Uh-huh."

"He was a handsome man. Bobby's a nice looking boy too but you stay away from him. I think you play with him too much."

"I hardly play with him at all. He plays with those girls all day."

"Did he say anything about them?"

"He said some people are prejudiced."

"Oh, he did, did he? Where'd he get such an idea anyway? Must be his grandpa. You listen to me, there's nobody even talks that way anymore except for a few rabble rousers, and there's a reason for that. People are dead because of that family. You just remember that. Many, many people died because of them."

"You mean Bobby's, or the girls?"

"Well, both actually. But most especially those girls. He didn't eat anything, did he?"

I looked out the window, pretending a new interest in our backyard, then, at her, with a little start, as though suddenly awoken. "What? Uh, no."

She stared at me with squinted eyes. I pretended to be unconcerned. She tapped her red fingernails against the kitchen counter. "You listen to me," she said in a sharp voice, "there's a war going on."

I rolled my eyes.

"You don't even remember, do you? Well, how could you, you were just a toddler. But there was a time when this country didn't know war. Why, people used to fly in airplanes all the time."

I stopped my fork halfway to my mouth. "Well, how stupid was that?"

"You don't understand. Everybody did it. It was a way to get from one place to another. Your grandparents did it a lot, and your father and I did too."

"You were on an airplane?"

"Even you." She smiled. "See, you don't know so much, missy. The world used to be safe, and then, one day, it wasn't. And those people," she pointed at the kitchen window, straight at the Millers' house, but I knew that wasn't who she meant, "started it."

"They're just a couple of kids."

"Well, not them exactly, but I mean the country they come from. That's why I want you to be careful. There's no telling what they're doing here. So little Bobby and his radical grandpa can say we're all prejudiced but who even talks that way anymore?" She walked over to the table, pulled out a chair, and sat down in front of me. "I want you to understand, there's no way to know about evil. So just stay away from them. Promise me."

Evil. Hard to understand. I nodded.

"Well, all right." She pushed back the chair, stood up, grabbed her pack of cigarettes from the windowsill.

"Make sure not to leave any crumbs. This is the time of year for ants."

From the kitchen window I could see my mother sitting on the picnic table, a gray plume of smoke spiraling away from her. I rinsed my dishes, loaded the dishwasher, wiped the table, and went outside to sit on the front steps and think about the world I never knew. The house on top of the hill blazed in the full sun. The broken windows had been covered by some sort of plastic that swallowed the light.

That night one flew over Oakgrove. I woke up and put my helmet on. My mother was screaming in her room, too frightened to help. My hands didn't shake the way hers did, and I didn't lie in my bed screaming. I put the helmet on and listened to it fly past. Not us. Not our town. Not tonight. I fell asleep with the helmet on and in the morning woke up with the marks of it dented on my cheeks.

Now, when summer approaches, I count the weeks when the apple trees and lilacs are in blossom, the tulips and daffodils in bloom before they droop with summer's heat, and I think how it is so much like that period of our innocence, that waking into the world with all its incandescence, before being subdued by its shadows into what we have become.

"You should have known the world then," my father says, when I visit him at the nursing home.

We've heard it so much it doesn't mean anything. The cakes, the money, the endless assortment of everything.

"We used to have six different kinds of cereal at one time," he raises his finger instructively, "coated in sugar, can you imagine? It used to go stale. We threw it out. And the planes. The sky used to be filled with them. Really. People traveled that way, whole families did. It didn't matter if someone moved away. Hell, you just got on a plane to see them."

Whenever he speaks like this, whenever any of them do, they sound bewildered, amazed. He shakes his head, he sighs. "We were so happy."

I cannot hear about those times without thinking of spring flowers, children's laughter, the sound of bells and clatter of goats. Smoke.

Bobby sits in the cart, holding the reigns, a pretty dark-skinned girl on either side of him. They ride up and down the street all morning, laughing and crying, their gauzy scarves blowing behind them like rainbows.

The flags droop listlessly from flagpoles and porches. Butterflies flit in and out of gardens. The Whitehall twins play in their backyard and the squeaky sound of their unoiled swings echoes through the neighborhood. Mrs. Renquat has taken the day off to take several kids to the park. I am not invited, probably because I hate Becky Renquat and told her so several times during the school year, pulling her hair, which was a stream of white gold so bright I could not resist it. It is Ralph Paterson's birthday and most of the little kids are spending the day with him and his dad at The Snowman's Cave Amusement Park where they get to do all the things kids used to do when snow was still safe, like sledding, and building snowmen. Lina Breedsore and Carol Minstreet went to the mall with their baby-sitter who has a boyfriend who works at the movie theater and can sneak them in to watch movies all day long. The town is empty except for the baby Whitehall twins, Trina Needles who is sucking her thumb and reading a book on her porch swing, and Bobby, going up and down the street with the Manmensvitzender girls and their goats. I sit on my porch picking at the scabs on my knees but Bobby speaks only to them, in a voice so low I can't hear what he says. Finally I stand up and block their way. The goats and cart stutter to a stop, the bells still jingling as Bobby says, "What's up, Weyers?"

He has eyes so blue, I recently discovered, I cannot look into them for more than thirty seconds, as though they burn me. Instead I look at the girls who are both smiling, even the one who is crying.

"What's your problem?" I say.

Her dark eyes widen, increasing the pool of milky white around them. She looks at Bobby. The sequins of her scarf catch the sun.

"Jesus Christ, Weyers, what are you talking about?"

"I just wanta know," I say still looking at her, "what it is with all this crying all the time, I mean like is it a disease, or what?"

"Oh for Christ's sake." The goats' heads rear, and the bells jingle. Bobby pulls on the reigns. The goats step back with clomps and the rattle of wheels but I continue to block their path. "What's your problem?"

"It's a perfectly reasonable question," I shout at his shadow against the bright sun. "I just wanta know what her problem is."

"It's none of your business," he shouts and at the same time the smaller girl speaks.

"What?" I say to her.

"It's the war, and all the suffering."

Bobby holds the goats steady. The other girl holds onto his arm. She smiles at me but continues to weep.

"Well, so? Did something happen to her?"

"It's just how she is. She always cries."

"That's stupid."

"Oh for Christ's sake, Weyers!"

"You can't cry all the time, that's no way to live."

Bobby steers the goats and cart around me. The younger girl turns and stares at me until, at some distance, she waves but I turn away without waving back.

Before it was abandoned and then occupied by the Manmensvitzenders the big house on the hill had been owned by the Richters. "Oh, sure they were rich," my father says when I tell him I am researching a book. "But you know, we all were. You should have seen the cakes! And the catalogs. We used to get these catalogs in the mail and you could buy anything that way, they'd mail it to you, even cake. We used to get this catalog, what was it called, Henry and Danny? Something like that. Two guys' names. Anyhow, when we were young it was just fruit but then, when the whole country was rich you could order spongecake with buttercream, or they had these towers of packages they'd send you, filled with candy and nuts and cookies, and chocolate, and oh my God, right in the mail."

"You were telling me about the Richters."

"Terrible thing what happened to them, the whole family."

"It was the snow, right?"

"Your brother, Jaime, that's when we lost him."

"We don't have to talk about that."

"Everything changed after that, you know. That's what

got your mother started. Most folks just lost one, some not even, but you know those Richters. That big house on the hill and when it snowed they all went sledding. The world was different then."

"I can't imagine."

"Well, neither could we. Nobody could of guessed it. And believe me, we were guessing. Everyone tried to figure what they would do next. But snow? I mean how evil is that anyway?"

"How many?"

"Oh, thousands. Thousands."

"No, I mean how many Richters?"

"All six of them. First the children and then the parents."

"Wasn't it unusual for adults to get infected?"

"Well, not that many of us played in the snow the way they did."

"So you must have sensed it, or something."

"What? No. We were just so busy then. Very busy. I wish I could remember. But I can't. What we were so busy with." He rubs his eyes and stares out the window. "It wasn't your fault. I want you to know I understand that."

"Pop."

"I mean you kids, that's just the world we gave you, so full of evil you didn't even know the difference."

"We knew, Pop."

"You still don't know. What do you think of when you think of snow?"

"I think of death."

"Well, there you have it. Before that happened it meant joy. Peace and joy."

"I can't imagine."

"Well, that's my point."

* * *

"Are you feeling all right?" She dishes out the macaroni, puts the bowl in front of me, and stands, leaning against the counter, to watch me eat.

I shrug.

She places a cold palm on my forehead. Steps back and frowns. "You didn't eat anything from those girls, did you?"

I shake my head. She is just about to speak when I say, "But the other kids did."

"Who? When?" She leans so close that I can see the lines of makeup sharp against her skin.

"Bobby. Some of the other kids. They ate candy."

Her hand comes palm down, hard, against the table. The macaroni bowl jumps, and the silverware. Some milk spills. "Didn't I tell you?" she shouts.

"Bobby plays with them all the time now."

She squints at me, shakes her head, then snaps her jaw with grim resolve. "When? When did they eat this candy?"

"I don't know. Days ago. Nothing happened. They said it was good."

Her mouth opens and closes like a fish. She turns on her heels and grabs the phone as she leaves the kitchen. The door slams. I can see her through the window, pacing the backyard, her arms gesturing wildly.

My mother organized the town meeting and everybody came, dressed up like it was church. The only people who weren't there were the Manmensvitzenders, for obvious reasons. Most people brought their kids, even the babies who sucked thumbs or blanket corners. I was there and so was Bobby with his grandpa who chewed the stem of a cold pipe and kept leaning over and whispering to his grandson during the proceedings, which quickly became heated, though there wasn't much argument, the heat being fueled by just the general excitement of it, my mother especially in her roses dress, her lips painted a bright red so that even I came to some understanding that she had a certain beauty though I was too young to understand what about that beauty wasn't entirely pleasing. "We have to remember that we are all soldiers in this war," she said to much applause.

Mr. Smyths suggested a sort of house arrest but my mother pointed out that would entail someone from town bringing groceries to them. "Everybody knows these people are starving. Who's going to pay for all this bread anyway?" she said. "Why should we have to pay for it?"

Mrs. Mathers said something about justice.

Mr. Hallensway said, "No one is innocent anymore."

My mother, who stood at the front of the room, leaning slightly against the village board table, said, "Then it's decided."

Mrs. Foley, who had just moved to town from the recently destroyed Chesterville, stood up, in that way she had of sort of crouching into her shoulders, with those eyes that looked around nervously so that some of us had secretly taken to calling her Bird Woman, and with a shaky voice, so soft everyone had to lean forward to hear, said, "Are any of the children actually sick?"

The adults looked at each other and each other's children. I could tell that my mother was disappointed that no one reported any symptoms. The discussion turned to the bright colored candies when Bobby, without standing or raising his hand, said in a loud voice, "Is that what this is about? Do you mean these?" He leaned back in his chair to wiggle his hand into his pocket and pulled out a handful of them.

There was a general murmur. My mother grabbed the edge of the table. Bobby's grandfather, grinning around his dry pipe, plucked one of the candies from Bobby's palm, unwrapped it, and popped it into his mouth.

Mr. Galvin Wright had to use his gavel to hush the noise. My mother stood up straight and said, "Fine thing, risking your own life like that, just to make a point."

"Well, you're right about making a point, Maylene," he said, looking right at my mother and shaking his head as if they were having a private discussion, "but this is candy I keep around the house to get me out of the habit of smoking. I order it through the Government Issue catalog. It's perfectly safe."

"I never said it was from them," said Bobby, who looked first at my mother and then searched the room until he found my face, but I pretended not to notice.

When we left, my mother took me by the hand, her red fingernails digging into my wrist. "Don't talk," she said, "just don't say another word." She sent me to my room and I fell asleep with my clothes on still formulating my apology.

The next morning when I hear the bells, I grab a loaf of bread and wait on the porch until they come back up the hill. Then I stand in their path.

"Now what d'you want?" Bobby says.

I offer the loaf, like a tiny baby being held up to God in church. The weeping girl cries louder, her sister clutches Bobby's arm. "What d'you think you're doing?" he shouts.

"It's a present."

"What kind of stupid present is that? Put it away! Jesus Christ, would you put it down?"

My arms drop to my sides, the loaf dangles in its bag from my hand. Both girls are crying. "I just was trying to be nice," I say, my voice wavering like the Bird Woman's.

"God, don't you know anything?" Bobby says. "They're afraid of our food, don't you even know that?"

"Why?"

"'Cause of the bombs, you idiot. Why don't you think once in a while?"

"I don't know what you're talking about."

The goats rattle their bells and the cart shifts back and forth. "The bombs! Don't you even read your history books? In the beginning of the war we sent them food packages all wrapped up the same color as these bombs that would go off when someone touched them."

"We did that?"

"Well, our parents did." He shakes his head and pulls the reigns. The cart rattles past, both girls pressed against him as if I am dangerous.

"Oh, we were so happy!" my father says, rocking into the memory. "We were like children, you know, so innocent, we didn't even know."

"Know what, Pop?"

"That we had enough."

"Enough what?"

"Oh, everything. We had enough everything. Is that a plane?" he looks at me with watery blue eyes.

"Here, let me help you put your helmet on."

He slaps at it, bruising his fragile hands.

"Quit it, Dad. Stop!"

He fumbles with arthritic fingers to unbuckle the strap but finds he cannot. He weeps into his spotted hands. It drones past.

Now that I look back on how we were that summer, before the tragedy, I get a glimmer of what my father's been trying to say all along. It isn't really about the cakes, and the mail order catalogs, or the air travel they used to take. Even though he uses stuff to describe it that's not what he means. Once there was a different emotion. People used to have a way of feeling and being in the world that is gone, destroyed so thoroughly we inherited only its absence.

"Sometimes," I tell my husband, "I wonder if my happiness is really happiness."

"Of course it's really happiness," he says, "what else would it be?"

We were under attack is how it felt. The Manmensvitzenders with their tears and fear of bread, their strange clothes and stinky goats were children like us and we could not get the town meeting out of our heads, what the adults had considered doing. We climbed trees, chased balls, came home when called, brushed our teeth when told, finished our milk, but we had lost that feeling we'd had before. It is true we didn't understand what had been taken from us, but we knew what we had been given and who had done the giving.

We didn't call a meeting the way they did. Ours just happened on a day so hot we sat in Trina Needles's playhouse fanning ourselves with our hands and complaining about the weather like the grownups. We mentioned house arrest but that seemed impossible to enforce. We discussed things like water balloons, T.P.ing. Someone mentioned dog shit in brown paper bags set on fire. I think that's when the discussion turned the way it did.

You may ask, who locked the door? Who made the stick piles? Who lit the matches? We all did. And if I am to find solace, twenty-five years after I destroyed all ability to feel that my happiness, or anyone's, really exists, I find it in this. It was all of us.

Maybe there will be no more town meetings. Maybe this plan is like the ones we've made before. But a town meeting is called. The grownups assemble to discuss how we will not be ruled by evil, and also, the possibility of widening Main Street. Nobody notices when we children sneak out. We had to leave behind the babies, sucking thumbs or blanket corners and not really part of our plan for redemption. We were children. It wasn't well thought out.

When the police came we were not "careening in some wild imitation of barbaric dance" or having seizures as has been reported. I can still see Bobby, his hair damp against his forehead, the bright red of his cheeks as he danced beneath the white flakes that fell from a sky we never trusted; Trina spinning in circles, her arms stretched wide, and the Manmensvitzender girls with their goats and cart piled high with rocking chairs, riding away from us, the jingle bells ringing, just like in the old song. Once again the world was safe and beautiful. Except by the town hall where the large white flakes rose like ghosts and the flames ate the sky like a hungry monster who could never get enough.

HOW WE GOT IN TOWN AND OUT AGAIN

BY JONATHAN LETHEM

Jonathan Lethem is the best-selling author of *The Fortress of Solitude, Motherless Brooklyn,* and several other novels, his most recent being *Chronic City.* His first novel, *Gun, with Occasional Music,* won the William L. Crawford Award, the Locus Award, and was a finalist for the Nebula Award. Lethem has published more than sixty short stories, in a diverse range of markets, from *The New Yorker* and *McSweeney's* to *F&SF* and *Asimov's*; his first collection, *The Wall of the Sky, the Wall of the Eye,* won the World Fantasy Award. In 2005, he was presented with the MacArthur Foundation "genius" grant for his contributions to literature.

"How We Got In Town and Out Again" is one of a sequence of stories by Lethem railing against virtual reality technologies. In an interview in *Science Fiction Studies*, Lethem said, "I didn't set out...to write a series of stories...examining my own resistance to that technology. But living in San Francisco during the years of an intense kind of utopian ideological boom in virtual reality and computer technologies, I felt an instinctive need to represent my own skepticism about claims that were being made that seemed to me naïve. …And so I found these resistance stories coming out of me."

Combine that with Lethem's research into 1930s dance marathons, and you've got this story.

When we first saw somebody near the mall Gloria and I looked around for sticks. We were going to rob them if they were few enough. The mall was about five miles out of the town we were headed for, so nobody would know. But when we got closer Gloria saw their vans and said they were scapers. I didn't know what that was, but she told me.

It was summer. Two days before this Gloria and I had broken out of a pack of people that had food but we couldn't stand their religious chanting anymore. We hadn't eaten since then.

"So what do we do?" I said.

"You let me talk," said Gloria.

"You think we could get into town with them?"

"Better than that," she said. "Just keep quiet."

I dropped the piece of pipe I'd found and we walked in across the parking lot. This mall was long past being good for finding food anymore but the scapers were taking out folding chairs from a store and strapping them on top of their vans. There were four men and one woman.

"Hey," said Gloria.

Two guys were just lugs and they ignored us and kept lugging. The woman was sitting in the front of the van. She was smoking a cigarette.

The other two guys turned. This was Kromer and Fearing, but I didn't know their names yet.

"Beat it," said Kromer. He was a tall squinty guy with a gold tooth. He was kind of worn but the tooth said he'd never lost a fight or slept in a flop. "We're busy," he said.

He was being reasonable. If you weren't in a town you were nowhere. Why talk to someone you met nowhere?

But the other guy smiled at Gloria. He had a thin face and a little mustache. "Who are you?" he said. He didn't look at me.

"I know what you guys do," Gloria said. "I was in one before."

"Oh?" said the guy, still smiling.

"You're going to need contestants," she said.

"She's a fast one," this guy said to the other guy. I'm Fearing," he said to Gloria.

"Fearing what?" said Gloria.

"Just Fearing."

"Well, I'm just Gloria."

"That's fine," said Fearing. "This is Tommy Kromer. We run this thing. What's your little friend's name?"

"I can say my own name," I said. "I'm Lewis."

"Are you from the lovely town up ahead?"

"Nope," said Gloria. "We're headed there."

"Getting in exactly how?" said Fearing.

"Anyhow," said Gloria, like it was an answer. "With you, now."

"That's assuming something pretty quick."

"Or we could go and say how you ripped off the last

town and they sent us to warn about you," said Gloria.

"Fast," said Fearing again, grinning, and Kromer shook his head. They didn't look too worried.

"You ought to want me along," said Gloria. "I'm an attraction."

"Can't hurt," said Fearing.

Kromer shrugged, and said, "Skinny, for an attraction."

"Sure, I'm skinny," she said. "That's why me and Lewis ought to get something to eat."

Fearing stared at her. Kromer was back to the van with the other guys.

"Or if you can't feed us—" started Gloria.

"Hold it, sweetheart. No more threats."

"We need a meal."

"We'll eat something when we get in." Fearing said. "You and Lewis can get a meal if you're both planning to enter."

"Sure," she said. "We're gonna enter—right, Lewis?"

I knew to say right.

The town militia came out to meet the vans, of course. But they seemed to know the scapers were coming, and after Fearing talked to them for a couple of minutes they opened up the doors and had a quick look then waved us through. Gloria and I were in the back of a van with a bunch of equipment and one of the lugs, named Ed. Kromer drove. Fearing drove the van with the woman in it. The other lug drove the last one alone.

I'd never gotten into a town in a van before, but I'd only gotten in two times before this anyway. The first time by myself, just by creeping in, the second because Gloria went with a militia guy.

Towns weren't so great anyway. Maybe this would be different.

We drove a few blocks and a guy flagged Fearing down. He came up to the window of the van and they talked, then went back to his car, waving at Kromer on his way. Then we followed him.

"What's that about?" said Gloria.

"Gilmartin's the advance man." said Kromer. "I thought you knew everything,"

Gloria didn't talk. I said, "What's an advance man?"

"Gets us a place, and the juice we need," said Kromer. "Softens the town up. Gets people excited."

It was getting dark. I was pretty hungry, but I didn't say anything. Gilmartin's car led us to this big building shaped like a boathouse only it wasn't near any water. Kromer said it used to be a bowling alley.

The lugs started moving stuff and Kromer made me help. The building was dusty and empty inside, and some of the lights didn't work. Kromer said just to get things inside for now. He drove away one of the vans and came back and we unloaded a bunch of little cots that Gilmartin the advance man had rented, so I had an idea where I was going to be sleeping. Apart from that it was stuff for the contest. Computer cables and plastic spacesuits, and loads of televisions.

Fearing took Gloria and they came back with food, fried chicken and potato salad, and we all ate. I couldn't stop going back for more but nobody said anything. Then I went to sleep on a cot. No one was talking to me. Gloria wasn't sleeping on a cot. I think she was with Fearing.

* * *

Gilmartin the advance man had really done his work. The town was sniffing around first thing in the morning. Fearing was out talking to them when I woke up. "Registration begins at noon, not a minute sooner," he was saying. "Beat the lines and stick around. We'll be serving coffee. Be warned, only the fit need apply—our doctor will be examining you, and he's never been fooled once. It's Darwinian logic, people. The future is for the strong. The meek will have to inherit the here and now."

Inside, Ed and the other guy were setting up the gear. They had about thirty of those wired-up plastic suits stretched out in the middle of the place, and so tangled up with cable and little wires that they were like husks of fly bodies in a spiderweb.

Under each of the suits was a light metal frame, sort of like a bicycle with a seat but no wheels, but with a headrest too. Around the web they were setting up the televisions in an arc facing the seats. The suits each had a number on the back, and the televisions had numbers on top that matched.

When Gloria turned up she didn't say anything to me but she handed me some donuts and coffee.

"This is just the start," she said, when she saw my eyes get big. "We're in for three squares a day as long as this thing lasts. As long as we last, anyway."

We sat and ate outside where we could listen to Fearing. He went on and on. Some people were lined up like he said. I didn't blame them since Fearing was such a talker. Others listened and just got nervous or excited and went away, but I could tell they were coming back later, at least to watch. When we finished the donuts Fearing came over and told us to get on line too.

"We don't have to," said Gloria.

"Yes, you do," said Fearing.

On line we met Lane. She said she was twenty like Gloria but she looked younger. She could have been sixteen, like me.

"You ever do this before?" asked Gloria.

Lane shook her head. "You?"

"Sure," said Gloria. "You ever been out of this town?"

"A couple of times," said Lane. "When I was a kid. I'd like to now."

"Why?"

"I broke up with my boyfriend."

Gloria stuck out her lip, and said, "But you're scared to leave town, so you're doing this instead."

Lane shrugged.

I liked her, but Gloria didn't.

The doctor turned out to be Gilmartin the advance man. I don't think he was a real doctor, but he listened to my heart. Nobody ever did that before, and it gave me a good feeling.

Registration was a joke, though. It was for show. They asked a lot of questions but they only sent a couple of women and one guy away, Gloria said for being too old. Everyone else was okay, despite how some of them looked pretty hungry, just like me and Gloria. This was a hungry town. Later I figured out that's part of why Fearing and Kromer picked it. You'd think they'd want to go where the money was, but you'd be wrong.

After registration they told us to get lost for the afternoon. Everything started at eight o'clock.

* * *

We walked around downtown but almost all the shops were closed. All the good stuff was in the shopping center and you had to show a town ID card to get in and me and Gloria didn't have those.

So, like Gloria always says, we killed time since time was what we had.

The place looked different. They had spotlights pointed from on top of the vans and Fearing was talking through a microphone. There was a banner up over the doors. I asked Gloria and she said, "Scape-Athon." Ed was selling beer out of a cooler and some people were buying, even though he must have just bought it right there in town for half the price he was selling at. It was a hot night. They were selling tickets but they weren't letting anybody in yet. Fearing told us to get inside.

Most of the contestants were there already. Anne, the woman from the van, was there, acting like any other contestant. Lane was there too and we waved at each other. Gilmartin was helping everybody put on the suits. You had to get naked but nobody seemed to mind. Just being contestants made it all right, like we were invisible to each other.

"Can we be next to each other?" I said to Gloria.

"Sure, except it doesn't matter," she said. "We won't be able to see each other inside."

"Inside where?" I said.

"The scapes," she said. "You'll see."

Gloria got me into my suit. It was plastic with wiring everywhere and padding at my knees and wrists and elbows and under my arms and in my crotch. I tried on the mask but it was heavy and I saw nobody else was wearing theirs so I kept it off until I had to. Then Gilmartin tried to help Gloria but she said she could do it herself.

So there we were, standing around half naked and dripping with cable in the big empty lit-up bowling alley, and then suddenly Fearing and his big voice came inside and they let the people in and the lights went down and it all started.

"Thirty-two young souls ready to swim out of this world, into the bright shiny future," went Fearing. "The question is, how far into that future will their bodies take them? New worlds are theirs for the taking—a cornucopia of scapes to boggle and amaze and gratify the senses. These lucky kids will be immersed in an ocean of data overwhelming to their undernourished sensibilities—we've assembled a really brilliant collection of environments for them to explore—and you'll be able to see everything they see, on the monitors in front of you. But can they make it in the fast lane? How long can they ride the wave? Which of them will prove able to outlast the others, and take home the big prize—one thousand dollars? That's what we're here to find out."

Gilmartin and Ed were snapping everybody into their masks and turning all the switches to wire us up and getting us to lie down on the frames. It was comfortable on the bicycle seat with your head on the headrest and a belt around your waist. You could move your arms and legs like you were swimming, the way Fearing said. I didn't mind putting on the mask now because the audience was making me nervous. A lot of them I couldn't see because of the lights, but I could tell they were there, watching.

The mask covered my ears and eyes. Around my chin

there was a strip of wire and tape. Inside it was dark and quiet at first except Fearing's voice was still coming into the earphones.

"The rules are simple. Our contestants get a thirty-minute rest period every three hours. These kids'll be well fed, don't worry about that. Our doctor will monitor their health. You've heard the horror stories, but we're a class outfit: you'll see no horrors here. The kids earn the quality care we provide one way: continuous, waking engagement with the data stream. We're firm on that. To sleep is to die—you can sleep on your own time, but not ours. One lapse, and you're out of the game—them's the rules."

The earphones started to hum. I wished I could reach out and hold Gloria's hand, but she was too far away.

"They'll have no help from the floor judges, or one another, in locating the perceptual riches of cyberspace. Some will discover the keys that open the doors to a thousand worlds, others will bog down in the antechamber to the future. Anyone caught coaching during rest periods will be disqualified—no warnings, no second chances."

Then Fearing's voice dropped out, and the scapes started.

I was in a hallway. The walls were full of drawers, like a big cabinet that went on forever. The drawers had writing on them that I ignored. First I couldn't move except my head, then I figured out how to walk, and just did that for a while. But I never got anywhere. It felt like I was walking in a giant circle, up the wall, across the ceiling, and then back down the other wall.

So I pulled open a drawer. It only looked big enough

to hold some pencils or whatever but when I pulled, it opened like a door and I went through.

"Welcome to Intense Personals," said a voice. There were just some colors to look at. The door closed behind me. "You must be eighteen years of age or older to use this service. To avoid any charges, please exit now."

I didn't exit because I didn't know how. The space with colors was kind of small except it didn't have any edges. But it felt small.

"This is the main menu. Please reach out and make one of the following selections: women seeking men, men seeking women, women seeking women, men seeking men, or alternatives."

Each of them was a block of words in the air. I reached up and touched the first one.

"After each selection touch *one* to play the recording again, *two* to record a message for this person, or *three* to advance to the next selection. You may touch three at any time to advance to the next selection, or four to return to the main menu."

Then a woman came into the colored space with me. She was dressed up and wearing lipstick.

"Hi, my name is Kate," she said. She stared like she was looking through my head at something behind me and poked at her hair while she talked. "I live in San Francisco. I work in the financial district, as a personnel manager, but my real love is the arts, currently painting and writing—"

"How did you get into San Francisco?" I said.

"—just bought a new pair of hiking boots and I'm hoping to tackle Mount Tam this weekend," she said, ignoring me.

"I never met anyone from there," I said.

"—looking for a man who's not intimidated by intelligence," she went on. "It's important that you like what you do, like where you are. I also want someone who's confident enough that I can express my vulnerability. You should be a good listener—"

I touched three. I can read numbers.

Another woman came in, just like that. This one was as young as Gloria, but kind of soft-looking.

"I continue to ask myself why in the *heck* I'm doing this personals thing," she said, sighing. "But I know the reason—I want to date. I'm new to the San Francisco area. I like to go to the theater, but I'm really open-minded. I was born and raised in Chicago, so I think I'm a little more east coast than west. I'm fast-talking and cynical. I guess I'm getting a little cynical about these ads, the sky has yet to part, lightning has yet to strike—"

I got rid of her, now that I knew how.

"—I have my own garden and landscape business—"

"—someone who's fun, not nerdy—"

"—I'm tender, I'm sensuous—"

I started to wonder how long ago these women were from. I didn't like the way they were making me feel, sort of guilty and bullied at the same time. I didn't think I could make any of them happy the way they were hoping but I didn't think I was going to get a chance to try, anyway.

It took pretty long for me to get back out into the hallway. From then on I paid more attention to how I got into things.

The next drawer I got into was just about the opposite. All space and no people. I was driving an airplane over

136

almost the whole world, as far as I could tell. There was a row of dials and switches under the windows but it didn't mean anything to me. First I was in the mountains and I crashed a lot, and that was dull because a voice would lecture me before I could start again, and I had to wait. But then I got to the desert and I kept it up without crashing much. I just learned to say "no" whenever the voice suggested something different like "engage target" or "evasive action." I wanted to fly awhile, that's all. The desert looked good from up there, even though I'd been walking around in deserts too often.

Except that I had to pee I could have done that forever. Fearing's voice broke in, though, and said it was time for the first rest period.

"—still fresh and eager after their first plunge into the wonders of the future," Fearing was saying to the people in the seats. The place was only half full. "Already this world seems drab by comparison. Yet, consider the irony, that as their questing minds grow accustomed to these splendors, their bodies will begin to rebel—"

Gloria showed me how to unsnap the cables so I could walk out of the middle of all that stuff still wearing the suit, leaving the mask behind. Everybody lined up for the bathroom. Then we went to the big hall in the back where they had the cots, but nobody went to sleep or anything. I guessed we'd all want to next time, but right now I was too excited and so was everybody else. Fearing just kept talking like us taking a break was as much a part of the show as anything else.

"Splendors, hah," said Gloria. "Bunch of second-hand cyberjunk."

"I was in a plane," I started.

"Shut up," said Gloria. "We're not supposed to talk about it. Only, if you find something you like, remember where it is."

I hadn't done that, but I wasn't worried.

"Drink some water," she said. "And get some food."

They were going around with sandwiches and I got a couple, one for Gloria. But she didn't seem to want to talk.

Gilmartin the fake doctor was making a big deal of going around checking everybody even though it was only the first break. I figured that the whole point of taking care of us so hard was to remind the people in the seats that they might see somebody get hurt.

Ed was giving out apples from a bag. I took one and went over and sat on Lane's cot. She looked nice in her suit.

"My boyfriend's here," she said.

"You're back together?"

"I mean ex-. I'm pretending I didn't see him."

"Where?"

"He's sitting right in front of my monitor." She tipped her head to point.

I didn't say anything but I wished I had somebody watching me from the audience.

When I went back the first thing I got into was a library of books. Every one you took off the shelf turned into a show, with charts and pictures, but when I figured out that it was all business stuff about how to manage your money, I got bored.

Then I went into a dungeon. It started with a wizard growing me up from a bug. We were in his workshop, which was all full of jars and cobwebs. He had a face like a melted candle and he talked as much as Fearing. There were bats flying around.

"You must resume the quest of Kroyd," he said to me and started touching me with his stick. I could see my arms and legs, but they weren't wearing the scaper suit. They were covered with muscles. When the wizard touched me I got a sword and a shield. "These are your companions, Rip and Batter," said the wizard. "They will obey you and protect you. You must never betray them for any other. That was Kroyd's mistake."

"Okay," I said.

The wizard sent me into the dungeon and Rip and Batter talked to me. They told me what to do. They sounded a lot like the wizard.

We met a Wormlion. That's what Rip and Batter called it. It had a head full of worms with little faces and Rip and Batter said to kill it, which wasn't hard. The head exploded and all the worms started running away into the stones of the floor like water.

Then we met a woman in sexy clothes who was holding a sword and shield too. Hers were loaded with jewels and looked a lot nicer than Rip and Batter. This was Kroyd's mistake, anyone could see that. Only I figured Kroyd wasn't here and I was, and so maybe his mistake was one I wanted to make too.

Rip and Batter started screaming when I traded with the woman, and then she put them on and we fought. When she killed me I was back in the doorway to the wizard's room, where I first ran in, bug-sized. This time I went the other way, back to the drawers.

Which is when I met the snowman.

I was looking around in a drawer that didn't seem to

have anything in it. Everything was just black. Then I saw a little blinking list of numbers in the corner. I touched the numbers. None of them did anything except one.

It was still black but there were five pictures of a snowman. He was three balls of white, more like plastic than snow. His eyes were just o's and his mouth didn't move right when he talked. His arms were sticks but they bent like rubber. There were two pictures of him small and far away, one from underneath like he was on a hill and one that showed the top of his head, like he was in a hole. Then there was a big one of just his head, and a big one of his whole body. The last one was of him looking in through a window, only you couldn't see the window, just the way it cut off part of the snowman.

"What's your name?" he said.

"Lewis."

"I'm Mr. Sneeze." His head and arms moved in all five pictures when he talked. His eyes got big and small.

"What's this place you're in?"

"It's no place," said Mr. Sneeze. "Just a garbage file."

"Why do you live in a garbage file?"

"Copyright lawyers," said Mr. Sneeze. "I made them nervous." He sounded happy no matter what he was saying.

"Nervous about what?"

"I was in a Christmas special for interactive television. But at the last minute somebody from the legal department thought I looked too much like a snowman on a video game called *Mud Flinger*. It was too late to redesign me so they just cut me out and dumped me in this file."

"Can't you go somewhere else?"

"I don't have too much mobility." He jumped and

twirled upside down and landed in the same place, five times at once. The one without a body spun too.

"Do you miss the show?"

"I just hope they're doing well. Everybody has been working so hard.

I didn't want to tell him it was probably a long time ago.

"What are you doing here, Lewis?" said Mr. Sneeze.

"I'm in a Scape-Athon."

"What's that?"

I told him about Gloria and Fearing and Kromer, and about the contest. I think he liked that he was on television again.

There weren't too many people left in the seats. Fearing was talking to them about what was going to happen tomorrow when they came back. Kromer and Ed got us all in the back. I looked over at Lane's cot. She was already asleep. Her boyfriend was gone from the chair out front.

I lay down on the cot beside Gloria. "I'm tired now," I said.

"So sleep a little," she said, and put her arm over me. But I could hear Fearing outside talking about a "Sexathon" and I asked Gloria what it was.

"That's tomorrow night," she said. "Don't worry about it now." Gloria wasn't going to sleep, just looking around.

I found the SmartHouse Showroom. It was a house with a voice inside. At first I was looking around to see who the voice was but then I figured out it was the house.

"Answer the phone!" it said. The phone was ringing.

I picked up the phone, and the lights in the room changed to a desk light on the table with the phone.

The music in the room turned off.

"How's that for responsiveness?"

"Fine," I said. I hung up the phone.

There was a television in the room, and it turned on. It was a picture of food. "See that?"

"The food, you mean?" I said.

"That's the contents of your refrigerator!" it said. "The packages with the blue halo will go bad in the next twenty-four hours. The package with the black halo has already expired! Would you like me to dispose of it for you?"

"Sure."

"Now look out the windows!"

I looked. There were mountains outside.

"Imagine waking up in the Alps every morning!"

"I—"

"And when you're ready for work, your car is already warm in the garage!"

The windows switched from the mountains to a picture of a car in a garage.

"And your voicemail tells callers that you're not home when it senses the car is gone from the garage!"

I wondered if there was somewhere I could get if I went down to drive the car. But they were trying to sell me this house, so probably not.

"And the television notifies you when the book you're reading is available this week as a movie!"

The television switched to a movie, the window curtains closed, and the light by the phone went off.

"I can't read," I said.

"All the more important, then, isn't it?" said the house.

"What about the bedroom?" I said. I was thinking about sleep.

"Here you go!" A door opened and I went in. The bedroom had another television. But the bed wasn't right. It had a scribble of electronic stuff over it.

"What's wrong with the bed?"

"Somebody defaced it," said the house. "Pity."

I knew it must have been Fearing or Kromer who wrecked the bed because they didn't want anyone getting that comfortable and falling asleep and out of the contest. At least not yet.

"Sorry!" said the house. "Let me show you the work center!"

Next rest I got right into Gloria's cot and curled up and she curled around me. It was real early in the morning and nobody was watching the show now and Fearing wasn't talking. I think he was off taking a nap of his own.

Kromer woke us up. "He always have to sleep with you, like a baby?"

Gloria said, "Leave him alone. He can sleep where he wants."

"I can't figure," said Kromer. "Is he your boyfriend or your kid brother?"

"Neither," said Gloria. "What do you care?"

"Okay," said Kromer. "We've got a job for him to do tomorrow, though."

"What job?" said Gloria. They talked like I wasn't there.

"We need a hacker boy for a little sideshow we put on." said Kromer "He's it."

"He's never been in a scape before," said Gloria. "He's no hacker."

"He's the nearest we've got. We'll walk him through it."

"I'll do it," I said.

"Okay, but then leave him out of the Sexathon," said Gloria.

Kromer smiled. "You're protecting him? Sorry. Everybody plays in the Sexathon, sweetheart. That's bread and butter. The customers don't let us break the rules." He pointed out to the rigs. "You'd better get out there."

I knew Kromer thought I didn't know about Gloria and Fearing, or other things. I wanted to tell him I wasn't so innocent, but I didn't think Gloria would like it, so I kept quiet.

I went to talk to Mr. Sneeze. I remembered where he was from the first time.

"What's a Sexathon?" I said.

"I don't know, Lewis."

"I've never had sex," I said.

"Me neither," said Mr. Sneeze.

"Everybody always thinks I do with Gloria just because we go around together. But we're just friends."

"That's fine," said Mr. Sneeze. "It's okay to be friends."

"I'd like to be Lane's boyfriend," I said.

Next break Gloria slept while Gilmartin and Kromer told me about the act. A drawer would be marked for me to go into, and there would be a lot of numbers and letters but I just had to keep pressing "1-2-3" no matter what. It was supposed to be a security archive, they said. The people watching would think I was breaking codes but it was just for show. Then something else would happen but they wouldn't say what, just that I should keep quiet and let Fearing talk. So I knew they were going to pull me out of my mask. I didn't know if I should tell Gloria.

Fearing was up again welcoming some people back in. I couldn't believe anybody wanted to start watching first thing in the morning but Fearing was saying "the gritty determination to survive that epitomizes the frontier spirit that once made a country called America great" and "young bodies writhing in agonized congress with the future" and that sounded like a lot of fun, I guess.

A woman from the town had quit already. Not Lane though.

A good quiet place to go was Mars. It was like the airplane, all space and no people, but better since there was no voice telling you to engage targets, and you never crashed.

I went to the drawer they told me about. Fearing's voice in my ear told me it was time. The place was a storeroom of information like the business library. No people, just files with a lot of blinking lights and complicated words. A voice kept asking me for "security clearance password" but there was always a place for me to touch "1-2-3" and I did. It was kind of a joke, like a wall made out of feathers that falls apart every time you touch it.

I found a bunch of papers with writing. Some of the words were blacked out and some were bright red and blinking. There was a siren sound. Then I felt hands pulling on me from outside and somebody took off my mask.

There were two guys pulling on me who I had never seen before, and Ed and Kromer were pulling on them. Everybody was screaming at each other but it was kind of fake, because nobody was pulling or yelling very hard. Fearing said, "The feds, the feds!" A bunch of people were crowded around my television screen I guess looking at the papers I'd dug up, but now they were watching the action.

Fearing came over and pulled out a toy gun and so did Kromer, and they were backing the two men away from me. I'm sure the audience could tell it was fake. But they were pretty excited, maybe just from remembering when feds were real.

I got off my frame and looked around. I didn't know what they were going to do with me now that I was out but I didn't care. It was my first chance to see what it was like when the contestants were all in their suits and masks, swimming in the information. None of them knew what was happening, not even Gloria, who was right next to me the whole time. They just kept moving in the scapes. I looked at Lane. She looked good, like she was dancing.

Meanwhile Fearing and Kromer chased those guys out the back. People were craning around to see. Fearing came out and took his microphone and said, "It isn't his fault, folks. Just good hacker instincts for ferreting out corruption from encrypted data. The feds don't want us digging up their trail, but the kid couldn't help it."

Ed and Kromer started snapping me back into my suit. "We chased them off," Fearing said, patting his gun. "We do take care of our own. You can't tell who's going to come sniffing around, can you? For his protection and ours we're going to have to delete that file, but it goes to show, there's no limit to what a kid with a nose for data's going to root out of cyberspace. We can't throw him out of the contest for doing what comes natural. Give him a big hand, folks."

People clapped and a few threw coins. Ed picked the change up for me, then told me to put on my mask.

Meanwhile Gloria and Lane and everybody else just went on through their scapes.

I began to see what Kromer and Fearing were selling. It wasn't any one thing. Some of it was fake and some was real, and some was a mix so you couldn't tell.

The people watching probably didn't know why they wanted to, except it made them forget their screwed-up lives for a while to watch the only suckers bigger than themselves—us.

"Meanwhile, the big show goes on," said Fearing. "How long will they last? Who will take the prize?"

I told Gloria about it at the break. She just shrugged and said to make sure I got my money from Kromer. Fearing was talking to Anne, the woman from the van, and Gloria was staring at them like she wanted them dead.

A guy was lying in his cot talking to himself as if nobody could hear and Gilmartin and Kromer went over and told him he was kicked out. He didn't seem to care.

I went to see Lane but we didn't talk. We sat on her cot and held hands. I didn't know if it meant the same thing to her that it did to me but I liked it

After the break I went and talked to Mr. Sneeze. He told me the story of the show about Christmas. He said it wasn't about always getting gifts. Sometimes you had to give gifts too.

The Sexathon was late at night. They cleared the seats and everyone had to pay again to get back in, because it was a special event. Fearing had built it up all day, talking about how it was for adults only, it would separate the men from the boys, things like that. Also that people would get knocked out of the contest. So we were pretty nervous by the time he told us the rules.

"What would scapes be without virtual sex?" he said. "Our voyagers must now prove themselves in the sensual realm—for the future consists of far more than cold, hard information. It's a place of desire and temptation, and, as always, survival belongs to the fittest. The soldiers will now be steered onto the sexual battlescape—the question is, will they meet with the Little Death, or the Big one?"

Gloria wouldn't explain. "Not real death," is all she said.

"The rules again are so simple a child could follow them. In the Sex-Scape environment our contestants will be free to pick from a variety of fantasy partners. We've packed this program with options, there's something for every taste, believe you me. We won't question their selections, but—here's the catch—we will chart the results. Their suits will tell us who does and doesn't attain sexual orgasm in the next session, and those who don't will be handed their walking papers. The suits don't lie. Find bliss or die, folks, find bliss or die."

"You get it now?" said Gloria to me.

"I guess," I said.

"As ever, audience members are cautioned never to interfere with the contestants during play. Follow their fantasies on the monitors, or watch their youthful bodies strain against exhaustion, seeking to bridge virtual lust and bona fide physical response. But no touchee."

Kromer was going around, checking the suits. "Who's gonna be in your fantasy, kid?" he said to me. "The snowman?"

I'd forgotten how they could watch me talk to Mr.

Sneeze on my television. I turned red.

"Screw you, Kromer," said Gloria.

"Whoever you want, honey," he said, laughing.

Well I found my way around their Sex-Scape and I'm not too embarrassed to say I found a girl who reminded me of Lane, except for the way she was trying so hard to be sexy. But she looked like Lane. I didn't have to do much to get the subject around to sex. It was the only thing on her mind. She wanted me to tell her what I wanted to do to her and when I couldn't think of much she suggested things and I just agreed. And when I did that she would move around and sigh as if it were really exciting to talk about even though she was doing the talking. She wanted to touch me but she couldn't really so she took off her clothes and got close to me and touched herself. I touched her too but she didn't really feel like much and it was like my hands were made of wood, which couldn't have felt too nice for her though she acted like it was great.

I touched myself a little too. I tried not to think about the audience. I was a little confused about what was what in the suit and with her breathing in my ear so loud but I got the desired result. That wasn't hard for me.

Then I could go back to the drawers but Kromer had made me embarrassed about visiting Mr. Sneeze so I went to Mars even though I would have liked to talk to him.

The audience was all stirred up at the next break. They were sure getting their money's worth now. I got into Gloria's cot. I asked her if she did it with her own hands too. "You didn't have to do that," she said.

"How else?"

"I just pretended. I don't think they can tell. They just want to see you wiggle around."

Well some of the women from the town hadn't wiggled around enough I guess because Kromer and Ed were taking them out of the contest. A couple of them were crying.

"I wish I hadn't," I said.

"It's the same either way," said Gloria. "Don't feel bad. Probably some other people did it too."

They didn't kick Lane out but I saw she was crying anyway.

Kromer brought a man into the back and said to me, "Get into your own cot, little snowman."

"Let him stay," said Gloria. She wasn't looking at Kromer.

"I've got someone here who wants to meet you," said Kromer to Gloria. "Mr. Warren, this is Gloria."

Mr. Warren shook her hand. He was pretty old. "I've been admiring you," he said. "You're very good."

"Mr. Warren is wondering if you'd let him buy you a drink," said Kromer.

"Thanks, but I need some sleep," said Gloria.

"Perhaps later," said Mr. Warren.

After he left, Kromer came back and said, "You shouldn't pass up easy money."

"I don't need it," said Gloria. "I'm going to win your contest, you goddamn pimp."

"Now, Gloria," said Kromer. "You don't want to give the wrong impression."

"Leave me alone."

I noticed now that Anne wasn't around in the rest area and I got the idea that the kind of easy money Gloria didn't want Anne did. I'm not so dumb.

* * *

Worrying about the Sexathon had stopped me from feeling how tired I was. Right after that I started nodding off in the scapes. I had to keep moving around. After I'd been to a few new things I went to see the snowman again. It was early in the morning and I figured Kromer was probably asleep and there was barely any audience to see what I was doing on my television. So Mr. Sneeze and I talked and that helped me stay awake.

I wasn't the only one who was tired after that night. On the next break I saw that a bunch of people had dropped out or been kicked out for sleeping. There were only seventeen left. I couldn't stay awake myself. But I woke up when I heard some yelling over where Lane was.

It was her parents. I guess they heard about the Sexathon, maybe from her boyfriend, who was there too. Lane was sitting crying behind Fearing who was telling her parents to get out of there, and her father just kept saying, "I'm her father! I'm her father!" Her mother was pulling at Fearing but Ed came over and pulled on her.

I started to get up but Gloria grabbed my arm and said, "Stay out of this."

"Lane doesn't want to see that guy," I said.

"Let the townies take care of themselves, Lewis. Let Lane's daddy take her home if he can. Worse could happen to her."

"You just want her out of the contest," I said.

Gloria laughed. "I'm not worried about your girlfriend outlasting me," she said. "She's about to break no matter what."

So I just watched. Kromer and Ed got Lane's parents

and boyfriend pushed out of the rest area, back toward the seats. Fearing was yelling at them, making a scene for the audience. It was all part of the show as far as he was concerned.

Anne from the van was over talking to Lane, who was still crying, but quiet now.

"Do you really think you can win?" I said to Gloria.

"Sure, why not?" she said. "I can last."

"I'm pretty tired." In fact my eyeballs felt like they were full of sand.

"Well if you fall out stick around. You can probably get food out of Kromer for cleaning up or something. I'm going to take these bastards."

"You don't like Fearing anymore," I said.

"I never did," said Gloria.

That afternoon three more people dropped out. Fearing was going on about endurance and I got thinking about how much harder it was to live the way me and Gloria did than it was to be in town and so maybe we had an advantage. Maybe that was why Gloria thought she could win now. But I sure didn't feel it myself. I was so messed up that I couldn't always sleep at the rest periods, just lie there and listen to Fearing or eat their sandwiches until I wanted to vomit.

Kromer and Gilmartin were planning some sideshow but it didn't involve me and I didn't care. I didn't want coins thrown at me. I just wanted to get through.

If I built the cities near the water the plague always killed all the people and if I built the cities near the mountains the volcanoes always killed all the people and if I built the cities on the plain the other tribe always came over and killed all the people and I got sick of the whole damn thing.

"When Gloria wins we could live in town for a while," I said. "We could even get jobs if there are any. Then if Lane doesn't want to go back to her parents she could stay with us."

"You could win the contest," said Mr. Sneeze.

"I don't think so," I said. "But Gloria could."

Why did Lewis cross Mars? To get to the other side. Ha ha.

I came out for the rest period and Gloria was already yelling and I unhooked my suit and rushed over to see what was the matter. It was so late it was getting light outside and almost nobody was in the place. "She's cheating!" Gloria screamed. She was pounding on Kromer and he was backing up because she was a handful mad. "That bitch is cheating! You let her sleep!" Gloria pointed at Anne from the van. "She's lying there asleep, you're running tapes in her monitor you goddamn cheater!"

Anne sat up in her frame and didn't say anything. She looked confused. "You're a bunch of cheaters!" Gloria kept saying. Kromer got her by the wrists and said, "Take it easy, take it easy. You're going scape-crazy, girl."

"Don't tell me I'm crazy!" said Gloria. She twisted away from Kromer and ran to the seats. Mr. Warren was there, watching her with his hat in his hands. I ran after Gloria and said her name but she said, "Leave me alone!" and went over to Mr. Warren. "You saw it, didn't you?" she said.

"I'm sorry?" said Mr. Warren.

"You must have seen it, the way she wasn't moving at all," said Gloria. "Come on, tell these cheaters you saw it. I'll go on that date with you if you tell them."

"I'm sorry, darling. I was looking at you."

Kromer knocked me out of the way and grabbed Gloria from behind. "Listen to me, girl. You're hallucinating. You're scape-happy. We see it all the time." He was talking quiet but hard. "Any more of this and you're out of the show, you understand? Get in the back and lie down now and get some sleep. You need it."

"You bastard," said Gloria.

"Sure, I'm a bastard, but you're seeing things." He held Gloria's wrist and she sagged.

Mr. Warren got up and put his hat on. "I'll see you tomorrow, darling. Don't worry. I'm rooting for you." He went out.

Gloria didn't look at him.

Kromer took Gloria back to the rest area but suddenly I wasn't paying much attention myself. I had been thinking Fearing wasn't taking advantage of the free action by talking about it because there wasn't anyone much in the place to impress at this hour. Then I looked around and I realized there were two people missing and that was Fearing and Lane.

I found Ed and I asked him if Lane had dropped out of the contest and he said no.

"Maybe there's a way you could find out if Anne is really scaping or if she's a cheat," I said to Mr. Sneeze.

"I don't see how I could," he said. "I can't visit her, she

has to visit me. And nobody visits me except you." He hopped and jiggled in his five places. "I'd like it if I could meet Gloria and Lane."

"Let's not talk about Lane," I said.

When I saw Fearing again I couldn't look at him. He was out talking to the people who came by in the morning, not in the microphone but one at a time, shaking hands and taking compliments like it was him doing the scaping.

There were only eight people left in the contest. Lane was still in it but I didn't care.

I knew if I tried to sleep I would just lie there thinking. So I went to rinse out under my suit, which was getting pretty rank. I hadn't been out of that suit since the contest started. In the bathroom I looked out the little window at the daylight and I thought about how I hadn't been out of that building for five days either, no matter how much I'd gone to Mars and elsewhere.

I went back in and saw Gloria asleep and I thought all of a sudden that I should try to win.

But maybe that was just the idea coming over me that Gloria wasn't going to.

I didn't notice it right away because I went to other places first. Mr. Sneeze had made me promise I'd always have something new to tell him about so I always opened a few drawers. I went to a tank game but it was boring. Then I found a place called the American History Blood and Wax Museum and I stopped President Lincoln from getting murdered a couple of times. I tried to stop President Kennedy from getting murdered but if I stopped it one way it always happened a different way. I don't know why.

So then I was going to tell Mr. Sneeze about it and that's when I found out. I went into his drawer and touched the right numbers but what I got wasn't the usual five pictures of the snowman. It was pieces of him but chopped up and stretched into thin white strips, around the edge of the black space, like a band of white light.

I said, "Mr. Sneeze?"

There wasn't any voice.

I went out and came back in but it was the same. He couldn't talk. The band of white strips got narrower and wider, like it was trying to move or talk. It looked a bit like a hand waving open and shut. But if he was still there he couldn't talk.

I would have taken my mask off then anyway, but the heat of my face and my tears forced me to.

I saw Fearing up front talking and I started for him without even getting my suit unclipped, so I tore up a few of my wires. I didn't care. I knew I was out now. I went right out and tackled Fearing from behind. He wasn't so big, anyway. Only his voice was big. I got him down on the floor.

"You killed him," I said, and I punched him as hard as I could, but you know Kromer and Gilmartin were there holding my arms before I could hit him more than once. I just screamed at Fearing, "You killed him, you killed him."

Fearing was smiling at me and wiping his mouth. "Your snowman malfunctioned, kid."

"That's a lie!"

"You were boring us to death with that snowman, you little punk. Give it a rest, for chrissake."

I kept kicking out even though they had me pulled away from him. "I'll kill you!" I said.

"Right," said Fearing. "Throw him out of here."

He never stopped smiling. Everything suited his plans, that was what I hated.

Kromer the big ape and Gilmartin pulled me outside into the sunlight and it was like a knife in my eyes. I couldn't believe how bright it was. They tossed me down in the street and when I got up Kromer punched me, hard.

Then Gloria came outside. I don't know how she found out, if she heard me screaming or if Ed woke her. Anyway she gave Kromer a pretty good punch in the side and said, "Leave him alone!"

Kromer was surprised and he moaned and I got away from him. Gloria punched him again. Then she turned around and gave Gilmartin a kick in the nuts and he went down. I'll always remember in spite of what happened next that she gave those guys a couple they'd be feeling for a day or two.

The gang who beat the crap out of us were a mix of the militia and some other guys from the town, including Lane's boyfriend. Pretty funny that he'd take out his frustration on us, but that just shows you how good Fearing had that whole town wrapped around his finger.

Outside of town we found an old house that we could hide in and get some sleep. I slept longer than Gloria. When I woke up she was on the front steps rubbing a spoon back and forth on the pavement to make a sharp point, even though I could see it hurt her arm to do it.

"Well, we did get fed for a couple of days," I said.

Gloria didn't say anything.

"Let's go up to San Francisco," I said. "There's a lot of lonely women there."

I was making a joke of course.

Gloria looked at me. "What's that supposed to mean?"

"Just that maybe I can get us in for once."

Gloria didn't laugh, but I knew she would later.

DARK, DARK WERE THE TUNNELS

BY GEORGE R. R. MARTIN

George R. R. Martin is the wildly popular author of the A Song of Ice and Fire epic fantasy series (which is currently being adapted for television on HBO as *Game of Thrones*), as well as other novels, such as *Dying of the Light* and *The Armageddon Rag*. His short fiction—which has appeared in numerous anthologies and in most if not all of the genre's major magazines—has garnered him four Hugos, two Nebulas, the Stoker, and the World Fantasy Award. Martin is also known for editing the *Wild Cards* series of shared world superhero anthologies, and for his work as a screenwriter on such television projects as the 1980s version of *The Twilight Zone* and *Beauty and the Beast*.

Before Martin became the king of epic fantasy (or "The American Tolkien," as *Time* magazine likes to call him), much of his fiction was science fictional in nature, such as the multiple award-winning "Sandkings" and the story included here.

* * *

In the story that follows, you'll meet Greel. He is a scout of the People. He's penetrated the Oldest Tunnels, where the taletellers said the People had come from a million years ago. He is no coward, but he is afraid, and with good reason. You see, he's very used to being in the dark, but some visitors have come to the tunnels, and they've brought with them light...

Greel was afraid.

He lay in the warm, rich darkness beyond the place where the tunnel curved, his thin body pressed against the strange metal bar that ran along the floor. His eyes were closed. He strained to remain perfectly still.

He was armed. A short barbed spear was clenched tightly in his right fist. But that did not lessen his fear.

He had come far, far. He had climbed higher and ranged further than any other scout of the People in long generations. He had fought his way through the Bad Levels, where the worm-things still hunted the People relentlessly. He had stalked and slain the glowing killer mole in the crumbling Middle Tunnels. He had wiggled through dozens of unmapped and unnamed passages that hardly looked big enough for a man to pass.

And now he had penetrated to the Oldest Tunnels, the great tunnels and halls of legend, where the taletellers said the People had come from a million years ago.

He was no coward. He was a scout of the People, who dared to walk in tunnels where men had not trod in centuries.

But he was afraid, and was not ashamed for his fear.

A good scout knows when to be afraid. And Greel was a very good scout. So he lay silent in the darkness, and clutched his spear, and thought.

Slowly the fear began to wane. Greel steeled himself, and opened his eyes. Quickly he shut them again.

The tunnel ahead was on fire.

He had never seen fire. But the taletellers had sung of it many times. Hot it was. And bright, so bright it hurt the eyes. Blindness was the lot of those who looked too long.

So Greel kept his eyes shut. A scout needed his eyes. He could not allow the fire ahead to blind him.

Back here, in the darkness beyond the bend of the tunnel, the fire was not so bad. It still hurt the eyes to look at it, as it hung upon the curving tunnel wall. But the pain was one that could be borne.

But earlier, when he had first seen the fire, Greel had been unwise. He had crept forward, squinting, to where the wall curved away. He had touched the fire that hung upon the stone. And then, foolishly, he had peered beyond the curve.

His eyes still ached. He had gotten only one quick glimpse before whirling and scrambling silently back to where he lay. But it was enough. Beyond the bend the fire had been brighter, much brighter, brighter than ever he could have imagined. Even with his eyes closed he could still see it, two dancing, aching spots of horrible intense brightness. They would not go away. The fire had burned part of his eyes, he thought.

But still, when he had touched the fire that hung upon the wall, it had not been like the fire of which the taletellers sing. The stone had felt like all other stone, cool and a little damp. Fire was hot, the taletellers said. But the fire on the stone had not been hot to the touch.

It was not fire, then, Greel decided after thought. What it was he did not know. But it could not be fire if it was not hot.

He stirred slightly from where he lay. Barely moving, he reached out and touched H'ssig in the darkness.

His mind-brother was several yards distant, near one of the other metal bars. Greel stroked him with his mind, and could feel H'ssig quiver in response. Thoughts and sensations mingled wordlessly.

H'ssig was afraid, too. The great hunting rat had no eyes. But his scent was keener than Greel's, and there was a strange smell in the tunnel. His ears were better, too. Through them Greel could pick up more of the odd noises that came from within the fire that was not a fire.

Greel opened his eyes again. Slowly this time, not all at once. Squinting.

The holes the fire had burned in his vision were still there. But they were fading. And the dimmer fire that moved on the curving tunnel wall could be endured, if he did not look directly at it.

Still. He could not go forward. And he must not creep back. He was a scout. He had a duty.

He reached out to H'ssig again. The hunting rat had run with him since birth. He had never failed him. He would not fail him now. The rat had no eyes that could be burned, but his ears and his nose would tell Greel what he must know about the thing beyond the curve.

H'ssig felt the command more than he heard it. He crept forward slowly towards the fire.

"A treasurehouse!"

Ciffonetto's voice was thick with admiration. The layer

of protective grease smeared onto his face could hardly hide the grin.

Von der Stadt looked doubtful. Not just his face, but his whole body radiated doubt. Both men were dressed alike, in featureless grey coveralls woven of a heavy metallic cloth. But they could never be mistaken. Von der Stadt was unique in his ability to express doubt while remaining absolutely still.

When he moved, or spoke, he underlined the impression. As he did now.

"Some treasurehouse," he said, simply.

It was enough to annoy Ciffonetto. He frowned slightly at his larger companion. "No, I mean it," he said. The beam from his heavy flashlight sliced through the thick darkness, and played up and down one of the rust-eaten steel pillars that stretched from the platform to the roof. "Look at that," Ciffonetto said.

Von der Stadt looked at it. Doubtfully. "I see it," he said. "So where's the treasure?"

Ciffonetto continued to move his beam up and down. "That's the treasure," he said. "This whole place is a major historical find. I knew this was the place to search. I told them so."

"What's so great about a steel beam, anyway?" Von der Stadt asked, letting his own flash brush against the pillar.

"The state of preservation," Ciffonetto said, moving closer. "Most everything above ground is radioactive slag, even now. But down here we've got some beautiful artifacts. It will give us a much better picture about what the old civilization was like, before the disaster."

"We know what the old civilization was like," Von der Stadt protested. "We've got tapes, books, films, everything.

All sorts of things. The war didn't even touch Luna."

"Yes, yes, but this is different," Ciffonetto said. "This is reality." He ran his gloved hand lovingly along the pillar. "Look here," he said.

Von der Stadt moved closer.

There was writing carved into the metal. Scratched in, rather. It didn't go very deep, but it could still be read, if but faintly.

Ciffonetto was grinning again. Von der Stadt looked doubtful. "Rodney loves Wanda," he said.

He shook his head. "Shit, Cliff," he said, "you can find the same thing in every public john in Luna City."

Ciffonetto rolled his eyes. "Von der Stadt," he said, "if we found the oldest cave painting in the world, you'd probably say it was a lousy picture of a buffalo." He jabbed at the writing with his free hand. "Don't you understand? This is old. It's history. It's the remains of a civilization and a nation and a planet that perished almost half a millennium ago."

Von der Stadt didn't reply, but he still looked doubtful. His flashlight wandered. "There's some more if that's what you're after," he said, holding his beam steady on another pillar a few feet distant.

This time it was Ciffonetto who read the inscription. "Repent or ye are doomed." he said, smiling, after his flash melted into Von der Stadt's.

He chuckled slightly. "The words of the prophets are written on the subway walls," he said softly.

Von der Stadt frowned. "Some prophet," he said. "They must have had one hell of a weird religion."

"Oh, Christ," Ciffonetto groaned. "I didn't mean it literally. I was quoting. A mid-twentieth-century poet named Simon. He wrote that only fifty years or so before the great disaster."

Von der Stadt wasn't interested. He wandered away impatiently, his flash darting here and there amid the pitch-black ruins of the ancient subway station. "It's hot down here," he complained.

"Hotter up there," Ciffonetto said, already lost in a new inscription.

"Not the same kind of hot," Von der Stadt replied.

Ciffonetto didn't bother to answer. "This is the biggest find of the expedition," he said when he looked up at last. "We've got to get pictures. And get the others down here. We're wasting our time on the surface."

"We'll do better down here?" Von der Stadt said. Doubtfully, of course.

Ciffonetto nodded. "That's what I've said all along. The surface was plastered. It's still a radioactive hell up there, even after all these centuries. If anything survived, it was underground. That's where we should look. We should branch out and explore this whole system of tunnels." His hands swept out expansively.

"You and Nagel have been arguing about that the whole trip," Von der Stadt said. "All the way from Luna City. I don't see that it's done you much good."

"Doctor Nagel is a fool," Ciffonetto said carefully.

"I don't think so," Von der Stadt said. "I'm a soldier, not a scientist. But I've heard his side of the argument, and it makes sense. All this stuff down here is great, but it's not what Nagel wants. It's not what the expedition was sent to Earth to look for."

"I know, I know," Ciffonetto said. "Nagel wants life. Human life, especially. So every day he sends the flyers out further and further. And so far all he's come up with is a few species of insects and a handful of mutated birds."

Von der Stadt shrugged.

"If he'd look down here, he'd find what he's after," Ciffonetto continued. "He doesn't realize how deep the cities had dug before the war. There are miles of tunnels under our feet. Level after level. That's where the survivors would be, if there are any survivors."

"How do you figure?" Von der Stadt asked.

"Look, when war hit, the only ones to live through it would be those down in deep shelters. Or in the tunnels beneath the cities. The radioactivity would have prevented them from coming up for years. Hell, the surface still isn't very attractive. They'd be trapped down there. They'd adjust. After a few generations they wouldn't want to come up."

But Von der Stadt's attention had wandered, and he was hardly listening any more. He had walked to the edge of the platform, and was staring down onto the tracks.

He stood there silently for a moment, then reached a decision. He stuffed his flashlight into his belt, and began to climb down. "Come on," he said. "Let's go look for some of these survivors of yours."

H'ssig stayed close to the metal bar as he edged forward. It helped to hide him, and kept away the fire, so he moved in a little band of almost darkness. Hugging it as best he could, he crept silently around the curve, and halted.

Through him Greel watched: watched with the rat's ears and with his nose.

The fire was talking.

There were two scents, alike but not the same. And

there were two voices. Just as there had been two fires. The bright things that had burned Greel's eyes were living creatures of some sort.

Greel listened. The sounds H'ssig heard so clearly were words. A language of some sort. Greel was sure of that. He knew the difference between the roars and grunts of animals and the patterns of speech.

But the fire things were talking in a language he did not know. The sounds meant no more to him than to H'ssig who relayed them.

He concentrated on the scent. It was strange, unlike anything he had encountered before. But somehow it felt like a man-scent, though it could not be that.

Greel thought. An almost man-scent. And words. Could it be that the fire things were men? They would be strange men, much unlike the People. But the taletellers sung of men in ancient times that had strange powers and forms. Might not these be such men? Here, in the Oldest Tunnels, where the legends said the Old Ones had created the People—might not such men still dwell here?

Yes.

Greel stirred. He moved slowly from where he lay, raising himself to a crouching position to squint at the curve ahead. A silent snap brought H'ssig back to safety from the fiery tunnel beyond the curve.

There was one way to make sure, Greel thought Trembling, he reached out cautiously with his mind.

Von der Stadt had adapted to Earth's gravity a lot more successfully than Ciffonetto. He reached the floor of the tunnel quickly, and waited impatiently while his companion climbed down from the platform.

Ciffonetto let himself drop the last foot or so, and landed with a thud. He looked up at the platform apprehensively. "I just hope I can make it back up," he said.

Von der Stadt shrugged. "You were the one who wanted to explore all the tunnels."

"Yes," said Ciffonetto, shifting his gaze from the platform to look around him. "And I still do. Down here, in these tunnels, are the answers we're seeking."

"That's your theory, anyway," Von der Stadt said. He looked in both directions, chose one at random, and moved forward, his flashlight beam spearing out before him. Ciffonetto followed a half-step behind.

The tunnel they entered was long, straight, and empty.

"Tell me," Von der Stadt said in an offhand manner as they walked, "even if your survivors did make it through the war in shelters, wouldn't they have been forced to surface eventually to survive? I mean—how could anyone actually live down here?" He looked around the tunnel with obvious distaste.

"Have you been taking lessons from Nagel or something?" Ciffonetto replied. "I've heard that so often I'm sick of it. I admit it would be difficult. But not impossible. At first, there would be access to large stores of canned goods. A lot of that stuff was kept in basements. You could get to it by tunneling. Later, you could raise food. There are plants that will grow without light. And there would be insects and boring animals too, I imagine."

"A diet of bugs and mushrooms. It doesn't sound too healthy to me."

Ciffonetto stopped suddenly, not bothering to reply. "Look there," he said, pointing with his flashlight.

The beam played over a jagged break in the tunnel wall. It looked as though someone had smashed through the stone a long time ago.

Von der Stadt's flash joined Ciffonetto's to light the area better. There was a passage descending from the break. Ciffonetto moved towards it with a start.

"What the hell do you say to this, Von der Stadt?" he asked, grinning. He stuck head and flashlight into the crude tunnel, but re-emerged quickly.

"Not much there," he said. "The passage is caved in after a few feet. But still, it confirms what I've been saying."

Von der Stadt looked vaguely uneasy. His free hand drifted to the holstered pistol at his side. "I don't know," he said.

"No, you don't," said Ciffonetto, triumphantly. "Neither does Nagel. Men have lived down here. They may still live here. We've got to organize a more efficient search of the whole underground system."

He paused, his mind flickering back to Von der Stadt's argument of a few seconds earlier. "As for your bugs and mushrooms, men can learn to live on a lot of things. Men adapt. If men survived the war—and this says they did—then they survived the aftermath, I'll wager."

"Maybe," Von der Stadt said. "I can't see what you are so hot on discovering survivors for anyway, though. I mean, the expedition is important and all that. We've got to re-establish spaceflight, and this is a good test for our new hardware. And I guess you scientists can pick up some good stuff for the museums. But humans? What did Earth ever get us besides the Great Famine?"

Ciffonetto smiled tolerantly. "It's because of the Great Famine that we want to find humans," he said. He paused.

"We've got enough to entice even Nagel now. Let's head back."

He started walking back in the direction they had come, and resumed talking. "The Great Famine was an unavoidable result of the war on Earth," he said. "When supplies stopped coming, there was absolutely no way to keep all the people in the lunar colony alive. Ninety per cent starved.

"Luna could be made self-sufficient, but only with a very small population. That's what happened. The population adjusted itself. But we recycled our air and our water, grew foods in hydroponic tanks. We struggled, but we survived. And began to rebuild.

"But we lost a lot. Too many people died. Our genetic pool was terribly small, and not too diverse. The colony had never had a lot of racial diversity to begin with.

"That hasn't helped. Population actually declined for a long time after we had the physical resources to support more people. The idea of in-breeding didn't go over. Now population's going up again, but slowly. We're stagnant, Von der Stadt. It's taken us nearly five centuries to get space travel going again, for example. And we still haven't duplicated many of the things they had back on Earth before the disaster."

Von der Stadt frowned. "Stagnant's a strong word," he said. "I think we've done pretty good."

Ciffonetto dismissed the comment with a wave of his flashlight. "Pretty good," he said. "Not good enough. We're not going anywhere. There's so damn few changes, so little in the way of new ideas. We need fresh viewpoints, fresh genetic stock. We need the stimulation of contact with a foreign culture.

"Survivors would give us that. After all Earth's been through, they'd have to have changed in some ways. And they'd be proof that human life can still flourish on Earth. That's crucial if we're going to establish a colony here."

The last point was tacked on almost as an afterthought, but caught Von der Stadt's approval. He nodded gravely.

They had reached the station again. Ciffonetto headed straight for the platform. "C'mon," he said, "let's get back to base. I can't wait to see Nagel's face drop when I tell him what we've found."

They were men.

Greel was almost sure of it. The texture of their minds was curious, but manlike. Greel was a strong mind-mingler. He knew the coarse, dim feel of an animal's mind, the obscene shadows that were the thoughts of the worm-things. And he knew the minds of men.

They were men.

Yet there was a strangeness. Mind-mingling was true communication only with a mind-brother. But always it was a sharing with other men. A dark and murky sharing, full of clouds and flavors and smells and emotions. But a sharing.

Here there was no sharing. Here it was like mind-mingling with a lower animal. Touch, feel, stroke, savor—all that a strong mind-mingler could do with an animal. But never would he feel a response. Men and mind-brothers responded; animals did not.

These men did not respond. These strange fire-men had minds that were silent and crippled.

In the darkness of the tunnel, Greel straightened from his crouch. The fire had faded suddenly from the wall.

The men were going away, down the tunnel away from him. The fire went with them.

He edged forward slowly, H'ssig at his side, spear in hand. Distance made mind-mingling difficult. He must keep them in range. He must find out more. He was a scout. He had a duty.

His mind crept out again, to taste the flavor of the other minds. He had to be sure.

Their thoughts moved around him, swirling chaos shot through with streaks of brightness and emotions and dancing, half-seen concepts. Greel understood little. But here he recognized something. And there something else came to him.

He lingered and tasted fully of their minds, and learned. But still it was like mind-mingling with an animal. He could not make himself felt. He could not get an answer.

Still they moved away, and their thoughts dimmed, and the mind-mingling became harder. Greel advanced. He hesitated when he got to the place where the tunnel curved. But he knew he must go on. He was a scout.

He lowered himself to the floor, squinted, and moved around the curve on hands and knees.

Beyond the curve, he started and gasped. He was in a great hall, an immense cavern with a vaulting roof and giant pillars that held up the sky. And the hall was bright with light, a strange, fiery light that danced over everything.

It was a place of legend. A hall of the Old Ones. It had to be. Never had Greel seen a chamber so vast. And he of all the People had wandered furthest and climbed highest.

The men were not in sight, but their fire danced around

the mouth of the tunnel at the other end of the hall. It was intense, but not unbearable. The men had gone around another curve. Greel realized that he looked only at the dim reflection of their fire. So long as he did not see it direct, he was safe.

He moved out into the hall, the scout in him crying to climb the stone wall and explore the upper chamber from which the mighty pillars reared. But no. The fire-men were more important. The hall he could return to.

H'ssig rubbed up against his leg. He reached down and stroked the rat's soft fur reassuringly. His mind-brother could sense the turmoil of his thoughts.

Men, yes, he was sure of that. And more he knew. Their thoughts were not those of the People, but they were man-thoughts, and some he could understand. One of them burned, burned to find other men. They seek the People, Greel thought.

That he knew. He was a scout and a mind-mingler. He did not make mistakes. But what he must do he did not know.

They sought the People. That might be good. When first that concept had touched him, Greel had quivered with joy. These fire-men were like the Old Ones of legend. If they sought the People, he would lead them. There would be rewards, and glory, and the taletellers would sing his name for generations.

More, it was his duty. Things went not well with the People in recent generations. The time of good had ended with the coming of the worm-things, who had driven the People from tunnel after tunnel. Even now, below his feet, the fight went on still in the Bad Levels and the tunnels of the People.

And Greel knew the People were losing.

It was slow. But certain. The worm-things were new to the People. More than animal, but less, less than men. They needed not the tunnels. They stalked through the earth itself, and nowhere were men safe.

The People fought back. Mind-minglers could sense the worm-things, and spears could slay them, and the great hunting rats could rip them to shreds. But always the worm-things fled back into the earth itself. And there were many worm-things, and few People.

But these new men, these fire-men, they could change the war. Legends said the Old Ones had fought with fire and stranger weapons, and these men lived in fire. They could aid the People. They could give mighty weapons to drive the worm-things back into the darkness from which they came.

But.

But these men were not quite men. Their minds were crippled, and much, much of their thought was alien to Greel. Only glimpses of it could he catch. He could not know them as he could know another of the People when they mingled minds.

He could lead them to the People. He knew the way. Back and down, a turn here, a twist there. Through the Middle Tunnels and the Bad Levels.

But what if he led them, and they were enemy to the People? What if they turned on the People with their fire? He feared for what they might do.

Without him, they would never find the People. Greel was certain of that. Only he, in long generations, had come this far. And only with stealth and mind-mingling and H'ssig alongside him. They would never find the ways he had come, the twisting tunnels that led deep, deep into the earth.

So the People were safe if he did not act. But then the worm-things would win, eventually. It might take many generations. But the People could not hold out.

His decision. No mind-mingler could reach a small part of the distance that separated him from the tunnels of the People. He alone must decide.

And he must decide soon. For he realized, with a shock, that the fire-men were coming back. Their odd thoughts grew stronger, and the light in the hall grew more and more intense.

He hesitated, then moved slowly backwards towards the tunnel from which be had come.

"Wait a minute," Von der Stadt said when Ciffonetto was a quarter of the way up the wall. "Let's try the other directions."

Ciffonetto craned his head around awkwardly to look at his companion, gave it up as a bad job, and dropped back to the tunnel floor. He looked disgruntled. "We should get back," he said. "We've got enough."

Von der Stadt shrugged. "C'mon. You're the one wanted to explore down here. So we might as well do a thorough job of it. Maybe we're only a few feet away from another one of your big finds."

"All right," said Ciffonetto, pulling his flashlight from his belt where he had stashed it for his intended assault on the platform. "I suppose you have a point. It would be tragic if we got Nagel down here and he tripped over something we had missed."

Von der Stadt nodded assent. Their flashlight beams

melted together, and they strode quickly towards the deeper darkness of the tunnel mouth.

They were coming. Fear and indecision tumbled in Greel's thoughts. He hugged the tunnel wall. Back he moved, fast and silent. He must keep away from their fire until he could decide what he must do.

But after the first turn, the tunnel ran long and straight. Greel was fast. But not fast enough. And his eyes were incautiously wide when the fire appeared suddenly in full fury.

His eyes burned. He squealed in sudden pain, and threw himself to the ground. The fire refused to go away. It danced before him even with his eyes closed, shifting colors horribly.

Greel fought for control. Still there was distance between them. Still he was armed. He reached out to H'ssig, nearby in the tunnel. The eyeless rat again would be his eyes.

Eyes still shut, Greel began to crawl back, away from the fire. H'ssig remained.

"What the hell was that?"

Von der Stadt's whispered question hung in the air for an instant. He was frozen where he had rounded the curve. Ciffonetto, by his side, had also stopped dead at the sound.

The scientist looked puzzled. "I don't know," he said. "It was—odd. Sounded like some sort of animal in pain. A scream, sort of. But as if the screamer were trying to remain silent, almost."

His flashlight darted this way and that, slicing ribbons of light from the velvet darkness, but revealing little. Von der Stadt's beam pointed straight ahead, unmoving.

"I don't like it," Von der Stadt stated doubtfully. "Maybe there is something down here. But that doesn't mean it's friendly." He shifted his flash to his left hand, and drew his pistol. "We'll see," he said.

Ciffonetto frowned, but said nothing. They started forward again.

They were big, and they moved fast. Greel realized with a sick despair that they would catch him. His choice had been made for him.

But perhaps it was right. They were men. Men like the Old Ones. They would help the People against the worm-things. A new age would dawn. The time of fear would pass. The horror would fade. The old glories of which the taletellers sing would return, and once again the People would build great halls and mighty tunnels.

Yes. They had decided for him, but the decision was right. It was the only decision. Man must meet man, and together they would face the worm-things.

He kept his eyes closed. But he stood.

And spoke.

Again they froze in mid-step. This time the sound was no muffled scream. It was soft, almost hissing, but it was too clear to be misunderstood.

Both flash beams swung wildly now, for seconds. Then one froze. The other hesitated, then joined it.

Together they formed a pool of light against a distant part of the tunnel wall. And in the pool stood—what?

"My God," said Von der Stadt. "Cliff, tell me what it is quick, before I shoot it."

"Don't," Ciffonetto replied. "It isn't moving."

"But—what?"

"I don't know." The scientist's voice had a strange, uncertain quiver in it.

The creature in the pool of light was small, barely over four feet. Small and sickening. There was something vaguely manlike about it, but the proportions of the limbs were all wrong, and the hands and feet were grotesquely malformed. And the skin, the skin was a sickly, maggoty white.

But the face was the worst. Large, all out of proportion to the body, yet the mouth and nose could hardly be seen. The head was all eyes. Two great, immense, grotesque eyes, now safely hidden by lids of dead white skin.

Von der Stadt was rock steady, but Ciffonetto shook a bit as he looked at it. Yet he spoke first.

"Look," he said, his voice soft. "In its hand. I think—I think that's a tool."

Silence. Long, strained silence. Then Ciffonetto spoke again. His voice was hoarse.

"I think that's a man."

Greel burned.

The fire had caught him. Even shut tight, his eyes ached, and he knew the horror that lurked outside if he opened them. And the fire had caught him. His skin itched strangely, and hurt. Worse and worse it hurt.

Yet he did not stir. He was a scout. He had a duty. He endured, while his mind mingled with those of the others.

And there, in their minds, he saw fear, but checked fear. In a distorted, blurry way he saw himself through their eyes, He tasted the awe and the revulsion that warred in one. And the unmixed revulsion that churned inside the other.

He angered, but he checked his anger. He must reach them. He must take them to the People. They were blind and crippled and could not help their feelings. But if they understood, they would aid. Yes.

He did not move. He waited. His skin burned, but he waited.

"That," said Von der Stadt. "That thing is a man?"

Ciffonetto nodded. "It must be. It carries tools. It spoke." He hesitated. "But—God, I never envisioned anything like this. The tunnels, Von der Stadt. The dark. For long centuries only the dark. I never thought—so much evolution in so little time."

"A man?" Still Von der Stadt doubted. "You're crazy. No man could become something like that."

Ciffonetto scarcely heard him. "I should have realized," he mumbled. "Should have guessed. The radiation, of course. It would speed up mutation. Shorter life-spans, probably. You were right, Von der Stadt. Men can't live on bugs and mushrooms. Not men like us. So they adapted. Adapted to the darkness, and the tunnels. It—"

Suddenly he started. "Those eyes," he said. He clicked off his flashlight, and the walls seemed to move closer. "He must be sensitive. We're hurting him. Divert your flash, Von der Stadt."

Von der Stadt gave him a doubtful sidelong glance. "It's dark enough down here already," he said. But he obeyed. His beam swung away.

"History," Ciffonetto said. "A moment that will live in—"

He never finished. Von der Stadt was tense, trigger-edged. As his beam swung away from the figure down the tunnel, he caught another flicker of movement in the darkness. He swung back and forth, found the thing again, pinned it against the tracks with a beam of light.

Almost he had shot before. But he had hesitated, because the manlike figure had been still and unfamiliar.

This new thing was not still. It squealed and scurried. Nor was it unfamiliar. This time Von der Stadt did not hesitate.

There was a roar, a flash. Then a second.

"Got it," said Von der Stadt. "A damn rat."

And Greel screamed.

After the long burning, there had come an instant of relief. But only an instant. Then, suddenly, pain flooded him. Wave after wave after wave. Rolled over him, blotting out the thoughts of the fire-men, blotting out their fear, blotting out his anger.

H'ssig died. His mind-brother died.

The fire-men had killed his mind-brother.

He shrieked in painrage. He darted forward, swung up his spear.

He opened his eyes. There was a flash of vision, then more pain and blindness. But the flash was enough. He struck. And struck again. Wildly, madly, blow after blow, thrust after thrust.

Then, again, the universe turned red with pain, and then again sounded that awful roar that had come when H'ssig died. Something threw him to the tunnel floor, and his eyes opened again, and fire, fire was everywhere.

But only for a while. Only for a while. Then, shortly, it was darkness again for Greel of the People.

* * *

The gun still smoked. The hand was still steady. But Von der Stadt's mouth hung open as he looked, unbelieving, from the thing he had blasted across the tunnel, to the blood dripping from his uniform, then back again.

Then the gun dropped, and he clutched at his stomach, clutched at the wounds. His hand came away wet with blood. He stared at it. Then stared at Ciffonetto.

"The rat," he said. There was pain in his voice. "I only shot a rat. It was going for him. Why, Cliff? I—?"

And he fell. Heavily. His flashlight shattered and went dark.

There was a long fumbling in the blackness. Then, at last, Ciffonetto's light winked on, and the ashen scientist knelt beside his companion.

"Von," he said, tugging at the uniform. "Are you all right?" He ripped away the fabric to expose the torn flesh.

Von der Stadt was mumbling. "I didn't even see him coming. I took my light away, like you said, Cliff. Why? I wasn't going to shoot him. Not if he was a man. I only shot a rat. Only a rat. It was going for him, too."

Ciffonetto, who had stood paralyzed through everything, nodded. "It wasn't your fault, Von. But you must have scared him. You need treating, now, though. He hurt you bad. Can you make it back to camp?"

He didn't wait for an answer. He slipped his arm under Von der Stadt's, and lifted him to his feet, and began to walk him down the tunnel, praying they could make it back to the platform.

"I only shot a rat," Von der Stadt kept saying, over and over, in a dazed voice.

"Don't worry," said Ciffonetto. "It won't matter. We'll

find others. We'll search the whole subway system if we have to. We'll find them."

"Only a rat. Only a rat."

They reached the platform. Ciffonetto lowered Von der Stadt back to the ground. "I can't make the climb carrying you, Von," he said. "I'll have to leave you here. Go for help." He straightened, hung the flash from his belt.

"Only a rat," Von der Stadt said again.

"Don't worry," said Ciffonetto. "Even if we don't find them, nothing will be lost. They were clearly sub-human. Men once, maybe. But no more. Degenerated. There was nothing they could have taught us, anyway."

But Von der Stadt was past listening, past hearing. He just sat against the wall, clutching his stomach and feeling the blood ooze from between his fingers, mumbling the same words over and over.

Ciffonetto turned to the wall. A few short feet to the platform, then the old, rusty escalator, and the basement ruins, and daylight. He had to hurry. Von der Stadt wouldn't last long.

He grabbed the rock, pulled himself up, hung on desperately as his other hand scrambled and found a hold. He pulled up again.

He was almost there, almost at the platform level, when his weak lunar muscles gave out on him. There was a sudden spasm, his hand slipped loose, his other hand couldn't take the weight.

He fell. On the flashlight.

The darkness was like nothing he had ever seen. Too thick, too complete. He fought to keep from screaming.

When he tried to rise again, he did scream. More than the flashlight had broken in the fall.

His scream echoed and re-echoed through the long, black tunnel he could not see. It was a long time dying. When it finally faded, he screamed again. And again.

Finally, hoarse, he stopped. "Von," he said. "Von, can you hear me?" There was no answer. He tried again. Talk, he must talk to hold his sanity. The darkness was all around him, and he could almost hear soft movements a few feet away.

Von der Stadt giggled, sounding infinitely far away. "It was only a rat," he said. "Only a rat."

Silence. Then, softly, Ciffonetto. "Yes, Von, yes."

"It was only a rat."

"It was only a rat."

"It was only a rat."

WAITING FOR THE ZEPHYR

BY TOBIAS S. BUCKELL

Tobias S. Buckell is the author of several novels, including the *New York Times* bestseller *Halo: The Cole Protocol*, the Xenowealth series, *Artic Rising*, and *Hurricane Fever*. His short fiction has appeared in magazines such as *Lightspeed*, *Analog*, *Clarkesworld*, and *Subterranean*, and in anthologies such as *Armored*, *The End is Nigh*, *Brave New Worlds*, and *Under the Moons of Mars*.

A native of the Caribbean, Buckell lived for a time aboard a boat powered by a wind generator. As a result, he has long felt it would be natural to bring wind power to a flat, desert-like area, and when he began speculating about a fossil fuel-less future he looked to his own background for an alternative.

Buckell says that post-apocalyptic SF is often a way of doing literary penance for all our imagined or real modern sins. This story, however, is perhaps the most optimistic in this volume.

The *Zephyr* was almost five days overdue.

Wind lifted the dust off in little devils of twisting columns that randomly touched down throughout the remains of the town. Further out beyond the hulks of the Super Wal-Mart and Kroger's Mara stood and swept the binoculars. The platform she stood on reached up a good hundred feet ending in the bulbous water tank that watered the town, affording her a look just over the edge of the horizon. She strained her eyes for the familiar shape of the *Zephyr*'s four blade-like masts, but saw nothing but dirt-twisters.

The old asphalt highway, laid down back in the time of plenty, had finally succumbed to the advancing dirt despite the town's best attempts to keep it out. The barriers lay on their side.

Mara still knew the twists and turns of the highway she'd memorized since twelve, when she'd first realized it led to other towns and people.

"Mara, it's getting dark."

"Yes, Ken."

Ken carefully put the binoculars into their pouch and climbed down the side of the tower. Pushing off down the dust piled at its feet she trudged down to Ken, now only a large silhouette in the suddenly approaching dusk.

"Your mother still wants to talk to you."

Mara didn't respond.

"She wants to work it out," Ken continued.

"I'm leaving. I've wanted to leave since I was twelve,

come on, Ken… don't start this again." Mara started walking quickly towards the house.

Ken matched her pace, and even though she could see him wondering what to say next, she could also see him examining the farm out of his peripheral vision. Their farm defied the dust and wind with lush green growth, but only because it lay underneath protective glass. Ken paused slightly twice, checking cracks in the façade, areas where dust tried to leak in.

"Their wind generator is down. They need help, Mara. I said I would go over tomorrow."

Mara sighed.

"I really don't want to."

Ken opened the outer door for her, stamping his boots clean and letting it shut, then passed through as she opened the second door. Dust slipped in everywhere and covered everything despite precautions. Brooms didn't quite get it all. Although Ken thought them a useless necessity, Mara thought the idea of a vacuum cleaner quite fetching.

"I need your help, Mara, just for an afternoon. You wouldn't feel right leaving someone without electricity, would you?"

Ken was right, without the wind-generator her parents would be without power.

"Okay. I'll help." Ken, she noticed, ever the wonder with his hands, already had a dinner set for the two of them. Despite being slightly cold from sitting out, it was wonderful.

The *Zephyr* was six days overdue.

Mara shimmied up the roof and joined Ken. He already

had parts of the wind-generator laying out on the roof. She had just managed to brush past her father without being physically stopped. Mother stood around, looking wounded and helpless.

Ken made a face.

"The blade is all right. But the alternator is burned out."

Simple enough to fix. The wind generators consisted of no more than an old automobile alternator attached to a propeller blade and swivel mounted on the roof. What electricity the houses had depended on deep cycle batteries that used the wind generators to recharge. Solar panels worked in some areas, but here the dust crept into them, and unlike wind generators, didn't work at night. Plus, it was easy enough to wander out to a car lot and pick an alternator out of the thousands of dead cars.

Mara half suspected her father had called them for help just to get her out to his farm. Damnit.

"Mara," her father said from the edge of the dust gutter. "We need to talk." Mara looked straight out over the edge, out at the miles and miles of brown horizon. "Mara, look at me. Mara, we spoke harshly. We're sorry."

"We like Ken," her mother chimed in from below. "But you're young. You can't move out just yet."

"Come back, honey. We could use your help on the farm. You wouldn't be as busy as you are with Ken."

Ken looked up at that with a half-pained grin. Mara swore and slid off the low end off the roof, hitting the dust with a grunt. Her father started back down the ladder but Mara was already in the cart, pulling up the sail and bouncing out across the dust back towards the relative safety of Ken's farm, leaving her mother's plaintive entreaties in the dusk air behind her.

Damn, how could she have fallen for that? Her parents were so obvious. And Ken, she fumed on her way back. He shouldn't have taken her over.

Even after he showed up, sheepishly cooking yet another marvelous meal, she tried to remain angry. But the anger eventually subsided, as it always did.

On the seventh and eighth day of waiting reception cleared up enough for the both of them to catch some broadcasts from further north. Ken had enough charge in the house batteries for almost eight hours of television shows, and they both cuddled on the couch.

Mara began to wonder if the *Zephyr* would ever show. The last visit was two years ago, when the giant, wheeled caravan sailed into town for a day. Traders and merchants festooned its various decks with smiles and stalls.

The *Zephyr*, Mara knew from talks to its bridge crew, was one of the few links the outer towns of America still had with the large cities, and each other. Ever since the petroleum collapse, with the Middle East nuked into oblivion and portions of Europe glowing, the country had been trying to replace an entire infrastructure based on oil.

Almost two generations later it was succeeding.

The large cities used more nuclear power, or even harnessed the sewer systems, but small towns were hit the hardest. Accustomed to power, but dropped off the line, isolated, a minor Dark Age had descended on them. Life based itself here on bare essentials; water and wind.

Mara wanted to see a city lit up in a wanton electrical blaze of light, forcing away the dusk and night with artificial man-made day.

* * *

On the tenth day Ken found her in the bedroom frantically packing.

"They spotted the *Zephyr* coming in from the east," Mara said, hoisting a pack onto her shoulders.

"Are you sure you want to do this?"

"What?"

"Go. You don't know what's out there. Strange places, strange people. Danger."

Mara looked at him.

"Of course."

Ken looked down at the ground.

"I thought we had something. You, me."

"Of course." Mara paused. "I told you that I would be going."

"But I'd hoped…"

"Ken. I can't."

"Go." His voice hardened, and he walked into the kitchen. Mara sat on the edge of the bed biting back tears, then snatched the two packs and left angrily.

The *Zephyr* rolled through Main Street, slowing down to a relative crawl to allow people to run alongside and leap up. Kids thronged the sides of the street, and furious trade went on. The four tall masts of the *Zephyr* towered above the small two- and three-story town buildings. The masts looked like vertical wings, and used the same principles. Air flowing across the shorter edge of the blade-like mast caused a vacuum, drawing the massive wheeled ship forward.

Mara followed the eager crowd behind the ship. She nodded to the occasional familiar face.

Plastic beads, more precious than gold due the rarity of oils, were draped across stalls that slid out of the side of the hull. Mara aimed her quick walk for one of these, but instead found herself blocked by a familiar form.

"Uncle Dan?"

"Hi." He had her arm in a firm grip. Mara saw the bulk of the *Zephyr* slowly moving away. She tried to pull out of his grip, but couldn't. Her dad pushed through the crowd.

"Dad! What are you doing?"

"It's for your own good, Mara," Uncle Dan said. "You don't know what you're doing."

"Yes I do," she yelled, kicking at her uncle's shins. The crowd around them paid no obvious attention, although Mara knew full well that by nighttime it would be the talk of the area.

She begged, pleaded, yelled, kicked, scratched and fought. But the men of the house already had their minds made. They locked her into the basement.

"You'll be out when the *Zephyr* leaves," Mom promised.

There were no windows. Mara could only imagine the *Zephyr*'s slow progress out of the town. She tried to put a brave face on, then crawled into a corner and cried. After that she beat on the door, but no came to let her out.

The basement was a comfortable area. The family den, it held several couches and carpet. The door creaked open, and from looking out Mara guessed it to be dusk. Ken came down the stairs carefully.

"It's me, Mara."

"I suppose you're in on this too?"

"Actually, no. You're family wants me to speak some sense into you. I won't lie to you, Mara. I want you to stay.

But holding you here like this is ridiculous."

"The longer we all stay out here, away from the cities, the crazier it gets."

"Maybe. You're family's scared. They don't want to lose you."

"That doesn't give them the right to lock me up like a damn dog!" Mara yelled.

Ken came closer.

"My sail-cart is outside. That's as far as you need to get. You're a better sailor than anyone else, once in you can outrun everyone. The *Zephyr* is still reachable on a long tack. Hey, I never did get along with your uncle anyway."

Mara looked up at him and gave him a long hug.

"Thank you so much."

"If you're ever back in town, look me up."

"Will you come with me, then?"

"Ask me then."

Ken pulled away and stepped up the stairs.

"Stay close."

He launched himself into her uncle and dad, tackling them with a loud yell. Mara ran past, losing only a shoe, pushing past her mom and out into the yard.

The cart's sail puffed out with a snap, and she was bouncing her way over the sand before she looked back to see two figures at the door watching her go. No one bothered to chase her. They all knew her skill with the sail.

It took the better part of a few hours before the four masts showed up. Mara could hear distant shouting as she overhauled the giant land ship.

"Ahoy *Zephyr*," she shouted.

Someone tossed a ladder down, and Mara hauled

herself up. The small sail-cart veered off and tipped into the dust, snapping its tiny mast in two. It felt faintly liberating to land on the deck with a smile.

The merchant with the ladder stepped aside, letting an officer in khaki step forward.

"We've been watching you approach for the past few hours," he said. "We like the way you handle the wind."

"Can you read a map?" asked a woman in uniform. She wore strange braids on her shoulders.

"No."

"You looking for a position on board the ship?"

"Yes." Mara felt her stomach flip-flop.

"Then we'll teach you how to read charts," the woman said. She stuck out a hand. "Welcome aboard, kid, I'm Captain Shana. Ever cross me or give me a reason to, I'll toss you off the side of the ship and leave you to the vultures. Understood?"

"Yes ma'am."

"Good. Give her a hammock."

Mara stood on the deck of the *Zephyr*, enjoying the moment. Then the man in uniform touched her shoulder.

"It isn't fun and games, it's a lot of hard work, but worth it. Come on."

Mara paused and looked out at the flat horizon, full of tempting futures. Then she followed him belowdecks.

NEVER DESPAIR

BY JACK MCDEVITT

Jack McDevitt is the author of more than a dozen novels, including the post-apocalyptic gem *Eternity Road*, with which this story shares its milieu. His short fiction has appeared in *Analog*, *Asimov's*, *Lightspeed* and *F&SF*, and in numerous anthologies. He has been nominated for the Nebula Award sixteen times, and won for the first time in 2007 for his novel *Seeker*. Other awards include the Locus Award for his first novel, *The Hercules Text*, and the John W. Campbell Memorial Award for his novel *Omega*.

"Never Despair" tells the story of Chaka Milana, a woman who leaves her hometown in search of a storied place that holds the secrets of the Roadmakers, the almost-mythical builders of the concrete strips that cover the land, and the ruined cities with towers so high that a person could not ascend one in a day. In the course of her journey, Chaka encounters a historical avatar of a man she doesn't recognize, but whom the reader most certainly will.

* * *

The rain began to fall as they threw the last few spadefuls of earth onto the grave.

Quait bowed his head and murmured the traditional farewell. Chaka looked at the wooden marker, which bore Flojian's name, his dates, and the legend FAR FROM HOME.

She hadn't cared all that much for Flojian. He was self-centered and he complained a lot and he always knew better ways to do things. But you could count on him to pull his weight, and now there were only two of them.

Quait finished, looked up, and nodded. Her turn. She was glad it was over. The poor son of a bitch had fallen on his head out of the upper level of a ruin, and during four excruciating days, they'd been able to do little for him. Pointless, silly way to die. "Flojian," she said, "we'll miss you." She let it go at that because she meant it, and the rain was coming harder.

They retreated to their horses. Quait packed his spade behind his saddle and mounted in that awkward way that always left her wondering whether Lightfoot would chuck him off on the other side.

She stood looking up at him.

"What's wrong?" He wiped the back of his hand against his cheek. His hat was jammed down on his head. Water spilled out of it onto his shoulders.

"It's time to give it up," Chaka said. "Go home. If we can." Thunder rumbled. It was getting very dark.

"Not the best time to discuss this." Quait waited for her to get on her horse. The rain pounded the soft earth, fell into the trees.

She looked back toward the grave. Flojian lay with the

ruins now, buried like them beneath the rolling hills and the broad forest. It was the sort of grave he would have preferred, she supposed. He liked stuff that had been dead a long time. She pulled her jacket tight and climbed into the saddle. Quait moved off at a brisk trot.

They'd buried him at the top of the highest ridge in the area. Now they rode slowly along the crest, picking their way among broken concrete casts and petrified timbers and corroded metal, the detritus of the old world, sinking slowly into the ground. The debris had been softened by time: earth and grass had rounded the rubble, spilled over it, absorbed its sharp edges. Eventually, she supposed, nothing would be left, and visitors would stand on the ruins and not know they were even here.

Quait bent against the rain, his hat pulled low over his eyes, his right hand pressed against Lightfoot's flank. He looked worn and tired and discouraged, and Chaka realized for the first time that he too had given up. That he was only waiting for someone else to take responsibility for admitting failure.

They dropped down off the ridge, and rode through a narrow defile bordered by blocks and slabs.

"You okay?" he asked.

Chaka was fine. Scared. Exhausted. Wondering what they would say to the widows and mothers when they got home. There had been six when they started. "Yes," she said. "I'm okay."

The grotto lay ahead, a square black mouth rimmed by chalkstone and half-hidden by a bracken. They'd left a fire burning, and it looked warm and good. They dismounted, and led their horses inside.

Quait threw a couple of logs onto the blaze. "Cold out there," he said.

Lightning flashed in the entrance.

They put the teapot onto its boiling rock, fed and watered the animals, changed into dry clothes, and sank down in front of the fire. They didn't talk much for a long time. Chaka sat, wrapped in a blanket, enjoying being warm and away from the rain. Quait made some notes in the journal, trying to establish the site of Flojian's grave, so that future travelers, if there were any, could find it. After a while he sighed and looked up, not at her, but over her shoulder, into the middle distance. "You really think we should turn around?"

"Yeah. I think we've had enough. Time to go home."

He nodded. "I hate to go back like this."

"Me too. But it's time." It was hard to guess what the grotto had been. It was not a cave. The walls were artificial. Whatever color they might once have possessed had been washed away. Now they were gray and stained, and they curved into a high ceiling. A pattern of slanted lines, probably intended for decorative effect, cut through them. The grotto was wide, wider than the council hall, which could accommodate a hundred people; and it went far back under the hill. Miles, maybe.

As a general principle, she avoided the ruins when she could. It wasn't easy because they were everywhere. But all sorts of critters made their homes among them. And the structures were dangerous, as Flojian had found out. Prone to cave-ins, collapsing floors, you name it. The real reason, though, was that she had heard too many stories about spectres and demons among the crumbling walls. She was not superstitious, and would never have admitted her discomfort to Quait. Still, you never knew.

They had found the grotto a few hours after Flojian got hurt, and moved in, grateful for the shelter. But she was anxious to be gone now.

Thunder shook the walls, and they could hear the steady rhythm of rainwater pouring off the ridge. It was still late afternoon, but all the light had drained out of the day.

"Tea should be ready," said Chaka.

Quait shook his head. "I hate to give it up. We'll always wonder if it might have been over the next hill."

She had just picked up the pot and begun to pour when a bolt exploded directly overhead. "Close," she said, grateful for the protection of the grotto.

Quait smiled, took his tea, and lifted it in a mock toast to whatever powers lived in the area. "Maybe you're right," he said. "Maybe we should take the hint."

The bolt was drawn by a corroded crosspiece, a misshapen chunk of dissolving metal jutting from the side of the hill. Most of the energy dissipated into the ground. But some of it leaped to a buried cable, followed it down to a melted junction box, flowed through a series of conduits, and lit up several ancient circuit boards. One of the circuit boards relayed power into a long-dormant auxiliary system; another turned on an array of sensors which began to take note of sounds in the grotto. And a third, after an appropriate delay, threw a switch and activated the only program that still survived.

They ate well. Chaka had come across an unlucky turkey that morning, and Quait added some berries and fresh-baked biscuit. They'd long since exhausted their store of wine, but a brook ran through the grotto about sixty yards back, and the water was clear and cold.

"It's not as if we have any reason to think we're close," said Chaka. "I'm not sure I believe in it anyway. Even if it is out there, the price is too high."

The storm eased with the coming of night. Rain still fell steadily, but it was light rain, not much more than mist.

Quait talked extensively through the evening, about his ambitions, about how important it was to find out who had built the great cities scattered through the wilderness, and what had happened to them, and about mastering the ancient wizardries. But she was correct, he kept saying, glancing her way, pausing to give her a chance to interrupt. It was better to be safe than sorry.

"Damn right," said Chaka.

It was warm near the fire, and after a while Quait fell asleep. He'd lost twenty pounds since they'd left Illyria ten weeks before. He had aged, and the good-humored nonchalance that had attracted her during the early days had disappeared. Quait was all business now.

She tried to shake off her sense of despair. They were a long way from home, alone in a wilderness filled with savages and demons and dead cities in which lights blinked and music played and mechanical things moved. She shrank down in her blankets and listened to the water dripping off the trees. A log broke and fell into the fire.

She was not sure what brought her out of it, but she was suddenly awake, senses alert.

Someone, outlined in moonlight, illuminated from behind by the fire, was standing at the exit to the grotto, looking out.

Beside her, Quait's chest gently rose and fell.

She was using her saddle bag for a pillow. Without any visible movement, she eased her gun out of it.

The figure appeared to be a man, somewhat thick at the waist, dressed in peculiar clothes. He wore a dark jacket and dark trousers of matching style, a hat with a rounded top, and he carried a walking stick. There was a red glow near his mouth that alternately dimmed and brightened. She detected an odor that might have been burning weed.

"Don't move," she said softly, rising to confront the apparition. "I have a gun."

He turned, looked curiously at her, and a cloud of smoke rose over his head. He was indeed puffing on something. And the smell was vile. "So you do," he said. "I hope you won't use it."

He didn't seem sufficiently impressed. "I mean it," she said.

"I'm sorry." He smiled. "I didn't mean to wake you." He wore a white shirt and a dark blue ribbon tied in a bow at his throat. The ribbon was sprinkled with white polka dots. His hair was white, and he had gruff, almost fierce, features. There was something of the bulldog about him. He advanced a couple of paces and removed his hat.

"What are you doing here?" she asked. "Who are you?"

"I live here, young lady."

"Where?" She glanced around at the bare walls, which seemed to move in the flickering light.

"Here." He lifted his arms to indicate the grotto and took another step forward.

She glanced at the gun and back at him. "That's far enough," she said. "Don't think I would hesitate."

"I'm sure you wouldn't, young lady." The stern cast of his features dissolved into an amiable smile. "I'm really not dangerous."

"Are you alone?" she asked, taking a quick look behind her. Nothing stirred in the depths of the cave.

"I am now. Franklin used to be here. And Abraham Lincoln. And an American singer. A guitar player, as I recall. Actually there used to be a considerable crowd of us."

Chaka didn't like the way the conversation was going. It sounded as if he were trying to distract her. "If I get any surprises," she said, "the first bullet's for you."

"It is good to have visitors again. The last few times I've been up and about, the building's been empty."

"Really?" What building?

"Oh, yes. We used to draw substantial crowds. But the benches and the gallery have gone missing." He looked slowly around. "I wonder what happened."

"What is your name?" she said.

He looked puzzled. Almost taken aback. "You don't know?" He leaned on his cane and studied her closely. "Then I think there is not much point to this conversation."

"How would I know you? We've never met." She waited for a response. When none came, she continued: "I am Chaka of Illyria."

The man bowed slightly. "I suppose, under the circumstances, you must call me Winston." He drew his jacket about him. "It is drafty. Why don't we retire to the fireside, Chaka of Illyria?"

If he were hostile, she and Quait would already be dead. Or worse. She lowered the weapon and put it in her belt. "I'm surprised to find anyone here. No offense, but this place looks as if it has been deserted a long time."

"Yes. It does, doesn't it?"

She glanced at Quait, dead to the world. Lot of good he'd have been if Tuks came sneaking up in the night. "Where have you been?" she asked.

"I beg your pardon?"

"We've been here several days. Where have you been?"

He looked uncertain. "I'm not sure," he said. "I was certainly here. I'm always here." He lowered himself unsteadily to the ground and held his hands up to the fire. "Feels good."

"It is cold."

"You haven't any brandy, by chance, I don't suppose?"

What was brandy? "No," she said. "We don't."

"Pity. It's good for old bones." He shrugged and looked around. "Strange," he said. "Do you know what's happened?"

"No." She didn't even understand the question. "I have no idea."

Winston placed his hat in his lap. "The place looks quite abandoned," he said. Somehow, the fact of desolation acquired significance from his having noted it. "I regret to say I have never heard of Illyria. Where is it, may I ask?"

"Several weeks to the southwest. In the valley of the Mawagondi."

"I see." His tone suggested very clearly that he did not see. "And who are the Mawagondi?"

"It is a river. Do you really not know of it?"

He peered into her eyes. "I fear there is a great deal I do not know." His mood seemed to have darkened. "Are you and your friend going home?" he asked.

"No," she said. "We seek Haven."

"You are welcome to stay here," said Winston. "But I do not think you will find it very comfortable."

"Thank you, no. I was referring to the Haven. And I know how that sounds."

Winston nodded, and his forehead crinkled. There was a brooding fire in his eyes. "Is it near Boston?"

Chaka looked over at Quait and wondered whether she should wake him. "I don't know," she said. "Where is Boston?"

That brought a wide smile. "Well," he said, "it certainly appears one of us is terribly lost. I wonder which of us it is."

She saw the glint in his eye and returned the smile. She understood what he was saying in his oddly accented diction: they were both lost.

"Where's Boston?" she asked again.

"Forty miles east. Straight down the highway."

"What highway? There's no highway out there anywhere. At least none that I've seen."

The cigar tip brightened and dimmed. "Oh, my. It must be a long time."

She pulled up her knees and wrapped her arms around them. "Winston, I really don't understand much of this conversation."

"Nor do I." His eyes looked deep into hers. "What is this Haven?"

She was shocked at his ignorance. "You are not serious."

"I am quite serious. Please enlighten me."

Well, after all he was living out here in the wilderness. How could she expect him to know such things? "Haven was the home of Abraham Polk," she said hopefully.

Winston shook his head sheepishly. "Try again," he said.

"Polk lived at the end of the age of the Roadmakers. He knew the world was collapsing, that the cities were dying.

He saved what he could. The treasures. The knowledge. The history. Everything. And he stored it in a fortress with an undersea entrance."

"An undersea entrance," said Winston. "How do you propose to get in?"

"I don't think we shall," said Chaka. "I believe we will give it up at this point and go home."

Winston nodded. "The fire's getting low," he said.

She poked at it, and added a log. "No one even knows whether Polk really lived. He may only be a legend."

Light filled the grotto entrance. Seconds later, thunder rumbled. "Haven sounds quite a lot like Camelot," he said.

What the devil was Camelot?

"You've implied," he continued after taking a moment to enjoy his weed, "that the world outside is in ruins."

"Oh, no. The world outside is lovely."

"But there are ruins?"

"Yes."

"Extensive?"

"They fill the forests, clog the rivers, lie in the shallow waters of the harbors. They are everywhere. Some are even active, in strange ways. There is, for example, a train that still runs, on which no one rides."

"And what do you know of their builders?"

She shrugged. "Very little. Almost nothing."

"Their secrets are locked in this Haven?"

"Yes."

"Which you are about to turn your back on."

"We're exhausted, Winston."

"Your driving curiosity, Chaka, leaves me breathless."

Damn. "Look, it's easy enough for you to point a finger. You have no idea what we've been through. None."

Winston stared steadily at her. "I'm sure I don't. But the prize is very great. And the sea is close."

"There are only two of us left," she said.

"The turnings of history are never directed by crowds," he said. "Nor by the cautious. Always, it is the lone captain who sets the course."

"It's over. We'll be lucky to get home alive."

"That may also be true. And certainly going on to your goal entails a great risk. But you must decide whether the prize is not worth the risk."

"We will decide. I have a partner in the enterprise."

"He will abide by your decision. It is up to you."

She tried to hold angry tears back. "We've done enough. It would be unreasonable to go on."

"The value of reason is often exaggerated, Chaka. It would have been reasonable to accept Hitler's offer of terms in 1940."

"What?"

He waved the question away. "It's of no consequence. But reason, under pressure, usually produces prudence when boldness is called for."

"I am not a coward, Winston."

"I did not imply you are." He bit down hard on his weed. A blue cloud drifted toward her. It hurt her eyes and she backed away.

"Are you a ghost?" she asked. The question did not seem at all foolish.

"I suspect I am. I'm something left behind by the retreating tide." The fire glowed in his eyes. "I wonder whether, when an event is no longer remembered by any living person, it loses all significance? Whether it is as if it never happened?"

Quait stirred in his sleep, but did not wake.

"I'm sure I don't know," said Chaka.

For a long time, neither of them spoke.

Winston got to his feet. "I'm not comfortable here," he said.

She thought he was expressing displeasure with her.

"The floor is hard on an old man. And of course you are right: you must decide whether you will go on. Camelot was a never-never land. Its chief value lay in the fact that it existed only as an idea. Perhaps the same thing is true of Haven."

"No," she said. "It exists."

"And is anyone else looking for this place?"

"No one. We will be the second mission to fail. I think there will be no more."

"Then for God's sake, Chaka of Illyria, you must ask yourself why you came all this way. Why your companions died. What you seek."

"Money. Pure and simple. Ancient manuscripts are priceless. We'd have been famous throughout the League. That's why we came."

His eyes grew thoughtful. "Then go back," he said. "If this is a purely commercial venture, write it off and put your money in real estate."

"Beg pardon?"

"But I would put it to you that those are not the reasons you dared so much. And that you wish to turn back because you have forgot why you came."

"That's not so," she said.

"Of course it's so. Shall I tell you why you undertook to travel through an unknown world, on the hope that you might, *might*, find a place that's half-mythical?"

Momentarily he seemed to fade, to lose definition. "Haven has nothing to do with fame or wealth. If you got there, if you were able to read its secrets, you would have all that, provided you could get home with it. But you would have acquired something infinitely more valuable, and I believe you know that: you would have discovered who you really are. You would have learned that you are a daughter of the people who designed the Acropolis, who wrote Hamlet, who visited the moons of Neptune. Do you know about Neptune?"

"No," she said. "I don't think so."

"Then we've lost everything, Chaka. But you can get it back. If you are willing to take it. And if not you, then someone else. But it is worth the taking, at whatever cost."

Momentarily, he became one with the dark.

"Winston," she said, "I can't see you. Are you still there?"

"I am here. The system is old, and will not keep a charge." She was looking through him. "You really are a ghost," she said.

"It is possible you will not succeed. Nothing is certain, save difficulty and trial. But have courage. Never surrender."

She stared at him.

"Never despair," he said.

A sudden chill whispered through her, a sense that she had been here before, had known this man in another life. "You seem vaguely familiar. Have I seen your picture somewhere?"

"I'm sure I do not know."

"Perhaps it is the words. They have an echo."

He looked directly at her. "Possibly." She could see the cave entrance and a few stars through his silhouette.

"Keep in mind, whatever happens, you are one of a select company. A proud band of brothers. And sisters. You will never be alone."

As she watched, he faded until only the glow of the cigar remained. "It is your own true self you seek."

"You presume a great deal."

"I know you, Chaka." Everything was gone now. Except the voice. "I know who you are. And you are about to learn."

"Was it his first or last name?" asked Quait, as they saddled the horses.

"Now that you mention it, I really don't know." She frowned. "I'm not sure whether he was real or not. He left no prints. No marks."

Quait looked toward the rising sun. The sky was clear. "That's the way of it in these places. Some of it's illusion; some of it's something else. But I wish you'd woke me."

"So do I." She climbed up and patted Brak's shoulder. "He said the sea is only forty miles."

Warm spring air flowed over them. "You want to go on?"

"Quait, you ever hear of Neptune?"

He shook his head.

"Maybe," she said, "we can try that next."

WHEN SYSADMINS RULED THE EARTH

BY CORY DOCTOROW

Cory Doctorow is the author of several novels, including *Down and Out in the Magic Kingdom*, *Makers*, *For the Win*, *Pirate Cinema*, and *Little Brother*. His short fiction, which has appeared in a variety of magazines—from *Asimov's Science Fiction* to *Salon.com*—has been collected in *A Place So Foreign and Eight More*, *With a Little Help*, and *Overclocked: Stories of the Future Present*. He is a four-time winner of the Locus Award, a winner of the Canadian Starburst Award, has been nominated for both the Hugo and Nebula Awards, and in 2000, he won the John W. Campbell Award for Best New Writer. Doctorow is also the co-editor of *Boing Boing*, an online "directory of wonderful things."

"When Sysadmins Ruled the Earth" first appeared in the online magazine *Jim Baen's Universe*, and won the 2007 Locus Award for best novelette. In this story, sysadmins—computer systems administrators—

huddle in their network operations centers, after a series of disasters ends civilization. The Internet was supposedly designed to withstand a nuclear blast; in this story, Doctorow—a former sysadmin himself— asks: If the Internet *did* survive the apocalypse, what would the surviving techs do after the world ended?

When Felix's special phone rang at two in the morning, Kelly rolled over and punched him in the shoulder and hissed, "Why didn't you turn that fucking thing off before bed?"

"Because I'm on call," he said.

"You're not a fucking doctor," she said, kicking him as he sat on the bed's edge, pulling on the pants he'd left on the floor before turning in. "You're a goddamned *systems administrator*."

"It's my job," he said.

"They work you like a government mule," she said. "You know I'm right. For Christ's sake, you're a father now, you can't go running off in the middle of the night every time someone's porn supply goes down. Don't answer that phone."

He knew she was right. He answered the phone.

"Main routers not responding. BGP not responding." The mechanical voice of the systems monitor didn't care if he cursed at it, so he did, and it made him feel a little better.

"Maybe I can fix it from here," he said. He could login to the UPS for the cage and reboot the routers. The UPS was in a different netblock, with its own independent routers on their own uninterruptible power-supplies.

Kelly was sitting up in bed now, an indistinct shape

against the headboard. "In five years of marriage, you have never once been able to fix anything from here." This time she was wrong—he fixed stuff from home all the time, but he did it discreetly and didn't make a fuss, so she didn't remember it. And she was right, too—he had logs that showed that after 1 A.M., nothing could ever be fixed without driving out to the cage. Law of Infinite Universal Perversity—AKA Felix's Law.

Five minutes later Felix was behind the wheel. He hadn't been able to fix it from home. The independent routers' netblock was offline, too. The last time that had happened, some dumbfuck construction worker had driven a ditch-witch through the main conduit into the data-center and Felix had joined a cadre of fifty enraged sysadmins who'd stood atop the resulting pit for a week, screaming abuse at the poor bastards who labored 24-7 to splice ten thousand wires back together.

His phone went off twice more in the car and he let it override the stereo and play the mechanical status reports through the big, bassy speakers of more critical network infrastructure offline. Then Kelly called.

"Hi," he said.

"Don't cringe, I can hear the cringe in your voice."

He smiled involuntarily. "Check, no cringing."

"I love you, Felix," she said.

"I'm totally bonkers for you, Kelly. Go back to bed."

"2.0's awake," she said. The baby had been Beta Test when he was in her womb, and when her water broke, he got the call and dashed out of the office, shouting, *The Gold Master just shipped!* They'd started calling him 2.0 before he'd finished his first cry. "This little bastard was born to suck tit."

213

"I'm sorry I woke you," he said. He was almost at the data-center. No traffic at 2 A.M. He slowed down and pulled over before the entrance to the garage. He didn't want to lose Kelly's call underground.

"It's not waking me," she said. "You've been there for seven years. You have three juniors reporting to you. Give them the phone. You've paid your dues."

"I don't like asking my reports to do anything I wouldn't do," he said.

"You've done it," she said. "Please? I hate waking up alone in the night. I miss you most at night."

"Kelly—"

"I'm over being angry. I just miss you is all. You give me sweet dreams."

"OK," he said.

"Simple as that?"

"Exactly. Simple as that. Can't have you having bad dreams, and I've paid my dues. From now on, I'm only going on night call to cover holidays."

She laughed. "Sysadmins don't take holidays."

"This one will," he said. "Promise."

"You're wonderful," she said. "Oh, gross. 2.0 just dumped core all over my bathrobe."

"That's my boy," he said.

"Oh that he is," she said. She hung up, and he piloted the car into the data-center lot, badging in and peeling up a bleary eyelid to let the retinal scanner get a good look at his sleep-depped eyeball.

He stopped at the machine to get himself a guarana/medafonil power-bar and a cup of lethal robot-coffee in a spill-proof clean-room sippy-cup. He wolfed down the bar and sipped the coffee, then let the inner door read his hand-geometry and size him up for a moment. It sighed open and gusted the airlock's load of positively pressurized air over him as he passed finally to the inner sanctum.

It was bedlam. The cages were designed to let two or three sysadmins maneuver around them at a time. Every other inch of cubic space was given over to humming racks of servers and routers and drives. Jammed among them were no fewer than twenty other sysadmins. It was a regular convention of black tee-shirts with inexplicable slogans, bellies overlapping belts with phones and multitools.

Normally it was practically freezing in the cage, but all those bodies were overheating the small, enclosed space. Five or six looked up and grimaced when he came through. Two greeted him by name. He threaded his belly through the press and the cages, toward the Ardent racks in the back of the room.

"Felix." It was Van, who wasn't on call that night.

"What are you doing here?" he asked. "No need for both of us to be wrecked tomorrow."

"What? Oh. My personal box is over there. It went down around 1:30 and I got woken up by my process-monitor. I should have called you and told you I was coming down—spared you the trip."

Felix's own server—a box he shared with five other friends—was in a rack one floor down. He wondered if it was offline too.

"What's the story?"

"Massive flashworm attack. Some jackass with a zero-day exploit has got every Windows box on the net running Monte Carlo probes on every IP block, including IPv6. The big Ciscos all run administrative interfaces over v6, and they all fall over if they get more than ten simultaneous probes, which means that just about every interchange has gone down. DNS is screwy, too—like maybe someone poisoned the zone transfer last night. Oh, and there's an email and IM component that sends pretty lifelike messages to everyone in your address book, barfing up Eliza-dialog that keys off of your logged email and messages to get you to open a trojan."

"Jesus."

"Yeah." Van was a type-two sysadmin, over six feet tall, long ponytail, bobbing Adam's apple. Over his toast-rack chest, his tee said CHOOSE YOUR WEAPON and featured a row of polyhedral RPG dice.

Felix was a type-one admin, with an extra seventy or eighty pounds all around the middle, and a neat but full beard that he wore over his extra chins. His tee said HELLO CTHULHU and featured a cute, mouthless, Hello-Kitty-style Cthulhu. They'd known each other for fifteen years, having met on Usenet, then f2f at Toronto Freenet beer-sessions, a Star Trek convention or two, and eventually Felix had hired Van to work under him at Ardent. Van was reliable and methodical. Trained as an electrical engineer, he kept a procession of spiral notebooks filled with the details of every step he'd ever taken, with time and date.

"Not even PEBKAC this time," Van said. Problem Exists Between Keyboard And Chair. Email trojans fell into that category—if people were smart enough not to open suspect attachments, email trojans would be a thing of the past. But worms that ate Cisco routers weren't a problem with the lusers—they were the fault of incompetent engineers.

"No, it's Microsoft's fault," Felix said. "Any time I'm at work at 2 A.M., it's either PEBKAC or Microsloth."

They ended up just unplugging the frigging routers from the Internet. Not Felix, of course, though he was itching to do it and get them rebooted after shutting down their IPv6 interfaces. It was done by a couple bull-goose Bastard Operators From Hell who had to turn two keys at once to get access to their cage—like guards in a Minuteman silo. Ninety-five percent of the long-distance traffic in Canada went through this building. It had *better* security than most Minuteman silos.

Felix and Van got the Ardent boxes back online one at a time. They were being pounded by worm-probes—putting the routers back online just exposed the downstream cages to the attack. Every box on the Internet was drowning in worms, or creating worm-attacks, or both. Felix managed to get through to NIST and Bugtraq after about a hundred timeouts, and download some kernel patches that should reduce the load the worms put on the machines in his care. It was 10 A.M., and he was hungry enough to eat the ass out of a dead bear, but he recompiled his kernels and brought the machines back online. Van's long fingers flew over the administrative keyboard, his tongue protruding as he ran load-stats on each one.

"I had two hundred days of uptime on Greedo," Van said. Greedo was the oldest server in the rack, from the days when they'd named the boxes after Star Wars characters. Now they were all named after Smurfs, and they were running out of Smurfs and had started in on McDonaldland characters, starting with Van's laptop, Mayor McCheese.

"Greedo will rise again," Felix said. "I've got a 486 downstairs with over five years of uptime. It's going to break my heart to reboot it."

"What the everlasting shit do you use a 486 for?"

"Nothing. But who shuts down a machine with five years uptime? That's like euthanizing your grandmother."

"I wanna eat," Van said.

"Tell you what," Felix said. "We'll get your box up, then mine, then I'll take you to the Lakeview Lunch for breakfast pizzas and you can have the rest of the day off."

"You're on," Van said. "Man, you're too good to us grunts. You should keep us in a pit and beat us like all the other bosses. It's all we deserve."

"It's your phone," Van said. Felix extracted himself from the guts of the 486, which had refused to power up at all. He had cadged a spare power-supply from some guys who ran a spam operation and was trying to get it fitted. He let Van hand him the phone, which had fallen off his belt while he was twisting to get at the back of the machine.

"Hey, Kel," he said. There was an odd, snuffling noise in the background. Static, maybe? 2.0 splashing in the bath? "Kelly?"

The line went dead. He tried to call back, but didn't get anything—no ring nor voicemail. His phone finally timed out and said NETWORK ERROR.

"Dammit," he said, mildly. He clipped the phone to his belt. Kelly wanted to know when he was coming home, or wanted him to pick something up for the family. She'd leave voicemail.

He was testing the power-supply when his phone rang again. He snatched it up and answered it. "Kelly, hey, what's up?" He worked to keep anything like irritation out of his voice. He felt guilty: technically speaking, he had discharged his obligations to Ardent Financial LLC once the Ardent servers were back online. The past three hours had been purely personal—even if he planned on billing them to the company.

There was sobbing on the line.

"Kelly?" He felt the blood draining from his face and his toes were numb.

"Felix," she said, barely comprehensible through the sobbing. "He's dead, oh Jesus, he's dead."

"Who? *Who*, Kelly?"

"Will," she said.

Will? he thought. *Who the fuck is*—He dropped to his knees. William was the name they'd written on the birth certificate, though they'd called him 2.0 all along. Felix made an anguished sound, like a sick bark.

"I'm sick," she said, "I can't even stand anymore. Oh, Felix. I love you so much."

"Kelly? What's going on?"

"Everyone, everyone—" she said. "Only two channels left on the tube. Christ, Felix, it looks like dawn of the dead out the window—" He heard her retch. The phone started to break up, washing her puke-noises back like an echoplex.

"Stay there, Kelly," he shouted as the line died. He punched 911, but the phone went NETWORK ERROR again as soon as he hit SEND.

He grabbed Mayor McCheese from Van and plugged it into the 486's network cable and launched Firefox off the command line and googled for the Metro Police site. Quickly, but not frantically, he searched for an online contact form. Felix didn't lose his head, ever. He solved problems, and freaking out didn't solve problems.

He located an online form and wrote out the details of his conversation with Kelly like he was filing a bug report, his fingers fast, his description complete, and then he hit SUBMIT.

Van had read over his shoulder. "Felix—" he began.

"God," Felix said. He was sitting on the floor of the cage and he slowly pulled himself upright. Van took the laptop and tried some news sites, but they were all timing out. Impossible to say if it was because something terrible was happening or because the network was limping under the superworm.

"I need to get home," Felix said.

"I'll drive you," Van said. "You can keep calling your wife."

They made their way to the elevators. One of the building's few windows was there, a thick, shielded porthole. They peered through it as they waited for the elevator. Not much traffic for a Wednesday. Were there more police cars than usual?

"Oh my God—" Van pointed.

The CN Tower, a giant white-elephant needle of a building loomed to the east of them. It was askew, like a branch stuck in wet sand. Was it moving? It was. It was heeling over, slowly, but gaining speed, falling northeast toward the financial district. In a second, it slid over the tipping point and crashed down. They felt the shock, then heard it, the whole building rocking from the impact. A cloud of dust rose from the wreckage, and there was more thunder as the world's tallest freestanding structure crashed through building after building.

"The Broadcast Centre's coming down," Van said. It

was—the CBC's towering building was collapsing in slow motion. People ran every way, were crushed by falling masonry. Seen through the porthole, it was like watching a neat CGI trick downloaded from a file-sharing site.

Sysadmins were clustering around them now, jostling to see the destruction.

"What happened?" one of them asked.

"The CN Tower fell down," Felix said. He sounded far away in his own ears.

"Was it the virus?"

"The worm? What?" Felix focused on the guy, who was a young admin with just a little type-two flab around the middle.

"Not the worm," the guy said. "I got an email that the whole city's quarantined because of some virus. Bioweapon, they say." He handed Felix his Blackberry.

Felix was so engrossed in the report—purportedly forwarded from Health Canada—that he didn't even notice that all the lights had gone out. Then he did, and he pressed the Blackberry back into its owner's hand, and let out one small sob.

The generators kicked in a minute later. Sysadmins stampeded for the stairs. Felix grabbed Van by the arm, pulled him back.

"Maybe we should wait this out in the cage," he said.

"What about Kelly?" Van said.

Felix felt like he was going to throw up. "We should get into the cage, now." The cage had microparticulate air-filters.

They ran upstairs to the big cage. Felix opened the door and then let it hiss shut behind him.

"Felix, you need to get home—"

"It's a bioweapon," Felix said. "Superbug. We'll be OK in here, I think, so long as the filters hold out."

"What?"

"Get on IRC," he said.

They did. Van had Mayor McCheese and Felix used Smurfette. They skipped around the chat channels until they found one with some familiar handles.

```
> pentagons gone/white house too
> MY NEIGHBORS BARFING BLOOD OFF HIS BALCONY
  IN SAN DIEGO
> Someone knocked over the Gherkin. Bankers
  are fleeing the City like rats.
> I heard that the Ginza's on fire
```

Felix typed: I'm in Toronto. We just saw the CN Tower fall. I've heard reports of bioweapons, something very fast.

Van read this and said, "You don't know how fast it is, Felix. Maybe we were all exposed three days ago."

Felix closed his eyes. "If that were so we'd be feeling some symptoms, I think."

```
> Looks like an EMP took out Hong Kong and
  maybe Paris—real-time sat footage shows
  them completely dark, and all netblocks
  there aren't routing
> You're in Toronto?
```

It was an unfamiliar handle.

```
> Yes—on Front Street
```

```
> my sisters at UofT and i cnt reach her—can
  you call her?
> No phone service
```

Felix typed, staring at NETWORK ERROR.

"I have a soft phone on Mayor McCheese," Van said, launching his voice-over-IP app. "I just remembered."

Felix took the laptop from him and punched in his home number. It rang once, then there was a flat, blatting sound like an ambulance siren in an Italian movie.

```
> No phone service
```

Felix typed again.

He looked up at Van, and saw that his skinny shoulders were shaking. Van said, "Holy motherfucking shit. The world is ending."

Felix pried himself off of IRC an hour later. Atlanta had burned. Manhattan was hot—radioactive enough to screw up the webcams looking out over Lincoln Plaza. Everyone blamed Islam until it became clear that Mecca was a smoking pit and the Saudi Royals had been hanged before their palaces.

His hands were shaking, and Van was quietly weeping in the far corner of the cage. He tried calling home again, and then the police. It didn't work any better than it had the last twenty times.

He sshed into his box downstairs and grabbed his mail. Spam, spam, spam. More spam. Automated messages. There—an urgent message from the intrusion detection system in the Ardent cage.

He opened it and read quickly. Someone was crudely, repeatedly probing his routers. It didn't match a worm's signature, either. He followed the traceroute and discovered that the attack had originated in the same building as him, a system in a cage one floor below.

He had procedures for this. He portscanned his attacker and found that port 1337 was open—1337 was "leet" or "elite" in hacker number/letter substitution code. That was the kind of port that a worm left open to slither in and out of. He googled known sploits that left a listener on port 1337, narrowed this down based on the fingerprinted operating system of the compromised server, and then he had it.

It was an ancient worm, one that every box should have been patched against years before. No mind. He had the client for it, and he used it to create a root account for himself on the box, which he then logged into, and took a look around.

There was one other user logged in, "scaredy," and he checked the process monitor and saw that scaredy had spawned all the hundreds of processes that were probing him and plenty of other boxen.

He opened a chat:

```
> Stop probing my server
```

He expected bluster, guilt, denial. He was surprised.

```
> Are you in the Front Street data-center?
> Yes
> Christ I thought I was the last one alive.
  I'm on the fourth floor. I think there's
```

```
a bioweapon attack outside. I don't want
to leave the clean room.
```

Felix whooshed out a breath.

```
> You were probing me to get me to trace
  back to you?
> Yeah
> That was smart
```

Clever bastard.

```
> I'm on the sixth floor, I've got one more
  with me.
> What do you know?
```

Felix pasted in the IRC log and waited while the other guy digested it. Van stood up and paced. His eyes were glazed over.

"Van? Pal?"

"I have to pee," he said.

"No opening the door," Felix said. "I saw an empty Mountain Dew bottle in the trash there."

"Right," Van said. He walked like a zombie to the trash can and pulled out the empty magnum. He turned his back.

```
> I'm Felix
> Will
```

Felix's stomach did a slow somersault as he thought about 2.0.

"Felix, I think I need to go outside," Van said. He was moving toward the airlock door. Felix dropped his keyboard and struggled to his feet and ran headlong to Van, tackling him before he reached the door.

"Van," he said, looking into his friend's glazed, unfocused eyes. "Look at me, Van."

"I need to go," Van said. "I need to get home and feed the cats."

"There's something out there, something fast-acting and lethal. Maybe it will blow away with the wind. Maybe it's already gone. But we're going to sit here until we know for sure or until we have no choice. Sit down, Van. Sit."

"I'm cold, Felix."

It was freezing. Felix's arms were broken out in gooseflesh and his feet felt like blocks of ice.

"Sit against the servers, by the vents. Get the exhaust heat." He found a rack and nestled up against it."

```
> Are you there?
> Still here—sorting out some logistics
> How long until we can go out?
> I have no idea
```

No one typed anything for quite some time then.

Felix had to use the Mountain Dew bottle twice. Then Van used it again. Felix tried calling Kelly again. The Metro Police site was down.

Finally, he slid back against the servers and wrapped his arms around his knees and wept like a baby.

After a minute, Van came over and sat beside him, with his arm around Felix's shoulder.

"They're dead, Van," Felix said. "Kelly and my s—son. My family is gone."

"You don't know for sure," Van said.

"I'm sure enough," Felix said. "Christ, it's all over, isn't it?"

"We'll gut it out a few more hours and then head out. Things should be getting back to normal soon. The fire department will fix it. They'll mobilize the Army. It'll be OK."

Felix's ribs hurt. He hadn't cried since—since 2.0 was born. He hugged his knees harder.

Then the doors opened.

The two sysadmins who entered were wild-eyed. One had a tee that said TALK NERDY TO ME and the other one was wearing an Electronic Frontiers Canada shirt.

"Come on," TALK NERDY said. "We're all getting together on the top floor. Take the stairs."

Felix found he was holding his breath.

"If there's a bioagent in the building, we're all infected," TALK NERDY said. "Just go, we'll meet you there."

"There's one on the sixth floor," Felix said, as he climbed to his feet.

"Will, yeah, we got him. He's up there."

TALK NERDY was one of the Bastard Operators From Hell who'd unplugged the big routers. Felix and Van climbed the stairs slowly, their steps echoing in the deserted shaft. After the frigid air of the cage, the stairwell felt like a sauna.

There was a cafeteria on the top floor, with working toilets, water and coffee and vending machine food. There was an uneasy queue of sysadmins before each. No one met anyone's eye. Felix wondered which one was Will and then he joined the vending machine queue.

He got a couple more energy bars and a gigantic cup of vanilla coffee before running out of change. Van had scored them some table space and Felix set the stuff down before him and got in the toilet line. "Just save some for me," he said, tossing an energy bar in front of Van.

By the time they were all settled in, thoroughly evacuated, and eating, TALK NERDY and his friend had returned again. They cleared off the cash-register at the end of the food-prep area and TALK NERDY got up on it. Slowly the conversation died down.

"I'm Uri Popovich, this is Diego Rosenbaum. Thank you all for coming up here. Here's what we know for sure: the building's been on generators for three hours now. Visual observation indicates that we're the only building in central Toronto with working power—which should hold out for three more days. There is a bioagent of unknown origin loose beyond our doors. It kills quickly, within hours, and it is aerosolized. You get it from breathing bad air. No one has opened any of the exterior doors to this building since five this morning. No one will open the doors until I give the go-ahead.

"Attacks on major cities all over the world have left emergency responders in chaos. The attacks are electronic, biological, nuclear and conventional explosives, and they are very widespread. I'm a security engineer, and where I come from, attacks in this kind of cluster are usually viewed as opportunistic: group B blows up a bridge because everyone is off taking care of group A's dirty nuke event. It's smart. An Aum Shinrikyo cell in Seoul gassed the subways there about 2 A.M. Eastern—that's the earliest event we can locate, so it may have been the Archduke that broke the camel's back. We're pretty sure that Aum

Shinrikyo couldn't be behind this kind of mayhem: they have no history of infowar and have never shown the kind of organizational acumen necessary to take out so many targets at once. Basically, they're not smart enough.

"We're holing up here for the foreseeable future, at least until the bioweapon has been identified and dispersed. We're going to staff the racks and keep the networks up. This is critical infrastructure, and it's our job to make sure it's got five nines of uptime. In times of national emergency, our responsibility to do that doubles."

One sysadmin put up his hand. He was very daring in a green Incredible Hulk ring-tee, and he was at the young end of the scale.

"Who died and made you king?"

"I have controls for the main security system, keys to every cage, and passcodes for the exterior doors— they're all locked now, by the way. I'm the one who got everyone up here first and called the meeting. I don't care if someone else wants this job, it's a shitty one. But someone needs to have this job."

"You're right," the kid said. "And I can do it every bit as well as you. My name's Will Sario."

Popovich looked down his nose at the kid. "Well, if you'll let me finish talking, maybe I'll hand things over to you when I'm done."

"Finish, by all means." Sario turned his back on him and walked to the window. He stared out of it intensely. Felix's gaze was drawn to it, and he saw that there were several oily smoke plumes rising up from the city.

Popovich's momentum was broken. "So that's what we're going to do," he said.

The kid looked around after a stretched moment of

silence. "Oh, is it my turn now?"

There was a round of good-natured chuckling.

"Here's what I think: the world is going to shit. There are coordinated attacks on every critical piece of infrastructure. There's only one way that those attacks could be so well coordinated: via the Internet. Even if you buy the thesis that the attacks are all opportunistic, we need to ask how an opportunistic attack could be organized in minutes: the Internet."

"So you think we should shut down the Internet?" Popovich laughed a little, but stopped when Sario said nothing.

"We saw an attack last night that nearly killed the Internet. A little DoS on the critical routers, a little DNS-foo, and down it goes like a preacher's daughter. Cops and the military are a bunch of technophobic lusers, they hardly rely on the net at all. If we take the Internet down, we'll disproportionately disadvantage the attackers, while only inconveniencing the defenders. When the time comes, we can rebuild it."

"You're shitting me," Popovich said. His jaw literally hung open.

"It's logical," Sario said. "Lots of people don't like coping with logic when it dictates hard decisions. That's a problem with people, not logic."

There was a buzz of conversation that quickly turned into a roar.

"Shut UP!" Popovich hollered. The conversation dimmed by one watt. Popovich yelled again, stamping his foot on the countertop. Finally there was a semblance of order. "One at a time," he said. He was flushed red, his hands in his pockets.

One sysadmin was for staying. Another for going. They should hide in the cages. They should inventory their supplies and appoint a quartermaster. They should go outside and find the police, or volunteer at hospitals. They should appoint defenders to keep the front door secure.

Felix found to his surprise that he had his hand in the air. Popovich called on him.

"My name is Felix Tremont," he said, getting up on one of the tables, drawing out his PDA. "I want to read you something.

"'Governments of the Industrial World, you weary giants of flesh and steel, I come from Cyberspace, the new home of Mind. On behalf of the future, I ask you of the past to leave us alone. You are not welcome among us. You have no sovereignty where we gather.

"'We have no elected government, nor are we likely to have one, so I address you with no greater authority than that with which liberty itself always speaks. I declare the global social space we are building to be naturally independent of the tyrannies you seek to impose on us. You have no moral right to rule us nor do you possess any methods of enforcement we have true reason to fear.

"'Governments derive their just powers from the consent of the governed. You have neither solicited nor received ours. We did not invite you. You do not know us, nor do you know our world. Cyberspace does not lie within your borders. Do not think that you can build it, as though it were a public construction project. You cannot. It is an act of nature and it grows itself through our collective actions.'

"That's from the Declaration of Independence of Cyberspace. It was written twelve years ago. I thought it was one of the most beautiful things I'd ever read. I wanted my kid to grow up in a world where cyberspace was free—and where that freedom infected the real world, so meatspace got freer too."

He swallowed hard and scrubbed at his eyes with the back of his hand. Van awkwardly patted him on the shoe.

"My beautiful son and my beautiful wife died today. Millions more, too. The city is literally in flames. Whole cities have disappeared from the map."

He coughed up a sob and swallowed it again.

"All around the world, people like us are gathered in buildings like this. They were trying to recover from last night's worm when disaster struck. We have independent power. Food. Water.

"We have the network, that the bad guys use so well and that the good guys have never figured out.

"We have a shared love of liberty that comes from caring about and caring for the network. We are in charge of the most important organizational and governmental tool the world has ever seen. We are the closest thing to a government the world has right now. Geneva is a crater. The East River is on fire and the UN is evacuated.

"The Distributed Republic of Cyberspace weathered this storm basically unscathed. We are the custodians of a deathless, monstrous, wonderful machine, one with the potential to rebuild a better world.

"I have nothing to live for but that."

There were tears in Van's eyes. He wasn't the only one. They didn't applaud him, but they did one better. They maintained respectful, total silence for seconds that stretched to a minute.

"How do we do it?" Popovich said, without a trace of sarcasm.

* * *

The newsgroups were filling up fast. They'd announced them in news.admin.net-abuse.email, where all the spamfighters hung out, and where there was a tight culture of camaraderie in the face of full-out attack.

The new group was alt.november5-disaster.recovery, with .recovery.governance, .recovery.finance, .recovery.logistics and .recovery.defense hanging off of it. Bless the wooly alt. hierarchy and all those who sail in her.

The sysadmins came out of the woodwork. The Googleplex was online, with the stalwart Queen Kong bossing a gang of rollerbladed grunts who wheeled through the gigantic data-center swapping out dead boxen and hitting reboot switches. The Internet Archive was offline in the Presidio, but the mirror in Amsterdam was live and they'd redirected the DNS so that you'd hardly know the difference. Amazon was down. PayPal was up. Blogger, TypePad and LiveJournal were all up, and filling with millions of posts from scared survivors huddling together for electronic warmth.

The Flickr photostreams were horrific. Felix had to unsubscribe from them after he caught a photo of a woman and a baby, dead in a kitchen, twisted into an agonized hieroglyph by the bioagent. They didn't look like Kelly and 2.0, but they didn't have to. He started shaking and couldn't stop.

Wikipedia was up, but limping under load. The spam poured in as though nothing had changed. Worms roamed the network.

.recovery.logistics was where most of the action was.

> We can use the newsgroup voting mechanism

```
to hold regional elections
```

Felix knew that this would work. Usenet newsgroup votes had been running for more than twenty years without a substantial hitch.

```
> We'll elect regional representatives and
  they'll pick a Prime Minister.
```

The Americans insisted on President, which Felix didn't like. Seemed too partisan. His future wouldn't be the American future. The American future had gone up with the White House. He was building a bigger tent than that.

There were French sysadmins online from France Telecom. The EBU's data-center had been spared in the attacks that hammered Geneva, and it was filled with wry Germans whose English was better than Felix's. They got on well with the remains of the BBC team in Canary Wharf.

They spoke polyglot English in .recovery.logistics, and Felix had momentum on his side. Some of the admins were cooling out the inevitable stupid flamewars with the practice of long years. Some were chipping in useful suggestions.

Surprisingly few thought that Felix was off his rocker.

```
> I think we should hold elections as soon
  as possible. Tomorrow at the latest. We
  can't rule justly without the consent of
  the governed.
```

Within seconds the reply landed in his inbox.

> You can't be serious. Consent of the governed? Unless I miss my guess, most of the people you're proposing to govern are puking their guts out, hiding under their desks, or wandering shell-shocked through the city streets. When do THEY get a vote?

Felix had to admit she had a point. Queen Kong was sharp. Not many women sysadmins, and that was a genuine tragedy. Women like Queen Kong were too good to exclude from the field. He'd have to hack a solution to get women balanced out in his new government. Require each region to elect one woman and one man?

He happily clattered into argument with her. The elections would be the next day; he'd see to it.

"Prime Minister of Cyberspace? Why not call yourself the Grand Poobah of the Global Data Network? It's more dignified, sounds cooler and it'll get you just as far." Will had the sleeping spot next to him, up in the cafeteria, with Van on the other side. The room smelled like a dingleberry: twenty-five sysadmins who hadn't washed in at least a day all crammed into the same room. For some of them, it had been much, much longer than a day.

"Shut up, Will," Van said. "You wanted to try to knock the Internet offline."

"Correction: I *want* to knock the Internet offline. Present-tense."

Felix cracked one eye. He was so tired, it was like lifting weights.

"Look, Sario—if you don't like my platform, put one of your own forward. There are plenty of people who think I'm full of shit and I respect them for that, since they're all running opposite me or backing someone who is. That's your choice. What's not on the menu is nagging and complaining. Bedtime now, or get up and post your platform."

Sario sat up slowly, unrolling the jacket he had been using for a pillow and putting it on. "Screw you guys, I'm out of here."

"I thought he'd never leave," Felix said, and turned over, lying awake a long time, thinking about the election.

There were other people in the running. Some of them weren't even sysadmins. A US Senator on retreat at his summer place in Wyoming had generator power and a satellite phone. Somehow he'd found the right newsgroup and thrown his hat into the ring. Some anarchist hackers in Italy strafed the group all night long, posting broken-English screeds about the political bankruptcy of "governance" in the new world. Felix looked at their netblock and determined that they were probably holed up in a small Interaction Design institute near Turin. Italy had been hit very bad, but out in the small town, this cell of anarchists had taken up residence.

A surprising number were running on a platform of shutting down the Internet. Felix had his doubts about whether this was even possible, but he thought he understood the impulse to finish the work and the world. Why not? From every indication, it seemed that the work to date had been a cascade of disasters, attacks, and opportunism, all of it adding up to Götterdämmerung. A terrorist attack here, a lethal counteroffensive there from an overreactive government… Before long, they'd made short work of the world.

He fell asleep thinking about the logistics of shutting down the Internet, and dreamed bad dreams in which he was the network's sole defender.

He woke to a papery, itchy sound. He rolled over and saw that Van was sitting up, his jacket balled up in his lap, vigorously scratching his skinny arms. They'd gone the color of corned beef, and had a scaly look. In the light streaming through the cafeteria windows, skin motes floated and danced in great clouds.

"What are you doing?" Felix sat up. Watching Van's fingernails rip into his skin made him itch in sympathy. It had been three days since he'd last washed his hair and his scalp sometimes felt like there were little egg-laying insects picking their way through it. He'd adjusted his glasses the night before and had touched the back of his ears; his finger came away shining with thick sebum. He got blackheads in the backs of his ears when he didn't shower for a couple days, and sometimes gigantic, deep boils that Kelly finally popped with sick relish.

"Scratching," Van said. He went to work on his head, sending a cloud of dandruff-crud into the sky, there to join the scurf that he'd already eliminated from his extremities. "Christ, I itch all over."

Felix took Mayor McCheese from Van's backpack and plugged it into one of the Ethernet cables that snaked all over the floor. He googled everything he could think of that could be related to this. "Itchy" yielded 40,600,000 links. He tried compound queries and got slightly more discriminating links.

"I think it's stress-related eczema," Felix said, finally.

"I don't get eczema," Van said.

Felix showed him some lurid photos of red, angry skin flaked with white. "Stress-related eczema," he said, reading the caption.

Van examined his arms. "I have eczema," he said.

"Says here to keep it moisturized and to try cortisone cream. You might try the first aid kit in the second-floor toilets. I think I saw some there." Like all of the sysadmins, Felix had had a bit of a rummage around the offices, bathrooms, kitchen and storerooms, squirreling away a roll of toilet-paper in his shoulder-bag along with three or four power-bars. They were sharing out the food in the caf by unspoken agreement, every sysadmin watching every other for signs of gluttony and hoarding. All were convinced that there was hoarding and gluttony going on out of eyeshot, because all were guilty of it themselves when no one else was watching.

Van got up and when his face hove into the light, Felix saw how puffed his eyes were. "I'll post to the mailinglist for some antihistamine," Felix said. There had been four mailing lists and three wikis for the survivors in the building within hours of the first meeting's close, and in the intervening days they'd settled on just one. Felix was still on a little mailing list with five of his most trusted friends, two of whom were trapped in cages in other countries. He suspected that the rest of the sysadmins were doing the same.

Van stumbled off. "Good luck on the elections," he said, patting Felix on the shoulder.

Felix stood and paced, stopping to stare out the grubby windows. The fires still burned in Toronto, more than before. He'd tried to find mailing lists or blogs that

Torontonians were posting to, but the only ones he'd found were being run by other geeks in other data-centers. It was possible—likely, even—that there were survivors out there who had more pressing priorities than posting to the Internet. His home phone still worked about half the time but he'd stopped calling it after the second day, when hearing Kelly's voice on the voicemail for the fiftieth time had made him cry in the middle of a planning meeting. He wasn't the only one.

Election day. Time to face the music.

```
> Are you nervous?
> Nope
```

Felix typed.

```
> I don't much care if I win, to be honest.
  I"m just glad we're doing this. The
  alternative was sitting around with our
  thumbs up our ass, waiting for someone to
  crack up and open the door.
```

The cursor hung. Queen Kong was very high latency as she bossed her gang of Googloids around the Googleplex, doing everything she could to keep her data- center online. Three of the offshore cages had gone offline and two of their six redundant network links were smoked. Lucky for her, queries-per-second were way down.

```
> There's still China
```

she typed. Queen Kong had a big board with a map

of the world colored in Google-queries-per-second, and could do magic with it, showing the drop-off over time in colorful charts. She'd uploaded lots of video clips showing how the plague and the bombs had swept the world: the initial upswell of queries from people wanting to find out what was going on, then the grim, precipitous shelving off as the plagues took hold.

> China's still running about ninety percent
  nominal.

Felix shook his head.

> You can't think that they're responsible
> No

She typed, but then she started to key something and then stopped.

> No of course not. I believe the Popovich
  Hypothesis. This is a bunch of assholes
  all using the rest for cover. But China
  put them down harder and faster than anyone
  else. Maybe we've finally found a use for
  totalitarian states.

Felix couldn't resist. He typed:

> You're lucky your boss can't see you type
  that. You guys were pretty enthusiastic
  participants in the Great Firewall of
  China.

```
> Wasn't my idea
```

she typed.

```
> And my boss is dead. They're probably all
  dead. The whole Bay Area got hit hard, and
  then there was the quake.
```

They'd watched the USGS's automated data-stream from the 6.9 that trashed Northern Cal from Gilroy to Sebastopol. Some webcams revealed the scope of the damage—gas main explosions, seismically retrofitted buildings crumpling like piles of children's blocks after a good kicking. The Googleplex, floating on a series of gigantic steel springs, had shook like a plateful of jello, but the racks had stayed in place and the worst injury they'd had was a badly bruised eye on a sysadmin who'd caught a flying cable-crimper in the face.

```
> Sorry. I forgot.
> It's OK. We all lost people, right?
> Yeah. Yeah. Anyway, I'm not worried about
  the election. Whoever wins, at least we're
  doing SOMETHING
> Not if they vote for one of the fuckrags
```

Fuckrag was the epithet that some of the sysadmins were using to describe the contingent that wanted to shut down the Internet. Queen Kong had coined it—apparently it had started life as a catch-all term to describe clueless IT managers that she'd chewed up through her career.

```
> They won't. They're just tired and sad is
  all. Your endorsement will carry the day
```

The Googloids were one of the largest and most powerful blocs left behind, along with the satellite uplink crews and the remaining transoceanic crews. Queen Kong's endorsement had come as a surprise and he'd sent her an email that she'd replied to tersely: "can't have the fuckrags in charge."

```
> gtg
```

she typed and then her connection dropped. He fired up a browser and called up google.com. The browser timed out. He hit reload, and then again, and then the Google front-page came back up. Whatever had hit Queen Kong's workplace—power failure, worms, another quake—she had fixed it. He snorted when he saw that they'd replaced the Os in the Google logo with little planet Earths with mushroom clouds rising from them.

"Got anything to eat?" Van said to him. It was midafternoon, not that time particularly passed in the data-center. Felix patted his pockets. They'd put a quartermaster in charge, but not before everyone had snagged some chow out of the machines. He'd had a dozen power-bars and some apples. He'd taken a couple sandwiches but had wisely eaten them first before they got stale.

"One power-bar left," he said. He'd noticed a certain looseness in his waistline that morning and had briefly relished it. Then he'd remembered Kelly's teasing about his weight and he'd cried some. Then he'd eaten two power-bars, leaving him with just one left.

"Oh," Van said. His face was hollower than ever, his shoulders sloping in on his toast-rack chest.

"Here," Felix said. "Vote Felix."

Van took the power-bar from him and then put it down on the table. "OK, I want to give this back to you and say, 'No, I couldn't,' but I'm fucking *hungry*, so I'm just going to take it and eat it, OK?"

"That's fine by me," Felix said. "Enjoy."

"How are the elections coming?" Van said, once he'd licked the wrapper clean.

"Dunno," Felix said. "Haven't checked in a while." He'd been winning by a slim margin a few hours before. Not having his laptop was a major handicap when it came to stuff like this. Up in the cages, there were a dozen more like him, poor bastards who'd left the house on Der Tag without thinking to snag something WiFi-enabled.

"You're going to get smoked," Sario said, sliding in next to them. He'd become famous in the center for never sleeping, for eavesdropping, for picking fights in RL that had the ill-considered heat of a Usenet flamewar. "The winner will be someone who understands a couple of fundamental facts." He held up a fist, then ticked off his bullet points by raising a finger one at a time. "Point: The terrorists are using the Internet to destroy the world, and we need to destroy the Internet first. Point: Even if I'm wrong, the whole thing is a joke. We'll run out of generator-fuel soon enough. Point: Or if we don't, it will be because the old world will be back and running, and it won't give a crap about your new world. Point: We're gonna run out of food before we run out of shit to argue about or reasons not to go outside. We have the chance to do something to help the world recover: we can kill the net and cut it off as a tool for bad guys. Or we can rearrange some more deck chairs on the bridge of your personal *Titanic* in the service of some sweet dream about an 'independent cyberspace.'"

The thing was that Sario was right. They would be out of fuel in two days—intermittent power from the grid had stretched their generator lifespan. And if you bought his hypothesis that the Internet was primarily being used as a tool to organize more mayhem, shutting it down would be the right thing to do.

But Felix's daughter and his wife were dead. He didn't want to rebuild the old world. He wanted a new one. The old world was one that didn't have any place for him. Not anymore.

Van scratched his raw, flaking skin. Puffs of dander and scruff swirled in the musty, greasy air. Sario curled a lip at him. "That is disgusting. We're breathing recycled air, you know. Whatever leprosy is eating you, aerosolizing it into the air supply is pretty anti-social."

"You're the world's leading authority on anti-social, Sario," Van said. "Go away or I'll multitool you to death." He stopped scratching and patted his sheathed multipliers like a gunslinger.

"Yeah, I'm anti-social. I've got Asperger's and I haven't taken any meds in four days. What's your fucking excuse?"

Van scratched some more. "I'm sorry," he said. "I didn't know."

Sario cracked up. "Oh, you are priceless. I'd bet that three-quarters of this bunch is borderline autistic. Me, I'm just as asshole. But I'm one who isn't afraid to tell the truth, and that makes me better than you, dickweed."

"Fuckrag," Felix said, "fuck off."

They had less than a day's worth of fuel when Felix was elected the first ever Prime Minister of Cyberspace. The first count was spoiled by a bot that spammed the voting process and they lost a critical day while they added up the votes a second time.

But by then, it was all seeming like more of a joke. Half the data-centers had gone dark. Queen Kong's net-maps of Google queries were looking grimmer and grimmer as more of the world went offline, though she maintained a leader-board of new and rising queries—largely related to health, shelter, sanitation and self-defense.

Worm-load slowed. Power was going off to many home PC users, and staying off, so their compromised PCs were going dark. The backbones were still lit up and blinking, but the missives from those data-centers were looking more and more desperate. Felix hadn't eaten in a day and neither had anyone in a satellite Earth-station of transoceanic head-end.

Water was running short, too.

Popovich and Rosenbaum came and got him before he could do more than answer a few congratulatory messages and post a canned acceptance speech to newsgroups.

"We're going to open the doors," Popovich said. Like all of them, he'd lost weight and waxed scruffy and oily. His BO was like a cloud coming off trash-bags behind a fish-market on a sunny day. Felix was quite sure he smelled no better.

"You're going to go for a reccy? Get more fuel? We can charter a working group for it—great idea."

Rosenbaum shook his head sadly. "We're going to go find our families. Whatever is out there has burned itself out. Or it hasn't. Either way, there's no future in here."

"What about network maintenance?" Felix said, though he knew the answers. "Who'll keep the routers up?"

"We'll give you the root passwords to everything," Popovich said. His hands were shaking and his eyes were bleary. Like many of the smokers stuck in the data-center, he'd gone cold turkey this week. They'd run out of caffeine products two days earlier, too. The smokers had it rough.

"And I'll just stay here and keep everything online?"

"You and anyone else who cares anymore."

Felix knew that he'd squandered his opportunity. The election had seemed noble and brave, but in hindsight all it had been was an excuse for infighting when they should have been figuring out what to do next. The problem was that there was nothing to do next.

"I can't make you stay," he said.

"Yeah, you can't." Popovich turned on his heel and walked out. Rosenbaum watched him go, then he gripped Felix's shoulder and squeezed it.

"Thank you, Felix. It was a beautiful dream. It still is. Maybe we'll find something to eat and some fuel and come back."

Rosenbaum had a sister whom he'd been in contact with over IM for the first days after the crisis broke. Then she'd stopped answering. The sysadmins were split among those who'd had a chance to say goodbye and those who hadn't. Each was sure the other had it better.

They posted about it on the internal newsgroup—they were still geeks, after all, and there was a little honor guard on the ground floor, geeks who watched them pass toward the double doors. They manipulated the keypads and the steel shutters lifted, then the first set of doors opened. They stepped into the vestibule and pulled the doors shut behind them. The front doors opened. It was very bright and sunny outside, and apart from how empty it was, it looked very normal. Heartbreakingly so.

The two took a tentative step out into the world. Then another. They turned to wave at the assembled masses. Then they both grabbed their throats and began to jerk and twitch, crumpling in a heap on the ground.

"Shiii—!" was all Felix managed to choke out before they both dusted themselves off and stood up, laughing so hard they were clutching their sides. They waved once more and turned on their heels.

"Man, those guys are sick," Van said. He scratched his arms, which had long, bloody scratches on them. His clothes were so covered in scurf they looked like they'd been dusted with icing sugar.

"I thought it was pretty funny," Felix said.

"Christ I'm hungry," Van said, conversationally.

"Lucky for you, we've got all the packets we can eat," Felix said.

"You're too good to us grunts, Mr. President," Van said.

"Prime Minister," he said. "And you're no grunt, you're the Deputy Prime Minister. You're my designated ribbon-cutter and hander-out of oversized novelty checks."

It buoyed both of their spirits. Watching Popovich and Rosenbaum go, it buoyed them up. Felix knew then that they'd all be going soon.

That had been preordained by the fuel-supply, but who wanted to wait for the fuel to run out, anyway?

```
> half my crew split this morning
```

Queen Kong typed. Google was holding up pretty good anyway, of course. The load on the servers was a lot lighter than it had been since the days when Google fit on a bunch of hand-built PCs under a desk at Stanford.

```
> we're down to a quarter
```

Felix typed back. It was only a day since Popovich and Rosenbaum left, but the traffic on the newsgroups had fallen down to near zero. He and Van hadn't had much time to play Republic of Cyberspace. They'd been too busy learning the systems that Popovich had turned over to them, the big, big routers that had went on acting as the major interchange for all the network backbones in Canada.

Still, someone posted to the newsgroups every now and again, generally to say goodbye. The old flamewars about who would be PM, or whether they would shut down the network, or who took too much food—it was all gone.

He reloaded the newsgroup. There was a typical message.

```
> Runaway processes on Solaris
> Uh, hi. I'm just a lightweight MSCE but
  I'm the only one awake here and four of the
  DSLAMs just went down. Looks like there's
  some custom accounting code that's trying
  to figure out how much to bill our corporate
  customers and it's spawned ten thousand
  threads and its eating all the swap. I
  just want to kill it but I can't seem to
  do that. Is there some magic invocation
```

```
I need to do to get this goddamned weenix
box to kill this shit? I mean, it's not
as if any of our customers are ever going
to pay us again. I'd ask the guy who wrote
this code, but he's pretty much dead as
far as anyone can work out.
```

He reloaded. There was a response. It was short, authoritative, and helpful—just the sort of thing you almost never saw in a high-caliber newsgroup when a noob posted a dumb question. The apocalypse had awoken the spirit of patient helpfulness in the world's sysop community.

Van shoulder-surfed him. "Holy shit, who knew he had it in him?"

He looked at the message again. It was from Will Sario. He dropped into his chat window.

```
> sario i thought you wanted the network dead
  why are you helping msces fix their boxen?
> <sheepish grin> Gee Mr PM, maybe I just
  can't bear to watch a computer suffer at
  the hands of an amateur.
```

He flipped to the channel with Queen Kong in it.

```
> How long?
> Since I slept? Two days. Until we run out
  of fuel? Three days. Since we ran out of
  food? Two days.
> Jeez. I didn't sleep last night either.
  We're a little short handed around here.
```

```
> asl? Im monica and I live in pasadena and
  Im bored with my homework. WOuld you like
  to download my pic???
```

The trojan bots were all over IRC these days, jumping to every channel that had any traffic on it. Sometimes you caught five or six flirting with each other. It was pretty weird to watch a piece of malware try to con another instance of itself into downloading a trojan.

They both kicked the bot off the channel simultaneously. He had a script for it now. The spam hadn't even tailed off a little.

```
> How come the spam isn't reducing? Half
  the goddamned data-centers have gone dark
```

Queen Kong paused a long time before typing. As had become automatic when she went high-latency, he reloaded the Google homepage. Sure enough, it was down.

```
> Sario, you got any food?
> You won't miss a couple more meals, Your
  Excellency
```

Van had gone back to Mayor McCheese but he was in the same channel.

"What a dick. You're looking pretty buff, though, dude."

Van didn't look so good. He looked like you could knock him over with a stiff breeze and he had a phlegmy, weak quality to his speech.

```
> hey kong everything ok?
```

```
> everything's fine just had to go kick
  some ass
```

"How's the traffic, Van?"

"Down twenty-five percent from this morning," he said. There were a bunch of nodes whose connections routed through them. Presumably most of these were home or commercial customers in places where the power was still on and the phone company's COs were still alive.

Every once in a while, Felix would wiretap the connections to see if he could find a person who had news of the wide world. Almost all of it was automated traffic, though: network backups, status updates. Spam. Lots of spam.

```
> Spam's still up because the services that
  stop spam are failing faster than the
  services that create it. All the anti-
  worm stuff is centralized in a couple
  places. The bad stuff is on a million
  zombie computers. If only the lusers had
  had the good sense to turn off their home
  PCs before keeling over or taking off
> at the rate were going well be routing
  nothing but spam by dinnertime
```

Van cleared his throat, a painful sound. "About that," he said. "I think it's going to hit sooner than that. Felix, I don't think anyone would notice if we just walked away from here."

Felix looked at him, his skin the color of corned-beef and streaked with long, angry scabs. His fingers trembled.

"You drinking enough water?"

Van nodded. "All frigging day, every ten seconds. Anything to keep my belly full." He pointed to a refilled Pepsi Max bottle full of water by his side.

"Let's have a meeting," he said.

There had been forty-three of them on D-Day. Now there were fifteen. Six had responded to the call for a meeting by simply leaving. Everyone knew without having to be told what the meeting was about.

"So that's it, you're going to let it all fall apart?" Sario was the only one with the energy left to get properly angry. He'd go angry to his grave. The veins on his throat and forehead stood out angrily. His fists shook angrily. All the other geeks went lids-down at the site of him, looking up in unison for once at the discussion, not keeping one eye on a chat-log or a tailed service log.

"Sario, you've got to be shitting me," Felix said. "You wanted to pull the goddamned plug!"

"I wanted it to go *clean*," he shouted. "I didn't want it to bleed out and keel over in little gasps and pukes forever. I wanted it to be an act of will by the global community of its caretakers. I wanted it to be an affirmative act by human hands. Not entropy and bad code and worms winning out. Fuck that, that's just what's happened out there."

Up in the top-floor cafeteria, there were windows all around, hardened and light-bending, and by custom, they were all blinds-down. Now Sario ran around the room, yanking on the blinds. *How the hell can he get the energy to run?* Felix wondered. He could barely walk up the stairs to the meeting room.

Harsh daylight flooded in. It was a fine sunny day

out there, but everywhere you looked across that commanding view of Toronto's skyline, there were rising plumes of smoke. The TD tower, a gigantic black modernist glass brick, was gouting flame to the sky. "It's all falling apart, the way everything does.

"Listen, listen. If we leave the network to fall over slowly, parts of it will stay online for months. Maybe years. And what will run on it? Malware. Worms. Spam. System-processes. Zone transfers. The things we use fall apart and require constant maintenance. The things we abandon don't get used and they last forever. We're going to leave the network behind like a lime-pit filled with industrial waste. That will be our fucking legacy—the legacy of every keystroke you and I and anyone, anywhere ever typed. You understand? We're going to leave it to die slow like a wounded dog, instead of giving it one clean shot through the head."

Van scratched his cheeks, then Felix saw that he was wiping away tears.

"Sario, you're not wrong, but you're not right either," he said. "Leaving it up to limp along is right. We're going to all be limping for a long time, and maybe it will be some use to someone. If there's one packet being routed from any user to any other user, anywhere in the world, it's doing it's job."

"If you want a clean kill, you can do that," Felix said. "I'm the PM and I say so. I'm giving you root. All of you." He turned to the white-board where the cafeteria workers used to scrawl the day's specials. Now it was covered with the remnants of heated technical debates that the sysadmins had engaged in over the days since the day.

He scrubbed away a clean spot with his sleeve and

began to write out long, complicated alphanumeric passwords salted with punctuation. Felix had a gift for remembering that kind of password. He doubted it would do him much good, ever again.

```
> Were going, kong. Fuels almost out anyway
> yeah well thats right then. it was an
  honor, mr prime minister
> you going to be ok?
> ive commandeered a young sysadmin to see
  to my feminine needs and weve found another
  cache of food thatll last us a coupel weeks
  now that were down to fifteen admins—im in
  hog heaven pal
> youre amazing, Queen Kong, seriously. Dont
  be a hero though. When you need to go go.
  Theres got to be something out there
> be safe felix, seriously—btw did i tell
  you queries are up in Romania? maybe theyre
  getting back on their feet
> really?
> yeah, really. we're hard to kill—like
  fucking roaches
```

Her connection died. He dropped to Firefox and reloaded Google and it was down. He hit reload and hit reload and hit reload, but it didn't come up. He closed his eyes and listened to Van scratch his legs and then heard Van type a little.

"They're back up," he said.

Felix whooshed out a breath. He sent the message to the newsgroup, one that he'd run through five drafts before settling on: "Take care of the place, OK? We'll be back, someday."

Everyone was going except Sario. Sario wouldn't leave. He came down to see them off, though.

The sysadmins gathered in the lobby and Felix made the safety door go up, and the light rushed in.

Sario stuck his hand out.

"Good luck," he said.

"You too," Felix said. He had a firm grip, Sario, stronger than he had any right to be. "Maybe you were right," he said.

"Maybe," he said.

"You going to pull the plug?"

Sario looked up at the drop-ceiling, seeming to peer through the reinforced floors at the humming racks above. "Who knows?" he said at last.

Van scratched and a flurry of white motes danced in the sunlight.

"Let's go find you a pharmacy," Felix said. He walked to the door and the other sysadmins followed.

They waited for the interior doors to close behind them and then Felix opened the exterior doors. The air smelled and tasted like mown grass, like the first drops of rain, like the lake and the sky, like the outdoors and the world, an old friend not heard from in an eternity.

"Bye, Felix," the other sysadmins said. They were drifting away while he stood transfixed at the top of the short concrete staircase. The light hurt his eyes and made them water.

"I think there's a Shopper's Drug Mart on King Street," he said to Van. "We'll throw a brick through the window and get you some cortisone, OK?"

"You're the Prime Minister," Van said. "Lead on."

* * *

They didn't see a single soul on the fifteen-minute walk. There wasn't a single sound except for some bird noises and some distant groans, and the wind in the electric cables overhead. It was like walking on the surface of the moon.

"Bet they have chocolate bars at the Shopper's," Van said.

Felix's stomach lurched. Food. "Wow," he said, around a mouthful of saliva.

They walked past a little hatchback and in the front seat was the dried body of a woman holding the dried body of a baby, and his mouth filled with sour bile, even though the smell was faint through the rolled-up windows.

He hadn't thought of Kelly or 2.0 in days. He dropped to his knees and retched again. Out here in the real world, his family was dead. Everyone he knew was dead. He just wanted to lie down on the sidewalk and wait to die, too.

Van's rough hands slipped under his armpits and hauled weakly at him. "Not now," he said. "Once we're safe inside somewhere and we've eaten something, then you can do this, but not now. Understand me, Felix? Not fucking now."

The profanity got through to him. He got to his feet. His knees were trembling.

"Just a block more," Van said, and slipped Felix's arm around his shoulders and led him along.

"Thank you, Van. I'm sorry."

"No sweat," he said. "You need a shower, bad. No offense."

"None taken."

The Shopper's had a metal security gate, but it had been torn away from the front windows, which had been rudely smashed. Felix and Van squeezed through the gap and stepped into the dim drug-store. A few of the displays were knocked over, but other than that, it looked OK. By the cash-registers, Felix spotted the racks of candy bars at the same instant that Van saw them, and they hurried over and grabbed a handful each, stuffing their faces.

"You two eat like pigs."

They both whirled at the sound of the woman's voice. She was holding a fire-axe that was nearly as big as she was. She wore a lab-coat and comfortable shoes.

"You take what you need and go, OK? No sense in there being any trouble." Her chin was pointy and her eyes were sharp. She looked to be in her forties. She looked nothing like Kelly, which was good, because Felix felt like running and giving her a hug as it was. Another person alive!

"Are you a doctor?" Felix said. She was wearing scrubs under the coat, he saw.

"You going to go?" She brandished the axe.

Felix held his hands up. "Seriously, are you a doctor? A pharmacist?"

"I used to be an RN, ten years ago. I'm mostly a Web-designer."

"You're shitting me," Felix said.

"Haven't you ever met a girl who knew about computers?"

"Actually, a friend of mine who runs Google's data-center is a girl. A woman, I mean."

"You're shitting me," she said. "A woman ran Google's data-center?"

"Runs," Felix said. "It's still online."

"NFW," she said. She let the axe lower.

"Way. Have you got any cortisone cream? I can tell you

the story. My name's Felix and this is Van, who needs any antihistamines you can spare."

"I can spare? Felix old pal, I have enough dope here to last a hundred years. This stuff's going to expire long before it runs out. But are you telling me that the net's still up?"

"It's still up," he said. "Kind of. That's what we've been doing all week. Keeping it online. It might not last much longer, though."

"No," she said. "I don't suppose it would." She set the axe down. "Have you got anything to trade? I don't need much, but I've been trying to keep my spirits up by trading with the neighbors. It's like playing Civilization."

"You have neighbors?"

"At least ten," she said. "The people in the restaurant across the way make a pretty good soup, even if most of the veg is canned. They cleaned me out of Sterno, though."

"You've got neighbors and you trade with them?"

"Well, nominally. It'd be pretty lonely without them. I've taken care of whatever sniffles I could. Set a bone—broken wrist. Listen, do you want some Wonder Bread and peanut butter? I have a ton of it. Your friend looks like he could use a meal."

"Yes please," Van said. "We don't have anything to trade, but we're both committed workaholics looking to learn a trade. Could you use some assistants?"

"Not really." She spun her axe on its head. "But I wouldn't mind some company."

They ate the sandwiches and then some soup. The restaurant people brought it over and made their manners at them, though Felix saw their noses wrinkle up and ascertained that there was working plumbing in the back room. Van went in to take a sponge bath and then he followed.

"None of us know what to do," the woman said. Her name was Rosa, and she had found them a bottle of wine and some disposable plastic cups from the housewares aisle. "I thought we'd have helicopters or tanks or even looters, but it's just quiet."

"You seem to have kept pretty quiet yourself," Felix said.

"Didn't want to attract the wrong kind of attention."

"You ever think that maybe there's a lot of people out there doing the same thing? Maybe if we all get together we'll come up with something to do."

"Or maybe they'll cut our throats," she said.

Van nodded. "She's got a point."

Felix was on his feet. "No way, we can't think like that. Lady, we're at a critical juncture here. We can go down through negligence, dwindling away in our hiding holes, or we can try to build something better."

"Better?" She made a rude noise.

"OK, not better. Something though. Building something new is better than letting it dwindle away. Christ, what are you going to do when you've read all the magazines and eaten all the potato chips here?"

Rosa shook her head. "Pretty talk," she said. "But what the hell are we going to do, anyway?"

"Something," Felix said. "We're going to do something. Something is better than nothing. We're going to take this patch of the world where people are talking to each other, and we're going to expand it. We're going to find everyone we can and we're going to take care of them and they're going to take care of us. We'll probably fuck it up. We'll probably fail. I'd rather fail than give up, though."

Van laughed. "Felix, you are crazier than Sario, you know it?"

"We're going to go and drag him out, first thing tomorrow. He's going to be a part of this, too. Everyone will. Screw the end of the world. The world doesn't end. Humans aren't the kind of things that have endings."

Rosa shook her head again, but she was smiling a little now. "And you'll be what, the Pope-Emperor of the World?"

"He prefers Prime Minister," Van said in a stagey whisper. The antihistamines had worked miracles on his skin, and it had faded from angry red to a fine pink.

"You want to be Minister of Health, Rosa?" he said.

"Boys," she said. "Playing games. How about this. I'll help out however I can, provided you never ask me to call you Prime Minister and you never call me the Minister of Health?"

"It's a deal," he said.

Van refilled their glasses, upending the wine bottle to get the last few drops out.

They raised their glasses. "To the world," Felix said. "To humanity." He thought hard. "To rebuilding."

"To anything," Van said.

"To anything," Felix said. "To everything."

"To everything," Rosa said.

They drank. He wanted to go see the house—see Kelly and 2.0, though his stomach churned at the thought of what he might find there. But the next day, they started to rebuild. And months later, they started over again, when disagreements drove apart the fragile little group they'd pulled together. And a year after that, they started over again. And five years later, they started again.

It was nearly six months before he went home. Van helped him along, riding cover behind him on the bicycles they used to get around town. The further north they rode, the stronger the smell of burnt wood became. There were lots of burnt-out houses. Sometimes marauders burnt the houses they'd looted, but more often it was just nature, the kinds of fires you got in forests and on mountains. There were six choking, burnt blocks where every house was burnt before they reached home.

But Felix's old housing development was still standing, an oasis of eerily pristine buildings that looked like maybe their somewhat neglectful owners had merely stepped out to buy some paint and fresh lawnmower blades to bring their old homes back up to their neat, groomed selves.

That was worse, somehow. He got off the bike at the entry of the subdivision and they walked the bikes together in silence, listening to the sough of the wind in the trees. Winter was coming late that year, but it was coming, and as the sweat dried in the wind, Felix started to shiver.

He didn't have his keys anymore. They were at the data-center, months and worlds away. He tried the door-handle, but it didn't turn. He applied his shoulder to the door and it ripped away from its wet, rotted jamb with a loud, splintering sound. The house was rotting from the inside.

The door splashed when it landed. The house was full of stagnant water, four inches of stinking pond-scummed water in the living room. He splashed carefully through it, feeling the floor-boards sag spongily beneath each step.

Up the stairs, his nose full of that terrible green mildewy stench. Into the bedroom, the furniture familiar as a childhood friend.

Kelly was in the bed with 2.0. The way they both lay, it was clear they hadn't gone easy—they were twisted double, Kelly curled around 2.0. Their skin was bloated, making them almost unrecognizable. The smell—God, the smell.

Felix's head spun. He thought he would fall over and clutched at the dresser. An emotion he couldn't name—rage, anger, sorrow?—made him breathe hard, gulp for air like he was drowning.

And then it was over. The world was over. Kelly and 2.0—over. And he had a job to do. He folded the blanket over them—Van helped, solemnly. They went into the front yard and took turns digging, using the shovel from the garage that Kelly had used for gardening. They had lots of experience digging graves by then. Lots of experience handling the dead. They dug, and wary dogs watched them from the tall grass on the neighboring lawns, but they were also good at chasing off dogs with well-thrown stones.

When the grave was dug, they laid Felix's wife and son to rest in it. Felix quested after words to say over the mound, but none came. He'd dug so many graves for so many men's wives and so many women's husbands and so many children—the words were long gone.

Felix dug ditches and salvaged cans and buried the dead. He planted and harvested. He fixed some cars and learned to make biodiesel. Finally he fetched up in a data-center for a little government—little governments came and went, but this one was smart enough to want to keep records and needed someone to keep everything running, and Van went with him.

They spent a lot of time in chat rooms and sometimes they happened upon old friends from the strange time they'd spent running the Distributed Republic of Cyberspace, geeks who insisted on calling him PM, though no one in the real world ever called him that anymore.

It wasn't a good life, most of the time. Felix's wounds never healed, and neither did most other people's. There were lingering sicknesses and sudden ones. Tragedy on tragedy.

But Felix liked his data-center. There in the humming of the racks, he never felt like it was the first days of a better nation, but he never felt like it was the last days of one, either.

```
> go to bed, felix
> soon, kong, soon—almost got this backup
  running
> youre a junkie, dude.
> look whos talking
```

He reloaded the Google homepage. Queen Kong had had it online for a couple years now. The Os in Google changed all the time, whenever she got the urge. Today they were little cartoon globes, one smiling the other frowning.

He looked at it for a long time and dropped back into a terminal to check his backup. It was running clean, for a change. The little government's records were safe.

```
> ok night night
> take care
```

Van waved at him as he creaked to the door, stretching out his back with a long series of pops.

"Sleep well, boss," he said.

"Don't stick around here all night again," Felix said. "You need your sleep, too."

"You're too good to us grunts," Van said, and went back to typing.

Felix went to the door and walked out into the night. Behind him, the biodiesel generator hummed and made its acrid fumes. The harvest moon was up, which he loved. Tomorrow, he'd go back and fix another computer and fight off entropy again. And why not?

It was what he did. He was a sysadmin.

THE LAST OF THE O-FORMS
BY JAMES VAN PELT

James Van Pelt is the author of the novel *Summer of the Apocalypse,* and more than one hundred short stories, which have mostly appeared in *Analog, Asimov's, Realms of Fantasy,* and *Talebones.* He also has four collections, *Strangers and Beggars, The Radio Magician and Other Stories, Flying in the Heart of the Lafayette Escadrille,* and *The Last of the O-Forms and Other Stories.*

Van Pelt had been writing a series of stories about slower-than-light ark ships fleeing Earth, when it occurred to him that he had generalized that the ark ship passengers were escaping from the "mutation plagues," and it might be interesting to write about what was going on back on Earth. Thus, "The Last of the O-Forms" was born.

This story, which was a finalist for the Nebula Award, takes place in a world where there are no more normal births. Each and every one is a mutation—which is both good and bad for Dr. Trevin's Traveling Zoological Extravaganza…

Beyond the big rig's open window, the Mississippi river lands rolled darkly by. Boggy areas caught the moon low on the horizon like a silver coin, flickering through black-treed hummocks, or strained by split-rail fence, mile after mile. The air smelled damp and dead-fish mossy, heavy as a wet towel, but it was better than the animal enclosures on a hot afternoon when the sun pounded the awnings and the exhibits huddled in weak shade. Traveling at night was the way to go. Trevin counted the distance in minutes. They'd blow through Roxie soon, then hit Hamburg, McNair, and Harriston in quick succession. In Fayette, there was a nice diner where they could get breakfast, but it meant turning off the highway and they'd hit the worst of Vicksburg's morning traffic if they stopped. No, the thing to do was to keep driving, driving to the next town, where he could save the show.

He reached across the seat to the grocery sack between him and Caprice. She was asleep, her baby-blonde head resting against the door, her small hands holding a Greek edition of the *Odyssey* open on her lap. If she were awake, she could glance at the map and tell him exactly how many miles they had left to Mayersville, how long to the minute at this speed it would take, and how much diesel, to the ounce, they'd have left in their tanks. Her little-girl eyes would pin him to the wall. "Why can't you figure this out on your own?" they'd ask. He thought about hiding her phone book so she'd have nothing to sit on and couldn't look out the window. That would show her.

She might look two years old, but she was really twelve, and had the soul of a middle-aged tax attorney.

At the sack's bottom, beneath an empty donut box, he found the beef jerky. It tasted mostly of pepper, but underneath it had a tingly, metallic flavor he tried not to think about. Who knew what it might have been made from? He doubted there were any original-form cows, the o-cows, left to slaughter.

After a long curve, a city limit sign loomed out of the dark. Trevin stepped on the brakes, then geared down. Roxie cops were infamous for speed traps, and there wasn't enough bribe money in the kitty to make a ticket go away. In his rearview mirror, the other truck and a car with Hardy the handyman and his crew of roustabouts closed ranks.

Roxie's traffic signal blinked yellow over an empty intersection, while the closed shops stood mute under a handful of streetlights. After the four-block-long downtown, another mile of beat-up houses and trailers lined the road, where broken washing machines and pickups on cinder blocks dotted moonlit front yards. Something barked at him from behind a chain-link fence. Trevin slowed for a closer look. Professional curiosity. It looked like an o-dog under a porch light, an original-form animal, an old one, if his stiff-gaited walk was an indicator. Weren't many of *those* left anymore. Not since the mutagen hit. Trevin wondered if the owners keeping an o-dog in the backyard had troubles with their neighbors, if there was jealousy.

A toddler voice said, "If we don't clear $2,600 in Mayersville, we'll have to sell a truck, Daddy."

"Don't call me Daddy, *ever*." He took a long curve

silently. Two-laned highways often had no shoulder, and concentration was required to keep safe. "I didn't know you were awake. Besides, a thousand will do it."

Caprice closed her book. In the darkness of the cab, Trevin couldn't see her eyes, but he knew that they were polar-ice blue. She said, "A thousand for diesel, sure, but we're weeks behind on payroll. The roustabouts won't stand for another delay, not after what you promised in Gulfport. The extension on the quarterly taxes is past, and I can't keep the feds off like the other creditors by pledging extra payments for a couple months. We've got food for most of the animals for ten days or so, but we have to buy fresh meat for the tigerzelle and the crocomouse or they'll die. We stay afloat with $2,600, but just barely."

Trevin scowled. It had been years since he'd found her little-girl voice and little-girl pronunciation to be cute, and almost everything she said was sarcastic or critical. It was like living with a pint-sized advocate for his own self-doubt. "So we need a house of . . ." He wrinkled his forehead. "$2,600 divided by four and a half bucks. . . ."

"Five hundred and seventy-eight. That'll leave you an extra dollar for a cup of coffee," Caprice said. "We haven't had a take that big since Ferriday last fall, and that was because Oktoberfest in Natchez closed early. Thank God for Louisiana liquor laws! We ought to admit the show's washed up, cut the inventory loose, sell the gear, and pay off the help."

She turned on the goosenecked reading light that arced from the dashboard and opened her book.

"If we can hold on until Rosedale . . ." He remembered Rosedale when they last came through, seven years ago. The city had recruited him. Sent letters and e-mails.

They'd met him in New Orleans with a committee, including a brunette beauty who squeezed his leg under the table when they went out to dinner.

"We can't," Caprice said.

Trevin recalled the hand on his leg feeling good and warm. He'd almost jumped from the table, his face flushed. "The soybean festival draws them in. Everything's made out of soybeans. Soybean pie. Soybean beer. Soybean ice cream." He chuckled. "We cleaned up there. I got to ride down Main Street with the Rosedale Soybean Queen."

"We're dead. Take your pulse." She didn't look up.

The Rosedale Soybean Queen had been friendly too, and oh so grateful that he'd brought the zoo to town. He wondered if she still lived there. He could look her up. "Yeah, if we make the soybean festival, we'll do fine. One good show and we're sailing again. I'll repaint the trucks. Folks love us when we come into town, music playing. World's greatest traveling novelty zoo! You remember when *Newsweek* did that story? God, that was a day!" He glanced out the window again. The moon rested on the horizon now, pacing them, big as a beachball, like a burnished hubcap rolling with them in the night, rolling up the Mississippi twenty miles to the west. He could smell the river flowing to the sea. How could she doubt that they would make it big? I'll show her, he thought. Wipe that smirk off her little-girl face. I'll show her in Mayersville and then Rosedale. Money'll be falling off the tables. We'll have to store it in sacks. She'll see. Grinning, he dug deep for another piece of beef jerky, and he didn't think at all what it tasted like this time.

Trevin pulled the truck into Mayersville at half past ten, keeping his eyes peeled for their posters and flyers.

He'd sent a box of them up two weeks earlier, and if the boy he'd hired had done his job, they should have been plastered everywhere, but he only saw one, and it was torn nearly in half. There were several banners welcoming softball teams to the South-Central Spring Time Regional Softball Tourney, and the hotels sported NO VACANCY signs, so the crowds were there. He turned the music on, and it blared from the loudspeakers on top of the truck. Zoo's in town, he thought. Come see the zoo! But other than a couple of geezers sitting in front of the barbershop, who watched them coolly as they passed, no one seemed to note their arrival.

"They can't play ball *all* day, eh, Caprice. They've got to do something in between games."

She grunted. Her laptop was open on the seat beside her, and she was double-entering receipts and bills into the ledger.

The fairgrounds were on the north edge of town, next to the ball fields. A park attendant met them at the gates, then climbed onto the running board so his head was just below the window.

"There's a hundred dollar occupancy fee," he said, his face hidden beneath a wide-brimmed straw hat that looked like it had been around the world a few times.

Trevin drummed his fingers on the steering wheel and stayed calm. "We paid for the site up front."

The attendant shrugged. "It's a hundred dollars or you find some other place to plant yourself."

Caprice, on her knees, leaned across Trevin. She deepened her voice in her best Trevin impersonation. "Do we make that check out to Mayersville City Parks or to Issaquena County?"

Startled, the attendant looked up before Caprice could duck out of sight, his sixty-year-old face as dusty as his hat. "Cash. No checks."

"That's what I thought," she said to Trevin as she moved back from the window. "Give him twenty. There better be the portable potties and the electrical hookups we ordered."

Trevin flicked the bill to him, and the attendant caught it neatly in flight as he stepped off the running board. "Hey, mister," he said. "How old's your little girl?"

"A million and ten, asshole," said Trevin, dropping the clutch to move the big rig forward. "I've *told* you to stay out of sight. We'll get into all kinds of trouble if the locals find out I've got a mutant keeping the books. They have labor laws, you know. Why'd you tell me to give him any money anyway? We could have bought a day or two of meat with that."

Caprice stayed on her knees to look out her window. "He's really a janitor. Never piss off the janitor. Hey, they cleaned this place up a bit! There was a patch of woods between us and the river last time."

Trevin leaned on the wheel. Turning the truck was tough at anything less than highway speed. "Would you want trees and brush next to where *you* were playing softball? You chase a foul shot into the undergrowth and never come back. . . ."

Beyond the fairgrounds, the land sloped down to the levee, and past that flowed the Mississippi, less than a hundred yards away, a great, muddy plain marked with lines of sullen grey foam drifting under the mid-morning sun. A black barge so distant that he couldn't hear it chug up-stream. Trevin noted with approval the endless stretch of ten-foot-tall chain-link fence between them and the river. Who knew what god-awful thing might come crawling out of there?

As always, it took most of the day to set up. The big animals, stinking of hot fur and unwashed cage bottoms in their eight-foot-high enclosures, came out of the semi-trailers first. Looking lethargic and sick, the tigerzelle, a long-legged, hoofed animal sporting almost no neck below an impressive face filled with saber-like teeth, barely looked up as its cage was lowered to the soggy ground. It hooted softly. Trevin checked its water. "Get a tarp over it right away," he said to handyman Harper, a big, grouchy man who wore old rock concert T-shirts inside out. Trevin added, "That trailer had to be a hundred and twenty degrees inside." Looking at the animal fondly, Trevin remembered when he'd acquired it from a farm in Illinois, one of the first American mutababies, before the mutagen was recognized and named, before it became a plague. The tigerzelle's sister was almost as bizarre: heavy legs, scaly skin, and a long, thin head, like a whippet, but the farmer had already killed it by the time Trevin arrived. Their mother, as ordinary a cow as you'd ever see, looked at its children with dull confusion. "What the *hell's* wrong with my cow?" asked the farmer several times, until they started dickering for the price. Once Trevin had paid him, the man said, "If'n I get any other weird-lookin' animal, you want I should give you a call?"

Trevin smelled profit. Charging twenty dollars per customer, he cleared ten thousand a week in June and July, showing the tigerzelle from the back of his pickup. He thought, I may not be too smart, but I do know how to make a buck. By the end of the summer, Dr. Trevin's Traveling Zoological Extravaganza was born. That was the year Caprice rode beside him in a child's car seat, her momma dead in childbirth. In August, they were going north from Senetobia to Memphis, and, at eleven months old, Caprice said her first words: "Isn't eighty over the speed limit?" Even then, there was a biting, sardonic tone to her voice. Trevin nearly wrecked the truck.

The crocomouse snarled and bit at the bars as it came out, its furry snout banging against the metal. It threw its two hundred pounds against the door and almost tipped the cage out of the handlers' grip. "Keep your hands away," snapped Harper to his crew, "or you'll be taping a pencil to a stub to write your mommas!"

Then the rest of the animals were unloaded: a porcumander, the warped child of a bullfrog that waved its wet, thorny hide at every shadow; the unigoose, about the size of a wild turkey atop four tiny legs, shedding ragged feathers by the handful below the pearl-like glinting horn, and each of the other mutababies, the unrecognizable progeny of cats and squirrels and horses and monkeys and seals and every other animal Trevin could gather to the zoo. Big cages, little ones, aquariums, terrariums, little corrals, bird cages, tethering poles—all came out for display.

By sunset, the last animal had been arranged and fed. Circus flags fluttered from the semi-trailer truck tops. The loudspeakers perched atop their posts.

The park attendant wandered through the cages, his hands pushed deep into his pockets, as casual and friendly as if he hadn't tried to rip them off earlier in the day. "Y'all best stay in your trucks once the sun sets if you're camping here."

Suspicious, Trevin asked, "Why's that?"

The man raised his chin toward the river, which was glowing red like a bloody stain in the setting sun. "Water level was up a couple days ago, over the fences. The levee held, but any sorta teethy mutoid might be floppin' around on our side now. It's got so you can't step in a puddle without somethin' takin' a bite outta ya! Civil Defense volunteers walk the banks every day, lookin' for the more cantankerous critters, but it's a big old river. You got a gun?"

Trevin shrugged. "Baseball bat. Maybe we'll get lucky and add something to the zoo. You expecting crowds for the softball tournament?"

"Thirty-two teams. We shipped in extra bleachers."

Trevin nodded. If he started the music early in the morning, maybe he'd attract folks waiting for games. Nothing like a little amusement before the heat set in. After a couple of minutes, the park attendant left. Trevin was glad to see him walk away. He had the distinct impression that the man was looking for something to steal.

After dinner, Caprice clambered into the upper bunk, her short legs barely giving her enough of a reach to make it. Trevin kicked his blanket aside. Even though it was after ten, it was still over ninety degrees, and there wasn't a hint of a breeze. Most of the animals had settled in their cages. Only the tigerzelle made noise, one long warbling hoot after another, a soft, melodic call that hardly fit its ferocious appearance.

"You lay low tomorrow. I'm not kidding," said Trevin after he'd turned off the light. "I don't want you driving people off."

Caprice sniffed loudly. "It's pretty ironic that I can't show myself at a mutoid zoo. I'm tired of hiding away like a freak. Another fifty years and there won't be any of your kind left anyway. Might as well accept the inevitable. I'm the future. They should be able to deal with that."

Trevin put his hands behind his head and stared up at her bunk. Through the screen he'd fitted over the windows, he could hear the Mississippi lapping against the bank. An animal screeched in the distance, its call a cross between a whistle and a bad cough. He tried to imagine what would make a sound like that. Finally he said, "People don't like human mutoids, at least ones that look human."

"Why's that?" she asked, all the sarcasm and bitterness suddenly gone. "I'm not a bad person, if they'd get to know me. We could discuss books, or philosophy. I'm a *mind,* not just a body."

The animal cried out again in the dark, over and over, until in mid-screech, it stopped. A heavy thrashing sound followed by splashes marked the creature's end. "I guess it makes them sad, Caprice."

"Do I make *you* sad?" In the truck cab's dim interior, she sounded exactly like a two-year-old. He remembered when she *was* a little girl, before he knew that she wasn't normal, that she'd never "grow up," that her DNA showed that she wasn't human. Before she started talking uppity and making him feel stupid with her baby-doll eyes. Before he'd forbidden her to call him Dad. He'd thought she looked a little like her mother then. He still caught echoes of her when Caprice combed her hair, or when she fell asleep and her lips parted to take a breath, just like her mother. The air caught in his throat thinking of those times.

"No, Caprice. You don't make me sad."

Hours later, long after Caprice had gone to sleep, Trevin drifted off into a series of dreams where he was being smothered by steaming Turkish towels, and when he threw the towels off, his creditors surrounded him. They carried payment-overdue notices, and none of them were human.

Trevin was up before dawn to feed the animals. Half the trick of keeping the zoo running was in figuring out what the creatures ate. Just because the parent had been, say, an o-form horse didn't mean hay was going to do the trick. Caprice kept extensive charts for him: the animal's weight, how much food it consumed, what vitamin supplements seemed most helpful. There were practicalities to running a zoo. He dumped a bucket of corn on the cob into the pigahump's cage. It snorted, then lumbered out of the doghouse it stayed in, not looking much like a pig, or any other animal Trevin knew. Eyes like saucers, it gazed at him gratefully before burying its face in the trough.

He moved down the rows. Mealworms in one cage. Grain in the next. Bones from the butcher. Dog food. Spoiled fish. Bread. Cereal. Old vegetables. Oats. The tigerzelle tasted the rump roast he tossed in, its delicate tongue, so like a cat's, lapping at the meat before it tore a small chunk off to chew delicately. It cooed in contentment.

At the end of the row, closest to the river, two cages were knocked off their display stands and smashed. Black blood and bits of meat clung to the twisted bars, and both animals the cages had contained, blind, leathery bird-like creatures, were gone. Trevin sighed and walked around the cages, inspecting the ground. In a muddy patch, a single webbed print a foot across, marked with four deep claw indents, showed the culprit. A couple of partial prints led up from the river. Trevin put his finger in the track, which was a half-inch deep. The ground was wet but firm. It took a hard press to push just his fingertip a half-inch. He wondered at the weight of the creature, and made a note to himself that tonight they'd have to store the smaller cages in the truck, which would mean more work. He sighed again.

By eight, the softball fields across the park had filled. Players warmed up outside the fences, while games took place. Tents to house teams or for food booths sprang up. Trevin smiled and turned on the music. Banners hung from the trucks. DR. TREVIN'S TRAVELING ZOOLOGICAL EXTRAVAGANZA. SEE NATURE'S ODDITIES! EDUCATIONAL! ENTERTAINING! By noon, there had been fifteen paying customers.

Leaving Hardy in charge of tickets, Trevin loaded a box with handbills, hung a staple gun to his belt, then marched to the ball fields, handing out flyers. The sun beat down like a humid furnace, and only the players in the field weren't under tents or umbrellas. Several folks offered him a beer—he took one—but his flyers, wrinkly with humidity, vanished under chairs or behind coolers. "We're doing a first day of the tournament special," he said. "Two bucks each, or three for you and a friend." His shirt clung to his back. "We'll be open after sunset, when it's cooler. These are displays not to be missed, folks!"

A woman in her twenties, her cheeks sun-reddened, her blonde hair tied back, said, "I don't need to *pay* to see a reminder, damn it!" She crumpled the paper and dropped it. One of her teammates, sitting on the ground, a beer between his knees, said, "Give him a break, Doris. He's just trying to make a living."

Trevin said, "We were in *Newsweek*. You might have read about us."

"Maybe we'll come over later, fella," said the player on the ground.

Doris popped a can open. "It might snow this afternoon, too."

"Maybe it will," said Trevin congenially. He headed toward town, on the other side of the fairgrounds. The sun pressured his scalp with prickly fire. By the time he'd gone a hundred yards, he wished he'd worn a hat, but it was too hot to go back.

He stapled a flyer to the first telephone pole he came to. "Yep," he said to himself. "A little publicity and we'll rake it in!" The sidewalk shimmered in white heat waves as he marched from pole to pole, past the hardware, past the liquor store, past the Baptist Church—SUFFER THE CHILDREN read the marquee—past the pool hall, and the auto supply shop. He went inside every store and asked the owner to post his sign. Most did. Behind Main Street stood several blocks of homes. Trevin turned up one street and down the next, stapling flyers, noting with approval the wire mesh over the windows. "Can't be too careful, nowadays," he said, his head swimming in the heat. The beer seemed to be evaporating through his skin all at once, and he felt sticky with it. The sun pulsed against his back. The magic number is five-seventy-eight, he thought. It beat within him like a song. Call it six hundred. Six hundred folks, come to the zoo, come to the zoo, come to the *zoo!*

When he finally made his way back to the fairgrounds, the sun was on its way down. Trevin dragged his feet, but the flyers were gone.

Evening fell. Trevin waited at the ticket counter in his zoo-master's uniform, a broad-shouldered red suit with gold epaulets. The change box popped open with jingly joy; the roll of tickets was ready. Circus music played softly from the loudspeakers as fireflies flickered in the darkness above the river. Funny, he thought, how the mutagen affected only the bigger vertebrate animals, not mice-sized mammals or little lizards, not small fish or bugs or plants. What would a bug mutate *into* anyway? They look alien to begin with. He chuckled to himself, his walking-up-the-sidewalk song still echoing: six hundred folks, come to the zoo, come to the zoo, come to the *zoo*.

Every car that passed on the highway, Trevin watched, waiting for it to slow for the turn into the fairgrounds.

From sunset until midnight, only twenty customers bought admissions; most of them were ball players who'd discovered that there wasn't much night-life in Mayersville. Clouds had moved in, and distant lightning flickered within their steel-wool depths.

Trevin spun the roll of tickets back and forth on its spool. An old farmer couple wearing overalls, their clothes stained with rich, Mississippi soil, shuffled past on their way out. "You got some strange animals here, mister," said the old man. His wife nodded. "But nothing stranger than what I've found wandering in my fields for the last few years. Gettin' so I don't remember what o-form normal looks like."

"Too close to the river," said his wife. "That's our place right over there." She pointed at a small farm house under a lone light, just beyond the last ball field. Trevin wondered if they ever retrieved home-run balls off their porch.

The thin pile of bills in the cash box rustled under

Trevin's fingers. The money should be falling off the tables, he thought. We should be drowning in it. The old couple stood beside him, looking back into the zoo. They reminded him of his parents, not in their appearance, but in their solid patience. They weren't going anywhere fast.

He had no reason to talk to them, but there was nothing else left to do. "I was here a few years ago. Did really well. What's happened?"

The wife held her husband's hand. She said, "This town's dyin', mister. Dyin' from the bottom up. They closed the elementary school last fall. No elementary-age kids. If you want to see a *real* zoo display, go down to Issaquena County Hospital pediatrics. The penalty of parenthood. Not that many folks are having babies, though."

"Or whatever you want to call them," added the old man. "Your zoo's depressin'."

"I'd heard you had somethin' special, though," said the woman shyly.

"Did see the crocomouse?" asked Trevin. "There's quite a story about that one. And the tigerzelle. Have you seen that one?"

"Saw 'em," she said, looking disappointed.

The old couple climbed into their pickup, and it rattled into life after a half-dozen starter-grinding tries.

"I found a buyer in Vicksburg for the truck," said Caprice.

Trevin whirled. She stood in the shadows beside the ticket counter, a notebook jammed under her arm. "I told you to stay out of view."

"Who's going to see me? You can't get customers even on a discount!" She gazed at the vacant lot. "We don't have to deliver it. He's coming to town next week on other business. I can do the whole transaction, transfer the deed, take the money, all of it, over the Internet."

One taillight out, the farmer's pickup turned from the fairgrounds and onto the dirt road that led to their house, which wasn't more than two hundred yards away. "What would we do with the animals?" He felt like weeping.

"Let the safe ones go. Kill the dangerous ones."

Trevin rubbed his eyes. She stamped her foot. "Look, this is no time for sentimentality! The zoo's a bust. You're going to lose the whole thing soon anyway. If you're too stubborn to give it all up, sell this truck now and you get a few extra weeks, maybe a whole season if we economize."

Trevin looked away from her. The fireflies still flickered above the river. "I'll have to make some decisions," he said heavily.

She held out the notebook. "I've already made them. This is what will fit in one semi-trailer. I already let Hardy and the roustabouts go with a severance check, postdated."

"What about the gear, cages?"

"The county dump is north of here."

Was that a note of triumph he detected in her voice? Trevin took the notebook. She dropped her hands to her side, chin up, staring at him. The zoo's lights cast long shadows across her face. I could kick her, he thought, and for a second his leg trembled with the idea of it.

He tucked the notebook under his arm. "Go to bed."

Caprice opened her mouth, then clamped it shut on whatever she might have said. She turned away.

Long after she'd vanished into the cab, Trevin sat on the stool, elbow on his knee, chin in his hand, watching insects circle the lights. The tigerzelle squatted on its haunches, alert, looking toward the river. Trevin remembered a ghastly cartoon he'd seen once. A couple of crones sat on the seat of a wagon full of bodies. The one holding the reins turned to the other and said, "You know, once the plague is over, we're out of a job."

The tigerzelle rose to its feet, focusing on the river. It paced intently in its cage, never turning its head from the darkness. Trevin straightened. What did it see out there? For a long moment, the tableau remained the same: insects swirled around the lights, which buzzed softly, highlighting the cages; shining metal against the enveloping spring night, the pacing tigerzelle, the ticket counter's polished wood against Trevin's hand, and the Mississippi's pungent murmuring in the background.

Beyond the cages, from the river, a piece of blackness detached itself from the night. Trevin blinked in fascinated paralysis, all the hairs dancing on the back of his neck. The short-armed creature stood taller than a man, surveyed the zoo, then dropped to all fours like a bear, except that its skin gleamed with salamander wetness. Its triangular head sniffed at the ground, moving over the moist dirt as if following a scent. When it reached the first cage, a small one that held the weaselsnake, the river creature lifted its forelegs off the ground, grasping the cage in web-fingered claws. In an instant, the cage was unrecognizable, and the weaselsnake was gone.

"Hey!" Trevin yelled, shaking off his stupor. The creature looked at him. Reaching under the ticket counter, Trevin grabbed the baseball bat and advanced. The monster turned away to pick up the next cage. Trevin's face flushed. "No, no, no, damn it!" He stepped forward again, stepped again, and suddenly he was running, bat held overhead. "Get away! Get away!" He brought the bat down on the animal's shoulder with a meaty whump.

It shrieked.

Trevin fell back, dropping the bat to cover his ears. It shrieked again, loud as a train whistle. For a dozen heartbeats, it stood above him, claws extended, then it seemed to lose interest and moved to the next cage, dismantling it with one jerk on the bars.

His ears ringing, Trevin snatched the bat off the ground and waded in, swinging. On its rear legs, the monster bared its teeth, dozens of glinting needles in the triangular jaw. Trevin nailed the creature in the side. It folded with surprising flexibility, backing away, claws distended, snarling in a deafening roar. Trevin swung. Missed. The monster swiped at his leg, ripping his pants and almost jerking his feet out from under him.

The thing moved clumsily, backing down the hill toward the levee fence as Trevin swung again. Missed. It howled, tried to circle around him. Trevin scuttled sideways, careful of his balance on the slick dirt. If he should fall! The thing charged, mouth open, but pulled back like a threatened dog when Trevin raised the bat. He breathed in short gasps, poked the bat's end at it, always shepherding it away from the zoo. Behind him, a police siren sounded, and car engines roared, but he didn't dare look around. He could only stalk and keep his bat at the ready.

After a long series of feints, its back to the fence, the nightmare stopped, hunched its back, and began to rise just as Trevin brought the bat down in a two-handed, over-the-head chop. Through the bat, he felt the skull crunch, and the creature dropped into a shuddery mass in the mud. Trevin, his pulse pounding, swayed for a moment, then sat beside the beast.

Up the hill, under the zoo's lights, people shouted into the darkness. Were they ball players? Town people? A police cruiser's lights blinked blue then red, and three or four cars, headlights on, were parked near the trucks. Obviously they couldn't see him, but he was too tired to call. Ignoring the wet ground, he lay back.

The dead creature smelled of blood and river mud. Trevin rested a foot on it, almost sorry that it was dead. If he could have captured it, what an addition it would have made to the zoo! Gradually, the heavy beat in his chest calmed. The mud felt soft and warm. Overhead, the clouds thinned a bit, scudding across the full moon.

At the zoo, there was talking. Trevin craned his head around to see. People jostled about, and flashlights cut through the air. They started down the hill. Trevin sighed. He hadn't saved the zoo, not really. Tomorrow would come and they'd leave one of the trucks behind. In a couple of months, it would all be gone, the other truck, the animals—he was most sorry about the tigerzelle—the pulling into town with music blaring and flags flapping and people lined up to see the menagerie. No more reason to wear the zoo-master's uniform with its beautiful gold epaulets. *Newsweek* would never interview him again. It was all gone. If he could only sink into the mud and disappear, then he wouldn't have to watch the dissolving of his own life.

He sat up so that they wouldn't think he was dead; waved a hand when the first flashlight found him. Mud dripped from his jacket. The policemen arrived first.

"God almighty, that's a big one!" The cop trained his

light on the river creature.

"Told you the fences warn't no good," said the other.

Everyone stayed back except the police. The first cop turned the corpse over. Laying on its back, its little arms flopped to the side, it didn't look nearly as big or intimidating. More folk arrived: some townies he didn't recognize, the old couple from the farmhouse across the ball fields, and finally, Caprice, the flashlight looking almost too big for her to carry.

The first cop knelt next to the creature, shoved his hat up off his forehead, then said low enough that Trevin guessed that only the other cop could hear him, "Hey, doesn't this look like the Andersons' kid? They said they'd smothered him."

"He wasn't half that big, but I think you're right." The other cop threw a coat over the creature's face, then stood for a long time looking down at it. "Don't say anything to them, all right? Maggie Anderson is my wife's cousin."

"Nothing here to see, people," announced the first cop in a much louder voice. "This is a dead 'un. Y'all can head back home."

But the crowd's attention wasn't on them anymore. The flashlights turned on Caprice.

"It's a baby girl!" someone said, and they moved closer.

Caprice shined her flashlight from one face to the other. Then, desperation on her face, she ran clumsily to Trevin, burying her face in his chest.

"What are we going to do?" she whispered.

"Quiet. Play along." Trevin stroked the back of her head, then stood. A sharp twinge in his leg told him he'd pulled something. The world was all bright lights, and he couldn't cover his eyes. He squinted against them.

"Is that your girl, mister?" someone said.

Trevin gripped her closer. Her little hands fisted in his coat.

"I haven't seen a child in ten years," said another voice. The flashlights moved in closer.

The old farmer woman stepped into the circle, her face suddenly illuminated. "Can I hold your little girl, son? Can I just hold her?" She extended her arms, her hands quivering.

"I'll give you fifty bucks if you let me hold her," said a voice behind the lights.

Trevin turned slowly, lights all around, until he faced the old woman again. A picture formed in his mind, dim at first but growing clearer by the second. One semi-trailer truck, the trailer set up like a child's room—no, like a nursery! Winnie-the-Pooh wallpaper. A crib. One of those musical rotating things, what cha' call ums—a mobile! A little rocking chair. Kid's music. And they'd go from town to town. The banner would say THE LAST O-FORM GIRL CHILD, and he would *charge* them, yes he would, and they would line *up*. The money would fall off the table!

Trevin pushed Caprice away from him, her hands clinging to his coat. "It's okay, darling. The nice woman just wants to hold you for a bit. I'll be right here."

Caprice looked at him, despair clear in her face. Could she already see the truck with the nursery? Could she picture the banner and the unending procession of little towns?

The old woman took Caprice in her arms like a precious vase. "That's all right, little girl. That's all right." She faced Trevin, tears on her cheeks. "She's just like the granddaughter I always wanted! Does she talk yet? I haven't heard a baby's voice in forever. Does she talk?"

"Go ahead, Caprice dear. Say something to the nice lady."

Caprice locked eyes with him. Even by flashlight, he could see the polar blue. He could hear her sardonic voice night after night as they drove across country. "It's not financially feasible to continue," she'd say in her two-year-old voice. "We should admit the inevitable."

She looked at him, lip trembling. She brought her fist up to her face. No one moved. Trevin couldn't even hear them breathing.

Caprice put her thumb in her mouth. "Daddy," she said around it. "Scared, Daddy!"

Trevin flinched, then forced a smile. "That's a good girl."

"Daddy, *scared*."

Up the hill, the tigerzelle hooted, and, just beyond the fence, barely visible by flashlight, the Mississippi gurgled and wept.

STILL LIFE WITH APOCALYPSE

BY RICHARD KADREY

Richard Kadrey is the bestselling author of several novels, including the six books in the Sandman Slim series, and the quintessential cyberpunk novel *Metrophage*. His short fiction has appeared in numerous anthologies, as well as the magazines *Asimov's*, *Interzone*, *Omni*, and *Wired*.

"Still Life with Apocalypse" first appeared in the online magazine *The Infinite Matrix*. The version that appears here is revised and slightly expanded.

Kadrey says that the story came from a dream image of horse carcasses being dragged from canals under industrial lights. He took that image and turned it into a snapshot of life after everything has fallen apart—about the people left behind and the jobs they do to fill their days, about the poor slobs who have to clean up the mess at the end of the world.

* * *

They're dragging another horse from the canal, its chestnut coat sheened bubblegum-pink from the freon. Each night, more pools bubble to the surface from deep underground. Freon. Old engine oil. Heavy water from forgotten nukes. Every day, a few dozen more hungry animals drown in the stagnant pools.

Loose-limbed in death, the horse sways, raglike, as the little diesel crane pulls it noisily from the muck and sets in on the pier with the other bodies. In the blue-tinted work lights, we divide the dead into Human and Animal, subdivide the Animals into Mammals and Other, then subdivide the Others into Vertebrates and Invertebrates, and so on.

I started out on Information Retrieval, looking for documents in submerged government offices, old libraries and bookstores. Once, I came up in a police records vault, surrounded by mug shots and photos of murder scenes and rapes. I came up in an IRS office where a dissatisfied citizen had gutted an auditor, then placed the bureaucrat's viscera on a photocopier. I swam through hundreds of grainy duplicates of his liver and intestines. I came up in adult bookshops and brought back waterlogged sex toys and old issues of *Wet & Messy Fun*. Bring back anything useful they said, so why not? Everything I brought back went into one big pile to be sorted by Information Classification.

I wish there had been a war, a plague or some new, grand Chernobyl. Something we could point to and say, "That's it. That's what killed the world." But it wasn't like that.

It started in New York. Or London. Mumbai, possibly. A minor traffic accident—just a fender bender—and someone missed a meeting, which meant someone else couldn't send a fax, which made someone else miss a plane. That someone got into an argument with the cabbie and was shot. No one knows by whom. Whatever happened, the shooting sparked a riot. TV cameras broadcast the riot live to a country so knotted with fury and tension that riots broke out from Maine to Hawaii. When the footage hit the satellites, riots spontaneously exploded around the world.

In the Helinski-Vantaa airport, a group of baggage handlers and striking sex workers pushed vending machines from third floor windows into the parking lot, killing a visiting Spanish diplomat. In Shanghai, farmers and students went on a rampage, destroying the newly built ocean-front casinos, burning the buildings and tossing billions of yen into the harbor. In New Orleans, children invaded the above-ground cemeteries and dragged the dead through the streets.

Ancient national rivalries and recent jealousies surfaced. Around the world, governments went into emergency sessions. Many politicians saw the sudden eruption of violence as an attack on their citizens as the work of terrorist cells. Others claimed it was a biblical plague, Ragnarok or the early return of the Rudras.

I can't say how long it's been since the world went to pieces. All the clocks seem to have stopped. A couple of kids built a sundial, but with half the cities in the world still burning the sky is mostly a swirling soup of ash. We keep warm by looting the libraries I used to wade through, burning first the old periodicals, then the card catalogs, bestsellers and self-help books, finally working our way up to the first editions.

Some days, the sky bursts open and rains fish. Sometimes stones or Barbie dolls. Last night, I cooked a sky salmon over an autographed copy of *The Great Gatsby*. I shared the fish with Natasha, a mute girl who runs one of the cranes, hauling carcasses from the freon pools. She's been staying with me out by the docks, in the cargo container I commandeered. I killed a man to get the container and still have to slice and dice the occasional house crasher. Natasha's not shy with a knife or length of rebar and has done more than a few intruders herself. I assume the ones she did were intruders. Anyway, it keeps us in meat.

I'm not sure that you'd call what we have a typical romance. I live with a girl who can make gloves from a poodle's hide and scavenges boots and clothes for me, and they're always my size. She grows herbs in a bathtub on the roof and decorates our home with wind-up toys and parts of smashed statues from looted museums. I miss ice cream, convertibles and going to the movies. I'm not fool enough to say that I'm happier since the world went away, but except for the rains of stones, I'm no more miserable.

They found a layer of zoo animals under the collapsed roadway of the Williamsburg Bridge. People over there have been living large on elephant steaks and giraffe burgers. The local government wants us to help gather up the remaining body parts, so we do. No one asks why. It's something to do. Besides, the paper pushers refuse to let the world end until every form is turned in, timestamped and properly initialed. Apocalypse is the last gasp of bureaucracy.

After dinner, Natasha and I sit on top of the cargo container watching a field full of cop cars sink slowly into a newly risen tar pit. Everyone from the docks is there. We give a mighty Whoop! as the last car slides, bubbling, below the surface.

Will the last person on the planet please turn off the lights?

ARTIE'S ANGELS

BY CATHERINE WELLS

Catherine Wells is the author of several books, including the post-apocalyptic novel *Mother Grimm* and the Coconino trilogy: *The Earth Is All That Lasts, Children of the Earth,* and *The Earth Saver.* Her latest is *Stones of Destiny*, her first foray into historical fiction. Her short fiction has appeared in *Asimov's* and *Analog*, and the anthologies *Redshift* and *The Doom of Camelot.*

This story, which first appeared in *Realms of Fantasy,* was inspired by a disturbing dream Wells had more than thirty years ago. In the dream, a young man shimmied up a drainpipe in a tenement to visit his friend; and although he was a good person, someone came to his bicycle shop and fired a shotgun through the plate-glass window. The senselessness and injustice of that dream event haunted Wells, and years later, as she rode a tandem bicycle along the back roads of Arizona, she imagined a post-apocalyptic society involving bicycles and young men such as the one in her dream, and "Artie's Angels" was the result.

When you set out to perpetrate a lie, I suppose it's counterproductive to write down the truth like this. But whatever population survives here on Earth is not likely to read this, much less believe it. Most of them can't read anymore as it is—not BookEnglish, anyway—and it will probably get worse before it gets better. Much, much worse.

My birth name is Faye, but I have not used it since I was ten. That's the year we moved inside the radiation shield, into a wreck of a building in Kansas Habitat. My mother cried, because my little brother died just before we got there, and she kept moaning that if only we'd gotten inside sooner, he might have lived. But you had to have either money or skills to get inside the radiation shield, and my parents had neither. So we fried our skins and our eyeballs in Earth's unfiltered sunlight until enough rich people moved offworld to make room for us under the shield.

Artie knocked at my window the first night; he'd shinnied up the drainpipe from his apartment just below. The artificial rain no longer worked in our sector, of course, because the infrastructure was well on the road to hell, but the drainpipe was still there. Artie D'Angelo was this skinny kid, just my age, a little goofy-looking, but agile as a monkey. When I saw him hanging on that drainpipe, I was more amazed than frightened. "Hi!" he said through the glass, grinning widely. He had dark, curly hair, deep brown eyes, and big ears.

I climbed onto my bed, which was under the window, and stared at him. "You gonna open up?" he asked. "Or let me hang on this drainpipe all night?"

With a glance over my shoulder to make sure my door was shut, I lifted the sash and Artie climbed in. "I'm Artie," he introduced. "I live downstairs."

"Faye," I replied. "You can't use the door?"

"I knocked before," he said, "but no one would answer."

I knew the cause of that. "My dad's scared to open the door," I told Artie.

He shrugged. "In this neighborhood, you're better off. But I saw you moving in, and I thought you must be from outside, so you'd probably need someone to show you around."

During the next months, Artie did just that. Born in KanHab, he knew its grid upground and under. If not for his tutelage, I would probably have died in that first year. By the time they got around to letting dregs like my family in, half the sectors were more or less lawless, and a ten-year-old kid could easily get snuffed if she didn't know where to run and where to hide. Artie taught me that and more. In those early days, he was my salvation; in these latter days, I shall be his.

It was while we were hiding from the Citizen Patrols in B4 that he first spoke the name I took as my own. That was back when the Sisters of Literacy still tried to run schools in B4, which was as close as they would get to B9 where Artie and I lived. School didn't excite me, but Mom wanted me to go, and Artie insisted crossing into B4 was at least as safe as living in B9. Most of the time that was true, but not when the Citizen Patrols were out.

We knew there was going to be trouble that day,

because Melissa's desk had been empty at roll call, and word got around by recess that she'd been found in a trash bin, missing a few parts. So the Citizen Patrols were out that afternoon, looking for someone to punish. B9ers were a favorite target. Artie and I ran from shadow to shaft, upground and under, trying to stay out of their way. We watched from beneath an abandoned maintenance cart as they rousted three teenage boys playing hoops in the street.

The boys must have scanned as B4s, because the CPs started to walk away; but then one of the boys said something. Something dirty, and cruel. And a CP just shot him. With a crossbow, that is, because no pulse or projectile weapons were ever allowed in the habitats—too much danger of damaging the shielding. When the other two boys went for their knives, the CPs shot them, too.

I'd seen people die before—things were even worse outside than under the shield. But this was the first time I knew—I knew—if I twitched, I'd be next. One CP went over to kick the boys and make sure they were dead. Another one cut open the mouthy boy's pants and sliced off his privates. "That's for Melissa," I heard him say, and he flung the bloody flesh across the street. It landed right beside the cart where we lay hidden.

The sight of it there, so close to my face, made me gag in horror. I stuffed my fist in my mouth to keep from screaming, and Artie pulled me to him, pushing my face against his scrawny chest and holding me tight. "Sh," he breathed in my ear, knowing both how terrified I was and how bad it would be if the CP heard us. "They can't hurt you. They can't hurt you, Faye, because—because you're magic."

I was so startled I stopped crying, wondering what in the dying world he was talking about. I couldn't see the Civilian Patrol, the way he had me pressed up against him, but after a minute or two he let go of me so I knew they had gone. "What you say, magic?" I demanded in the barest of whispers, not knowing how far away they were.

"They left, didn't they?" he whispered back. "Magic. You've got the magic name."

I told him what I thought he was full of.

"Maybe," he agreed, checking the street carefully to be sure it really was clear. "But your name, 'Faye,' that's like Morgan LeFey, right?" He started to squirm out from under the cart.

I squirmed right after him. "Who?"

"King Arthur's sister," he said. "She was magic. She took Arthur to the Isle of Avalon where he couldn't die."

Later that night, Artie shinnied up the drainpipe to my room, and we sat there for hours in the dark while he told me stories of King Arthur and his knights: men who defended the helpless instead of victimizing them, men who fought against the villains of their age and inevitably prevailed. Not until many years later did I learn what a spin he put on the stories for me that night, to make me believe that once, there had been people who cared about the likes of me, who stood for justice and nobility of spirit, who made it honorable to protect the weak.

That night I took the name of Morgan, not because I ever believed it was magic, but because I wanted to be a part of that ideal. I needed the hope that King Arthur represented, and I saw it in my Arthur—Artie. To think of myself as his sister pleased me in a quiet, deep way I could not explain.

Nor was I the only one so drawn to Artie. He had already begun to acquire a following when I met him: children he had grown up with, and others like myself whom he befriended along the way. There was safety in numbers, as long as no crossbows were involved. A pack offered the protection of a dozen knives that could not all be taken away at once. And then we discovered another form of protection—or rather, Artie discovered it, and it changed him. It changed us all.

We were thieves in those days; I hate to say it, but that's what we were. Artie was a thief. I was a thief. There was an ethic to our larceny, for we never stole from people poorer and weaker than we were—the rather rude beginnings of the Code. But we took things we did not own and thought no more of it than a goat thinks of cropping grass. That's how we came by the first bicycles.

José started it. A procurement convoy had come in from outside, loaded with goods for the Launch Pad. That's what we called the sectors where the engineers and administrators and other elite live, those who will surely have berths on the next transport ship carrying people away from this dying planet. While the last driver stopped to flirt with the gatekeeper, José jimmied the lock on his truck and slipped inside. He was working for some older kids, of course, but by the time they roadblocked the convoy in G5, José had the cargo mapped out so they knew which crates to snatch. One of them had six bicycles.

The bike was his fee. No one could have been prouder than José when he showed up with that bicycle. He carried it on his shoulder, because he didn't know how to ride, and it had slipped its chain, anyway. Artie looked at it, and looked at it, and I could see the ideas spinning through his head like a cyclone. He was thirteen by then, and though he was still skinny, he'd grown into his ears and his teeth enough so the girls were starting to give him second looks; but when an idea possessed him, he still looked like a goofy kid, his mouth hanging slack and his eyes glazed over.

"You can ride it, right?" José asked, because like most of the younger kids, he believed implicitly that Artie knew everything worth knowing and had all skills worth acquiring. Artie had even wrangled his way into Spark Academy, which amazed everyone. Kids from B9 didn't get into Spark Academy. Most of them didn't bother with school at all.

Artie had not answered José's question; I wasn't sure he had even heard it. I nudged him. "I can ride," I told him softly. "Learned outside. Bikes lay around free-for-nothing; my old man, he fix one up for me."

Finally Artie's eyes left the bicycle and fastened on me, still whirling with the enchantment of his racing thoughts. "Your dad can fix bicycles?"

I shrugged. "He know machines 'n' things. That how we got under shield, finally. Learned him welding."

At that, Artie scowled and came back to the present. "Don't talk street, Morgan," he chided. "You've got to practice BookEnglish if you're going to get into the Academy with me."

That was his dream for me, that I would pass the entrance exams to go to Spark Academy, too. I worked at it, because he thought I should, but I never had much hope. "Yes, Artie, he knows something about bicycles," I said with exaggerated articulation. "I'm not sure how much."

It was enough. When my father got off shift, he had the

bike running in less than fifteen minutes; then Artie took it, and me, and found a deserted stretch of tunnel where he could master the two-wheeler without an audience. I was the only one he trusted to witness the ignominy of his early failures. A week later when he returned the bike to José, he rode into the street where the others waited, braked to a smooth stop, and dismounted with practiced ease.

"We need more of these," Artie announced. "We need every one of us to be mounted. We can outrun anyone on these things. We can pick up our families' rations and not worry about being mugged on the way home, because no one will be able to catch us. We can get to a friend who's in trouble, and we can get away from trouble when it comes looking for us. Bicycles are the answer."

And because he was Artie, we all believed him.

Over the next year, bicycles sprouted like primalloy mushrooms in the streets of B9. We lost one kid in the process—Torey got shot by Security making a run out of F5, where he should never have been grazing—but that left seventeen of us on wheels. Knights of the Wheel Round, I laughed.

You might wonder how Artie could develop such a following, win the loyalty of so many people who would—and sometimes did—sacrifice themselves and their own well-being to follow his Code. The answer, I'm convinced, lies in three qualities Artie possessed in greater measure than other human beings: compassion, conviction, and compulsion. When Artie latched onto a notion, he pursued it with a focus ordinary mortals can't hope to achieve, and the intensity of his devotion sucked other people in like a black hole.

Bicycles became his world. Between my father's sketchy knowledge and some books we found online, Artie not only learned how to maintain and repair the bikes, he also learned frame geometry and stress factors and performance metrics. I learned some, too, because you couldn't hang around Artie and not learn, but mostly I stuck with maintenance and repair. It wasn't enough for him, though, that we should all learn to ride and care for our bikes—we had to train. He had us up before dawn each day, racing along the empty streets of B9 and B7. Our legs grew thick with muscle as we vied with each other for dominance in speed and endurance.

Soon we ventured out of our home sectors, becoming a familiar sight throughout the upground Bs and Gs, and even in parts of the As. Seventeen cyclists whooshing along in a pack at twenty-plus miles an hour is an impressive sight—that was both good and bad. A pack of thugs in A12 called the Big Dogs tried to lay traps for us whenever we crossed their sector, and we crossed it often escorting Artie to and from Spark Academy. But we were always too quick and too smart and too mobile for them.

There were two reasons Artie kept running the gauntlet to get to Spark Academy. Okay, three. The third was that he couldn't stand for someone to tell him he couldn't do something. But the first was that he liked learning. It charged his batteries. He was into mechanical engineering, and the teachers at Spark actually encouraged him in that. I guess they thought he could help keep habitat infrastructure from collapsing around us.

But the second reason he kept going to the Academy was Yvonne.

Now, Artie had girlfriends in the neighborhood, and had since he was old enough to understand why a man would want to insert Tab A into Slot B. He didn't exactly tell me the first time he got laid—he did have some notion that I was a girl and wouldn't appreciate hearing about his conquests—but I knew it had happened, because I saw the girl try to take ownership of him. Fat chance she had. Artie always had champagne taste when it came to girls, and you don't find champagne in B9.

Yvonne was champagne. I never met her, but I knew because Artie told me all about her. He'd lost his heart, and it wasn't the kind of thing you could tell other guys, so he told me. Most of what he was learning in Spark Academy, he confided, he could pick up out of books and vids that were available remotely, even on the archaic B9 equipment. And besides, he could earn a ration just running the courier service he'd started, so he didn't really need to get into a university program. But a girl like Yvonne wouldn't marry a courier and live in B9. So he had to get a degree, and a better housing assignment, so he could make a life with Yvonne.

For the record, I think he would have gone to the Academy anyway. Not that he didn't like running courier—he liked using his cycling skills, evading obstacles, flirting with danger only to escape. He liked organizing the rest of us as couriers, and he liked being able to deliver packages quickly and safely for people who were afraid to walk the streets. As with protecting smaller children, and helping outsiders adjust to the habitat, it was a way for him to touch people's lives and make them better. The need to do that was deep in him, and it was the foundation of the Code he established.

For Yvonne, though, he needed to be more than a courier. The others in our pack knew Artie had an Academy girlfriend, but they assumed she was no different than the girls he fooled around with in B9—except it was somehow more exciting to get your rocks off with some C5 princess, so the rest of the guys looked at Artie in awe. That was why, when Yvonne dumped him, he climbed the drainpipe to my room and cried in my arms.

We were never lovers, Artie and I. He never wanted me that way, and I knew better than to try enticing him. It would have been laughable: I am a homely woman, and I was an ugly child. My mother said it was the radiation I endured outside—she blamed everything on radiation—but I didn't have to look far to find the long jaw and the close-set eyes I inherited, or the limp, colorless hair and crooked teeth. My shape, too, eschews beauty: I have a bony frame and tiny breasts. There are boys who don't care what Slot B looks like, as long as it will accommodate Tab A, but Artie was never one of them.

So I held him the night Yvonne rejected his love, knowing this was as close to him as I would ever get. The next day he went out and built his first bicycle.

Before he graduated from Spark Academy, the counselors there tried to push him into vocational training because he was so gifted in working with his hands: carving, molding, welding. "Wouldn't you be happier," they asked, "crafting components? Building machines? Turning out a product?" If Yvonne had dumped him earlier, he might have yielded to their pressure; but he had told them he could do both: design and build. With his heart torn to shreds, he needed to prove that.

It was no work of art, that first bicycle: primalloy tubes patch-welded together. But it was serviceable, and it was a start. DeRon and I took over running the courier business—we already handled the routine maintenance and repair of our pack bicycles—so Artie would have time to build. His instructors in the university engineering program derided him, he told me, for wasting his time building "toys." New robots to evacuate clogged water and sewer lines, or innovative geometries to prop up the sagging tunnels of KanHab—those were projects worthy of a mechanical engineer, they said. Not swift transportation through the unsavory streets of lawless sectors.

But he did all they asked of him by day, and when darkness blanketed KanHab, he locked the front door of the abandoned storefront that served as our headquarters, called up his drawings, and began to build.

Artie made it his business to see that every child in B9 who kept the Code had a sleek, efficient machine that could carry him or her away from danger. The Code was fairly simple at that point: Take care of your bike and your friends; never fight when you can run; study and learn; make things better for everyone, not just yourself. Those same tenets were required of everyone in his pack.

By this time we had left thievery behind and were a legitimate business, recognized by Admin, delivering parcels and providing reconnaissance for electric cart convoys and groups of pedestrians throughout KanHab. We wore patches that showed we were part of Artie's pack—Artie's Angels, we called ourselves—with authorization to cross sectors and ride through public tunnels and buildings. Admin gave us helmets, gloves, and light body armor as part of our ration, and they stamped out cleats for Artie to fasten on flexible, steel-shanked shoes so we could lock into our pedals. When we rode as a pack, armored and shod identically, people stood aside, gaping.

As our customer base expanded to other sectors, our fees—originally accepted as comestibles, tools, and clothing—were paid more and more in ExCees, or Exchange Credits, flushed through habitat accounting and redeemable in rations, entertainment, or just about anything else we could want. I drew a single ration for myself and gave everything else I earned to Artie, to buy materials for the bicycles that gave the kids of B9 a chance: a chance to learn, a chance to grow, a chance to believe in the goodness and worth of other people.

But it's hard to give hope to a dying planet.

All the time Artie was trying to make things better in B9, outside KanHab, life became more and more futile. Plants and animals died in the unfiltered sunlight, people starved to death, babies were born with mutations so horrible their own parents killed them. Brutality reigned, for life was short and ugly, and people snatched what pleasure they could; too often that meant the adrenalin rush gained by inflicting one's will on someone or something else. How long the Reapers were a problem outside, I don't know; but the day they broke through Security into KanHab is a day we will never forget.

They rode old combustion-engine motorcycles, powered by whatever alcohol they could manufacture to fuel them. Their philosophy was nihilistic: Earth and its inhabitants were doomed, so why not help them along the path to destruction? Whether or not they died in the process seemed of no consequence to the Reapers. Of the twenty or so who crashed the gate that day, only two made any effort to escape the certain death they found at the hands of KanHab's defenders. But before they died, eighteen Security officers and over a hundred civilians fell to the Reapers' projectile weapons—not to mention the people they simply rode down. Hundreds more burned to death in the fires they started.

Infrastructure at the gate, including the radiation shield, was so badly damaged that Admin sealed off the entire sector and simply built a new gate further in. They did nothing to repair the collapsed tunnels and fire-gutted buildings of A7 and 8. Why should they? Physical space was not what kept people out of KanHab, but the lack of food from our greenhouses. Housing was plentiful, and it was only residential areas the Reapers had terrorized in their eighteen-hour frenzy of destruction.

Artie got two months off from classes while he and other students helped repair the damage to the shield and other critical parts of the infrastructure. One day as we worked in C17 underground—Artie as field engineer and DeRon and I as his crew chiefs—the most strikingly beautiful woman I have ever seen approached us: tall and lithe, with high cheekbones in an oval face and dark, unblemished skin.

"Mr. D'Angelo?" she asked, and her voice was like thick cream, a smooth, rich fluid that spilled out and soaked into the thirsty air.

Artie was smitten; it was written all over his face as he stepped down from the ladder he had just mounted. "I'm Artie D'Angelo," he said.

I tried to see what Saronda was seeing: a wiry young man well shy of six feet, with a flat gut and thighs like tree trunks; dark hair clumped in curls from sweating beneath his hard hat; red-rimmed eyes and two days' growth of beard telling how little he had done the past fourty-eight hours except work to salvage something from the destruction.

But she smiled, a smile as warm and sincere as it was brilliantly white. "I'm Saronda McCabe. I understand you build bicycles."

She was an electrical engineering student, and her father worried about her traveling from her home in F3 to her practicum in C7. She thought a bicycle might be the answer. Artie agreed, provided she also got some practical training in avoiding danger—which he, of course, would be happy to provide at no charge. DeRon and I exchanged a look, then took our crew in search of some lunch while the two of them made eyes and traded compliments. "Ten ExCees he's in her pants before morning," DeRon muttered as we turned a corner.

I didn't think so—she was high-class stuff—but I wasn't stupid enough to take the bet. Good thing—I would have lost.

Once Saronda's bicycle was made, we started swinging through F3 on our morning rides to pick her up for a couple of miles, after which she and Artie would break off and go their own way—because, he said, she couldn't keep up with us quite yet. That was true, and they did stay with us longer as she improved. But she had a housing assignment separate from her parents—her father was high up in Admin—and within a couple of months we were picking up Artie in F3, too.

His bicycle building went by the wayside. All the kids in B9 had bikes by this time, anyway, and every Angel had a top-notch custom machine. On weekends he came back to B9 to check on the courier operation and hang with his pack, and he was still the same Artie: same huge smile, same warm laugh, same abiding concern for his neighborhood. But the kids missed him, and some of them started acting out, breaking the Code. That brought him back for a while, because he recognized that his presence was necessary to keep them on track, to keep them believing. I worried more about him then, though, because when night came and things started locking up, that's when he'd get on his bicycle and head for F3 to see Saronda. It was a bad hour to be out without your pack.

I told myself that Artie was making a terrible mistake, that he was headed for another fall like with Yvonne; but I don't think I really believed that. He was too happy, and Saronda—blast her sculpted, perfect face—was a nice person. Genuinely nice. I liked her, hard as I tried not to. Once she came with us into B9, because she wanted to see where Artie and the rest of us lived, to meet the children and hear them recite the Code. "I wanted to join the Sisters of Literacy when I was younger," she confided to me as Artie explained to a nine-year-old how the derailleur worked and the easiest way to replace a slipped chain. "But my dad wouldn't hear of it. He pointed out that where we're going—"

She broke off suddenly, and I saw the pain on her face before she changed the topic quickly. But I knew. I knew. And I wanted to scream at Artie for being so stupid, and at Saronda for not stopping this, and at myself for not shaking them both and making them face reality—but they were so in love. All we have here in B9 is moments. I figured they were entitled to theirs.

It was September when the transport ship arrived and began to load those who could pay the co-op fee for their passage offworld. There was a brief stir of excitement as a renegade Reaper popped out from wherever he'd been hiding for ten months to throw a home-made grenade at the shuttle when it docked. He died with six crossbow bolts in his chest, and some heroic Security officer threw himself on the grenade so there was no damage to the shuttle. But I watched it all on the news without much interest, waiting instead for the tap at my window.

Artie's grin through the glass was forced. "You gonna open up?" he asked. "Or let me hang on this drainpipe all night?"

I expected a repeat of the night Yvonne dumped him, because I knew what had happened: Saronda's family was departing on the transport, and she'd chosen life offworld—where you can live for hundreds of years in peace and comfort—over a couple of decades with a boy from B9.

But I was wrong. Her father had purchased Artie's passage, as well, for Saronda's happiness and because he found Artie to be a man worth saving, a man with a contribution to make.

"Then this is good-bye," I said, my voice choked with my loss.

But Artie shook his head. "I'm not going," he said, as though he had never seriously considered it.

"What do you mean?" I demanded. "You have to go, Artie. You have to get out."

"And leave you guys here to have all the fun?" he asked, though his voice broke and his eyes swam with tears. "Naa."

"You have to!" I shouted again, and I struck his chest with my fist. "You have to, Artie! For all of us! You're the only B9er who's ever, ever been offered transport out of here, and you have to go! You have to go where you can live for hundreds of years, you have to do it for us. You have to live all those years for us, Artie—you're the only one who can."

Still he shook his head, though it took him a moment longer to speak this time. "Naa," he repeated. "Who'd make bikes for the kids? Who'd make them live by the Code? You saw what happened when I was gone for just a couple of months." He smiled at me, though he had to brush his eyes with the back of his hand. "Besides, I can't leave the Angels. DeRon would go mercenary inside of six weeks, and Stash is already smuggling on the side—I'm going to have to come down on him before he drags the whole operation lawless. And you know, there are bike packs in five other sectors now, and three of them follow the Code. I've got to stick around and make sure it stays that way."

"And Saronda?" I challenged, desperate for some way to talk him into going.

He drew a deep breath. "She thinks I'm already onboard. Her dad won't tell her till they launch, he promised me." Then he looked out my window as a bright streak of light flashed across the darkened sky: the shuttle leaping upward to meet the waiting transport.

"Damn you, Artie!" I screamed at him, as though I were the one he had abandoned. "Damn you, Artie, you should have gone with her!" And I hit him again, and again, and again, until he grabbed my fists to make me stop and I dissolved in weeping. Then he held me close and we both wept until, exhausted, we finally slept in each other's arms; and our dreams echoed with the whisper of Saronda's anguished wails.

What a story it would be, if it ended there. You would understand, then, and perhaps believe, all the legends that surround Artie and his Angels. You would think that he devoted the rest of his life to protecting the children of B9, and eventually of other sectors, and that he restored pride and honor and—dare I say—chivalry to a society that had lost all that. That was his intention, certainly. But he never had the chance.

We had known for months there was a Reaper hanging with the Big Dogs, one who had escaped death on the day of their invasion. We knew because the Reapers' insidious philosophy began creeping out of A12. When the assault was made on the shuttle, though, we all supposed that was him, and the assailant's death put an end to the threat.

We were wrong.

It was six months later, and Artie was in his shop building a bicycle for a kid who had just come in from outside. I was in my room, just across the street, studying Taninger's treatise on folk myths. Although I was never accepted for advanced schooling, Artie had insisted that I keep studying remotely. With his help, I was working at the first-year university level in math and science, and higher in social studies. It had just occurred to me, reading Taninger, that the Arthurian cycle had many parallels to the Christ cycle, when I heard the double shotgun blasts.

I bolted for the door, not even pausing to look out my window. Though the sound was foreign to me, and I wouldn't know until much later what had made it, I was seized with a dread conviction that it had come from Artie's shop.

The Reaper hadn't stuck around, but his handiwork was all too evident. The fiberforced glass in the storefront window was not meant to withstand the onslaught of outlaw projectile weapons; it had shattered into a million harmless shards that crunched under my feet as I stumbled through the wreckage to the back of the room. Artie was on the floor between the truing stand and his framebuilding jig, in a litter of primalloy tubing and joining patches. His chest was shredded where the brunt of one blast had caught him, and spots of blood glistened on his legs and arms from a spray of pellets.

Someone else entered behind me—Louis, it turned out. "Get a doctor!" I screamed. "Call for med-evac!"

But the light was already fading from Artie's eyes. "Wanted to take you with me," he slurred, blood foaming with the words from his lips.

"Don't talk," I commanded. "Lie still. Help is coming."

"Said I'd go if you could, too," he managed.

"Shut up, Artie!" I shouted. "Don't you lay that on me! Don't you do it!"

Then, impossibly, he smiled. "Morgan LeFey," he whispered. "Take me to Avalon…"

The story goes that we got him to a hospital, and the doctors were able to stabilize him enough to put him in a cryogenic chamber. That chamber went on the next transport ship to a distant world where Saronda was waiting, and where they have the medical science to heal him. Someday, when he's recovered, he'll come back to Earth again, to KanHab. In the meantime, Artie's Angels are still here, seeing that what he started doesn't die.

That's the story. But Artie died in my arms that night, and no med-evac bothered to come. Not to B9. Louis and I took him underground, to a place where a collapsed tunnel had left only a crawl space. We laid him in there and sealed it up, and we didn't tell anyone else. Then I concocted that story about the cryogenic chamber. Ha. As if KanHab had any such thing.

So that is the truth of what happened to Artie D'Angelo, but don't try to tell that to anyone in KanHab. He has become larger in death than he ever was in life—I have seen to that. A brutal act of nihilism deprived me of my friend, my pack leader, my guiding light, but I will not let it deprive KanHab of hope. The stories of Artie's exploits grow richer with each telling; and in them he succeeds, in ways he could only dream of, in protecting the helpless and improving the lives of those he left behind.

For us, he turned down a chance to live hundreds of years in comfort and peace with his beloved. I will give him, in its place, immortality.

Sleep well in Avalon, my Arthur. KanHab will not forget.

JUDGMENT PASSED
BY JERRY OLTION

Jerry Oltion is the author the novels *Paradise Passed*, *The Getaway Special*, *Anywhere But Here*, and several others. In 1998, he won the Nebula Award for his novella "Abandon in Place," which he later expanded into a novel. He is also the author of more than 100 short stories, most of which have appeared in the pages of *F&SF* and *Analog*.

"Judgment Passed," which is original to this volume, tells of the Biblical day of judgment from a rationalist viewpoint; a starship crew returns to Earth to find that the rapture has occurred without them. Oltion has strong views on religion—namely that it's a scourge on humanity—that led him to write this story, which speculates on whether or not being "left behind" would be such a bad thing.

It was cold that morning, and the snow squeaked beneath my boots as I walked up the lane in search of Jody. Last night's storm had left an ankle-deep layer of fresh powder over the week-old crust, and her tracks stood out sharp and clear as they led away through the bare skeletons of aspen trees and out of sight around the bend. She had gone toward the mountains. I didn't need to see her tracks to know that she had gone alone.

Except for Jody's footprints there was no sign of humanity anywhere. My boots on the snow made the only sound in the forest, and the only motion other than my own was in the clouds that puffed away behind me with every breath. Insulated as I was inside my down-filled coat, I felt an overwhelming sense of solitude. I knew why Jody had come this way. In a place that was supposed to be empty, she wouldn't find herself looking for people who weren't there.

I found her sitting on a rail fence, staring out across a snow-covered field at the mountains. She sat on the bottom rail with her chin resting on her mittened hands on the top rail. Her shoulder-length brown hair stuck out below a green stocking cap. There were trenches dug in the snow where she had been swinging her feet. She turned her head as I squeaked up behind her, said, "Hi, Gregor," then turned back to the mountains. I sat down beside her, propping my chin on my hands like she had, and looked up at them myself.

Sunlight was shining full on the peaks, making the snowfields glow brilliant white and giving the rocks a color of false warmth. No trees grew on their jagged flanks. They were nothing but rock and ice.

The Tetons, I thought. God's country. How true that had proved to be.

"I'd forgotten how impressive mountains could be," I

said, my breath frosting the edges of my gloves.

"So had I," she said. "It's been a long time."

Twelve years. Five years going, five years coming, and two years spent there, on a dusty planet around a foreign star.

She said, "There was nothing like this on Dessica."

"No glaciers. It takes glaciers to carve up a mountain like that."

"Hmm."

We stared up at the sunlit peaks, each thinking our own thoughts. I thought about Dessica. We'd waited two months after landing to name it, but the decision was unanimous. Hot, dry, with dust storms that could blow for weeks at a time—if ever there was a Hell, that place had to be it. But eight of us had stayed there for two years, exploring and collecting data; the first interstellar expedition at work. And then we had packed up and come back—to an empty Earth. Not a soul left anywhere. Nothing to greet us but wild animals and abandoned cities full of yellowed newspapers, four years old.

According to those papers, this was where Jesus had first appeared. Not in Jerusalem, nor at the Vatican, nor even Salt Lake City. The Grand Teton. Tallest of the range, ruggedly beautiful, a fitting monument to the Son of God. I could almost see Him myself, floating down from the peak and alighting next to the Chapel of the Transfiguration back by the lodge where we'd spent the night. Hard as it was to believe, it was easy to imagine.

What came next was the hard part. He'd apparently given people six days to prepare themselves, then on the seventh He had called them all to judgment. No special call for the faithful, no time of tribulation for the unbelievers; He'd hauled everyone off at once, presumably to sort them out later. The newspapers were silent on the method He'd used, all the reporters and editors and press operators apparently caught up in the moment along with everyone else, but I couldn't imagine how it had worked. Most people had expected to rise into the sky; but above 15,000 feet they would start to asphyxiate and above 40,000 or so their blood would boil. Not quite the sort of thing I imagined even the Old Testament God would want His faithful to endure. Slipping into an alternate dimension seemed more likely, but I couldn't imagine what that would be like, either.

Trying to visualize the unimaginable reminded me why I'd come looking for Judy. "The captain's going to be holding services in a little while. She thought maybe you'd like to be there."

Jody looked over at me with an expression usually reserved for a stupid younger brother. "Why, to pray? To try getting God's attention?"

I nodded. "Dave talked her into it. He figures the more of us doing it, the stronger the signal."

"Very scientific."

"Dave's an engineer. Gwen agrees with him."

"I suppose she's going to ask God to send Jesus back for us."

"That's the general idea, yeah," I said, beginning to get embarrassed.

She gave me the look again. "You don't really think it'll work, do you?"

"It's worth a try. It can't hurt, can it?"

She laughed. "Spoken like a true agnostic."

I shifted my weight so a knot on the fence rail would

stop poking me in the thigh. The joint where the rail met the post squeaked. "We're all agnostic," I pointed out. "Or were." When the mission planners selected the crew, they had wanted people who made decisions based on the information at hand, not wishful thinking or hearsay. Those sort of people tended to be agnostic.

"I still am," she said.

I looked at her in surprise. "How can you be? The entire population of the world disappears, every newspaper we find has stories about the Second Coming of Christ—complete with pictures—and all the graveyards are empty. Doesn't that make a believer out of you?"

She shook her head and asked simply, "Why are we here?"

"What do you mean?"

"I mean if I'm supposed to believe that Jesus came back for the second time, called the day of judgment and took every human soul to Heaven, then what are we doing here? Why didn't He take us, too?"

"We weren't on Earth."

"Neither were three thousand Lunar colonists, and they got taken."

"We were doing ninety-eight percent of the speed of light. We were three and a half light-years away."

"And so God missed us. That's my point. If He was omniscient He would have known we were there."

I'd been thinking about that myself in the days since we'd been home. "Maybe He did," I said.

"Huh?"

"Maybe God did know about us. Maybe He left us behind on purpose, as punishment for not believing in Him."

She snorted. "What about atheists, then? What about other agnostics? Why just us eight?"

I held up my gloved hands, palms up. "I don't know. I'm not God."

"If you were, you'd have done a better job."

I wasn't sure whether to take that as a compliment or what, so I decided to ignore it. "What do you think happened, then, if it wasn't God?"

"I don't know. Maybe aliens came and took us all for slaves. Maybe we were a lab experiment and they got all the data they needed. Maybe we taste like chicken. There are plenty of more believable explanations than God."

"What about the photos of Jesus?" I asked.

She rubbed her red nose with a mitten. "If you were going to harvest an entire planet's population, wouldn't you use their local religion to keep them in line?"

"Jesus wouldn't have much sway with Jews," I pointed out. "Or Moslems. Or atheists."

"So says the former agnostic who believes in him because of what he read in the paper." She said it kindly, but it still stung.

"Look," I said, "Gwen's going to start pretty soon. You coming or not?"

She shrugged. "What the hell. It ought to be fun listening to an agnostic sermon."

We swung our legs around off the fence rail and stood up, then started following our tracks back to the lodge, an enormous log hotel built around the turn of the last century to house the crush of tourists who came to visit one of the last unspoiled places on Earth.

I took Jody's right hand in my left as we walked. It was an unconsciously natural act; we weren't a pair at the moment, but we had been a few times. With the small crew on the ship and lots of time to experiment, we had tried just about every combination at least once. The warmth and comfort I felt as we walked through the fresh snow together made me glad we'd never broken up hard. It felt like maybe we were headed for another stretch of time together.

Jody must have been feeling the same way. When we got down in among the aspen trees, she said, "Assuming God really is behind all this, and it's not just some sort of enormous practical joke, then maybe this is a reward."

"A reward?"

She nodded. "I like it here. It's pretty, and peaceful. The last time I was here it was a zoo. Tourists wherever you looked, lines of motor homes and SUVs on the road as far as you could see, trash blowing all around. I feel like now I'm finally getting to see it the way it's supposed to be."

"The way God intended?"

"Yeah, maybe." She grinned an agnostic-theologian grin and said, "Maybe we're the next Ark. We were all set to start our own colony, after all. We're the best genetic stock the UN Space Authority could find, and we've got more fertilized ova in the freezer. Maybe God decided it would be a good time to clear away all the riff-raff and give humanity a fresh start."

"It's a little cold for Eden," I said.

"We've got the whole world," she pointed out.

I thought about that. I supposed we did, at least until the airplanes and hovercars all fell apart. There was no way eight people could maintain a technological civilization indefinitely. Our colonization equipment was designed to keep us at what the UN's social scientists called an "artificially augmented industrial age" until we could increase the population enough to build our own factories and so forth, but that level wasn't particularly cosmopolitan. The idea had been to pick a spot and settle in rather than to play tourist on a new planet. Of course the planet needed at least one habitable spot, which was why we'd given up after two years of searching and come home.

"I'd never considered just going on with our lives," I said. "I mean, after the Second Coming of Christ, that simply never occurred to me."

Jody shrugged. "We just landed; we've all been too busy trying to figure out what happened. Give 'em time, though, and I think most of us will start thinking about it. I mean, this could be all the Heaven we need if we do it right."

A sudden chill ran up my spine, and it wasn't from the snow. "We may not have time," I said. "If Gwen's little prayer meeting works, God may come back for us today."

Jody looked up at me, her face mirroring the concern in my own. "Damn," she said, then she took off running for the chapel. I took off after her, both of us shouting, "Gwen! Gwen, wait up!"

Running in snow isn't easy. Our feet punched right through the crust that had supported us when we'd been walking, and we wound up struggling for every step. We were both sweating and panting when we burst into the chapel, gasping for enough breath to cry out, "Don't pray!"

Gwen was standing behind the pulpit, wearing a long white robe with gold hems a hand's width wide. She'd found it in a closet in the priest's sacristy. The wall behind her was mostly window, affording the congregation— Dave and Maria and Hammad and Arjuna and Keung in the front pew—a fantastic view of the Tetons behind her own splendor. Everyone turned and looked at us as Jody said again, "Don't pray. We've got to think this through first."

Gwen frowned. "What's there to think through? We've got to contact God."

"Do we?"

"What do you mean? Of course we do. He left us behind!"

"Maybe that's a good thing." Tugging off her mittens, stocking hat, and coat as she talked, Jody told her what she'd told me, ending with, "So maybe we ought to just keep quiet and go on about our business."

Gwen had been shaking her head the whole time Jody had been speaking. She was a big woman, with a thick halo of curly black hair that wagged from side to side as she shook it. Now she said, "We don't know what that business is. This could just as easily be a test of some sort."

"Exactly! It could be a test, so I think we'd be smart to be careful what we ask for. We might get it."

Dave had been listening with as much impatience as Gwen. Before she could answer, he said, "If God intends for us to repopulate the Earth, wouldn't He have told us so? He told Noah what He wanted him to do."

Jody shrugged. "God was a lot more talkative in those days."

"If you believe the Judeo-Christian bible," Hammad put in.

"The Christian Day of Judgment has come and gone," Gwen said. "What else are we supposed to believe?"

Hammad spread his hands to indicate the chapel, and by implication everything beyond it. "We should believe what we have always believed: the evidence of our own senses. The Earth has been depopulated. Newspapers left behind tell us a being calling himself Jesus Christ claimed responsibility. Beyond that we can only speculate."

"Wait a minute," Maria said, but before she had a chance to finish her thought Arjuna said, "We can too—" and Keung said, "Yeah, what about—" and the room descended into babble.

Gwen hadn't been chosen captain for nothing. She let it go on for a few seconds, then shouted at top volume, "Quiet!"

The chapel grew quiet.

"All right," she said into the silence. "I obviously made a false assumption when I thought we all wanted to ask God to come back for us. Jody doesn't think we should try to contact Him at all. What do the rest of you think?"

A chorus of voices nearly drowned her out again. "One at a time," she yelled. "You, Dave."

"I think we should ask His forgiveness and ask Him to take us with Him."

"Hammad?"

"Ask what He wants us to do, rather than just assume."

"Maria?"

"I…uh, I definitely think we should try to contact Him, but I think Hammad kind of makes sense, actually."

"Thank you," said Hammad.

Gwen looked at me. "Gregor?"

I looked at Hammad, then at Jody. "I'm not sure it's a good idea to call His attention to us at all. Depending on whose version of Christianity is true, we could do a lot worse than where we are now."

"Arjuna?"

Arjuna said, "I kind of agree with Jody and Gregor,

except I wonder what we'd do if God decides to turn out the lights."

"It's been four years," Hammad said.

"That doesn't mean—" Dave said, and the babble started up again.

"Quiet!" shouted Gwen. She snatched the wooden cross from the front of the pulpit and banged it down like a gavel on the angled top. "All right," she said when we'd quieted down, "let's try this again. Keung, what do you think?"

Keung shrugged. "I don't think it matters. If we can reach Him with prayer, then one of us would have done it already. I think if we can get His attention at all, then there's no point in hiding out because He'll eventually realize we're here."

"Is that a vote for or against praying to Him?"

"It's an 'I don't care.'"

Gwen nodded. "Well then, it looks like the prayer contingent wins, but I don't see anything wrong with asking politely what God intends for us to do before we start begging for divine intervention. Can we all agree on that?"

"No," Jody said, but Dave's and Maria's and Hammad's assent was louder.

Gwen said, "Jody, Keung's right; if prayer works, then somebody's bound to get God's attention sooner or later."

"No they're not," Jody said. "There's millions of guns lying around, but that doesn't mean we have to start shooting each other with them. We don't have to pray."

"I do," Dave said.

Jody stared at him a moment, then shook her head and picked up her coat and hat and mittens again. "I'll wait outside, then," she said, brushing past me toward the door. "Maybe He'll miss me again when he comes for you idiots."

I followed her out. I hadn't taken my coat off, just unzipped it; the cold air felt good through my shirt.

"Idiots," Jody said again when we were alone. "They're playing with dynamite in there. Worse. Antimatter."

"Maybe literally," I said. "Who knows what God might be made of."

"Aaahhh, God, God, God," she growled. "I'm sick of the whole subject. I wish He'd just stayed the hell out of my life."

I poked a finger in her ribs. "He did, silly."

"It's not funny."

"Sure it is. We've spent our whole lives saying it didn't matter what we thought or did about religion, since the truth is inherently unknowable, and now we're afraid somebody is going to pray us out of existence. I think it's hilarious."

We were walking back toward the guest lodge along a path surrounded by pine trees and snowbanks. On impulse I reached up and slapped a branch just as Jody walked under it. "Yow!" she screamed as a clump of snow went down her neck, and before I could back out of range she bent down, scooped up a handful, and hurled it at my face. I stumbled backward and sat down unexpectedly in a snowbank, which saved me from another faceful that flew over my head instead.

As long as I was on the ground I figured I might as well defend myself, so I started throwing snow back at her as fast as I could scoop it up. It was too cold to stick into balls, so we just shovelled it at each other, shrieking and laughing like fools while the rest of humanity prayed for a miracle.

The prayer meeting broke up a half hour or so later. By then Jody and I were snuggling on the bear rug in front of the lodge's main fireplace, an enormous flagstone construction with a firebox big enough to roast a hovercar in. Hammad found us first.

"We seem to have failed in raising the deity," he said as he stripped off his coat and hung it over a peg on the wall. "Unless of course there's a time-lag involved."

"Oh great," said Jody. "Now I'll be waiting all night for the skies to open and a choir of angels to wake me up."

"By the looks of you two, you won't be sleeping much in the first place, unless it's from exhaustion." He sat down in one of the overstuffed chairs beside us and stuck his feet toward the flames. "You know, I think you have the right of it," he said. "We should get on with our lives, and let God get on with His. I have to admit I feel greatly relieved to have missed all the commotion."

"Me too," I said. "Ever since we found out He exists, I've felt like an outsider in gang territory. I keep waiting for the tap on the shoulder that means I'm in big trouble."

"I wonder if that's how religious people normally felt?" asked Jody. "Tiptoeing through life so they wouldn't attract the wrong kind of attention."

Hammad shook his head. "I doubt if most people even considered it that way. They probably—"

The solid wood door banged open and Dave, Gwen, and the others came in, stomping snow from their boots and talking. Dave glared at Jody and me and took off for his room or somewhere, but Gwen, Maria, Arjuna, and

Keung took off their coats and joined us by the fire.

"Well, at least we can say we tried," Gwen said as she presented her backside to the flames. She had left the robe in the chapel and was wearing a regular shirt and pants.

"So what now?" asked Jody. "Travel? Sightsee? Play with the leftover toys before they all rust back into the ground? Or do we get straight to work starting a colony?"

Arjuna said, "No offense, but after twelve years of close contact with you guys I'm ready for some time alone."

Keung edged playfully away from her, but he said, "My sentiments exactly. I wouldn't mind having a whole continent to myself for a while."

Maria looked shocked. "Wait a minute. Splitting up could mean some of us might get left behind again if God comes back."

"He's not coming back," Keung said.

"What makes you so sure?"

He shrugged. "I'm not, actually, but I didn't spend my whole life disregarding the issue just to start worrying about it now. If He comes for me, He comes, and if not, that's fine too. I've got plenty to do on my own."

"That's kind of how I feel about it," I said. "I'd like to see the world a little while I've got the chance."

"Me too," said Jody.

Gwen turned around to face the fire, saying over her shoulder, "The satellite phone system still works, so it shouldn't be too hard to stay in touch. There's hundreds of cell phones right here in the hotel, and I'll bet at least some of them still have active accounts, paid automatically every month by credit card. It shouldn't be hard to find a working phone for each of us. Of course we don't all have to play tourist. Whoever wants to could start setting up the colony."

"Where?" Hammad asked.

"The Mediterranean," Arjuna said, just as I said, "California." We looked at each other for a moment, then I shrugged and said, "Okay, the Mediterranean."

A sharp bang sounded from the back of the lodge.

"That sounded like a gun," Gwen said, and she took off running down the hallway, shouting, "Dave! Dave!" the whole way. The rest of us followed close behind her, but I took the time to grab the fireplace poker. Maybe he'd committed suicide and maybe he hadn't. A poker wasn't much of a weapon against a gun, but it felt better than nothing.

We found Dave outside on the deck overlooking the Snake River, a shotgun in his hand and a mess of feathers and blood smeared across the snow. I could see bird seed among the feathers; evidently Dave had scattered a handful and waited for something to come for it. That something had been hardly bigger than a mouse by the looks of its remains.

"Kind of small for dinner, isn't it?" I asked, reaching out with the poker and flipping the tiny bird body over so I could see its underside.

"It's an experiment," Dave said. I was glad to see he was carefully pointing the shotgun away from everyone. "According to Jesus, not even a sparrow can fall without God noticing. I figured that would be pretty easy to test."

Jody had come up beside me and was examining the bird. "It would be if you'd managed to shoot a sparrow," she said. "This is a chickadee."

Dave blushed when we all laughed, but he said, "It's not the species; it's the concept."

"Whatever, it doesn't seem to be working."

"Maybe you should have tied a message to its foot first," I said.

Keung laughed. "You're supposed to use a pigeon for that."

"It's not funny," Dave snapped. He took a deep breath, then said, "I am trying to attract the attention of God. If you think it's funny or useless, I'm sorry, but I think it's important and I'm going to try everything I can until I get the job done."

"What's next?" Gwen asked him. "Sacrificing sheep? Rebuilding the Ark of the Covenant?"

"Whatever is necessary," Dave said.

I felt myself shivering, and when it didn't stop I suddenly realized all of us but Dave were out there without our coats.

"Come on," I said to Jody. "Let's get inside before we catch our death."

We left the next morning for Yellowstone Park. The rest of the crew split up for other parts of the globe, but Jody and I decided as long as we were that close we might as well visit the biggest tourist attraction in the world. We found a hovercar that still ran and whose diagnostics told us it would continue to run for another few hundred hours, tossed our personal belongings in the back, and flew low up the Snake River valley past Jackson Lake and into the park. We ignored the loading ramps and the rail cars that had ferried tourists through for the last fifty years, blowing right past the sign proclaiming it a federal crime to drive a private vehicle within the park's borders.

The forest seemed endless. We flew along the old

roadbed down among the trees so we could see more of it, including the animals the park was famous for. In parts of the world where the human population had been denser, the ecosystem was still out of whack from our sudden disappearance, but Yellowstone had already reached a balance without us before the Second Coming. We watched moose and elk and buffalo plodding along like great hoofed snowplows, and we even caught a glimpse of a wolf drinking out of a stream near Old Faithful.

The geysers were probably the same as always, too, but with just the two of us standing there on the snow-covered boardwalk in front of Old Faithful it seemed to me that we must be watching its best eruption ever. Steam and boiling water shot up over a hundred feet in the air, and the ground shook with the force of its eruption.

"You know," Jody said as it subsided, "I just realized how silly it is to come here right now."

"Silly how?" I asked.

"If Dave succeeds in reaching God, we might have all of eternity to watch this sort of thing in action."

I looked out at the steaming mound of reddish rock, then at the brilliant white snowfield and green forest beyond it. "You talking about the pretty parts, or the hot parts?"

"Who knows?"

Yeah, who knew? I'd lived a perfectly moral life, by agnostic standards, but who could tell if that would be good enough for God? For that matter, who knew whether Heaven or Hell really existed, even now? So Jesus had come and taken everyone away; he could have hauled them to Andromeda for all we knew.

All the same, I wondered if we were wise for leaving Dave free to pursue God. The crew had talked about it before we'd gone our separate ways, but none of us knew what else we could do about him. He wouldn't rest until he'd tried everything he could think of, and none of us wanted to attempt confining him to prevent it. I suppose after the prayer meeting and the chickadee incident none of us really believed he would succeed, which was why we weren't more concerned about it. We were all hoping he'd give it up after a while and become the normal—if somewhat obsessive—friend and crewmember we'd all learned to live with.

We realized we'd made a mistake when Gwen got a call from him a few days later. She had formally renounced her title as captain and flown to Hawaii, but she was still acting as our coordinator. Dave had called to find out where the rest of us were, and when she'd asked him why, he would only tell her to warn us away from Cheyenne, Wyoming, or any place downwind of it.

"Downwind?" I asked when Gwen called us to relay his message. "What the hell is he trying this time?"

Jody and I were in the car again, headed north toward Mammoth hot springs. A ghost of Gwen's face peered at us through the phone's heads-up windshield display. "He wouldn't tell me," she replied. "He just said to keep everyone away from the American Midwest for a while."

"I bet he's going to blow up a nuclear bomb," Jody said. "Cheyenne's one of the Air Force bases where they stored them."

"A nuclear bomb?" asked Gwen. "What does that have to do with God?"

I laughed. "Maybe he thinks we just need to knock loud enough to be heard."

"Yeah, but where's the door?" Jody asked. "Certainly not in Cheyenne. I've been there; it's a dirty little government town out on the prairie."

My smile faded. "If physical location matters at all, I'd guess the Grand Teton, considering that's where Jesus showed up."

"He wouldn't nuke the Tetons, would he?" Jody asked, horrified at the thought.

"I don't know," Gwen said. "Probably not for his first shot, at least. He'll probably just lob one into Nebraska or somewhere. But if that doesn't work, then he might."

We'd been passing through a long straight notch cut in an ocean of lodgepole pine; I let off the throttle and the hovercar slid to a stop, snow billowing up all around it. "We're still in Yellowstone," I told Gwen, "but we could get to Cheyenne in—what, four hours? Five?" We'd been dawdling along on ground-effect until now, but we could fly as high as we liked if we had to.

"I don't know if that's a good idea or not," Gwen said. "I don't like the idea of you two heading toward a nuclear explosion."

"I don't exactly like it either," I said, "but I'm even less happy about the idea of him blowing up an entire mountain range just to get God's attention."

"And screwing up the ecosystem just as it's starting to straighten out again," Jody put in.

Snow had quit swirling around us. The car's fans had blown it all away. I tilted the joystick to the side until the car pivoted halfway around, then pulled upward on it and shoved it forward again. The car rose up above the trees and began accelerating southeast.

I said, "Cheyenne itself should be safe enough. That's

where Dave will be, after all. Do you think we should call and let him know we're coming, or should we try to catch him off guard?"

"He'll just hide if we tell him we're coming," Jody said.

"But he might not blow the bomb if we make him think you're near the blast zone," Gwen said.

"Might not?" I asked. "Just how far around the bend do you figure he's gone?"

"Maybe not at all," Gwen said. "I don't know. This is a very emotionally charged issue for all of us. I doubt if any of us are behaving entirely rationally, but how can we tell if we are or we aren't? We're on completely new ground here."

"I don't think exploding a nuclear bomb is a rational act," Jody said.

"Not even if he succeeds in getting God to notice us?"

"Especially not then."

Gwen smiled wryly. "That's not entirely rational either, Jody."

"It's the way I feel."

"And Dave no doubt feels he has to get God to come back for him."

"No doubt. Well I feel like I have to stop him."

Nodding, Gwen said, "Just don't get yourself killed in the process."

Jody laughed. "That would kind of defeat the purpose, now, wouldn't it?"

We were flying over a windswept basin about a hundred kilometers northwest of Cheyenne when we saw the mushroom cloud peek up over the horizon.

For a second I was too stunned to move, watching the

way the shock wave raced upward in a spherical shell and how the surface of the cloud roiled and churned inside it. Then, remembering where we were, I shouted, "Christ!" and yanked the emergency descent handle under the dashboard. It was the first time I'd ever done that in a car; the air bags blossoming out of the doors and roof and dash slammed me back in the seat and completely blocked my view for ten or fifteen terrifying seconds while the automatic landing sequence took over and dropped us like a rock. We bobbed once, hard, like a cork smacking into water, then settled with a crunch on the ground. The air bags sucked back inside their cubbyholes and I fell forward against the dash. We were listing at about a thirty-degree angle toward the front.

Jody had caught herself with her hands before she fell forward. She looked out the window and said, "We're sitting on a sagebrush."

I looked out my side. Sure enough, a gnarled, knobby little bush was holding the rear end of the car in the air. Not a good position to be in when the shock wave rolled over us. I started the motor and lifted the joystick to raise us off it, and with a sound like ice cubes in a blender the car chopped the bush to shreds, blowing blue-gray bits of foliage everywhere and sending an eye-watering burst of sage smell in through the vents. We lifted up, though, and the wind shoved us forward a few meters before I could set us back down again. We sat there watching the cloud rise and waited for the blast to reach us.

And waited, and waited. The wind shifted a little, then shifted back, and after a while we realized we weren't going to feel anything more this far away so I cautiously took us up a few meters and started flying southeast again. The car had picked up a bad vibration from the sagebrush, but it still flew.

The mushroom cloud blew eastward in front of us as we approached, the wind at different altitudes slowly tearing it apart. We were moving faster than the wind, though, and as we approached it we realized the bomb couldn't have gone off very far out of Cheyenne.

Jody looked at me with a worried expression. "I thought Gwen said he'd lob one into Nebraska."

I was starting to worry, too. "Maybe it went off in the launch tube."

"We'd better call and see if he's okay."

I didn't want to blow our chances of surprising him, but if he was hurt I supposed we should know it. "Okay," I said, and Jody dialed his number.

When it rang half a dozen times without an answer I began worrying in earnest, but then the phone display flickered on and his face appeared before us. "Dave here," he said.

Jody put on a stern expression. "God called, and He told me to tell you to knock it off."

For just a moment, I could see hope blossom in Dave's face. Then he scowled and said, "Very funny. Did you call just to harass me or do you have something important to say?"

"We called to see if you were okay. That blast looked like it was pretty close to town."

"It was in town," said Dave. "At the Air Force base, anyway, which is pretty much the same thing. None of the rockets were in shape to fly, so I just blew one of the missiles in place."

"Where were you?" I asked.

Dave laughed. "Colorado Springs. NORAD control.

I've got a half mile of mountain over my head right now, in case you were thinking of trying to stop me."

In a teasing voice, Jody said, "Aren't you afraid God will miss you again?"

Dave shook his head. "You wouldn't believe the spy network they've got here. I've got satellite surveillance all over the world. If He shows up I'll know it, and I'll set off another one closer to home. He'll know I'm here."

And so did we, now. I angled the car straight south.

"Have you ever considered how God might feel about nuclear bombs?" Jody asked him. "Destroying so much of His handiwork all at once might make Him mad."

"It's a risk I'm willing to take," Dave said.

"But you're taking it for all of us, and I'm not willing."

"Not now," Dave said, "but you'll thank me when I succeed."

"And what if you don't? None of us are going to thank you for blowing a bunch of fallout into the air. We're going to have to live here, Dave. You too, probably."

He laughed. "That's what the environmentalists thought. So they quit cutting the forests and burning fossil fuels, and all for what? The environmentalists are gone and the forests and the fossil fuels are still here. It was a complete waste."

I could hardly believe my ears. "You really believe that?"

"I really do."

"Then you're a lot worse off than I thought."

His eyes narrowed. "Ah, why am I even talking to you?" He reached forward, and his image flicked out.

Jody looked over at me. "I don't think subduing him's going to be easy. If he's in the NORAD command center, then I don't know if we'll even be able to get to him."

"We'll figure out something when we get there," I said. I was trying to convince myself as well as her. I didn't have any idea what we'd do, but what else could we do but try?

Thin as our plans were, the car put an unexpected twist in them just south of the Wyoming-Colorado border. The vibration in the rear fans had been getting steadily worse, and I'd brought us down closer to the ground to reduce the strain on them, hoping to make it to another city before they died completely, but we were still quite a ways north of Fort Collins when the right one gave up with a shriek and the car dropped on that side, hit the ground, then slewed halfway around and flipped completely over. The air bags whooshed out to hold us in place again, but the one in front of Jody burst with a bang and I heard her shriek in surprise as she fell head first into the windshield.

"Jody!" I fought to reach her over the bags still holding me in place. We skidded to a stop, but with the car upside down they deflated slowly, so we wouldn't fall to the roof and break our necks. I managed to squeeze out through the gap between the one in front of me and the one between the seats. Jody lay in the hollow made by the roof and the curved windshield, her face bloody from a gash in her forehead. She was groping for something to pull herself up against.

My first thought was that she should lie flat in case she'd hurt her neck or spine, but then I realized there wasn't enough space for that and she'd probably be better off sitting upright anyway. I took her hand in mine and helped her twist around until she could sit on the roof. The seats were just over our heads. "Is anything broken?"

I asked as I looked in the gap between seats and floor for a medical kit.

"I don't know." She flexed her arms and legs, then said, "Doesn't feel like it." She held a hand to her forehead to keep the blood out of her eyes while she blinked to clear them. "Both eyes are okay," she said after a moment. Her voice was a little slurred but completely calm, the result of years of training for emergencies.

I couldn't find a medical kit, so I tore a strip of cloth from my shirt and used that to sop up the blood from her wound. She winced when I blotted her cut with it, but I was glad to see muscle instead of bone before the blood welled up again.

"I think you'll live," I said, trying not to let her hear the worry in my voice. Her injuries probably wouldn't kill her, but a night outside in Colorado in the wintertime just might. I bent down so I could look out the windows. The Sun was still fairly high over the mountains. We had a couple of hours of daylight left, but I couldn't see any houses and I didn't know how far we could walk to find one. The wind wasn't as strong here as it had been farther north, but it was still blowing hard enough to drop the chill factor by twenty degrees or so. It was already sucking the heat out of the car.

Jody had been thinking along the same lines. "All of a sudden I'm not so happy the world's empty," she said.

"We're not in trouble yet," I told her. "For one thing, the world's not empty." I flicked on the car's phone, dialed upside down, and waited, hoping the transmitter could make contact with its antenna underneath us.

"Who are you calling?" Jody asked. "Dave?"

"That's right. He's the only one anywhere close to us."

"What makes you think he'll help us?"

"I don't know if he will or not. But it can't hurt to ask."

We waited for ten or fifteen seconds while the phone tried to make a connection. Finally we saw a flickering, snowy phantom on the windshield, and Dave's voice, shot through with static, said, "What now?"

"This is Gregor," I said. "We've been in a wreck just north of Fort Collins. Jody's been hurt. Can you come get us?"

His upside-down face looked us over suspiciously. "This is a trick to get me out of here."

"No it's not," Jody said. "Here, have a look." She bent down toward the camera eye and took the blood-soaked rag from her forehead. Dave's expression grew a little more sympathetic, but not enough.

"Sorry," he said. "You got yourselves into this, you can get yourselves out."

I said, "Dave, we're not just asking a favor. We could die of exposure out here."

"Quit being melodramatic. You're resourceful—" His image broke up for a second, then came back. "—must have brought coats and hats and stuff."

"We're in an upside-down car in the middle of nowhere and you're telling us to put on our coats? Damn it, Jody's injured! We need to get her to a hospital and see if she's broken anything. She could have internal injuries."

It was hard to read his expression in the snowy, upside-down image. I thought he was scowling, then for a brief moment the scowl reversed itself. "All right," he said. "I'll come. It'll take me a while to get out of the mountain, and an hour or two more to get up there and find you. Just sit tight." Then before either of us could say anything more, he switched off.

I thought for a moment about his sudden capitulation. I didn't like the feel of it, and pretty soon I realized why.

"The bastard isn't going to come."

Jody looked around at me sharply. "What? He just said—"

"He wants us to think he's coming, but he's going to wait for us to die of exposure. Think about it. What better way to get God's attention than to send a couple of free souls to go knock on Heaven's gates for him?"

"But…he…would he do that?"

"Sure he would. He just said so. It's going to take him a 'while' to get out of the mountain, and a 'while' to fly up here, and a 'while' longer to find us. He'll make sure it takes a long while, so when he gets here he can honestly say he tried to rescue us, but he was just too late."

She shook her head. "No, I don't think he'd do that."

"I do. I'm not waiting around to find out the hard way."

"What are you going to do?"

I reached under the seats into the back for our coats. As I helped Jody into hers, I said, "I'm going to walk toward Fort Collins and see if I can find a house or another car that works. I won't go any farther than I can walk back before dark."

She thought about it, then said, "All right. While you're doing that I'll call Gwen and see who else might be able to come get us."

"Good." I pulled on my coat and hat and gloves, then opened the window and slid out onto the frozen ground. A cold blast of air swirled snow inside. I leaned in to give Jody a kiss, then backed away and made sure she closed the window tight before I stood up.

The car was a dark oblong against white snow; I wouldn't have much trouble finding it again if I got back before dark. I started off toward where I hoped town would be, turning back periodically to make sure I could spot the car again until the slope of the land hid it from view. The Colorado foothills didn't have nearly as much snow as Yellowstone, but there was enough to leave a pretty good set of tracks. It would take a few hours for them to fill in, so I wasn't that worried. I trudged along, hands in pockets and head tilted to the side to keep the wind from blowing down my neck, looking for any sign of civilization.

As I walked, I realized how much I was going to hate living a primitive life when all the machinery started falling apart. By the time I was an old man, I'd probably be walking everywhere I went. I might even be burning wood for heat, depending on how long the colony's power plant lasted. No wonder Dave was so desperate to have God come back for him.

I thought about Jody waiting for me in the car, possibly dying of injuries or exposure before I got back. At the moment I didn't mind the idea of a God watching over us, either, provided He'd actually do something to help if we needed it. Even if He wouldn't—or couldn't—keep her alive, the idea that I might somehow join her again after we both died was at least a little comfort. Not much, because I could never be sure it would happen until it did, but the possibility might keep me going for a while.

It came to me then that if Jody died, I could easily join Dave in his quest. But she wasn't going to die. All I needed was to find some shelter and we'd both be fine.

I eventually spotted what I was looking for down in a gentle valley: a house and barn set in among a stand of tall, bare cottonwood trees. There were a couple of vehicles parked out front and a long, winding road leading down to them from a highway off to my left. I kept going cross-country straight for it.

It was farther away than it looked, but I made it just as the Sun touched the mountains. The house was unlocked, so I didn't have to break in. It was also unheated, but it felt wonderful compared to outside. I tried to call Jody on my cell phone, but when I opened it up the screen had a big crack in it and it failed to light. I had apparently landed on it in the crash. The house phone was dead, too; no surprise after four years of weather like this. But I found a hook by the back door with a set of keys dangling from it, so I took them outside and tried them in the vehicles.

There was a hovercar and a four-wheeled pickup truck in the driveway. The hovercar was as dead as the phone, but the pickup lurched forward when I turned the key. I pushed in the clutch and tried again, and was rewarded with the whine of a flywheel winding up to speed. The power gauge read low, but I didn't think I'd need much just to reach Jody and come back.

While the flywheel spun up I checked in the glove box for a working phone, but all I found were a bunch of wrenches and fuses. That wasn't reassuring. I let out the clutch slowly and the truck began to roll forward, though, so I steered it around the driveway and began to bounce and spin my way up toward the highway. I'd heard it was easy to get a wheeled vehicle stuck in snow, so I figured I should drive on roads as much as I could until I got close enough to try driving cross-country.

It was a good idea, and it would have worked if there hadn't been a big drift about a kilometer down the road where it crossed the bottom of the valley and began to climb the other side. I realized too late that the road didn't rise up with the terrain, and by the time the pickup nosed into the bank, shuddered as it dug itself in a few more meters and came to a stop, it was thoroughly stuck. I couldn't back out or go forward, not even when I left it in gear and got out and pushed.

Of course there was no shovel in the truck. I would have to go back to the house to get one. Cursing my stupidity in not thinking ahead, I followed the tire tracks back the way I had come.

It was starting to get dark by the time I reached the house again, so I prowled through the kitchen drawers until I found a flashlight that worked, then went out to the barn and found a shovel. I jogged back to the truck and started digging it out, hoping Jody wasn't too worried that I hadn't come back yet. She was only a kilometer or two away; if I was careful not to get stuck again I could be there in a few minutes.

I had just dug a path for the left wheel and was starting in on the right when I saw a bright light descending toward me from the south. It slid on past, still dropping, right toward the car. Dave.

"Well I'll be damned," I said aloud. "He actually came." I leaned back against the pickup for a moment, catching my breath. I didn't have to break my back at it now; he and Jody would probably be coming for me pretty soon.

If they could find me. My tracks would be pretty hard to follow in a hovercar, and if they missed the farmhouse then they could very easily miss me out on the road in a pickup.

I reached inside and turned on the headlights. That would help. But I started digging again, too.

Ten minutes later I finished the other wheel track. They still hadn't come for me. I climbed into the pickup, put it in forward, and let out the clutch, but it didn't budge.

Back outside with the shovel, this time digging the snow out from underneath. It took another fifteen minutes. When I tried it again the truck moved a little, and I rocked it back and forth until it started rolling, then drove on up the road as fast as I could. Something wasn't right.

Dave had left his landing light on. As soon as I came up over the edge of the valley I saw it, shining straight at our overturned car. I could see a figure standing beside it, but I couldn't tell if it was Dave or Jody.

The road curved the wrong way. Cursing my luck, I gunned the pickup and swerved off the road, bouncing over rocks and sagebrush and trying to steer whenever the wheels touched ground. The tires spun and the flywheel motor screeched in protest, but I kept the throttle all the way to the floor and held on while the pickup bounced toward the two air cars. As I drew closer I could see that it was Dave standing in the light, and Jody was lying flat on the ground in front of him. She wasn't moving.

I popped open the glove box just as the truck hit a hard bump, scattering wrenches all over the seat and floor. I snatched one of the bigger ones in my right hand as I skidded to a stop beside Dave's car, leaped out with it upraised, and shouted, "What have you done to her?"

He didn't even try to defend himself. He just stood there with a beatific smile on his face and said, "Go ahead. It won't matter. I'll even tell God it was justified."

"God ain't the guy you'll be talking with," I said. I raised the wrench to cave in his head, but with him just standing there I found that I couldn't do it. Not even with Jody lying before us on the ground.

He'd taken off her coat and gloves. Her face and hands were white as the snow, and no breath rose from her open mouth.

"We should have realized right away that one of us would have to go get Him for the rest of us," Dave told me as I bent down to feel her neck for a pulse. "I would have gone myself once I figured it out, but Jody was already so close I figured she might as well be the one. It really doesn't matter."

I didn't see any wounds other than the one on her forehead. She must have been unconscious when he arrived, or he'd stunned her somehow. I couldn't find a pulse, but my fingers were so cold from digging snow that I probably couldn't have found my own. I bent down and felt for breath against my cheek, but there was none. Not knowing what else to do, I covered her mouth with mine and blew a breath into her lungs.

Dave grabbed me by the collar. "No, I can't allow that. You can't bring her back until we're sure she's done the job."

In one quick motion I stood up and smacked him in the left temple with the flat of the wrench. His head jerked sideways, and he fell over backwards with a thump that swirled snow up around him. I bent back down to Jody.

Five compressions of the chest, breath, five compressions of the chest, breath, over and over again. Sometime between forever and an eternity later, she shuddered, gasped a breath on her own, and moaned.

I whooped with joy, lifted her up in my arms, and carried her over to Dave's car, where I set her in the passenger seat and turned the heater up all the way.

I ran around to the other side and climbed in. She woke with a scream when I slammed the door, then she saw it was me and slumped back in the seat. "Christ you scared me," she said. "I had a hell of a crazy dre—wait a minute." She looked around at the car, a much bigger one than what we'd been flying.

"This is Dave's car," she said after a moment. "He did come."

"That's right, and he dragged you outside to die, too." I looked out to make sure he was still lying where he'd dropped. I had just enough time to realize he wasn't when the door beside me popped open and he stood there with my wrench in his hand.

I lunged for the lift controls, but he reached across me and rapped my hand with the wrench before the car even began to move. "No you don't," he said. "Get out. We're going to finish this experiment one way or another."

I cradled my suddenly numb right hand in my left, wondering if I could clench it into a fist, and whether I could do any good with it if I could.

Jody leaned over so he could see her. "It's already finished," she said.

"What do you mean? It can't be. You're still alive."

She laughed. "I'm alive again, idiot. I was dead. I was there. I saw your precious gates to Heaven, and they're slammed tight."

"You did?" I asked.

"They are?" asked Dave.

"Yup." Jody's eyes held a spark of elemental fire as she looked at him.

Dave let the wrench drop to the ground. In a subdued voice, he said, "Let me in. It's cold out here."

I thought about it a moment, much preferring the idea of leaving him outside a while longer, but Jody said, "Go ahead, I've got something I want to tell him," so I tilted my seat forward and let him climb in back. The moment he sat down I pulled on the lift control and took us straight up a hundred meters or so.

"Where are you going?" he asked.

"High enough to make you think twice about trying something cute," I replied.

"He won't try anything," Jody said. "Not now or ever again."

"What makes you so sure?" I asked.

She grinned like a whole pack of wolves surrounding a deer. "Because if he does, he might get hurt, and if you think it's lonely on this side of the great divide, wait 'til you see what's waiting for us over there."

"What?" Dave asked, leaning forward between the seats. "What did you find?"

She got a faraway look in her eyes. "I found the place where Heaven used to be. At the end of a long tunnel of light. There weren't gates really; it was more of a…a place. It's hard to describe physically. But I could tell that was where I was supposed to go, and I could tell it was closed."

"Permanently?" Dave asked.

"It felt that way. There was just the memory of a doorway, no promise of one to come. So I turned around to come back, but I couldn't find the way at first. I wandered around quite a while before I stumbled across it. If Gregor hadn't kept my body going, I don't think I would have found it."

"Wandered around where?" Dave demanded. "What was it like?"

"Like fog," Jody said. Her voice picked up a tremor as she added, "I was just a viewpoint in a formless, shapeless, gray fog. There wasn't any sound, any smell; I didn't even have a body to hear or smell or feel with. I don't even know if I was actually seeing anything. There was nothing there to see."

"Then how did you know where your body was?"

"How do you know where your chin is? It was just there." Jody turned away from him and leaned back in her seat. "Look, I'm tired and my head hurts and I've been dead once too often today. I just want to get some rest. I'll tell you all about it tomorrow."

I took the hint and flew us away in search of a hospital.

Later, after we'd bandaged her head and made sure she had no other injuries, we took the bridal suite at the top of the Fort Collins Hilton. Dave was in one of the rooms down below. I'd wanted to put him in the city jail, but Jody wouldn't let me.

"His teeth are pulled," she told me as we lay in the enormous bed, a dozen blankets pulled over us for warmth and as many candles providing light. "He'll believe anything I tell him now. Besides, we need him. The best thing we can do is treat him like a recovering alcoholic or something and just integrate him back into our lives as fast as we can."

"Integrate him back into our lives?" I asked incredulously. "After what he did to you? He murdered you. You were dead!"

She giggled. "Well, I'm not so sure about that."

"Huh? What about the tunnel of light, and the gates to Heaven and all that?"

She lowered her voice to a whisper. "That was all total vacuum. I told him what he wanted to hear. Well, what I wanted him to hear, anyway."

I stared at her in the flickering candlelight, dumbfounded.

She shrugged. "I don't remember a thing from the moment Dave knocked me out until the moment I woke up with you next to me."

"You don't?"

"No."

"You're one hell of an actress, then."

"Good, because I want him convinced."

I thought about that. "Even if we aren't?" I asked after a while.

"What?"

"You want Dave convinced, but we're still in the same shape we were before. We don't know anything at all about what's waiting for us after we die."

She giggled again and snuggled up closer to me under the covers. "Then God is just, if He exists," she said. "After all, I'm agnostic. I wouldn't have it any other way."

MUTE

BY GENE WOLFE

Gene Wolfe—who is perhaps best known for his multi-volume epic, *The Book of the New Sun*—is the author of more than 200 short stories and thirty novels, is a multiple winner of both the Nebula and World Fantasy Award, and was once praised as "the greatest writer in the English Language alive today" by author Michael Swanwick. His most recent novels are *The Sorcerer's House*, *Home Fires*, and *The Land Across*.

This story is about two children who return home, find an empty house, and are forced to grow up in a hurry. It first appeared in the program book for the 2002 World Horror Convention, where Wolfe was guest of honor.

In that same program book, Neil Gaiman offered up some advice on how to read Gene Wolfe. The first two points of his essay were:

(1) Trust the text implicitly. The answers are in there.

(2) Do not trust the text farther than you can throw it, if that far. It's tricksy and desperate stuff, and it may go off in your hand at any time.

Keep that in mind when you're reading this story. And when you're done, you might want to heed Gaiman's third point as well: "Reread. It's better the second time."

Jill was not certain it was a bus at all, although it was shaped like a bus and of a bus-like color. To begin with (she said to herself) Jimmy and I are the only people. If it's a school bus, why aren't there other kids? And if it's a pay-when-you-get-on bus, why doesn't anybody get on? Besides there was a sign that said BUS STOP, and it didn't.

The road was narrow, cracked and broken; the bus negotiated it slowly. Trees closed above it to shut out the sun, relented for a moment or two, then closed again.

As it seemed, forever.

There were no cars on the road, no trucks or SUVs, and no other buses. They passed a rusty sign with a picture of a girl on a horse, but there were no girls and no horses. A deer with wide, innocent eyes stood beside a sign showing a leaping buck and watched their bus (if it really was a bus) rumble past. It reminded Jill of a picture in a book: a little girl with long blond hair with her arm around the neck of just such a deer. That girl was always meeting bad animals and horrible, ugly people; and it seemed to Jill that the artist had been nice to give her this respite. Jill looked at the other pictures with horrified fascination, then turned to this one with a sense of relief. There were bad things, but there were good things too.

"Do you remember the knight falling off his horse?" she whispered to her brother.

"You never saw a knight, Jelly. Me neither."

"In my book. Most of the people that girl met were awful, but she liked the knight and he liked—"

The driver's voice cut through hers. "Right over yonder's where your ma's buried." He pointed, coughing. Jill tried to see it, and saw only trees.

After that she tried to remember Mother. No clear image would come, no tone of voice or remembered words. There had been a mother. Their mother. Her mother. She had loved her mother, and Mother had loved her. She would hold on to that, she promised herself. They could not bury that.

Trees gave way to a stone wall pierced by a wide gate of twisted bars, a gate flanked by stone pillars on which stone lions crouched and glared. An iron sign on the iron bars read POPLAR HILL.

Gate, sign, pillars, and lions were gone almost before she could draw breath. The stone wall ran on and on, with trees in front of it and more trees behind it. Alders in front, she decided, and maples and birches in back. No poplars.

"Did I ever read your storybook?"

She shook her head.

"I didn't think so. I was always going to, but I never got around to it. Was it good?"

Seeing her expression, he put his arm around her. "It's not gone forever, Jelly. Okay? Maybe they'll send it."

When she had dried her eyes, the bus had left the road and was creeping up a narrow winding drive between trees. It slowed for a curve, slowed more. Turned again. Through the windshield she glimpsed a big house. A man in a tweed jacket stood in what seemed to be its back doorway, smoking a pipe.

The driver coughed and spat. "This here's your papa's place," he announced. "He'll be around somewhere, and glad to see you. You be good kids so he's not sorry he was glad, you hear?"

Jill nodded.

The bus coasted to a stop and its door opened. "This's where you get out. Don't you forget them bags."

She would not have forgotten hers without the reminder. It held all the worldly goods she had been allowed to take, and she picked it up without difficulty. Her brother preceded her out of the bus carrying his own bag, and the door shut behind them.

She stared at the back door of the house. It was closed. "Dad was here," she said. "I saw him."

"I didn't," her brother said.

"He was standing in the door waiting for us."

Her brother shrugged. "Maybe the phone rang."

Behind them the bus backed up, pulled forward, backed a second time, and started down the drive. Jill waved. "Wait! Wait a minute!"

If its driver heard her, there was no sign of it.

"We ought to go in the house." Her brother strode away. "He might be in there waiting for us."

"Maybe it's locked." Reluctantly, Jill followed him.

It was not, and was not even closed enough to latch. There were leaves on the floor of the big kitchen, as though the door had stood open for hours while the wind blew. Jill pushed it solidly shut behind her.

"He might be" (her brother's voice cracked) "in front."

"If he was talking on the phone, we'd hear him."

"Not if the other person was talking." Her brother had already seen enough of the kitchen. "Come on."

She did not. There was an electric stove whose burners glowed crimson then fiery scarlet, a refrigerator containing a pound of cheese and two bottles of beer, and a pantry full of cans. There were dishes, pots, pans, knives, spoons, and forks in plenty.

Her brother returned. "The TV's on in the front room, but there's nobody there."

"Dad has to be around somewhere," Jill said. "I saw him."

"I didn't."

"Well, I did."

She followed her brother down a wide hall with high, dark windows on one side, past the big door to a big dining room where no one sat eating, and into a living room in which half a dozen drivers might have parked half a dozen buses, full of sunshine. "A man did this," she said, looking around.

"Did what?"

"In here. A man picked out this furniture, the rugs, and everything."

Her brother pointed. "Have a look over there. There's a chair made out of horns. I think that's hot."

She nodded. "So do I. Only I wouldn't have bought it. A room is—it's a frame, and the people in it are the pictures."

"You're crazy."

"No, I'm not." She shook her head in self-defense.

"You're saying Dad got this stuff to make him look good."

"To make him look right. You can't make people look good. If they don't, they don't. That's all there is to it. But you can make them look right and that's more important. Everybody looks right in the right place. If you had a picture of Dad—"

"I don't."

"If you did. And you were going to get a frame for it. The man in the frame store says take any of these you want. Would you take a pretty black one with silver flowers?"

"Heck no!"

"There you are. But I'd like a picture of me in a frame like that."

Her brother smiled. "I'll do it someday, Jelly. Did you notice the TV?"

She nodded. "I saw it as soon as we came in. Only you can't hear what that man's saying, because it's on mute."

"So he could talk on the phone, maybe."

"In another room?" The telephone was on an end table near the television; she lifted the receiver and held it to her ear.

"What's wrong? Could you hear him?"

"No." Gently, she returned the receiver to its cradle. "There's no noise at all. It's not hooked up."

"He's not on a phone in another room, then."

It was not logical, but she felt too drained to argue.

"I don't think he's here at all," her brother said.

"The TV is on." She sat down in a chair, bare waxed wood and brown-and-orange cushions. "Did you turn on these lights?"

Her brother shook his head.

"Besides, I saw him. He was standing in the door."

"Okay." Her brother was silent for a moment. He

was tall and blond, like Dad, with a face that was already beginning to discover that it had been made for seriousness. "I'd have heard the car if he went away. I've been listening for something like that."

"So have I." She sensed, although she did not say, that there was a presence in this empty house that made you listen. Listen, listen. All the time.

MUTE, said the screen, and made no sound.

"I'd like to know what that man on the TV's saying," she told her brother.

"It's on mute, and I can't find the remote. I looked."

She said nothing, snuggling back against the brown-and-orange cushion and staring at the screen. The chair made her feel that she was enclosed by some defense, however small.

"Want me to change the channel?"

"You said you couldn't find the changer."

"There's buttons." He swung back a hinged panel at the side of the screen. "On and off. Channel up and channel down, volume up and volume down. Only no Mute button."

"We don't need a Mute button," she whispered, "we need an Unmute button."

"Want to change the channel? Look."

The next channel was a gray screen with wavy lines and the yellow word mute in one corner, but the next one after it had a pretty, friendly looking woman sitting at a table and talking. The yellow MUTE was in the corner of her screen, too. She had a very sharp yellow pencil in her hands, and she played with it as she talked. Jill wished that she would write something instead, but she did not.

The next channel showed an almost empty street, and

the yellow MUTE. The street was not quite empty because two people, a man and a woman, were lying down in it. They did not move.

"You want to watch this?"

Jill shook her head. "Go back to the man Dad was watching."

"The first one?"

She nodded, and channels flicked past.

"You like—" Her brother froze in mid-sentence. Seconds crept past, fearful and somehow guilty.

"I—"Jill began.

"*Shhh!* Someone's walking around upstairs. Hear it?" Her brother dashed out of the room.

She, who had heard nothing, murmured to herself, "I really don't like him at all. But he talks slower than the woman, and I think maybe I can learn to read his lips if I watch him long enough."

She tried, and searched for the control between times.

There had been no one upstairs, but there was a big bedroom there with two small beds, one against the east wall and one against the south, three windows, and two dressers. Her brother had wanted a room of his own; but she, terrified at the thought of lying alone in the dark, promised that the room would be his room and she would have no room—that she would sweep and dust his room for him every day, and make his bed for him.

Reluctantly, he consented.

They ate canned chili the first night, and oatmeal the next morning. The house, they found, had three floors and fourteen rooms—fifteen counting the pantry. The TV, which Jill had turned off when she had left the room to heat their supper, was on again, still on mute.

There was an attached garage, with two cars. Her brother spent all afternoon hunting for the keys to one or the other without finding them. Indeed, without finding any keys at all.

In the living room, the man who had been (silently) talking talked silently still, on and on. Jill spent most of her time watching him, and eventually concluded that he was on tape. His last remark (at which he looked down at the polished top of his desk) being followed by his first.

That evening, as she prepared Vienna sausages and canned potato salad, she heard her brother shout, "Dad!" The shout was followed by the banging of a door and the sound of her brother's running feet.

She ran too, and caught up with him as he was looking through a narrow doorway in the back hall. "I saw him!" he said. "He was standing there looking right at me."

The narrow doorway opened upon darkness and equally narrow wooden steps.

"Then I heard this slam. I know it was this one. It had to be!"

Jill looked down, troubled by a draft from the doorway that was surely cold, dank, and foul. "It looks like the basement," she said.

"It *is* the basement. I've been down here a couple times, only I never could find the light. I kept thinking I'd find a flashlight and come down again." Her brother started down the steps, and turned in surprise when a single dim bulb suspended from a wire came on. "How'd you do that, Jelly?"

"The switch is here in the hall, on the wall behind the door."

"Well, come on! Aren't you coming?"

She did. "I wish we were back at that place."

Her brother did not hear her. Or if he heard her, chose to ignore her. "He's down here somewhere, Jelly—he's got to be. With two of us, he can't hide very long."

"Isn't there any other way out?"

"I don't think so. Only I didn't stay long. It was really dark, and it smelled bad."

They found the source of that smell in back of a bank of freestanding shelves heaped with tools and paint cans. It was rotting and had stained its clothing. In places its flesh had fallen in, and in others had fallen away. Her brother cleared scrap wood, a garden sprayer, and half a dozen bottles and jugs from the shelves so that the light might better reach the dead thing on the floor; after a minute or two, Jill helped him.

When they had done all they could, he said, "Who was it?" and she whispered, "Dad."

After that, she turned away and went back up the stairs, washed her hands and arms at the kitchen sink, and sat at the table until she heard the basement door close and her brother came in. "Wash," she told him. "We ought to take baths, really. Both of us."

"Then let's do it."

There were two bathrooms upstairs. Jill used the one nearest their room, her brother the other. When she had bathed and dried herself, she put on a robe that had perhaps been her mother's once, hitching it up and knotting the sash tight to keep the hem off the floor. So attired, she carried their clothes downstairs and into the laundry room, and put them in the machine.

In the living room, the man whose lips she had tried

to read was gone. The screen was gray and empty now save for the single word MUTE in glowing yellow. She found the panel her brother had shown her. Other channels she tried were equally empty, equally gray, equally muted.

Her brother came in, in undershorts and shoes. "Aren't you going to eat?"

"Later," Jill said. "I don't feel like it."

"You mind if I do?"

She shrugged.

"You think that was Dad, don't you? What we found in the basement."

"Yes," she said, "I didn't know being dead was like that."

"I saw him. I didn't believe you did, that time. But I did, and he closed the basement door. I heard it."

She said nothing.

"You think we'll see him any more?"

"No."

"Just like that? He wanted us to find him, and we did, and that was all he wanted?"

"He was telling us that he was dead." Her voice was flat, expressionless. "He wanted us to know he wouldn't be around to help us. Now we do. You're going to eat?"

"Yeah."

"Wait just a minute and I'll eat with you. Did you know there isn't any more TV?"

"There wasn't any before," her brother said.

"I guess. Tomorrow I'm going out. You remember that gate we passed on the bus?"

He nodded. "Poplar Hill."

"That's it. I'm going to walk there. Maybe it will be unlocked to let cars in. If it isn't, I can probably get over the wall some way. There were a lot of trees, and it wasn't very high. I'd like it if you came with me, but if you won't I'm going to anyhow."

"We'll both go," he said. "Come on, let's eat."

They set out next morning, shutting the kitchen door but making very certain that it was unlocked, and walking down the long, curving drive the bus had climbed. When the house was almost out of sight, Jill stopped to look back at it. "It's sort of like we were running away from home," she said.

"We're not," her brother told her.

"I don't know."

"Well, I do. Listen, that's our house. Dad's dead, so it belongs to you and me."

"I don't want it," Jill said; and then, when the house was out of sight, "but it's the only home we've got."

The drive was long, but not impossibly so, and the highway—if it could be called a highway—stretched away to right and left at the end of it. Stretched silent and empty. "I was thinking if there were some cars, we could flag one down," her brother said. "Or maybe the bus will come by."

"There's grass in the cracks."

"Yeah, I know. This way, Jelly." He set out, looking as serious as always, and very, very determined.

She trotted behind. "Are you going into Poplar Hill with me?"

"If we can flag down a car first, or a truck or anything, I'm going with them if they'll take me. So are you."

She shook her head.

"But if we can't, I'm going to Poplar Hill like you say.

Maybe there's somebody there, and if there is, maybe they'll help us."

"I'll bet somebody is." She tried to sound more confident than she felt.

"There's no picture on the TV. I tried all the channels." He was three paces ahead of her, and did not look back.

"So did I." It was a lie, but she had tried several.

"It means there's nobody in the TV stations. Not in any of them." He cleared his throat, and his voice suddenly deepened, as the voices of adolescent boys will. "Nobody alive, anyhow."

"Maybe there's somebody alive who doesn't know how to work it," she suggested. After a moment's thought she added, "Maybe they don't have any electricity where they are."

He stopped and looked around at her. "We do."

"So people are still alive. That's what I said."

"Right! And it means a car might come past, and that's what *I* said."

A small bush, fresh and green, sprouted from a crevice in the middle of the highway. Seeing it, Jill sensed that some unknown and unknowable power had overheard them and was gently trying to show them that they were wrong. She shuddered, and summoned up all the good reasons that argued that the bush was wrong instead. "There were live people back at that place. The bus driver was all right, too."

The iron gates were still there, just as she had seen them the previous day, graceful and strong between their pillars of cut stone. The lions still snarled atop those pillars, and the iron sign on the iron bars still proclaimed POPLAR HILL.

"They're locked," her brother announced. He rattled the lock to show her—a husky brass padlock that looked new.

"We've got to get in."

"Sure. I'm going to go along this wall, see? I'm going to look for a place where I can climb over, or maybe it's fallen down somewhere. When I find one, I'll come back and tell you."

"I want to go with you." Fear had come like a chill wind. What if Jimmy went away and she never saw him again?

"Listen, back at the house you were going to do this all by yourself. If you could do it by yourself, you can stay here for ten minutes to watch for cars. Now *don't follow me!*"

She did not; but an hour later she was waiting for him when he came back along the inside of the wall, scratched and dirty and intent on speaking to her through the gate. "How'd you get in?" he asked when she appeared at his shoulder.

She shrugged. "You first. How did you?"

"I found a little tree that had died and fallen over. It was small enough that I could drag it if I didn't try to pick up the root end. I leaned it on the wall and climbed up it, and jumped down."

"Then you can't get out," she told him, and started up a road leading away from the gate.

"I'll find some way. How did you get in?"

"Through the bars. It was tight and scrapy, though. I don't think you could." Somewhat maliciously, she added, "I've been waiting in here a long time."

The private road led up a hill between rows of slender trees that made her think of models showing off green gowns. The big front door of the big square house at the top of the hill was locked; and the big brass knocker produced only empty echoes from inside the house no matter how hard her brother pounded. The pretty pearl-colored button that she pressed sounded distant chimes that brought no one.

Peering though the window to the left of the door, she saw a mostly wooden chair with brown-and-orange cushions, and a gray TV screen. One corner of the gray screen read MUTE in bright yellow letters.

Circling the house they found the kitchen door unlocked, as they had left it. She was heaping corned beef hash out of her frying pan when the lights went out.

"That means no more hot food," she told her brother. "It's electric. My stove is."

"They'll come back on," he said confidently, but they did not.

That night she undressed in the dark bedroom they had made their own, in the lightless house, folding clothes she could not see and laying them as neatly as her fingers could manage upon an invisible chair before slipping between the sheets.

Warm and naked, her brother followed her half a minute later. "You know, Jelly," he said as he drew her to him, "we're probably the only live people in the whole world."

INERTIA

BY NANCY KRESS

Nancy Kress is the author of thirty-two books, including twenty-five novels, four collections of short stories, and three books about writing. Her work has won two Hugos ("Beggars in Spain" and "The Erdmann Nexus"), four Nebulas (all for short fiction), a Sturgeon ("The Flowers of Aulit Prison"), and a John W. Campbell Memorial award (for *Probability Space*). The novels include science fiction, fantasy, and thrillers; many concern genetic engineering. Her most recent works are the Nebula-winning and Hugo-nominated *After the Fall, Before the Fall, During the Fall* (Tachyon, 2012), a long novella of eco-disaster, time travel, and human resiliency and another short novel from Tachyon, *Yesterday's Kin* (Fall 2014).

"Inertia" tells the story of the victims of a disfiguring epidemic who are interned in the modern equivalent of leper colonies. Kress says that identity—who you are, why you're here, why you are who you are (and what you are supposed to be doing about it)—is a central idea in her work, and this story is no exception.

At dusk the back of the bedroom falls off. One minute it's a wall, exposed studs and cracked blue drywall, and the next it's snapped-off two-by-fours and an irregular fence as high as my waist, the edges both jagged and furry, as if they were covered with powder. Through the hole a sickly tree pokes upward in the narrow space between the back of our barracks and the back of a barracks in E Block. I try to get out of bed for a closer look, but today my arthritis is too bad, which is why I'm in bed in the first place. Rachel rushes into the bedroom.

"What happened, Gram? Are you all right?"

I nod and point. Rachel bends into the hole, her hair haloed by California twilight. The bedroom is hers, too; her mattress lies stored under my scarred four-poster.

"Termites! Damn. I didn't know we had them. You sure you're all right?"

"I'm fine. I was all the way across the room, honey. I'm fine."

"Well—we'll have to get Mom to get somebody to fix it."

I say nothing. Rachel straightens, throws me a quick glance, looks away. Still I say nothing about Mamie, but in a sudden flicker from my oil lamp I look directly at Rachel, just because she is so good to look at. Not pretty, not even here Inside, although so far the disease has affected only the left side of her face. The ridge of thickened, ropy skin, coarse as old hemp, isn't visible at all when she stands in right profile. But her nose is large, her eyebrows heavy and low, her chin a bony knob. An honest nose, expressive brows, direct gray eyes, chin that juts forward when she tilts her head in intelligent listening—to a grandmother's eye, Rachel is good to look at. They wouldn't think so, Outside. But they would be wrong.

Rachel says, "Maybe I could trade a lottery card for more drywall and nails, and patch it myself."

"The termites will still be there."

"Well, yes, but we have to do something." I don't contradict her. She is sixteen years old. "Feel that air coming in—you'll freeze at night this time of year. It'll be terrible for your arthritis. Come in the kitchen now, Gram—I've built up the fire."

She helps me into the kitchen, where the metal wood-burning stove throws a rosy warmth that feels good on my joints. The stove was donated to the colony a year ago by who-knows-what charity or special interest group for, I suppose, whatever tax breaks still hold for that sort of thing. If any do. Rachel tells me that we still get newspapers, and once or twice I've wrapped vegetables from our patch in some fairly new-looking ones. She even says that the young Stevenson boy works a donated computer news net in the Block J community hall, but I no longer follow Outside tax regulations. Nor do I ask why Mamie was the one to get the wood-burning stove when it wasn't a lottery month.

The light from the stove is stronger than the oil flame in the bedroom; I see that beneath her concern for our dead bedroom wall, Rachel's face is flushed with excitement. Her young skin glows right from intelligent chin to the ropy ridge of disease, which of course never changes color. I smile at her. Sixteen is so easy to excite. A new hair ribbon from the donations repository, a glance from a boy, a secret with her cousin Jennie.

"Gram," she says, kneeling beside my chair, her hands restless on the battered wooden arm, "Gram—there's a visitor. From Outside. Jennie saw him."

I go on smiling. Rachel—nor Jennie, either—can't remember when disease colonies had lots of visitors. First bulky figures in contamination suits, then a few years later, sleeker figures in the sani-suits that took their place. People were still being interred from Outside, and for years the checkpoints at the Rim had traffic flowing both ways. But of course Rachel doesn't remember all that; she wasn't born. Mamie was only twelve when we were interred here. To Rachel, a visitor might well be a great event. I put out one hand and stroke her hair.

"Jennie said he wants to talk to the oldest people in the colony, the ones who were brought here with the disease. Hal Stevenson told her."

"Did he, sweetheart?" Her hair is soft and silky. Mamie's hair had been the same at Rachel's age.

"He might want to talk to you!"

"Well, here I am."

"But aren't you excited? What do you suppose he wants?"

I'm saved from answering her because Mamie comes in, her boyfriend Peter Malone following with a string-bag of groceries from the repository.

At the first sound of the doorknob turning, Rachel gets up from beside my chair and pokes at the fire. Her face goes completely blank, although I know that part is only temporary. Mamie cries, "Here we are!" in her high, doll-baby voice, cold air from the hall swirling around her like bright water. "Mama darling—how are you feeling? And Rachel! You'll never guess—Pete had extra depository cards and he got us some chicken! I'm going to make a stew!"

"The back wall fell off the bedroom," Rachel says flatly. She doesn't look at Peter with his string-crossed chicken, but I do. He grins his patient, wolfish grin. I guess that he won the depository cards at poker. His fingernails are dirty. The part of the newspaper I can see says ESIDENT CONFISCATES C.

Mamie says, "What do you mean, 'fell off'?'"

Rachel shrugs. "Just fell off. Termites."

Mamie looks helplessly at Peter, whose grin widens. I can see how it will be: They will have a scene later, not completely for our benefit, although it will take place in the kitchen for us to watch. Mamie will beg prettily for Peter to fix the wall. He will demur, grinning. She will offer various smirking hints about barter, each hint becoming more explicit. He will agree to fix the wall. Rachel and I, having no other warm room to go to, will watch the fire or the floor or our shoes until Mamie and Peter retire ostentatiously to her room. It's the ostentation that embarrasses us. Mamie has always needed witnesses to her desirability.

But Peter is watching Rachel, not Mamie. "The chicken isn't from Outside, Rachel. It's from that chicken-yard in Block B. I heard you say how clean they are."

"Yeah," Rachel says shortly, gracelessly.

Mamie rolls her eyes. "Say 'thank you,' darling. Pete went to a lot of trouble to get this chicken."

"Thanks."

"Can't you say it like you mean it?" Mamie's voice goes shrill.

"Thanks," Rachel says. She heads towards our three-walled bedroom. Peter, still watching her closely, shifts the chicken from one hand to the other. The pressure of the string bag cuts lines across the chicken's yellowish skin.

"Rachel Anne Wilson—"

"Let her go," Peter says softly.

"No," Mamie says. Between the five crisscrossing lines of disease, her face sets in unlovely lines. "She can at least learn some manners. And I want her to hear our announcement! Rachel, you just come right back out here this minute!"

Rachel returns from the bedroom; I've never known her to disobey her mother. She pauses by the open bedroom door, waiting. Two empty candle scones, both blackened by old smoke, frame her head. It has been since at least last winter that we've had candles for them. Mamie, her forehead creased in irritation, smiles brightly.

"This is a special dinner, all of you. Pete and I have an announcement. We're going to get married."

"That's right," Peter says. "Congratulate us."

Rachel, already motionless, somehow goes even stiller. Peter watches her carefully. Mamie casts down her eyes, blushing, and I feel a stab of impatient pity for my daughter, propping up mid-thirties girlishness on such a slender reed as Peter Malone. I stare at him hard. If he ever touches Rachel...but I don't really think he would. Things like that don't happen anymore. Not Inside.

"Congratulations," Rachel mumbles. She crosses the room and embraces her mother, who hugs her back with theatrical fervor. In another minute, Mamie will start to cry. Over her shoulder I glimpse Rachel's face, momentarily sorrowing and loving, and I drop my eyes.

"Well! This calls for a toast!" Mamie cries gaily. She winks, makes a clumsy pirouette, and pulls a bottle from the back shelf of the cupboard Rachel got at the last donations lottery. The cupboard looks strange in our kitchen: gleaming white lacquer, vaguely Oriental-looking, amid the wobbly chairs and scarred table with the broken drawer no one has ever gotten around to mending. Mamie flourishes the bottle, which I didn't know was there. It's champagne.

What had they been thinking, the Outsiders who donated champagne to a disease colony? Poor devils, even if they never have anything to celebrate…Or here's something they won't know what to do with…Or better them than me—as long as the sickies stay Inside…It doesn't really matter.

"I just love champagne!" Mamie cries feverishly; I think she has drunk it once. "And oh look—here's someone else to help us celebrate! Come in, Jennie—come in and have some champagne!"

Jennie comes in, smiling. I see the same eager excitement that animated Rachel before her mother's announcement. It glows on Jennie's face, which is beautiful. She has no disease on her hands or her face. She must have it somewhere, she was born Inside, but one doesn't ask that. Probably Rachel knows. The two girls are inseparable. Jennie, the daughter of Mamie's dead husband's brother, is Rachel's cousin, and technically Mamie is her guardian. But no one pays attention to such things anymore, and Jennie lives with some people in a barracks in the next Block, although Rachel and I asked her to live here. She shook her head, the beautiful hair so blonde it's almost white bouncing on her shoulders, and blushed in embarrassment, painfully not looking at Mamie.

"I'm getting married, Jennie," Mamie says, again casting down her eyes bashfully. I wonder what she did, and with whom, to get the champagne.

"Congratulations!" Jennie says warmly. "You, too, Peter."

"Call me Pete," he says, as he has said before. I catch his hungry look at Jennie. She doesn't, but some sixth sense—even here, even Inside—makes her step slightly backwards. I know she will go on calling him "Peter."

Mamie says to Jennie, "Have some more champagne. Stay for dinner."

With her eyes Jennie measures the amount of champagne in the bottle, the size of the chicken bleeding slightly on the table. She measures unobtrusively, and then of course she lies. "I'm sorry, I can't—we ate our meal at noon today. I just wanted to ask if I could bring someone over to see you later, Gram. A visitor." Her voice drops to a hush, and the glow is back. "From Outside."

I look at her sparkling blue eyes, at Rachel's face, and I don't have the heart to refuse. Even though I can guess, as the two girls cannot, how the visit will be. I am not Jennie's grandmother, but she has called me that since she was three. "All right."

"Oh, thank you!" Jennie cries, and she and Rachel look at each other with delight. "I'm so glad you said yes, or else we might never get to talk to a visitor up close at all!"

"You're welcome," I say. They are so young. Mamie looks petulant; her announcement has been upstaged. Peter watches Jennie as she impulsively hugs Rachel. Suddenly I know that he too is wondering where Jennie's body is diseased, and how much. He catches my eye and looks at the floor, his dark eyes lidded, half-ashamed. But only half. A log cackles in the wooden stove, and for a brief moment the fire flares.

The next afternoon Jennie brings the visitor. He surprises me immediately: he isn't wearing a sani-suit, and he isn't a sociologist.

In the years following the internments, the disease colonies had a lot of visitors. Doctors still hopeful of a cure for the thick gray ridges of skin that spread slowly over a human body—or didn't, nobody knew why. Disfiguring. Ugly. Maybe eventually fatal. And communicable. That was the biggie: communicable. So doctors in sani-suits came looking for causes or cures. Journalists in sani-suits came looking for stories with four-color photo spreads. Legislative fact-finding committees in sani-suits came looking for facts, at least until Congress took away the power of colonies to vote, pressured by taxpayers who, increasingly pressured themselves, resented our dollar-dependent status. And the sociologists came in droves, minicams in hand, ready to record the collapse of the ill-organized and ill colonies into street-gang, dog-eat-dog anarchy.

Later, when this did not happen, different sociologists came in later-model sani-suits to record the reasons why the colonies were not collapsing on schedule. All these groups went away dissatisfied. There was no cure, no cause, no story, no collapse, no reasons.

The sociologists hung on longer than anybody else. Journalists have to be timely and interesting, but sociologists merely have to publish. Besides, everything in their cultural tradition told them that Inside must sooner or later degenerate into war zones: Deprive people of electricity (power became expensive), of municipal police (who refused to go Inside), of freedom to leave, of political clout, of jobs, of freeways and movie theaters and federal judges and state-administered elementary-school accreditation—and you get unrestrained violence to just survive. Everything in the culture said so. Bombed-out inner cities. Lord of the Flies. The Chicago projects. Western movies. Prison memoirs. The Bronx. East L.A. Thomas Hobbes. The sociologists knew.

Only it didn't happen.

The sociologists waited. And Inside we learned to grow vegetables and raise chickens who, we learned, will eat anything. Those of us with computer knowledge worked real jobs over modems for a few years—maybe it was as long as a decade—before the equipment became too obsolete and unreplaced. Those who had been teachers organized classes among the children, although the curriculum, I think, must have gotten simpler every year: Rachel and Jennie don't seem to have much knowledge of history or science. Doctors practiced with medicines donated by corporations for the tax write-offs, and after a decade or so they began to train apprentices. For a while—it might have been a long while—we listened to radios and watched TV. Maybe some people still do, if we have any working ones donated from Outside.

Eventually the sociologists remembered older models of deprivation and discrimination and isolation from the larger culture: Jewish shtetls. French Huguenots. Amish farmers. Self-sufficient models, stagnant but uncollapsed. And while they were remembering, we held goods lotteries, and took on apprentices, and rationed depository food according to who needed it, and replaced our broken-down furniture with other broken-down furniture, and got married and bore children. We paid no taxes, fought no wars, wielded no votes, provided no drama. After a while—a long while—the visitors stopped coming. Even the sociologists.

But here stands this young man, without a sani-suit, smiling from brown eyes under thick dark hair and taking my hand. He doesn't wince when he touches the ropes of disease. Nor does he appear to be cataloguing the kitchen furniture for later recording: three chairs, one donated imitation Queen Anne and one Inside genuine Joe Kleinschmidt; the table; the wood stove; the sparkling new Oriental lacquered cupboard; plastic sink with hand pump connected to the reservoir pipe from Outside; woodbox with donated wood stamped "Gift of Boise-Cascade"; two eager and intelligent and loving young girls he had better not try to patronize as diseased freaks. It has been a long time, but I remember.

"Hello, Mrs. Pratt. I'm Tom McHabe. Thank you for agreeing to talk to me."

I nod. "What are we going to talk about, Mr. McHabe? Are you a journalist?"

"No. I'm a doctor."

I didn't expect that. Nor do I expect the sudden strain that flashes across his face before it's lost in another smile. Although it is natural enough that strain should be there: Having come Inside, of course, he can never leave. I wonder where he picked up the disease. No other new cases have been admitted to our colony for as long as I could remember. Had they been taken, for some Outside political reason, to one of the other colonies instead?

McHabe says, "I don't have the disease, Mrs. Pratt."

"Then why on earth—"

"I'm writing a paper on the progress of the disease in long-established colony residents. I have to do that from Inside, of course," he says, and immediately I know he is lying. Rachel and Jennie, of course, do not. They sit one on each side of him like eager birds, listening.

"And how will you get this paper out once it's written?" I said.

"Short-wave radio. Colleagues are expecting it," but he doesn't quite meet my eyes.

"And this paper is worth permanent internment?"

"How rapidly did your case of the disease progress?" he says, not answering my question. He looks at my face and hands and forearms, an objective and professional scrutiny that makes me decide at least one part of his story is true. He is a doctor.

"Any pain in the infected areas?"

"None."

"Any functional disability or decreased activity as a result of the disease?" Rachel and Jennie look slightly puzzled; he's testing me to see if I understand the terminology.

"None."

"Any change in appearance over the last few years in the first skin areas to be affected? Changes in color or tissue density or size of the thickened ridges?"

"None."

"Any other kinds of changes I haven't thought to mention?"

"None."

He nods and rocks back on his heels. He's cool, for someone who is going to develop non-dysfunctional ropes of disease himself. I wait to see if he's going to tell me why he's really here. The silence lengthens. Finally McHabe says, "You were a CPA," at the same time that Rachel says, "Anyone want a glass of 'ade?"

McHabe accepts gladly. The two girls, relieved to be in motion, busy themselves pumping cold water, crushing canned peaches, mixing the 'ade in a brown plastic pitcher with a deep wart on one side where it once touched the hot stove.

"Yes," I say to McHabe, "I was a CPA. What about it?"

"They're outlawed now."

"CPAs? Why? Staunch pillars of the establishment," I say, and realize how long it's been since I used words like that. They taste metallic, like old tin.

"Not anymore. IRS does all tax computations and sends every household a customized bill. The calculations on how they reach your particular customized figure is classified. To prevent foreign enemies from guessing at revenue available for defense."

"Ah."

"My uncle was a CPA."

"What is he now?"

"Not a CPA," McHabe says. He doesn't smile. Jennie hands glasses of 'ade to me and then to McHabe, and then he does smile. Jennie drops her lashes and a little color steals into her cheeks. Something moves behind McHabe's eyes. But it's not like Peter; not at all like Peter.

I glance at Rachel. She doesn't seem to have noticed anything. She isn't jealous, or worried, or hurt. I relax a little.

McHabe says to me, "You also published some magazine articles popularizing history."

"How do you happen to know that?"

Again he doesn't answer me. "It's an unusual combination of abilities, accounting and history writing."

"I suppose so," I say, without interest. It was so long ago.

Rachel says to McHabe, "Can I ask you something?"

"Sure."

"Outside, do you have medicines that will cure wood of termites?"

Her face is deadly serious. McHabe doesn't grin, and I admit—reluctantly—that he is likable. He answers her courteously. "We don't cure the wood, we do away with the termites. The best way is to build with wood saturated with creosote, a chemical they don't like, so that they don't get into the wood in the first place. But there must be chemicals that will kill them after they're already there. I'll ask around and try to bring you something on my next trip Inside."

His next trip Inside. He drops this bombshell as if easy passage In and Out were a given. Rachel's and Jennie's eyes grow wide; they both look at me. McHabe does, too, and I see that his look is a cool scrutiny, an appraisal of my reaction. He expects me to ask for details, or maybe even—it's been a long time since I thought in these terms, and it's an effort—to become angry at him for lying. But I don't know whether or not he's lying, and at any rate, what does it matter? A few people from Outside coming into the colony—how could it affect us? There won't be large immigration, and no emigration at all.

I say quietly, "Why are you really here, Dr. McHabe?"

"I told you, Mrs. Pratt. To measure the progress of the disease." I say nothing. He adds, "Maybe you'd like to hear more about how it is now Outside."

"Not especially."

"Why not?"

I shrug. "They leave us alone."

He weighs me with his eyes. Jennie says timidly, "I'd like to hear more about Outside." Before Rachel can add "Me, too," the door flings violently open and Mamie backs into the room, screaming into the hall behind her.

"And don't ever come back! If you think I'd ever let you touch me again after screwing that…that…I hope she's got a diseased twat and you get it on your—" She sees McHabe and breaks off, her whole body jerking in rage. A soft answer from the hall, the words unintelligible from my chair by the fire, makes her gasp and turn even redder. She slams the door, bursts into tears, and runs into her bedroom, slamming that door as well.

Rachel stands up. "Let me, honey," I say, but before I can rise—my arthritis is much better—Rachel disappears into her mother's room. The kitchen rings with embarrassed silence.

Tom McHabe rises to leave. "Sit down, Doctor," I say, hoping, I think, that if he remains Mamie will restrain her hysterics—maybe—and Rachel will emerge sooner from her mother's room.

McHabe looks undecided. Then Jennie says, "Yes, please stay. And would you tell us—" I see her awkwardness, her desire to not sound stupid "—about how people do Outside?"

He does. Looking at Jennie but meaning me, he talks about the latest version of martial law, about the failure of the National Guard to control protestors against the South American war until they actually reached the edge of the White House electro-wired zone; about the growing power of the Fundamentalist underground that the other undergrounds—he uses the plural—call "the God gang." He tells us about the industries losing out steadily to Korean and Chinese competitors, the leaping unemployment rate, the ethnic backlash, the cities in flames. Miami. New York. Los Angeles—these had been rioting for years. Now it's Portland, St. Louis, Atlanta, Phoenix. Grand Rapids burning. It's hard to picture.

I say, "As far as I can tell, donations to our repositories haven't fallen off."

He looks at me again with that shrewd scrutiny, weighing something I can't see, then touches the edge of the stove with one boot. The boot, I notice, is almost as old and scarred as one of ours. "Korean-made stove. They make nearly all the donations now. Public relations. Even a lot of martial-law Congressmen had relatives interred, although they won't admit it now. The Asians cut deals warding off complete protectionism, although of course your donations are only a small part of that. But just about everything you get Inside is Chink or Splat." He uses the words casually, this courteous young man giving me the news from such a liberal slant, and that tells me more about the Outside than all his bulletins and summaries.

Jennie says haltingly, "I saw ... I think it was an Asian man. Yesterday."

"Where?" I say sharply. Very few Asian-Americans contract the disease; something else no one understands. There are none in our colony.

"At the Rim. One of the guards. Two other men were kicking him and yelling names at him—we couldn't hear too clearly over the intercom boxes."

"We? You and Rachel? What were you two doing at the

Rim?" I say, and heard my own tone. The Rim, a wide empty strip of land, is electro-mined and barb-wired to keep us communicables Inside. The Rim is surrounded by miles of defoliated and disinfected land, poisoned by preventive chemicals, but even so it's patrolled by unwilling soldiers who communicate with the Inside by intercoms set up every half-mile on both sides of the barbed wire. When the colony used to have a fight or a rape or—once, in the early years—a murder, it happened on the Rim. When the hateful and the hating came to hurt us because before the elecro-wiring and barbed wire we were easy targets and no police would follow them Inside, the soldiers, and sometimes our men as well, stopped them at the Rim. Our dead are buried near the Rim. And Rachel and Jennie, dear gods, at the Rim...

"We went to ask the guards over the intercom boxes if they knew how to stop termites," Jennie says logically. "After all, their work is to stop things, germs and things. We thought they might be able to tell us how to stop termites. We thought they might have special training in it."

The bedroom door opens and Rachel comes out, her young face drawn. McHabe smiles at her, and then his gaze returns to Jennie. "I don't think soldiers are trained in stopping termites, but I'll definitely bring you something to do that the next time I come Inside."

There it is again. But all Rachel says is, "Oh, good. I asked around for more drywall today, but even if I get some, the same thing will happen again if we don't get something to stop them."

McHabe says, "Did you know that termites elect a queen? Closely monitored balloting system. Fact."

Rachel smiles, although I don't think she really understands.

"And ants can bring down a rubber tree plant." He begins to sing, an old song from my childhood. "High Hopes." Frank Sinatra on the stereo—before CDs, even, before a lot of things—iced tea and Coke in tall glasses on a Sunday afternoon, aunts and uncles sitting around the kitchen, football on the television in the living room beside a table with a lead-crystal vase of the last purple chrysanthemums from the garden. The smell of late Sunday afternoon, tangy but a little thin, the last of the weekend before the big yellow schoolbus labored by on Monday morning.

Jennie and Rachel, of course, see none of this. They hear light-hearted words in a good baritone and a simple rhythm they could follow, hope and courage in silly doggerel. They are delighted. They join in the chorus after McHabe has sung it a few times, then sing him three songs popular at Block dances, then make him more 'ade, then begin to ask questions about the Outside. Simple questions: What did people eat? Where did they get it? What did they wear? The three of them are still at it when I go to bed, my arthritis finally starting to ache, glancing at Mamie's closed door with a sadness I hadn't expected and can't name.

"That son-of-a-bitch better never come near me again," Mamie says the next morning. The day is sunny and I sit by our one window, knitting a blanket to loosen my fingers, wondering if the donated wool came from Chinese or Korean sheep. Rachel has gone with Jennie on a labor call to deepen a well in Block E; people had been talking about doing that for weeks, and apparently someone finally got around to organizing it. Mamie slumps at the table, her eyes red from crying. "I caught him screwing Mary Delbarton." Her voice splinters like a two-year-old's. "Mama—he was screwing Mary Delbarton."

"Let him go, Mamie."

"I'd be alone again." She says it with a certain dignity, which doesn't last. "That son-of-a-bitch goes off with that slut one day after we're engaged and I'm fucking alone again!"

I don't say anything; there isn't anything to say. Mamie's husband died eleven years ago, when Rachel was only five, of an experimental cure being tested by government doctors. The colonies were guinea pigs. Seventeen people in four colonies died, and the government discontinued funding and made it a crime for anyone to go in and out of a disease colony. Too great a risk of contamination, they said. For the protection of the citizens of the country.

"He'll never touch me again!" Mamie says, tears on her lashes. One slips down an inch until it hits the first of the disease ropes, then travels sideways towards her mouth. I reach over and wipe it away. "Goddamn fucking son-of-a-bitch!"

By evening, she and Peter are holding hands. They sit side by side, and his fingers creep up her thigh under what they think is the cover of the table. Mamie slips her hand under his buttocks. Rachel and Jennie look away, Jennie flushing slightly. I have a brief flash of memory, of the kind I haven't had for years: myself at eighteen or so, my first year at Yale, in a huge brass bed with a modern geometric-print bedspread and a red-headed man I met three hours ago. But here, Inside…here sex, like everything else, moves so much slowly, so much more carefully, so much more privately. For such a long time people were afraid that this disease, like that other earlier one, might be transmitted sexually. And then there was the shame of one's ugly body, crisscrossed with ropes of disease. I'm not sure that Rachel has ever seen a man naked.

I say, for the sake of saying something, "So there's a Block dance Wednesday."

"Block B," Jennie said. Her blue eyes sparkled. "With the band that played last summer for Block E."

"Guitars?"

"Oh, no! They've got a trumpet and a violin," Rachel says, clearly impressed. "You should hear how they sound together, Gram—it's a lot different than guitars. Come to the dance!"

"I don't think so, honey. Is Dr. McHabe going?" From both their faces I know this guess is right.

Jennie says hesitantly, "He wants to talk to you first, before the dance, for a few minutes. If that's all right."

"Why?"

"I'm not…not exactly sure I know all of it." She doesn't meet my eyes: unwilling to tell me, unwilling to lie. Most of the children Inside, I realize for the first time, are not liars. Or else they're bad ones. They're good at privacy, but it must be an honest privacy.

"Will you see him?" Rachel says eagerly.

"I'll see him."

Mamie looks away from Peter long enough to add sharply, "If it's anything about you or Jennie, he should see me, miss, not your grandmother. I'm your mother and Jennie's guardian, and don't you forget it."

"No, Mama," Rachel says.

"I don't like your tone, miss!"

"Sorry," Rachel says, in the same tone. Jennie drops her eyes, embarrassed. But before Mamie can get really started on indignant maternal neglect, Peter whispers something in her ear and she claps her hand over her mouth, giggling.

Later, when just the two of us are left in the kitchen, I say quietly to Rachel, "Try not to upset your mother, honey. She can't help it."

"Yes, Gram," Rachel says obediently. But I hear the disbelief in her tone, a disbelief muted by her love for me and even for her mother, but nonetheless there. Rachel doesn't believe that Mamie can't help it. Rachel, born Inside, can't possibly help her own ignorance of what it is that Mamie thinks she has lost.

On his second visit to me six days later, just before the Block dance, Tom McHabe seems different. I'd forgotten that there are people who radiate such energy and purpose that they seem to set the very air tingling. He stands with his legs braced slightly apart, flanked by Rachel and Jennie, both dressed in their other skirts for the dance. Jennie has woven a red ribbon through her blonde curls; it glows like a flower. McHabe touches her lightly on the shoulder, and I realize from her answering look what must be happening between them. My throat tightens.

"I want to be honest with you, Mrs. Pratt. I've talked to Jack Stevenson and Mary Kramer, as well as some others in Blocks C and E, and I've gotten a feel for how you live here. A little bit, anyway. I'm going to tell Mr.

Stevenson and Mrs. Kramer what I tell you, but I wanted you to be first."

"Why?" I say, more harshly than I intend. Or think I intend.

He isn't fazed. "Because you're one of the oldest survivors of the disease. Because you had a strong education Outside. Because your daughter's husband died of axoperidine."

At the same moment that I realize what McHabe is going to say next, I realize too that Rachel and Jennie have already heard it. They listen to him with the slightly open-mouthed intensity of children hearing a marvelous but familiar tale. But do they understand? Rachel wasn't present when her father finally died, gasping for air his lungs couldn't use.

McHabe, watching me, says, "There's been a lot of research on the disease since those deaths, Mrs. Pratt."

"No. There hasn't. Too risky, your government said."

I see that he caught the pronoun. "Actual administration of any cures is illegal, yes. To minimize contact with communicables."

"So how has this 'research' been carried on?"

"By doctors willing to go Inside and not come out again. Data is transmitted out by laser. In code."

"What clean doctor would be willing to go Inside and not come out again?"

McHabe smiles; again I'm struck by that quality of spontaneous energy. "Oh, you'd be surprised. We had three doctors inside the Pennsylvania colony. One past retirement age. Another, an old-style Catholic, who dedicated his research to God. A third nobody could figure out, a dour persistent guy who was a brilliant researcher."

Was. "And you."

"No," McHabe says quietly. "I go in and out."

"What happened to the others?"

"They're dead." He makes a brief aborted movement with his right hand and I realize that he is, or was, a smoker. How long since I had reached like that for a non-existent cigarette? Nearly two decades. Cigarettes are not among the things people donate; they're too valuable. Yet I recognize the movement still. "Two of the three doctors caught the disease. They worked on themselves as well as volunteers. Then one day the government intercepted the relayed data and went in and destroyed everything."

"Why?" Jennie asks.

"Research on the disease is illegal. Everyone Outside is afraid of a leak: a virus somehow getting out on a mosquito, a bird, even as a spore."

"Nothing has gotten out in all these years," Rachel says.

"No. But the government is afraid that if researchers start splicing and intercutting genes, it could make viruses more viable. You don't understand the Outside, Rachel. Everything is illegal. This is the most repressive period in American history. Everyone's afraid."

"You're not," Jennie says, so softly I barely hear her. McHabe gives her a smile that twists my heart.

"Some of us haven't given up. Research goes on. But it's all underground, all theoretical. And we've learned a lot. We've learned that the virus doesn't just affect the skin. There are—"

"Be quiet," I say, because I see that he's about to say something important. "Be quiet a minute. Let me think."

McHabe waits. Jennie and Rachel look at me, that glow of suppressed excitement on them both. Eventually I find it. "You want something, Dr. McHabe. All this research wants something from us besides pure scientific joy. With things Outside as bad as you say, there must be plenty of diseases Outside you could research without killing yourself, plenty of need among your own people—" he nods, his eyes gleaming "—but you're here. Inside. Why? We don't have any more new or interesting symptoms, we barely survive, the Outside stopped caring what happened to us a long time ago. We have nothing. So why are you here?"

"You're wrong, Mrs. Pratt. You do have something interesting going on here. You have survived. Your society has regressed but not collapsed. You're functioning under conditions where you shouldn't have."

The same old crap. I raise my eyebrows at him. He stares into the fire and says quietly, "To say Washington is rioting says nothing. You have to see a twelve-year-old hurl a homemade bomb, a man sliced open from neck to crotch because he still has a job to go to and his neighbor doesn't, a three-year-old left to starve because someone abandoned her like an unwanted kitten...You don't know. It doesn't happen Inside."

"We're better than they are," Rachel says. I look at my grandchild. She says it simply, without self-aggrandizement, but with a kind of wonder. In the firelight the thickened gray ropes of skin across her cheek glow dull maroon.

McHabe said, "Perhaps you are. I started to say earlier that we've learned that the virus doesn't affect just the skin. It alters neurotransmitter receptor sites in the brain as well. It's a relatively slow transformation, which is why the flurry of research in the early years of the disease missed it. But it's real, as real as the faster site-capacity transformations brought about by, say, cocaine. Are you following me, Mrs. Pratt?"

I nod. Jennie and Rachel don't look lost, although they don't know any of this vocabulary, and I recognize that McHabe must have explained all this to them, earlier, in some other terms.

"As the disease progresses to the brain, the receptors which receive excitory transmitters slowly become harder to engage, and the receptors which receive inhibiting transmitters become easier to engage."

"You mean that we become stupider."

"Oh, no! Intelligence is not affected at all. The results are emotional and behavioral, not intellectual. You become—all of you—calmer. Disinclined to action or innovation. Mildly but definitely depressed."

The fire burns down. I pick up the poker, bent slightly where someone once tried to use it as a crowbar, and poke at the log, which is a perfectly shaped molded-pulp synthetic stamped "Donated by Weyerhaeuser-Seyyed." "I don't feel depressed, young man."

"It's a depression of the nervous system, but a new kind—without the hopelessness usually associated with clinical depression."

"I don't believe you."

"Really? With all due courtesy, when was the last time you—or any of the older Block leaders—pushed for any significant change in how you do things Inside?"

"Sometimes things cannot be constructively changed. Only accepted. That's not chemistry, it's reality."

"Not Outside," McHabe says grimly. "Outside they don't change constructively or accept. They get violent.

Inside, you've had almost no violence since the early years, even when your resources tightened again and again. When was the last time you tasted butter, Mrs. Pratt, or smoked a cigarette, or had a new pair of jeans? Do you know what happens Outside when consumer goods become unavailable and there are no police in a given area? But Inside you just distribute whatever you have as fairly as you can, or make do without. No looting, no rioting, no cancerous envy. No one Outside knew why. Now we do."

"We have envy."

"But it doesn't erupt into anger."

Each time one of us speaks, Jennie and Rachel turn their heads to watch, like rapt spectators at tennis. Which neither of them has ever seen. Jennie's skin glows like pearl.

"Our young people aren't violent either, and the disease hasn't advanced very far in some of them."

"They learn how to behave from their elders—just like kids everywhere else."

"I don't feel depressed."

"Do you feel energetic?"

"I have arthritis."

"That's not what I mean."

"What do you mean, Doctor?"

Again that restless, furtive reach for a non-existent cigarette. But his voice is quiet. "How long did it take you to get around to applying that insecticide I got Rachel for the termites? She told me you forbid her to do it, and I think you were right; it's dangerous stuff. How many days went by before you or your daughter spread it around?"

The chemical is still in its can.

"How much anger are you feeling now, Mrs. Pratt?"

he goes on. "Because I think we understand each other, you and I, and that you guess now why I'm here. But you aren't shouting or ordering me out of here or even telling me what you think of me. You're listening, and you're doing it calmly, and you're accepting what I tell you even though you know what I want you to—"

The door opens and he breaks off. Mamie flounces in, followed by Peter. She scowls and stamps her foot. "Where were you, Rachel? We've been standing outside waiting for you all for ten minutes now! The dance has already started!"

"A few more minutes, Mama. We're talking."

"Talking? About what? What's going on?"

"Nothing," McHabe says. "I was just asking your mother some questions about life Inside. I'm sorry we took so long."

"You never ask me questions about life Inside. And besides, I want to dance!"

McHabe says, "If you and Peter want to go ahead, I'll bring Rachel and Jennie."

Mamie chews her bottom lip. I suddenly know that she wants to walk up the street to the dance between Peter and McHabe, an arm linked with each, the girls trailing behind. McHabe meets her eyes steadily.

"Well, if that's what you want," she says pettishly. "Come on, Pete!" She closes the door hard.

I look at McHabe, unwilling to voice the question in front of Rachel, trusting him to know the argument I want to make. He does. "In clinical depression, there's always been a small percentage for whom the illness is manifested not as passivity but as irritability. It may be the same. We don't know."

"Gram," Rachel says, as if she can't contain herself any longer, "he has a cure."

"For the skin manifestation only," McHabe says quickly, and I see that he wouldn't have chosen to blurt it out that way. Not for the effects on the brain."

I say, despite myself, "How can you cure one without the other?"

He runs his hand through his hair. Thick, brown hair. I watch Jennie watch his hand. "Skin tissue and brain tissue aren't alike, Mrs. Pratt. The virus reaches both the skin and the brain at the same time, but the changes to brain tissue, which is much more complex, take much longer to detect. And they can't be reversed—nerve tissue is non-regenerative. If you cut your fingertip, it will eventually break down and replace the damaged cells to heal itself. Shit, if you're young enough, you can grow an entire new fingertip. Something like that is what we think our cure will stimulate the skin to do.

"But if you damage your cortex, those cells are gone forever. And unless another part of the brain can learn to compensate, whatever behavior those cells governed is also changed forever."

"Changed into depression, you mean."

"Into calmness. Into restraint of action…The country desperately needs restraint, Mrs. Pratt."

"And so you want to take some of us Outside, cure the skin ropes, and let the 'depression' spread: the 'restraint,' the 'slowness to act'…"

"We have enough action out there. And no one can control it—it's all the wrong kind. What we need now is to slow everything down a little—before there's nothing left to slow down."

"You'd infect a whole population—"

"Slowly. Gently. For their own good—"

"Is that up to you to decide?"

"Considering the alternative, yes. Because it works. The colonies work, despite all your deprivations. And they work because of the disease!"

"Each new case would have skin ropes—"

"Which we'll then cure."

"Does your cure work, Doctor? Rachel's father died of a cure like yours!"

"Not like ours," he says, and I hear in his voice the utter conviction of the young. Of the energetic. Of the Outside. "This is new, and medically completely different. This is the right strain."

"And you want me to try this new right strain as your guinea pig."

There is a moment of electric silence. Eyes shift: gray, blue, brown. Even before Rachel rises from her stool or McHabe says, "We think the best chances to avoid scarring are with young people without heavy skin manifestations," I know. Rachel puts her arms around me. And Jennie—Jennie with the red ribbon woven in her hair, sitting on her broken chair as on a throne, Jennie who never heard of neurotransmitters or slow viruses or risk calculations—says simply, "It has to be me," and looks at McHabe with eyes shining with love.

I say no. I send McHabe away and say no. I reason with both girls and say no. They look unhappily at each other, and I wonder how long it will be before they realize they can act without permission, without obedience. But they never have.

We argue for nearly an hour, and then I insist they go on to the dance, and that I go with them. The night is cold. Jennie puts on her sweater, a heavy hand-knitted garment that covers her shapelessly from neck to knees. Rachel drags on her coat, a black donated synthetic frayed at cuffs and hem. As we go out the door, she stops me with a hand on my arm.

"Gram—why did you say no?"

"Why? Honey, I've been telling you for an hour. The risk, the danger…"

"Is it that? Or—" I can feel her in the darkness of the hall, gathering herself together "—or is it—don't be mad, Gram, please don't be mad at me—is it because the cure is a new thing, a change? A…different thing you don't want because it's exciting? Like Tom said?"

"No, it isn't that," I say, and feel her tense beside me, and for the first time in her life I don't know what the tensing means.

We go down the street towards Block B. There's a moon and stars, tiny high pinpoints of cold light. Block B is further lit by kerosene lamps and by torches stuck in the ground in front of the peeling barracks walls that form the cheerless square. Or does it only seem cheerless because of what McHabe said? Could we have done better than this blank utilitarianism, this subdued bleakness—this peace?

Before tonight, I wouldn't have asked.

I stand in the darkness at the head of the street, just beyond the square, with Rachel and Jennie. The band plays across from me, a violin, guitar, and trumpet with one valve that keeps sticking. People bundled in all the clothes they own ring the square, clustering in the circles of light around the torches, talking in quiet voices. Six or seven couples dance slowly in the middle of the barren earth, holding each other loosely and shuffling to a plaintive version of "Starships and Roses." The song was a hit the year I got the disease, and then had a revival a decade later, the year the first manned expedition left for Mars. The expedition was supposed to set up a colony.

Are they still there?

We had written no new songs.

Peter and Mamie circle among the other couples. "Starships and Roses" ends and the band begins "Yesterday." A turn brings Mamie's face briefly into full torchlight: it's clenched and tight, streaked with tears.

"You should sit down, Gram," Rachel says. This is the first time she's spoken to me since we left the barracks. Her voice is heavy but not angry, and there is no anger in Jennie's arm as she sets down the three-legged stool she carried for me. Neither of them is ever really angry.

Under my weight the stool sinks unevenly into the ground. A boy, twelve or thirteen years old, comes up to Jennie and wordlessly holds out his hand. They join the dancing couples. Jack Stevenson, much more arthritic than I, hobbles towards me with his grandson Hal by his side.

"Hello, Sarah. Been a long time."

"Hello, Jack." Thick disease ridges cross both his cheeks and snakes down his nose. Once, long ago, we were at Yale together.

"Hal, go dance with Rachel," Jack says. "Give me that stool first." Hal, obedient, exchanges the stool for Rachel, and Jack lowers himself to sit beside me. "Big doings, Sarah."

"So I hear."

"McHabe told you? All of it? He said he'd been to see you just before me."

"He told me."

"What do you think?"

"I don't know."

"He wants Hal to try the cure."

Hal. I hadn't thought. The boy's face is smooth and clear, the only visible skin ridges on his right hand.

I say, "Jennie, too."

Jack nods, apparently unsurprised. "Hal said no."

"Hal did?"

"You mean Jennie didn't?" He stares at me. "She'd even consider something as dangerous as an untried cure—not to mention this alleged passing Outside?"

I don't answer. Peter and Mamie dance from behind the other couples, disappear again. The song they dance to is slow, sad, and old.

"Jack—could we have done better here? With the colony?"

Jack watches the dancers. Finally he says, "We don't kill each other. We don't burn things down. We don't steal, or at least not much and not cripplingly. We don't hoard. It seems to me we've done better than anyone had ever hoped. Including us." His eyes search the dancers for Hal. "He's the best thing in my life, that boy."

Another rare flash of memory: Jack debating in some long-forgotten political science class at Yale, a young man on fire. He stands braced lightly on the balls of his feet, leaning forward like a fighter or a dancer, the electric lights brilliant on his glossy black hair. Young women watch him with their hands quiet on their open textbooks. He has the pro side of the debating question:

Resolved: Fomenting first-strike third-world wars is an effective method of deterring nuclear conflict among super-powers.

Abruptly the band stops playing. In the center of the square Peter and Mamie shout at each other.

"—saw the way you touched her! You bastard, you faithless prick!"

"For God's sake, Mamie, not here!"

"Why not here? You didn't mind dancing with her here, touching her back here, and ass and…and…" She starts to cry. People look away, embarrassed. A woman I don't know steps forward and puts a hesitant hand on Mamie's shoulder. Mamie shakes it off, her hands to her face, and rushes away from the square. Peter stands there dumbly a moment before saying to no one in particular, "I'm sorry. Please dance." He walks towards the band who begin, raggedly, to play "Didn't We Almost Have It All." The song is twenty-five years old. Jack Stevenson says, "Can I help, Sarah? With your girl?"

"How?"

"I don't know," he says, and of course he doesn't. He offers not out of usefulness but out of empathy, knowing how the ugly little scene in the torchlight depresses me.

Do we all so easily understand depression?

Rachel dances by with someone I don't know, a still-faced older man. She throws a worried glance over his shoulder: now Jennie is dancing with Peter. I can't see Peter's face. But I see Jennie's. She looks directly at no one, but then she doesn't have to. The message she's sending is clear: I forbade her to come to the dance with McHabe, but I didn't forbid her to dance with Peter and so she is, even though she doesn't want to, even though it's clear from her face that this tiny act of defiance terrifies her. Peter tightens his arm and she jerks backward against it, smiling hard.

Kara Desmond and Rob Cottrell come up to me, blocking my view of the dancers. They've been here as long as I. Kara has an infant great-grandchild, one of the rare babies born already disfigured by the disease. Kara's dress, which she wears over jeans for warmth, is torn at the hem; her voice is soft. "Sarah. It's great to see you out." Rob says nothing. He's put on weight in the few years since I saw him last. In the flickering torchlight his jowly face shines with the serenity of a diseased Buddha.

It's two more dances before I realize that Jennie has disappeared.

I look around for Rachel. She's pouring sumac tea for the band. Peter dances by with a woman not wearing jeans under her dress; the woman is shivering and smiling. So it isn't Peter that Jennie left with…

"Rob, will you walk me home? In case I stumble?" The cold is getting to my arthritis.

Rob nods, incurious. Kara says, "I'll come, too," and we leave Jack Stevenson on his stool, waiting for his turn at hot tea. Kara chatters happily as we walk along as fast as I can go, which isn't as fast as I want to go. The moon has set. The ground is uneven and the street dark except for the stars and fitful lights in barracks windows. Candles. Oil lamps. Once, a single powerful glow from what I guess to be a donated stored-solar light, the only one I've seen in a long time.

Korean, Tom said.

"You're shivering," Kara says. "Here, take my coat." I shake my head.

I make them leave me outside our barracks and they do, unquestioning. Quietly I open the door to our dark kitchen. The stove has gone out. The door to the back bedroom stands half-open, voices coming from the darkness. I shiver again, and Kara's coat wouldn't have helped.

But I am wrong. The voices aren't Jennie and Peter.

"—not what I wanted to talk about just now," Mamie says.

"But it's what I want to talk about."

"Is it?"

"Yes."

I stand listening to the rise and fall of their voices, to the petulance in Mamie's, the eagerness in McHabe's.

"Jennie is your ward, isn't she?"

"Oh, Jennie. Yes. For another year."

"Then she'll listen to you, even if your mother... the decision is yours. And hers."

"I guess so. But I want to think about it. I need more information."

"I'll tell you anything you ask."

"Will you? Are you married, Dr. Thomas McHabe?"

Silence. Then his voice, different. "Don't do that."

"Are you sure? Are you really sure?"

"I'm sure."

"Really, really sure? That you want me to stop?"

I cross the kitchen, hitting my knee against an unseen chair. In the open doorway a sky full of stars moves into view through the termite hole in the wall.

"Ow!"

"I said to stop it, Mrs. Wilson. Now please think about what I said about Jennie. I'll come back tomorrow morning and you can—"

"You can go straight to hell!" Mamie shouts. And then, in a different voice, strangely calm, "Is it because I'm diseased? And you're not? And Jennie is not?"

"No. I swear it, no. But I didn't come here for this."

"No," Mamie says in that same chill voice, and I realize that I have never heard it from her before, never, "you came to help us. To bring a cure. To bring the Outside. But not for everybody. Only for the few who aren't too far gone, who aren't too ugly—who you can use."

"It isn't like that—"

"A few who you can rescue. Leaving all the rest of us here to rot, like we did before."

"In time, research on the—"

"Time! What do you think time matters Inside? Time matters shit here! Time only matters when someone like you comes in from the Outside, showing off your healthy skin and making it even worse than it was before with your new whole clothing and your working wristwatch and your shiny hair and your…your…," She is sobbing. I step into the room.

"All right, Mamie. All right."

Neither of them react to seeing me. McHabe just stands there until I wave him towards the door and he goes, not saying a word. I put my arms around Mamie and she leans against my breast and cries. My daughter. Even through my coat I feel the thick ropy skin of her cheek pressing against me, and all I can think of is that I never noticed at all that McHabe wears a wristwatch.

Late that night, after Mamie has fallen into damp exhausted sleep and I have lain awake tossing for hours, Rachel creeps into our room to say that Jennie and Hal Stevenson have both been injected with an experimental disease cure by Tom McHabe. She's cold and trembling, defiant in her fear, afraid of all their terrible defiance. I hold her until she, too, sleeps, and I remember Jack Stevenson as a young man, classroom lights glossy on his thick hair, spiritedly arguing in favor of the sacrifice of one civilization for another.

Mamie leaves the barracks early the next morning. Her eyelids are still swollen and shiny from last night's crying. I guess that she's going to hunt up Peter, and I say nothing. We sit at the table, Rachel and I, eating our oatmeal, not looking at each other. It's an effort to even lift the spoon. Mamie is gone a long time.

Later, I picture it. Later, when Jennie and Hal and McHabe have come and gone, I can't stop picturing it: Mamie walking with her swollen eyelids down the muddy streets between the barracks, across the unpaved squares with their corner vegetable gardens of rickety bean poles and the yellow-green tops of carrots. Past the depositories with their donated Chinese and Japanese and Korean wool and wood stoves and sheets of alloys and unguarded medicines. Past the chicken runs and goat pens. Past Central Administration, that dusty cinder-block building where people stopped keeping records maybe a decade ago because why would you need to prove you'd been born or had changed barracks? Past the last of the communal wells, reaching deep into a common and plentiful water table. Mamie walking, until she reaches the rim, and is stopped, and says what she came to say.

They come a few hours later, dressed in full sani-suits and armed with automatic weapons that don't look American-made. I can see their faces through the clear shatter-proof plastic of their helmets. Three of them stare frankly at my face, at Rachel's, at Hal Stevenson's hands. The other two won't look directly at any of us, as if viruses could be transmitted over locked gazes.

They grab Tom McHabe from his chair at the kitchen table, pulling him up so hard he stumbles, and throw him against the wall. They are gentler with Rachel and Hal. One of them stares curiously at Jennie, frozen on the opposite side of the table. They don't let McHabe make any of the passionate explanations he had been trying to make to me. When he tries, the leader hits him across the face.

Rachel—Rachel—throws herself at the man. She wraps her strong young arms and legs around him from behind, screaming, "Stop it! Stop it!" The man shrugs her off like a fly. A second soldier pushes her into a chair. When he looks at her face he shudders. Rachel goes on yelling, sound without words.

Jennie doesn't even scream. She dives across the table and clings to McHabe's shoulder, and whatever is on her face is hidden by the fall of her yellow hair.

"Shut you fucking 'doctors' down once and for all!" the leader yells, over Rachel's noise. The words come through his helmet as clearly as if he weren't wearing one. "Think you can just go on coming Inside and Outside and diseasing us all?"

"I—" McHabe says.

"Fuck it!" the leader says, and shoots him.

McHabe slumps against the wall. Jennie grabs him, desperately trying to haul him up upright. The soldier fires again. The bullet hits Jennie's wrist, shattering the bone. A third shot, and McHabe slides to the floor.

The soldiers leave. There is little blood, only two small holes where the bullets went in and stayed in. We didn't know, Inside, that they have guns like that now. We didn't know bullets could do that. We didn't know.

"You did it," Rachel says.

"I did it for you," Mamie says. "I did!" They stand across the kitchen from each other, Mamie pinned against the door she just closed behind her when she finally came home, Rachel standing in front of the wall where Tom died. Jennie lies sedated in the bedroom. Hal Stevenson, his young face anguished because he had been useless against five armed soldiers, had run for the doctor who lives in Barracks J, who had been found setting the leg of a goat.

"You did it. You." Her voice is dull, heavy. Scream, I want to say. Rachel, scream.

"I did it so you would be safe!"

"You did it so I would be trapped Inside. Like you."

"You never thought it was a trap!" Mamie cries. "You were the one who was happy here!"

"And you never will be. Never. Not here, not anyplace else."

I close my eyes, to not see the terrible maturity on my Rachel's face. But the next moment she's a child again, pushing past me to the bedroom with a furious sob, slamming the door behind her.

I face Mamie. "Why?"

But she doesn't answer. And I see that it doesn't matter; I wouldn't have believed her anyway. Her mind is not her own. It is depressed, ill. I have to believe that now. She's my daughter, and her mind has been affected by the ugly ropes of skin that disfigure her. She is the victim of disease, and nothing she says can change anything at all.

It's almost morning. Rachel stands in the narrow aisle between the bed and the wall, folding clothes. The bedspread still bears the imprint of Jennie's sleeping shape; Jennie herself was carried by Hal Stevenson to her own barracks, where she won't have to see Mamie when she wakes up. On the crude shelf beside Rachel the oil lamp burns, throwing shadows on the newly whole wall that smells of termite exterminator.

She has few enough clothes to pack. A pair of blue tights, old and clumsily darned; a sweater with pulled threads; two more pairs of socks; her other skirt, the one she wore to the Block dance. Everything else she already has on.

"Rachel," I say. She doesn't answer, but I see what silence costs her. Even such a small defiance, even now. Yet she is going. Using McHabe's contacts to go Outside, leaving to find the underground medical research outfit. If they have developed the next stage of the cure, the one for people already disfigured, she will take it. Perhaps even if they have not. And as she goes, she will contaminate as much as she can with her disease, depressive and non-aggressive. Communicable.

She thinks she has to go. Because of Jennie, because of Mamie, because of McHabe. She is sixteen years old, and she believes—even growing up Inside, she believes this—that she must do something. Even if it is the wrong thing. To do the wrong thing, she has decided, is better than to do nothing.

She has no real idea of Outside. She has never watched television, never stood in a bread line, never seen a crack den or a slasher movie. She cannot define napalm, or political torture, or neutron bomb, or gang rape. To her, Mamie, with her confused and self-justifying fear, represents the height of cruelty and betrayal; Peter, with his shambling embarrassed lewdness, the epitome of danger; the theft of a chicken, the last word in criminality. She has never heard of Auschwitz, Cawnpore, the Inquisition, gladiatorial games, Nat Turner, Pol Pot, Stalingrad, Ted Bundy, Hiroshima, My Lai, Wounded Knee, Babi Yar, Bloody Sunday, Dresden or Dachau. Raised with a kind of mental inertia, she knows nothing of the savage inertia of destruction, that once set in motion in a civilization is as hard to stop as a disease.

I don't think she can find the underground researchers, no matter how much McHabe told her. I don't think her passage Outside will spread enough infection to make any difference at all. I don't think it's possible that she can get very far before she is picked up and either returned Inside or killed. She cannot change the world. It's too old, too entrenched, too vicious, too there. She will fail. There is no force stronger than destructive inertia.

I get my things ready to go with her.

AND THE DEEP BLUE SEA
BY ELIZABETH BEAR

Elizabeth Bear is the Hugo, Sturgeon, and Campbell Award-winning author of almost a hundred short stories and more than twenty-five novels, the most recent of which is *Steles of the Sky*, from Tor Books. Other books include the Jenny Casey trilogy—*Hammered*, *Scardown*, and *Worldwired*—*Undertow*, *Carnival*, the Promethean Age fantasy series, and, with Sarah Monette, *A Companion to Wolves*. She is a prolific short story writer, with nearly one hundred publications to her credit since 2003. Most of her short fiction has been collected in the volumes *The Chains That You Refuse*, *Jewels and Stones*, and *Shoggoths in Bloom*.

"And the Deep Blue Sea," which first appeared in the online magazine *SCI FICTION*, is Bear's take on the post-apocalyptic messenger story, reminiscent—without being derivative—of Roger Zelazny's *Damnation Alley*. Bear's fascination with abandoned places, and the fact that she lived for years in Las Vegas—"America's Nuclear City"—led her to write this story. As research for this piece, she says she learned how to move safely through a radioactive zone, which should come in handy should the events leading up to this story ever come to pass.

The end of the world had come and gone. It turned out not to matter much in the long run.

The mail still had to get through.

Harrie signed yesterday's paperwork, checked the dates against the calendar, contemplated her signature for a moment, and capped her pen. She weighed the metal barrel in her hand and met Dispatch's faded eyes. "What's special about this trip?"

He shrugged and turned the clipboard around on the counter, checking each sheet to be certain she'd filled them out properly. She didn't bother watching. She never made mistakes. "Does there have to be something special?"

"You don't pay my fees unless it's special, Patch." She grinned as he lifted an insulated steel case onto the counter.

"This has to be in Sacramento in eight hours," he said.

"What is it?"

"Medical goods. Fetal stem-cell cultures. In a climate-controlled unit. They can't get too hot or too cold, there's some arcane formula about how long they can live in this given quantity of growth media, and the customer's paying very handsomely to see them in California by eighteen hundred hours."

"It's almost oh ten hundred now. What's too hot or too cold?" Harrie hefted the case. It was lighter than it looked; it would slide effortlessly into the saddlebags on her touring bike.

"Any hotter than it already is," Dispatch said, mopping his brow. "Can you do it?"

"Eight hours? Phoenix to Sacramento?" Harrie leaned back to check the sun. "It'll take me through Vegas. The California routes aren't any good at that speed since the Big One."

"I wouldn't send anybody else. Fastest way is through Reno."

"There's no gasoline from somewhere this side of the dam to Tonopah. Even my courier card won't help me there—"

"There's a checkpoint in Boulder City. They'll fuel you."

"Military?"

"I did say they were paying very well." He shrugged, shoulders already gleaming with sweat. It was going to be a hot one. Harrie guessed it would hit a hundred and twenty in Phoenix.

At least she was headed north.

"I'll do it," she said, and held her hand out for the package receipt. "Any pickups in Reno?"

"You know what they say about Reno?"

"Yeah. It's so close to Hell that you can see Sparks." Naming the city's largest suburb.

"Right. You don't want anything in Reno. Go straight through," Patch said. "Don't stop in Vegas, whatever you do. The overpass's come down, but that won't affect you unless there's debris. Stay on the 95 through to Fallon; it'll see you clear."

"Check." She slung the case over her shoulder, pretending she didn't see Patch wince. "I'll radio when I hit Sacramento—"

"Telegraph," he said. "The crackle between here and

there would kill your signal otherwise."

"Check," again, turning to the propped-open door. Her prewar Kawasaki Concours crouched against the crumbling curb like an enormous, restless cat. Not the prettiest bike around, but it got you there. Assuming you didn't ditch the top-heavy son of a bitch in the parking lot.

"Harrie—"

"What?" She paused, but didn't turn.

"If you meet the Buddha on the road, kill him."

She glanced behind her, strands of hair catching on the strap of the insulated case and on the shoulder loops of her leathers. "What if I meet the Devil?"

She let the Concours glide through the curves of the long descent to Hoover Dam, a breather after the hard straight push from Phoenix, and considered her options. She'd have to average near enough a hundred sixty klicks an hour to make the run on time. It should be smooth sailing; she'd be surprised if she saw another vehicle between Boulder City and Tonopah.

She'd checked out a backup dosimeter before she left Phoenix, just in case. Both clicked softly as she crossed the dam and the poisoned river, reassuring her with alert, friendly chatter. She couldn't pause to enjoy the expanse of blue on her right side or the view down the escarpment on the left, but the dam was in pretty good shape, all things considered.

It was more than you could say for Vegas.

Once upon a time—she downshifted as she hit the steep grade up the north side of Black Canyon, sweat already soaking her hair—once upon a time a delivery like this would have been made by aircraft. There were places where it still would be. Places where there was money for fuel, money for airstrip repairs.

Places where most of the aircraft weren't parked in tidy rows, poisoned birds lined up beside poisoned runways, hot enough that you could hear the dosimeters clicking as you drove past.

A runner's contract was a hell of a lot cheaper. Even when you charged the way Patch charged.

Sunlight glinted off the Colorado River so far below, flashing red and gold as mirrors. Crumbling casino on the right, now, and the canyon echoing the purr of the sleek black bike. The asphalt was spiderwebbed but still halfway smooth—smooth enough for a big bike, anyway. A big bike cruising at a steady ninety kph, much too fast if there was anything in the road. Something skittered aside as she thought it, a grey blur instantly lost among the red and black blurs of the receding rock walls on either side. Bighorn sheep. Nobody'd bothered to tell them to clear out before the wind could make them sick.

Funny thing was, they seemed to be thriving.

Harrie leaned into the last curve, braking in and accelerating out just to feel the tug of g-forces, and gunned it up the straightaway leading to the checkpoint at Boulder City. A red light flashed on a peeling steel pole beside the road. The Kawasaki whined and buzzed between her thighs, displeased to be restrained, then gentled as she eased the throttle, mindful of dust.

Houses had been knocked down across the top of the rise that served as host to the guard's shielded quarters, permitting an unimpeded view of Boulder City stretching out below. The bulldozer that had done the work slumped nearby, rusting under bubbled paint, too radioactive to be taken away. Too radioactive even to be melted down for salvage.

Boulder City had been affluent once. Harrie could see the husks of trendy businesses on either side of Main Street: brick and stucco buildings in red and taupe, some whitewashed wood frames peeling in slow curls, submissive to the desert heat.

The gates beyond the checkpoint were closed and so were the lead shutters on the guard's shelter. A digital sign over the roof gave an ambient radiation reading in the mid double digits and a temperature reading in the low triple digits, Fahrenheit. It would get hotter—and "hotter"—as she descended into Vegas.

Harrie dropped the sidestand as the Kawasaki rolled to a halt, and thumbed her horn.

The young man who emerged from the shack was surprisingly tidy, given his remote duty station. Cap set regulation, boots shiny under the dust. He was still settling his breathing filter as he climbed down red metal steps and trotted over to Harrie's bike. Harrie wondered who he'd pissed off to draw this duty, or if he was a novelist who had volunteered.

"Runner," she said, her voice echoing through her helmet mike. She tapped the ID card visible inside the windowed pocket on the breast of her leathers, tugged her papers from the pouch on her tank with a clumsy gloved hand and unfolded them inside their transparent carrier. "You're supposed to gas me up for the run to Tonopah."

"You have an independent filter or just the one in your helmet?" All efficiency as he perused her papers.

"Independent."

"Visor up, please." He wouldn't ask her to take the

helmet off. There was too much dust. She complied, and he checked her eyes and nose against the photo ID.

"Angharad Crowther. This looks in order. You're with UPS?"

"Independent contractor," Harrie said. "It's a medical run."

He turned away, gesturing her to follow, and led her to the pumps. They were shrouded in plastic, one diesel and one unleaded. "Is that a Connie?"

"A little modified so she doesn't buzz so much." Harrie petted the gas tank with a gloved hand. "Anything I should know about between here and Tonopah?"

He shrugged. "You know the rules, I hope."

"Stay on the road," she said, as he slipped the nozzle into the fill. "Don't go inside any buildings. Don't go near any vehicles. Don't stop, don't look back, and especially don't turn around; it's not wise to drive through your own dust. If it glows, don't pick it up, and nothing from the black zone leaves."

"I'll telegraph ahead and let Tonopah know you're coming," he said, as the gas pump clicked. "You ever crash that thing?"

"Not in going on ten years," she said, and didn't bother to cross her fingers. He handed her a receipt; she fumbled her lacquered stainless Cross pen out of her zippered pocket and signed her name like she meant it. The gloves made her signature into an incomprehensible scrawl, but the guard made a show of comparing it to her ID card and slapped her on the shoulder. "Be careful. If you crash out there, you're probably on your own. Godspeed."

"Thanks for the reassurance," she said, and grinned at him before she closed her visor and split.

* * *

Digitized music rang over her helmet headset as Harrie ducked her head behind the fairing, the hot wind tugging her sleeves, trickling between her gloves and her cuffs. The Kawasaki stretched out under her, ready for a good hard run, and Harrie itched to give it one. One thing you could say about the Vegas black zone: there wasn't much traffic. Houses—identical in red tile roofs and cream stucco walls—blurred past on either side, flanked by trees that the desert had killed once people weren't there to pump the water up to them. She cracked a hundred and sixty kph in the wind shadow of the sound barriers, the tach winding up like a watch, just gliding along in sixth as the Kawasaki hit its stride. The big bike handled like a pig in the parking lot, but out on the highway she ran smooth as glass.

She had almost a hundred miles of range more than she'd need to get to Tonopah, God willing and the creek didn't rise, but she wasn't about to test that with any side trips through what was left of Las Vegas. Her dosimeters clicked with erratic cheer, nothing to worry about yet, and Harrie claimed the center lane and edged down to one forty as she hit the winding patch of highway near the old downtown. The shells of casinos on the left-hand side and godforsaken wasteland and ghetto on the right gave her back the Kawasaki's well-tuned shriek; she couldn't wind it any faster with the roads so choppy and the K-Rail canyons so tight.

The sky overhead was flat blue like cheap turquoise. A pall of dust showed burnt sienna, the inversion layer trapped inside the ring of mountains that made her horizon in four directions.

The freeway opened out once she cleared downtown, the overpass Patch had warned her about arching up and over, a tangle of banked curves, the crossroads at the heart of the silent city. She bid the ghosts of hotels good day as the sun hit zenith, heralding peak heat for another four hours or so. Harrie resisted the urge to reach back and pat her saddlebag to make sure the precious cargo was safe; she'd never know if the climate control failed on the trip, and moreover she couldn't risk the distraction as she wound the Kawasaki up to one hundred seventy and ducked her helmet into the slipstream off the fairing.

Straight shot to the dead town called Beatty from here, if you minded the cattle guards along the roads by the little forlorn towns. Straight shot, with the dosimeters clicking and vintage rock and roll jamming in the helmet speakers and the Kawasaki purring, thrusting, eager to spring and run.

There were worse days to be alive.

She dropped it to fourth and throttled back coming up on that overpass, the big one where the Phoenix to Reno highway crossed the one that used to run LA to Salt Lake, when there was an LA to speak of. Patch had said overpass's down, which could mean unsafe for transit and could mean littering the freeway underneath with blocks of concrete the size of a semi, and Harrie had no interest in finding out which it was with no room left to brake. She adjusted the volume on her music down as the rush of wind abated, and took the opportunity to sightsee a bit.

And swore softly into her air filter, slowing further before she realized she'd let the throttle slip.

Something—no, someone—leaned against a shotgunned, paint-peeled sign that might have given a speed limit once, when there was anyone to care about such things.

Her dosimeters clicked aggressively as she let the bike roll closer to the verge. She shouldn't stop. But it was a death sentence, being alone and on foot out here. Even if the sun weren't climbing the sky, sweat rolling from under Harrie's helmet, adhering her leathers to her skin.

She was almost stopped by the time she realized she knew him. Knew his ocher skin and his natty pinstriped double-breasted suit and his fedora, tilted just so, and the cordovan gleam of his loafers. For one mad moment, she wished she carried a gun.

Not that a gun would help her. Even if she decided to swallow a bullet herself.

"Nick." She put the bike in neutral, dropping her feet as it rolled to a stop. "Fancy meeting you in the middle of Hell."

"I got some papers for you to sign, Harrie." He pushed his fedora back over his hollow-cheeked face. "You got a pen?"

"You know I do." She unzipped her pocket and fished out the Cross. "I wouldn't lend a fountain pen to just anybody."

He nodded, leaning back against a K-Rail so he could kick a knee up and spread his papers out over it. He accepted the pen. "You know your note's about come due."

"Nick—"

"No whining now," he said. "Didn't I hold up my end of the bargain? Have you ditched your bike since last we talked?"

"No, Nick." Crestfallen.

"Had it stolen? Been stranded? Missed a timetable?"

"I'm about to miss one now if you don't hurry up with my pen." She held her hand out imperiously; not terribly convincing, but the best she could do under the circumstances.

"Mmm-hmmm." He was taking his own sweet time.

Perversely, the knowledge settled her. "If the debt's due, have you come to collect?"

"I've come to offer you a chance to renegotiate," he said, and capped the pen and handed it back. "I've got a job for you; could buy you a few more years if you play your cards right."

She laughed in his face and zipped the pen away. "A few more years?" But he nodded, lips pressed thin and serious, and she blinked and went serious too. "You mean it."

"I never offer what I'm not prepared to give," he said, and scratched the tip of his nose with his thumbnail. "What say, oh—three more years?"

"Three's not very much." The breeze shifted. Her dosimeters crackled. "Ten's not very much, now that I'm looking back on it."

"Goes by quick, don't it?" He shrugged. "All right. Seven—"

"For what?"

"What do you mean?" She could have laughed again, at the transparent and oh-so-calculated guilelessness in his eyes.

"I mean, what is it you want me to do for seven more years of protection." The bike was heavy, but she wasn't about to kick the sidestand down. "I'm sure it's bad news for somebody."

"It always is." But he tipped the brim of his hat down a centimeter and gestured to her saddlebag, negligently.

"I just want a moment with what you've got there in that bag."

"Huh." She glanced at her cargo, pursing her lips. "That's a strange thing to ask. What would you want with a box full of research cells?"

He straightened away from the sign he was holding up and came a step closer. "That's not so much yours to worry about, young lady. Give it to me, and you get seven years. If you don't—the note's up next week, isn't it?"

"Tuesday." She would have spat, but she wasn't about to lift her helmet aside. "I'm not scared of you, Nick."

"You're not scared of much." He smiled, all smooth. "It's part of your charm."

She turned her head, staring away west across the sun-soaked desert and the roofs of abandoned houses, abandoned lives. Nevada had always had a way of making ghost towns out of metropolises. "What happens if I say no?"

"I was hoping you weren't going to ask that, sweetheart," he said. He reached to lay a hand on her right hand where it rested on the throttle. The bike growled, a high, hysterical sound, and Nick yanked his hand back. "I see you two made friends."

"We get along all right," Harrie said, patting the Kawasaki's gas tank. "What happens if I say no?"

He shrugged and folded his arms. "You won't finish your run." No threat in it, no extra darkness in the way the shadow of his hat brim fell across his face. No menace in his smile. Cold fact, and she could take it how she took it.

She wished she had a piece of gum to crack between her teeth. It would fit her mood. She crossed her arms, balancing the Kawasaki between her thighs. Harrie liked bargaining. "That's not the deal. The deal's no spills, no crashes, no breakdowns, and every run complete on time. I said I'd get these cells to Sacramento in eight hours. You're wasting my daylight; somebody's life could depend on them."

"Somebody's life does," Nick answered, letting his lips twist aside. "A lot of somebodies, when it comes down to it."

"Break the deal, Nick—fuck with my ride—and you're in breach of contract."

"You've got nothing to bargain with."

She laughed, then, outright. The Kawasaki purred between her legs, encouraging. "There's always time to mend my ways—"

"Not if you die before you make it to Sacramento," he said. "Last chance to reconsider, Angharad, my princess. We can still shake hands and part friends. Or you can finish your last ride on my terms, and it won't be pretty for you"—the Kawasaki snarled softly, the tang of burning oil underneath it—"or your bike."

"Fuck off," Harrie said, and kicked her feet up as she twisted the throttle and drove straight at him, just for the sheer stupid pleasure of watching him dance out of her way.

Nevada had been dying slowly for a long time: perchlorate-poisoned groundwater, a legacy of World War Two titanium plants; cancer rates spiked by exposure to fallout from aboveground nuclear testing; crushing drought and climatic change; childhood leukemia clusters in rural towns. The explosion of the PEPCON plant in 1988 might have been perceived by a sufficiently imaginative mind as God's shot across the bow, but the real damage didn't occur until decades later, when a train carrying high-level nuclear waste to the Yucca Mountain storage facility collided with a fuel tanker stalled across the rails.

The resulting fire and radioactive contamination of the Las Vegas Valley proved to be a godsend in disguise. When the War came to Nellis Air Force Base and the nuclear mountain, Las Vegas was already as much a ghost town as Rhyolite or Goldfield—except deserted not because the banks collapsed or the gold ran out, but because the dust that blew through the streets was hot enough to drop a sparrow in midflight, or so people said.

Harrie didn't know if the sparrow story was true.

"So." She muttered into her helmet, crouched over the Kawasaki's tank as the bike screamed north by northwest, leaving eerie Las Vegas behind. "What do you think he's going to throw at us, girl?"

The bike whined, digging in. Central city gave way to desolate suburbia, and the highway dropped to ground level and straightened out, a narrow strip of black reflecting the summer heat in mirage silver.

The desert sprawled on either side, a dun expanse of scrub and hardpan narrowing as the Kawasaki climbed into the broad pass between two dusty ranges of mountains. Harrie's dosimeters clicked steadily, counting marginally more rads as she roared by the former nuclear testing site at Mercury at close to two hundred kph. She throttled back as a sad little township—a few discarded trailers, another military base and a disregarded prison—came up. There were no pedestrians to worry about, but the grated metal cattle guard was not something to hit at speed.

On the far side, there was nothing to slow her for fifty miles. She cranked her music up and dropped her head behind the fairing and redlined her tach for Beatty and the far horizon.

It got rocky again coming up on Beatty. Civilization in Nevada huddled up to the oases and springs that lurked at the foot of mountains and in the low parts in valleys. This had been mining country, mountains gnawed away by dynamite and sharp-toothed payloaders. A long gorge on the right side of the highway showed green clots of trees; water ran there, tainted by the broken dump, and her dosimeters clicked as the road curved near it. If she walked down the bank and splashed into the stream between the roots of the willows and cottonwoods, she'd walk out glowing, and be dead by nightfall.

She rounded the corner and entered the ghost of Beatty.

The problem, she thought, arose because every little town in Nevada grew up at the same place: a crossroads, and she half-expected Nick to be waiting for her at this one too. The Kawasaki whined as they rolled through tumbleweed-clogged streets, but they passed under the town's sole, blindly staring stoplight without seeing another creature. Despite the sun like a physical pressure on her leathers, a chill ran spidery fingers up her spine. She'd rather know where the hell he was, thank you very much. "Maybe he took a wrong turn at Rhyolite."

The Kawasaki snarled, impatient to be turned loose on the open road again, but Harrie threaded it through slumping cars and around windblown debris with finicky care. "Nobody's looking out for us anymore, Connie," Harrie murmured, and stroked the sun-scorched fuel tank with her gloved left hand. They passed a deserted gas station, the pumps crouched useless without power; the dosimeters chirped and warbled. "I don't want to kick up that dust if I can help it."

The ramshackle one- and two-story buildings gave way to desert and highway. Harrie paused, feet down on tarmac melted sticky-soft by the sun, and made sure the straw of her camel pack was fixed in the holder. The horizon shimmered with heat, ridges of mountains on either side and dun hardpan stretching to infinity. She sighed and took a long drink of stale water.

"Here we go," she said, hands nimble on the clutch and the throttle as she lifted her feet to the peg. The Kawasaki rolled forward, gathering speed. "Not too much further to Tonopah, and then we can both get fed."

Nick was giving her time to think about it, and she drowned the worries with the Dead Kennedys, Boiled in Lead, and the Acid Trip. The ride from Beatty to Tonopah was swift and uneventful, the flat road unwinding beneath her wheels like a spun-out tape measure, the banded mountains crawling past on either side. The only variation along the way was forlorn Goldfield, its wind-touched streets empty and sere. It had been a town of twenty thousand, abandoned before Vegas fell to radiation sickness, even longer before the nuke dump broke open. She pushed two hundred kph most of the way, the road all hers, not so much as the glimmer of sunlight off a distant windshield to contest her ownership. The silence and the empty road just gave her more to worry at, and she did, picking at her problem like a vulture picking at a corpse.

The fountain pen was heavy in her breast pocket as Tonopah shimmered into distant visibility. Her head swam with the heat, the helmet squelching over saturated hair. She sucked more water, trying to ration; the temperature was climbing toward one twenty, and she wouldn't last long without hydration. The Kawasaki coughed a little, rolling down a slow, extended incline, but the gas gauge gave her nearly a quarter of a tank—and there was the reserve if she exhausted the main. Still, instruments weren't always right, and luck wasn't exactly on her side.

Harrie killed her music with a jab of her tongue against the control pad inside her helmet. She dropped her left hand from the handlebar and thumped the tank. The sound she got back was hollow, but there was enough fluid inside to hear it refract off a moving surface. The small city ahead was a welcome sight; there'd be fresh water and gasoline, and she could hose the worst of the dust off and take a piss. God damn, you'd think with the sweat soaking her leathers to her body, there'd be no need for that last, but the devil was in the details, it turned out.

Harrie'd never wanted to be a boy. But some days she really wished she had the knack of peeing standing up.

She was only about half a klick away when she realized that there was something wrong about Tonopah. Other than the usual; her dosimeters registered only background noise as she came up on it, but a harsh reek like burning coal rasped the back of her throat even through the dust filters, and the weird little town wasn't the weird little town she remembered. Rolling green hills rose around it on all sides, thick with shadowy, leafless trees, and it was smoke haze that drifted on the still air, not dust. A heat shimmer floated over the cracked road, and the buildings that crowded alongside it weren't Tonopah's desert-weathered construction but peeling white shingle-sided houses, a storefront post office, a white church with the steeple caved in and half the facade dropped into a smoking sinkhole in the ground.

The Kawasaki whined, shivering as Harrie throttled back. She sat upright in the saddle, letting the big bike roll. "Where the hell are we?" Her voice reverberated. She startled; she'd forgotten she'd left her microphone on.

"Exactly," a familiar voice said at her left. "Welcome to Centralia." Nick wore an open-faced helmet and straddled the back of a Honda Goldwing the color of dried blood, if blood had gold dust flecked through it. The Honda hissed at the Kawasaki, and the Connie growled back, wobbling in eager challenge. Harrie restrained her bike with gentling hands, giving it a little more gas to straighten it out.

"Centralia?" Harrie had never heard of it, and she flattered herself that she'd heard of most places.

"Pennsylvania." Nick lifted his black-gloved hand off the clutch and gestured vaguely around himself. "Or Jharia, in India. Or maybe the Chinese province of Xinjiang. Subterranean coal fires, you know, anthracite burning in evacuated mines. Whole towns abandoned, sulfur and brimstone seeping up through vents, the ground hot enough to flash rain to steam. Your tires will melt. You'll put that bike into a crevasse. Not to mention the greenhouse gases. Lovely things." He grinned, showing shark's teeth, four rows. "Second time asking, Angharad, my princess."

"Second time saying no." She fixed her eyes on the road.

She could see the way the asphalt buckled, now, and the dim glow from the bottom of the sinkhole underneath the church. "You really are used to people doing your bidding, aren't you, Nick?"

"They don't usually put up much of a fight." He twisted the throttle while the clutch was engaged, coaxing a whining, competitive cough from his Honda.

Harrie caught his shrug sideways but kept her gaze trained grimly forward. Was that the earth shivering, or was it just the shimmer of heat-haze over the road? The Kawasaki whined. She petted the clutch to reassure herself.

The groaning rumble that answered her wasn't the Kawasaki. She tightened her knees on the seat as the ground pitched and bucked under her tires, hand clutching the throttle to goose the Connie forward. Broken asphalt sprayed from her rear tire. The road split and shattered, vanishing behind her. She hauled the bike upright by raw strength and nerved herself to check her mirrors; lazy steam rose from a gaping hole in the road.

Nick cruised along, unperturbed. "You sure, Princess?"

"What was that you said about Hell, Nick?" She hunkered down and grinned at him over her shoulder, knowing he couldn't see more than her eyes crinkle through the helmet. It was enough to draw an irritated glare.

He sat back on his haunches and tipped his toes up on the footpegs, throwing both hands up, releasing throttle and clutch, letting the Honda coast away behind her. "I said, welcome to it."

The Kawasaki snarled and whimpered by turns, heavy and agile between her legs as she gave it all the gas she dared. She'd been counting on the refuel stop here, but compact southwestern Tonopah had been replaced by a shattered sprawl of buildings, most of them obviously either bulldozed or vanished into pits that glared like a wolf's eye reflecting a flash, and a gas station wasn't one of the remaining options. The streets were broad, at least, and deserted, not so much winding as curving gently through shallow swales and over hillocks. Broad, but not intact; the asphalt rippled as if heaved by moles and some of the rises and dips hid fissures and sinkholes. Her tires scorched; she coughed into her filter, her mike amplifying it to a hyena's bark. The Cross pen in her pocket pressed her breast over her heart. She took comfort in it, ducking behind the fairing to dodge the stinking wind and the clawing skeletons of ungroomed trees. She'd signed on the line, after all. And either Nick had to see her and the Kawasaki safe or she got back what she'd paid.

As if Nick abided by contracts.

As if he couldn't just kill her and get what he wanted that way. Except he couldn't keep her, if he did.

"Damn," she murmured, to hear the echoes, and hunched over the Kawasaki's tank. The wind tore at her leathers. The heavy bike caught air coming over the last rise. She had to pee like she couldn't believe, and the vibration of the engine wasn't helping, but she laughed out loud to set the city behind.

She got out easier than she thought she would, although her gauge read empty at the bottom of the hill. She switched to reserve and swore. Dead trees and smoking stumps rippled into nonexistence around her, and the lone and level sands stretched to ragged mountains east and west. Back in Nevada, if she'd ever left it, hard westbound now, straight into the glare of the afternoon sun. Her polarized faceplate helped somewhat, maybe not enough, but the road was smooth again before and behind and she could see Tonopah sitting dusty and forsaken in her rearview mirror, inaccessible as a mirage, a city at the bottom of a well.

Maybe Nick could only touch her in the towns. Maybe he needed a little of man's hand on the wilderness to twist to his own ends, or maybe it amused him. Maybe it was where the roads crossed, after all. She didn't think she could make it back to Tonopah if she tried, however, so she pretended she didn't see the city behind her and cruised west, toward Hawthorne, praying she had enough gas to make it but not expecting her prayers to be answered by anybody she particularly wanted to talk to.

The 95 turned northwest again at the deserted Coaldale junction; there hadn't been a town there since long before the War, or even the disaster at Vegas. Mina was gone too, its outskirts marked by a peeling sign advertising an abandoned crawfish farm, the Desert Lobster Facility.

Harrie's camel bag went dry. She sucked at the straw forlornly one last time and spat it out, letting it sag against her jaw, damp and tacky. She hunkered down and laid a long line of smoking road behind, cornering gently when she had to corner, worried about her scorched and bruised tires. At least the day was cooling as evening encroached, as she progressed north and gained elevation. It might be down into the double digits, even, although it was hard to tell through the leather. On her left, the Sarcophagus Mountains rose between her and California.

The name didn't amuse her as much as it usually did.

And then they were climbing. She breathed a low sigh of relief and patted the hungry, grumbling Kawasaki on the fuel tank as the blistering blue of Walker Lake came into view, the dusty little town of Hawthorne huddled like a crab on the near shore. There was nothing moving there either, and Harrie chewed her lip behind the filter. Dust had gotten into her helmet somehow, gritting every time she blinked; weeping streaks marked her cheeks behind the visor. She hoped the dust wasn't the kind that was likely to make her glow, but her dosimeters had settled down to chickenlike clucking, so she might be okay.

The Kawasaki whimpered apologetically and died as she coasted into town.

"Christ," she said, and flinched at the echo of her own amplified voice. She reached to thumb the mike off, and, on second thought, left it alone. It was too damned quiet out here without the Kawasaki's commentary. She tongued her music back on, flipping selections until she settled on a tune by Grey Line Out.

She dropped her right foot and kicked the stand down on the left, then stood on the peg and slung her leg over the saddle. She ached with vibration, her hands stiff claws from clutching the handlebars. The stretch of muscle across her ass and thighs was like the reminder of a two-day-old beating but she leaned into the bike, boot sole slipping on grit as she heaved it into motion. She hopped on one foot to kick the stand up, wincing.

It wasn't the riding. It was the standing up, afterward.

She walked the Kawasaki up the deserted highway, between the deserted buildings, the pavement hot enough to sear her feet through the boot leather if she stood still for too long. "Good girl," she told the Kawasaki, stroking the forward brake handle. It leaned against her heavily, cumbersome at a walking pace, like walking a drunk friend home. "Gotta be a gas station somewhere."

Of course, there wouldn't be any power to run the pumps, and probably no safe water, but she'd figure that out when she got there. Sunlight glimmered off the lake; she was fine, she told herself, because she wasn't too dehydrated for her mouth to wet at the thought of all that cool, fresh water.

Except there was no telling what kind of poison was in that lake. There was an old naval base on its shore, and the lake itself had been used as a kind of kiddie pool for submarines. Anything at all could be floating around in its waters. Not, she admitted, that there wasn't a certain irony to taking the long view at a time like this.

She spotted a Texaco station, the red and white sign bleached pink and ivory, crazed by the relentless desert sun. Harrie couldn't remember if she was in the Mojave or the Black Rock desert now, or some other desert entirely. They all ran together. She jumped at her own slightly hysterical giggle. The pumps were off, as she'd anticipated, but she leaned the Kawasaki up on its sidestand anyway, grabbed the climate-controlled case out of her saddlebag, and went to find a place to take a leak.

The leather was hot on her fingers when she pulled her gloves off and dropped her pants. "Damned, stupid... First thing I do when I get back to civilization is buy a set of leathers and a helmet in white, dammit." She glanced at the Kawasaki as she fixed herself, expecting a hiss of agreement, but the black bike was silent. She blinked stinging eyes and turned away.

There was a garden hose curled on its peg behind one of the tan-faced houses huddled by the Texaco station, the upper side bleached yellow on green like the belly of a dead snake. Harrie wrenched it off the peg one-handed. The rubber was brittle from dry rot; she broke it twice trying to uncoil a section, but managed to get about seven feet clean. She pried the fill cap off the underground tank with a tire iron and yanked off her helmet and air filter to sniff, checking both dosimeters first.

It had, after all, been one of those days.

The gas smelled more or less like gasoline, though, and it tasted like fucking gasoline too, when she got a good mouthful of it from sucking it up her impromptu siphon. Not very good gasoline, maybe, but beggars and choosers. The siphon wouldn't work as a siphon because she couldn't get the top end lower than the bottom end, but she could suck fuel up into it and transfer it, hoseful by hoseful, into the Kawasaki's empty tank, the precious case leaning against her boot while she did.

Finally, she saw the dark gleam of fluid shimmer through the fill hole when she peered inside and tapped the side of the tank.

She closed the tank and spat and spat, wishing she had water to wash the gasoline away. The lake glinted, mocking her, and she resolutely turned her back on it and picked up the case.

It was light in her hand. She paused with one hand on the flap of the saddlebag, weighing that gleaming silver object, staring past it at her boots. She sucked on her lower lip, tasted gas, and turned her head and spat again. "A few more years of freedom, Connie," she said, and stroked the metal with a black-gloved hand. "You and me. I could drink the water. It wouldn't matter if that was bad gas I fed you. Nothing could go wrong…"

The Kawasaki was silent. Its keys jangled in Harrie's

hip pocket. She touched the throttle lightly, drew her hand back, laid the unopened case on the seat. "What do you say, girl?"

Nothing, of course. It was quiescent, slumbering, a dreaming demon. She hadn't turned it on.

With both thumbs at once, Harrie flicked up the latches and opened the case.

It was cool inside, cool enough that she could feel the difference on her face when she bent over it. She kept the lid at half-mast, trying to block that cool air with her body so it wouldn't drift away. She tipped her head to see inside: blue foam threaded through with cooling elements, shaped to hold the contents without rattling. Papers in a plastic folder, and something in sealed culture plates, clear jelly daubed with ragged polka dots.

There was a sticky note tacked on the plastic folder. She reached into the cool case and flicked the sticky note out, bringing it into the light. Patch's handwriting. She blinked.

"Sacramento next, if these don't get there," it said, thick black definite lines. "Like Faustus, we all get one good chance to change our minds."

If you meet the Buddha on the road—

"I always thought there was more to that son of a bitch than met the eye," she said, and closed the case, and stuffed the note into her pocket beside the pen. She jammed her helmet back on, double-checking the filter that had maybe started leaking a little around the edges in Tonopah, slung her leg over the Kawasaki's saddle, and closed the choke.

It gasped dry when she clutched and thumbed the start button, shaking between her legs like an asthmatic pony.

She gave it a little throttle, then eased up on it like easing up on a virgin lover. Coaxing, pleading under her breath. Gasoline fumes from her mouth made her eyes tear inside the helmet; the tears or something else washed the grit away. One cylinder hiccuped. A second one caught.

She eased the choke as the Kawasaki coughed and purred, shivering, ready to run.

Both dosimeters kicked hard as she rolled across the flat, open plain toward Fallon, a deadly oasis in its own right. Apparently Nick hadn't been satisfied with a leukemia cluster and perchlorate and arsenic tainting the ground water; the trees Harrie saw as she rolled up on the startling green of the farming town weren't desert cottonwoods but towering giants of the European forest, and something grey and massive, shimmering with lovely crawling blue Cherenkov radiation, gleamed behind them. The signs she passed were in an alphabet she didn't understand, but she knew the name of this place.

A light rain was falling as she passed through Chernobyl.

It drove down harder as she turned west on the 50, toward Reno and Sparks and a crack under the edge of the clouds that glowed a toxic, sallow color with evening coming on. Her tires skittered on slick, greasy asphalt.

Where the cities should have been, stinking piles of garbage crouched against the yellowing evening sky, and nearly naked, starvation-slender people picked their way over slumped rubbish, calling the names of loved ones buried under the avalanche. Water sluiced down her helmet, soaked her saddle, plastered her leathers to her body. She wished she dared drink the rain. It didn't make her cool. It only made her wet.

She didn't turn her head to watch the wretched victims of the garbage slide. She was one hour out of Sacramento, and in Manila of fifty years ago.

Donner Pass was green and pleasant, sunset staining the sky ahead as red as meat. She was in plenty of time. It was all downhill from here.

Nick wasn't about to let her get away without a fight.

The big one had rerouted the Sacramento River too, and Harrie turned back at the edge because the bridge was down and the water was on fire. She motored away, a hundred meters, two hundred, until the heat of the burning river faded against her back. "What's that?" she asked the slim man in the pinstriped suit who waited for her by the roadside.

"Cuyahoga River fire," he said. "1969. Count your blessings. It could have been Bhopal."

"Blessings?" She spared him a sardonic smile, invisible behind her helmet. He tilted the brim of his hat with a grey-gloved finger. "I suppose you could say that. What is it really?"

"Phlegethon."

She raised her visor and peeked over her shoulder, watching the river burn. Even here, it was hot enough that her sodden leathers steamed against her back. The back of her hand pressed her breast pocket. The paper from Patch's note crinkled; her Cross poked her in the tit.

She looked at Nick, and Nick looked at her. "So that's it."

"That's all she wrote. It's too far to jump."

"I can see that."

"Give me the case and I'll let you go home. I'll give

you the Kawasaki and I'll give you your freedom. We'll call it even."

She eyed him, tension up her right leg, toe resting on the ground. The great purring bike shifted heavily between her legs, lithe as a cat, ready to turn and spit gravel from whirring tires. "Too far to jump."

"That's what I said."

Too far to jump. Maybe. And maybe if she gave him what was in the case, and doomed Sacramento like Bhopal, like Chernobyl, like Las Vegas…Maybe she'd be damning herself even if he gave it back to her. And even if she wasn't, she wasn't sure she and the Kawasaki could live with that answer.

If he wanted to keep her, he had to let her make the jump, and she could save Sacramento. If he was willing to lose her, she might die on the way over, and Sacramento might die with her, but they would die free.

Either way, Nick lost. And that was good enough for her.

"Devil take the hindmost," she said under her breath, and touched the throttle one more time.

SPEECH SOUNDS

BY OCTAVIA E. BUTLER

Octavia E. Butler was the author of a dozen novels and several short stories—a giant of the field who died long before her time. She was the first science fiction writer to receive the MacArthur Foundation's prestigious "genius" grant, and she also received a lifetime achievement award for her writing from the PEN American Center. In the speculative fiction field, she was also well-appreciated, having won two Hugos, two Nebulas, and a Locus Award—with her novelette "Bloodchild" winning all three. She died in February 2006. A new, short collection of previously unpublished works of Butler's—*Unexpected Stories*—appeared from digital publisher Open Road in 2014.

Butler's work frequently explored the subject of life after apocalypse. Though none of her novel-length works would be classified *primarily* as post-apocalyptic, her three multi-book series—the *Xenogenesis* trilogy, the

Patternist series, and the *Parable* duology—all take place in post-apocalyptic settings, making her an important author to the read in the sub-genre, even if her books are not really a part of it.

This story, which won the Hugo Award in 1984, was conceived by Butler after witnessing a bloody, senseless fight while riding the bus. In her story collection, *Bloodchild and Other Stories*, Butler said that witnessing the fight made her wonder "whether the human species would ever grow up enough to learn to communicate without using fists of one kind or another." And then the first line of the story came to her.

There was trouble aboard the Washington Boulevard bus. Rye had expected trouble sooner or later in her journey. She had put off going until loneliness and hopelessness drove her out. She believed she might have one group of relatives left alive—a brother and his two children twenty miles away in Pasadena. That was a day's journey one-way, if she were lucky. The unexpected arrival of the bus as she left her Virginia Road home had seemed to be a piece of luck—until the trouble began.

Two young men were involved in a disagreement of some kind, or, more likely, a misunderstanding. They stood in the aisle, grunting and gesturing at each other, each in his own uncertain T stance as the bus lurched over the potholes. The driver seemed to be putting some effort into keeping them off balance. Still, their gestures stopped just short of contact—mock punches, hand games of intimidation to replace lost curses.

People watched the pair, then looked at one another and made small anxious sounds. Two children whimpered.

Rye sat a few feet behind the disputants and across from the back door. She watched the two carefully, knowing the fight would begin when someone's nerve broke or someone's hand slipped or someone came to the end of his limited ability to communicate. These things could happen anytime.

One of them happened as the bus hit an especially large pothole and one man, tall, thin, and sneering, was thrown into his shorter opponent.

Instantly, the shorter man drove his left fist into the disintegrating sneer. He hammered his larger opponent as though he neither had nor needed any weapon other than his left fist. He hit quickly enough, hard enough to batter his opponent down before the taller man could regain his balance or hit back even once.

People screamed or squawked in fear. Those nearby scrambled to get out of the way. Three more young men roared in excitement and gestured wildly. Then, somehow, a second dispute broke out between two of these three—probably because one inadvertently touched or hit the other.

As the second fight scattered frightened passengers, a woman shook the driver's shoulder and grunted as she gestured toward the fighting.

The driver grunted back through bared teeth. Frightened, the woman drew away.

Rye, knowing the methods of bus drivers, braced herself and held on to the crossbar of the seat in front of her. When the driver hit the brakes, she was ready and the combatants were not. They fell over seats and onto screaming passengers, creating even more confusion. At least one more fight started.

The instant the bus came to a full stop, Rye was on her feet, pushing the back door. At the second push, it opened and she jumped out, holding her pack in one arm. Several other passengers followed, but some stayed on the bus. Buses were so rare and irregular now, people rode when they could, no matter what. There might not be another bus today—or tomorrow. People started walking, and if they saw a bus they flagged it down. People making intercity trips like Rye's from Los Angeles to Pasadena made plans to camp out, or risked seeking shelter with locals who might rob or murder them.

The bus did not move, but Rye moved away from it. She intended to wait until the trouble was over and get on again, but if there was shooting, she wanted the protection of a tree. Thus, she was near the curb when a battered blue Ford on the other side of the street made a U-turn and pulled up in front of the bus. Cars were rare these days—as rare as a severe shortage of fuel and of relatively unimpaired mechanics could make them. Cars that still ran were as likely to be used as weapons as they were to serve as transportation. Thus, when the driver of the Ford beckoned to Rye, she moved away warily. The driver got out—a big man, young, neatly bearded with dark, thick hair. He wore a long overcoat and a look of wariness that matched Rye's. She stood several feet from him, waiting to see what he would do. He looked at the bus, now rocking with the combat inside, then at the small cluster of passengers who had gotten off. Finally he looked at Rye again.

She returned his gaze, very much aware of the old

forty-five automatic her jacket concealed. She watched his hands.

He pointed with his left hand toward the bus. The dark-tinted windows prevented him from seeing what was happening inside.

His use of the left hand interested Rye more than his obvious question. Left-handed people tended to be less impaired, more reasonable and comprehending, less driven by frustration, confusion, and anger.

She imitated his gesture, pointing toward the bus with her own left hand, then punching the air with both fists.

The man took off his coat revealing a Los Angeles Police Department uniform complete with baton and service revolver.

Rye took another step back from him. There was no more LAPD, no more *any* large organization, governmental or private. There were neighborhood patrols and armed individuals. That was all.

The man took something from his coat pocket, then threw the coat into the car. Then he gestured Rye back, back toward the rear of the bus. He had something made of plastic in his hand. Rye did not understand what he wanted until he went to the rear door of the bus and beckoned her to stand there. She obeyed mainly out of curiosity. Cop or not, maybe he could do something to stop the stupid fighting.

He walked around the front of the bus, to the street side where the driver's window was open. There, she thought she saw him throw something into the bus. She was still trying to peer through the tinted glass when people began stumbling out the rear door, choking and weeping. Gas.

Rye caught an old woman who would have fallen, lifted

two little children down when they were in danger of being knocked down and trampled. She could see the bearded man helping people at the front door. She caught a thin old man shoved out by one of the combatants. Staggered by the old man's weight, she was barely able to get out of the way as the last of the young men pushed his way out. This one, bleeding from nose and mouth, stumbled into another, and they grappled blindly, still sobbing from the gas.

The bearded man helped the bus driver out through the front door, though the driver did not seem to appreciate his help. For a moment, Rye thought there would be another fight. The bearded man stepped back and watched the driver gesture threateningly, watched him shout in wordless anger.

The bearded man stood still, made no sound, refused to respond to clearly obscene gestures. The least impaired people tended to do this—stand back unless they were physically threatened and let those with less control scream and jump around. It was as though they felt it beneath them to be as touchy as the less comprehending. This was an attitude of superiority, and that was the way people like the bus driver perceived it. Such "superiority" was frequently punished by beatings, even by death. Rye had had close calls of her own. As a result, she never went unarmed. And in this world where the only likely common language was body language, being armed was often enough. She had rarely had to draw her gun or even display it.

The bearded man's revolver was on constant display. Apparently that was enough for the bus driver. The driver spat in disgust, glared at the bearded man for a moment longer, then strode back to his gas-filled bus. He stared at it for a moment, clearly wanting to get in, but the gas was still too strong. Of the windows, only his tiny driver's window actually opened. The front door was open, but the rear door would not stay open unless someone held it. Of course, the air conditioning had failed long ago. The bus would take some time to clear. It was the driver's property, his livelihood. He had pasted old magazine pictures of items he would accept as fare on its sides. Then he would use what he collected to feed his family or to trade. If his bus did not run, he did not eat. On the other hand, if the inside of his bus was torn apart by senseless fighting, he would not eat very well either. He was apparently unable to perceive this. All he could see was that it would be some time before he could use his bus again. He shook his fist at the bearded man and shouted. There seemed to be words in his shout, but Rye could not understand them. She did not know whether this was his fault or hers. She had heard so little coherent human speech for the past three years, she was no longer certain how well she recognized it, no longer certain of the degree of her own impairment.

The bearded man sighed. He glanced toward his car, then beckoned to Rye. He was ready to leave, but he wanted something from her first. No. No, he wanted her to leave with him. Risk getting into his car when, in spite of his uniform, law and order were nothing—not even words any longer.

She shook her head in a universally understood negative, but the man continued to beckon.

She waved him away. He was doing what the less impaired rarely did—drawing potentially negative attention to another of his kind. People from the bus had begun to look at her.

One of the men who had been fighting tapped another on the arm, then pointed from the bearded man to Rye, and finally held up the first two fingers of his right hand as though giving two-thirds of a Boy Scout salute. The gesture was very quick, its meaning obvious even at a distance. She had been grouped with the bearded man. Now what?

The man who had made the gesture started toward her.

She had no idea what he intended, but she stood her ground. The man was half a foot taller than she was and perhaps ten years younger. She did not imagine she could outrun him. Nor did she expect anyone to help her if she needed help. The people around her were all strangers.

She gestured once—a clear indication to the man to stop. She did not intend to repeat the gesture. Fortunately, the man obeyed. He gestured obscenely and several other men laughed. Loss of verbal language had spawned a whole new set of obscene gestures. The man, with stark simplicity, had accused her of sex with the bearded man and had suggested she accommodate the other men present—beginning with him.

Rye watched him wearily. People might very well stand by and watch if he tried to rape her. They would also stand and watch her shoot him. Would he push things that far?

He did not. After a series of obscene gestures that brought him no closer to her, he turned contemptuously and walked away.

And the bearded man still waited. He had removed his service revolver, holster and all. He beckoned again, both hands empty. No doubt his gun was in the car and within easy reach, but his taking it off impressed her. Maybe he was all right. Maybe he was just alone. She had been alone herself for three years. The illness had stripped her, killing her children one by one, killing her husband, her sister, her parents. . . .

The illness, if it was an illness, had cut even the living off from one another. As it swept over the country, people hardly had time to lay blame on the Soviets (though they were falling silent along with the rest of the world), on a new virus, a new pollutant, radiation, divine retribution. . . . The illness was stroke-swift in the way it cut people down and strokelike in some of its effects. But it was highly specific. Language was always lost or severely impaired. It was never regained. Often there was also paralysis, intellectual impairment, death.

Rye walked toward the bearded man, ignoring the whistling and applauding of two of the young men and their thumbs-up signs to the bearded man. If he had smiled at them or acknowledged them in any way, she would almost certainly have changed her mind. If she had let herself think of the possible deadly consequences of getting into a stranger's car, she would have changed her mind. Instead, she thought of the man who lived across the street from her. He rarely washed since his bout with the illness. And he had gotten into the habit of urinating wherever he happened to be. He had two women already—one tending each of his large gardens. They put up with him in exchange for his protection. He had made it clear that he wanted Rye to become his third woman.

She got into the car and the bearded man shut the door. She watched as he walked around to the driver's door—watched for his sake because his gun was on the seat beside her. And the bus driver and a pair of young men had come a few steps closer. They did nothing, though, until the bearded man was in the car. Then one of them threw a rock. Others followed his example, and as the car drove away, several rocks bounced off harmlessly.

When the bus was some distance behind them, Rye wiped sweat from her forehead and longed to relax. The bus would have taken her more than halfway to Pasadena. She would have had only ten miles to walk. She wondered how far she would have to walk now—and wondered if walking a long distance would be her only problem.

At Figuroa and Washington where the bus normally made a left turn, the bearded man stopped, looked at her, and indicated that she should choose a direction. When she directed him left and he actually turned left, she began to relax. If he was willing to go where she directed, perhaps he was safe.

As they passed blocks of burned, abandoned buildings, empty lots, and wrecked or stripped cars, he slipped a gold chain over his head and handed it to her. The pendant attached to it was a smooth, glassy, black rock. Obsidian. His name might be Rock or Peter or Black, but she decided to think of him as Obsidian. Even her sometimes useless memory would retain a name like Obsidian.

She handed him her own name symbol—a pin in the shape of a large golden stalk of wheat. She had bought it long before the illness and the silence began. Now she wore it, thinking it was as close as she was likely to come to Rye. People like Obsidian who had not known her before probably thought of her as Wheat. Not that it mattered. She would never hear her name spoken again.

Obsidian handed her pin back to her. He caught her hand as she reached for it and rubbed his thumb over her calluses.

He stopped at First Street and asked which way again. Then, after turning right as she had indicated, he parked near the Music Center. There, he took a folded paper from the dashboard and unfolded it. Rye recognized it as a street map, though the writing on it meant nothing to her. He flattened the map, took her hand again, and put her index finger on one spot. He touched her, touched himself, pointed toward the floor. In effect, "We are here." She knew he wanted to know where she was going. She wanted to tell him, but she shook her head sadly. She had lost reading and writing. That was her most serious impairment and her most painful. She had taught history at UCLA. She had done freelance writing. Now she could not even read her own manuscripts. She had a houseful of books that she could neither read nor bring herself to use as fuel. And she had a memory that would not bring back to her much of what she had read before.

She stared at the map, trying to calculate. She had been born in Pasadena, had lived for fifteen years in Los Angeles. Now she was near L.A. Civic Center. She knew the relative positions of the two cities, knew streets, directions, even knew to stay away from freeways, which might be blocked by wrecked cars and destroyed overpasses. She ought to know how to point out Pasadena even though she could not recognize the word.

Hesitantly, she placed her hand over a pale orange patch in the upper right corner of the map. That should be right. Pasadena.

Obsidian lifted her hand and looked under it, then folded the map and put it back on the dashboard. He could read, she realized belatedly. He could probably write, too. Abruptly, she hated him—deep, bitter hatred. What did literacy mean to him—a grown man who played cops and robbers? But he was literate and she was not. She never would be. She felt sick to her stomach with hatred, frustration, and jealousy. And only a few inches from her hand was a loaded gun.

She held herself still, staring at him, almost seeing his blood. But her rage crested and ebbed and she did nothing.

Obsidian reached for her hand with hesitant familiarity. She looked at him. Her face had already revealed too much. No person still living in what was left of human society could fail to recognize that expression, that jealousy.

She closed her eyes wearily, drew a deep breath. She had experienced longing for the past, hatred of the present, growing hopelessness, purposelessness, but she had never experienced such a powerful urge to kill another person. She had left her home, finally, because she had come near to killing herself. She had found no reason to stay alive. Perhaps that was why she had gotten into Obsidian's car. She had never before done such a thing.

He touched her mouth and made chatter motions with thumb and fingers. Could she speak?

She nodded and watched his milder envy come and go. Now both had admitted what it was not safe to admit, and there had been no violence. He tapped his mouth and forehead and shook his head. He did not speak or comprehend spoken language. The illness had played with them, taking away, she suspected, what each valued most.

She plucked at his sleeve, wondering why he had

decided on his own to keep the LAPD alive with what he had left. He was sane enough otherwise. Why wasn't he at home raising corn, rabbits, and children? But she did not know how to ask. Then he put his hand on her thigh and she had another question to deal with.

She shook her head. Disease, pregnancy, helpless, solitary agony...no.

He massaged her thigh gently and smiled in obvious disbelief.

No one had touched her for three years. She had not wanted anyone to touch her. What kind of world was this to chance bringing a child into even if the father were willing to stay and help raise it? It was too bad, though. Obsidian could not know how attractive he was to her—young, probably younger than she was, clean, asking for what he wanted rather than demanding it. But none of that mattered. What were a few moments of pleasure measured against a lifetime of consequences?

He pulled her closer to him and for a moment she let herself enjoy the closeness. He smelled good—male and good. She pulled away reluctantly.

He sighed, reached toward the glove compartment. She stiffened, not knowing what to expect, but all he took out was a small box. The writing on it meant nothing to her. She did not understand until he broke the seal, opened the box, and took out a condom. He looked at her, and she first looked away in surprise. Then she giggled. She could not remember when she had last giggled.

He grinned, gestured toward the backseat, and she laughed aloud. Even in her teens, she had disliked backseats of cars. But she looked around at the empty streets and ruined buildings, then she got out and into the backseat. He let her put the condom on him, then seemed surprised at her eagerness.

Sometime later, they sat together, covered by his coat, unwilling to become clothed near-strangers again just yet. He made rock-the-baby gestures and looked questioningly at her.

She swallowed, shook her head. She did not know how to tell him her children were dead.

He took her hand and drew a cross in it with his index finger, then made his baby-rocking gesture again.

She nodded, held up three fingers, then turned away, trying to shut out a sudden flood of memories. She had told herself that the children growing up now were to be pitied. They would run through the downtown canyons with no real memory of what the buildings had been or even how they had come to be. Today's children gathered books as well as wood to be burned as fuel. They ran through the streets chasing one another and hooting like chimpanzees. They had no future. They were now all they would ever be.

He put his hand on her shoulder, and she turned suddenly, fumbling for his small box, then urging him to make love to her again. He could give her forgetfulness and pleasure. Until now, nothing had been able to do that. Until now, every day had brought her closer to the time when she would do what she had left home to avoid doing: putting her gun in her mouth and pulling the trigger.

She asked Obsidian if he would come home with her, stay with her.

He looked surprised and pleased once he understood.

But he did not answer at once. Finally, he shook his head as she had feared he might. He was probably having too much fun playing cops and robbers and picking up women.

She dressed in silent disappointment, unable to feel any anger toward him. Perhaps he already had a wife and a home. That was likely. The illness had been harder on men than on women—had killed more men, had left male survivors more severely impaired. Men like Obsidian were rare. Women either settled for less or stayed alone. If they found an Obsidian, they did what they could to keep him. Rye suspected he had someone younger, prettier keeping him.

He touched her while she was strapping her gun on and asked with a complicated series of gestures whether it was loaded.

She nodded grimly. He patted her arm.

She asked once more if he would come home with her, this time using a different series of gestures. He had seemed hesitant. Perhaps he could be courted.

He got out and into the front seat without responding. She took her place in front again, watching him. Now he plucked at his uniform and looked at her. She thought she was being asked something but did not know what it was.

He took off his badge, tapped it with one finger, then tapped his chest. Of course.

She took the badge from his hand and pinned her wheat stalk to it. If playing cops and robbers was his only insanity, let him play. She would take him, uniform and all. It occurred to her that she might eventually lose him to someone he would meet as he had met her. But she would have him for a while. He took the street map down again, tapped it, pointed vaguely northeast toward Pasadena, then looked at her.

She shrugged, tapped his shoulder, then her own, and held up her index and second fingers tight together, just to be sure.

He grasped the two fingers and nodded. He was with her.

She took the map from him and threw it onto the dashboard. She pointed back southwest—back toward home. Now she did not have to go to Pasadena. Now she could go on having a brother there and two nephews—three right-handed males. Now she did not have to find out for certain whether she was as alone as she feared. Now she was not alone.

Obsidian took Hill Street south, then Washington west, and she leaned back, wondering what it would be like to have someone again. With what she had scavenged, what she had preserved, and what she grew, there was easily enough food for them. There was certainly room enough in a four-bedroom house. He could move his possessions in. Best of all, the animal across the street would pull back and possibly not force her to kill him.

Obsidian had drawn her closer to him, and she had put her head on his shoulder when suddenly he braked hard, almost throwing her off the seat. Out of the corner of her eye, she saw that someone had run across the street in front of the car. One car on the street and someone had to run in front of it.

Straightening up, Rye saw that the runner was a woman, fleeing from an old frame house to a boarded-up storefront. She ran silently, but the man who followed her a moment later shouted what sounded like garbled words as he ran. He had something in his hand. Not a gun. A knife, perhaps.

The woman tried a door, found it locked, looked around desperately, finally snatched up a fragment of glass broken from the storefront window. With this she turned to face her pursuer. Rye thought she would be more likely to cut her own hand than to hurt anyone else with the glass.

Obsidian jumped from the car, shouting. It was the first time Rye had heard his voice—deep and hoarse from disuse He made the same sound over and over the way some speechless people did, "Da, da, da!"

Rye got out of the car as Obsidian ran toward the couple. He had drawn his gun. Fearful, she drew her own and released the safety. She looked around to see who else might be attracted to the scene. She saw the man glance at Obsidian, then suddenly lunge at the woman. The woman jabbed his face with her glass, but he caught her arm and managed to stab her twice before Obsidian shot him.

The man doubled, then toppled, clutching his abdomen. Obsidian shouted, then gestured Rye over to help the woman. Rye moved to the woman's side, remembering that she had little more than bandages and antiseptic in her pack. But the woman was beyond help. She had been stabbed with a long, slender boning knife.

She touched Obsidian to let him know the woman was dead. He had bent to check the wounded man who lay still and also seemed dead. But as Obsidian looked around to see what Rye wanted, the man opened his eyes. Face contorted, he seized Obsidian's just-holstered revolver and fired. The bullet caught Obsidian in the temple and he collapsed.

It happened just that simply, just that fast. An instant later, Rye shot the wounded man as he was turning the gun on her.

And Rye was alone—with three corpses.

She knelt beside Obsidian, dry-eyed, frowning, trying to understand why everything had suddenly changed. Obsidian was gone. He had died and left her—like everyone else.

Two very small children came out of the house from which the man and woman had run—a boy and girl perhaps three years old. Holding hands, they crossed the street toward Rye. They stared at her, then edged past her and went to the dead woman. The girl shook the woman's arm as though trying to wake her.

This was too much. Rye got up, feeling sick to her stomach with grief and anger. If the children began to cry, she thought she would vomit.

They were on their own, those two kids. They were old enough to scavenge. She did not need any more grief. She did not need a stranger's children who would grow up to be hairless chimps.

She went back to the car. She could drive home, at least. She remembered how to drive.

The thought that Obsidian should be buried occurred to her before she reached the car, and she did vomit.

She had found and lost the man so quickly. It was as though she had been snatched from comfort and security and given a sudden, inexplicable beating. Her head would not clear. She could not think.

Somehow, she made herself go back to him, look at him. She found herself on her knees beside him with no memory of having knelt. She stroked his face, his beard. One of the children made a noise and she looked at them, at the woman who was probably their mother. The children looked back at her, obviously frightened. Perhaps it was their fear that reached her finally.

She had been about to drive away and leave them. She had almost done it, almost left two toddlers to die. Surely there had been enough dying. She would have to take the children home with her. She would not be able to live with any other decision. She looked around for a place to bury three bodies. Or two. She wondered if the murderer were the children's father. Before the silence, the police had always said some of the most dangerous calls they went out on were domestic disturbance calls. Obsidian should have known that—not that the knowledge would have kept him in the car. It would not have held her back either. She could not have watched the woman murdered and done nothing.

She dragged Obsidian toward the car. She had nothing to dig with her, and no one to guard for her while she dug. Better to take the bodies with her and bury them next to her husband and her children. Obsidian would come home with her after all.

When she had gotten him onto the floor in the back, she returned for the woman. The little girl, thin, dirty, solemn, stood up and unknowingly gave Rye a gift. As Rye began to drag the woman by her arms, the little girl screamed, "No!"

Rye dropped the woman and stared at the girl.

"No!" the girl repeated. She came to stand beside the woman. "Go away!" she told Rye.

"Don't talk," the little boy said to her. There was no blurring or confusing of sounds. Both children had spoken and Rye had understood. The boy looked at the dead murderer and moved further from him. He took the girl's hand. "Be quiet," he whispered.

Fluent speech! Had the woman died because she could talk and had taught her children to talk? Had she been killed by a husband's festering anger or by a stranger's jealous rage?

And the children…they must have been born after the silence. Had the disease run its course, then? Or were these children simply immune? Certainly they had had time to fall sick and silent. Rye's mind leaped ahead. What if children of three or fewer years were safe and able to learn language? What if all they needed were teachers? Teachers and protectors.

Rye glanced at the dead murderer. To her shame, she thought she could understand some of the passions that must have driven him, whomever he was. Anger, frustration, hopelessness, insane jealousy…how many more of him were there—people willing to destroy what they could not have?

Obsidian had been the protector, had chosen that role for who knew what reason. Perhaps putting on an obsolete uniform and patrolling the empty streets had been what he did instead of putting a gun into his mouth. And now that there was something worth protecting, he was gone.

She had been a teacher. A good one. She had been a protector, too, though only of herself. She had kept herself alive when she had no reason to live. If the illness let these children alone, she could keep them alive.

Somehow she lifted the dead woman into her arms and placed her on the backseat of the car. The children began to cry, but she knelt on the broken pavement and whispered to them, fearful of frightening them with the harshness of her long unused voice.

"It's all right," she told them. "You're going with us, too. Come on." She lifted them both, one in each arm. They were so light. Had they been getting enough to eat?

The boy covered her mouth with his hand, but she moved her face away. "It's all right for me to talk," she told him. "As long as no one's around, it's all right." She put the boy down on the front seat of the car and he moved over without being told to, to make room for the girl. When they were both in the car, Rye leaned against the window, looking at them, seeing that they were less afraid now, that they watched her with at least as much curiosity as fear.

"I'm Valerie Rye," she said, savoring the words. "It's all right for you to talk to me."

KILLERS
BY CAROL EMSHWILLER

Carol Emshwiller is the author of six novels and more than 100 short stories. Her short work has appeared in numerous anthologies and magazines, and has been collected in several volumes, most recently in *The Collected Stories of Carol Emshwiller*. In her career spanning five decades, she has won the Nebula Award, the World Fantasy Award, and the Philip K. Dick Award. In 2005, she was presented the World Fantasy Award for Life-Time Achievement. Her most recent novel, *The Secret City*, was published in 2007.

Emshwiller can't help but wonder if our civilization will fall apart one of these days. But being the kind of person who loves the simple life—oil lamps, walking, pumping water for a shower, washing diapers at the shore of a lake on an old-fashioned washboard—-she's hesitant to say she's "afraid" it'll happen. She's not looking forward to it either, but she says it's just as much fun writing about regression and devastation as it is writing about a future full of new gadgets and inventions.

"Killers" grew out of Emshwiller's objections to the war in Iraq. The American people have been told that we're fighting terrorists over there so we don't have to fight them here. This story ponders what it would be like afterward if such a war did come to our shores.

Most people left because of no water. I don't know where they found a place where things were any better. Some of us felt safer here than anywhere else. And even way before the war wound down, it was hard to pick up and go someplace. No gas for civilians. Pretty soon no gas at all.

After the bombing of our pipeline (one man with a grenade could have done that), we got together and moved the town up higher, along a stream and put in ditches so that the water came past several houses. We have to carry water into the house in buckets and we have to empty the sink by hand, back out into the yard. At least the water flows into our kitchen gardens and past our fruit trees. In warm weather, we bathe in our irrigation ditch, in colder we sponge off inside, in basins, but there's hardly any cold weather anymore.

There wasn't much to moving the town since most of us were gone already. All the able-bodied men, of course, so it took us women to make the move ourselves and without horses or mules. The enemy stole them or killed them or maimed them just to make things harder for us.

No electricity, though some of the women think they can hook the dam back up and get some. Nobody has bothered to try it yet. In a way none of this bothers me as much as you'd think. I always liked walking, and we have rendered fat lamps and candles that send out a soft, cozy glow.

Our house was already well above where the town used to be. Good because I didn't want to move. I want my brother to have our old home to come back to. And besides, I couldn't move Mother.

Beyond our back yard there used to be the Department of Water and Power, after that Forest Service land, and then the John Muir wilderness. Now the town has moved above me, and of course there's no DWP or Forest Service anymore.

Our house has a good view. We always sat on the front steps and looked at the mountains. Now that everybody has moved up the mountain side, everybody has a good view.

The town below is empty. The Vons and Kmart are big looted barns. Up here there's one small store where we sell each other our produce or our sewing and knitting. Especially socks. Hard to get socks these days. Before the war we were so wasteful nobody darned anymore, but now we not only darn but reinforce the heels and toes of brand new socks before we wear them.

We moved the little library up. Actually it's got more books than before. We brought all the books we could find, ours and those from the people who left. We don't need a librarian. Everybody brings them back honor system.

We have a little hospital but no doctors, just a couple of elderly nurses who were too old to be recruited. They're in their seventies and still going. They've trained new ones. No medicines though. Only what we can get from local herbs. We went to the Paiute to find out more. There's a couple of Paiute nurses, who come to help out every now and then, though they have their own nursing to do on the reservation. (They moved the rez up, too, and they don't call it the reservation anymore.)

It's a woman's town now. Full of women's arts and crafts…. Quilt makers, sweater knitters…. And the women do the heavy work. There's a good roof repair group and there's carpenters….

Lots of women went to war along with the men, but I had to look after Mother. I was taking care of her even before my brother left. She wasn't exactly sick but she was fat and she drank. Her legs looked terrible, full of varicosities. It hurt her to walk so she didn't. When the war came she got a little better because of the shortages, though there was still plenty of homemade beer, but she couldn't walk. Or wouldn't. I think her muscles had all withered away. Looking after somebody who can't walk seems normal to me. I've done it since I can first remember anything.

Now that Mother's gone I have a chance to do something useful. If I knew the war was still going on in some specific place, I'd go fight, but it *seems* to be over. Maybe. It didn't stop exactly. I don't know how it ended or even if it's ended. We don't have a way to find out, but there hasn't been any action that we know of for quite some time. Overhead, nothing flies by. Not even anything old fashioned. (Not that we ever had any action to speak of way out here. Except for the bombing of our pipeline and stealing our livestock, nobody cared much about us.)

But that's the way the war was, hardly a beginning and hardly an end. Wars aren't like they used to be—with two clearly separated sides. The enemy was among us even before it started. They could never win a real old-fashioned war with us, they were weak and low tech, but low tech was good enough as long as there were lots of them. You never knew who to trust, and we still don't. Our side put all we could in internment camps, practically everybody with black eyes and hair and olive skin, but you can't get them all. And then the war went on so long we used up all our resources, but they still had theirs—sabotage doesn't ever have to stop. They escaped from the camps. Actually they just walked away. The guards had already walked away, too.

Lots of those men brought their injuries and craziness to our mountains. Both sides came here to get away from everything. They're hermits. They don't trust anybody. Some of them are still fighting each other up there. It's almost as bad as having left-over minefields. They're all damaged, physically or mentally. Of course most likely all of us are, too, and we probably don't even know it.

My brother might be out there somewhere. If he's alive he's got to be here. He loves this place. He hunted and trapped and fished. He'd get along fine and I know he'd do anything to come back.

Most of those men don't come down to us even if they're starving or cold or sick. Those that do, come to steal. They take our tomatoes and corn and radishes. Other things disappear, too. Kitchen knives, spoons, fishhooks…. And of course sweaters and woolen socks…. Those crazies live up even higher than we do. It does still get cold up there.

And they are crazies. And now one of them has been killing other men and dumping them at the edge of the village. They've all been shot in the back by wooden crossbow darts. Beautifully carved and polished. I hope it isn't one of our side. Though I don't suppose sides matter anymore.

Every time this happens, before we put them into the depository, I go to check if it's my brother. I wouldn't want my brother in the depository. Ever. But those men are always such a mess—dirty and bearded—I wonder, would I recognize him? I keep thinking: How could I not? But I was only fifteen when he left. He was eighteen. He'd be thirty-two now. If he's alive.

We're all a little edgy even if it's not us getting killed. And then last night I saw someone looking in my window. I'd been asleep but I heard a noise and woke up. I saw the silhouette of a lumpy hat and a mass of tangled hair flying out from under it, the moonlit sky glowing behind. I called out, "Clement!" I didn't mean to. I was half asleep and in that state I knew it was my brother. Whoever it was ducked down in a hurry and I heard the crunch, crunch of somebody running away. Afterwards I got scared. I could have been shot as I slept.

The next morning I saw footprints and it looked like somebody had spent some time behind my shed.

I keep hoping it's my brother, though I wouldn't want him to be the one killing those poor men, but you'd think he wouldn't be afraid of coming to his own house. Of course he doesn't know that Mother is dead. I can understand him being afraid of her. They never got along. When she was drunk she used to throw things at him. If he got close enough, she'd grab his arm and twist. Then he got too strong for her. But he couldn't be afraid of me. Could he? I'm the baby sister.

Mother was nicer to me. She got worried I'd stay out of reach or not help anymore. I could have just walked off and left her but until she died I didn't think of it. I actually didn't. I'd looked after her for so long I thought that's just the way life is. And I might not have left, anyway. She *was* my mother and there was nobody else to look after her but me.

If it's my brother been looking in the window, he must know Mother isn't here. She never left her bed. The house is small and all on one floor so he could have looked in all the windows. We have three tiny bedrooms, and one kitchen/living room combined. Mother and her big bed took up wall-to-wall space in the biggest bedroom.

I posted Clement's picture at the store and the library, but of course it was a picture from long ago. In it he has the usual army shaved head. I drew a version with wild hair. Then I drew another of him bald with wild hair around the sides. (Baldness runs in our family.) I drew a different kind of beard on each of them. I put up both versions.

Leo at the store said, "He might not want to talk to you…or anybody."

But I know that already.

"I think he's come looking in my window."

"Well, there you are. He'd a come in if he'd wanted to."

"You went to war. How come you're okay and most all the other men have gone wild?"

"I was lucky. I never saw real horror."

Actually he may not be so okay. Most of us never married. We never had the chance with all the men gone. He could have married one of us but he never did. He lives in a messy shed behind the store and he smells, even though the ditch passes right by his store. And he's always grumpy. You have to get used to him.

"If my brother comes around, tell him I'm going out to look for him in all his favorite spots."

"Even if you find him he won't come back."

"So then I'll go after that crazy person who's been killing those men."

Truth is, I don't know what to do with myself. I don't know how to live with just me to care about. I can go anywhere and do anything. I ought to find the man who's the killer. I have nothing else to do. Who better to do it than I?

But I might find that man right here, hiding at the edge of the village—or most likely looking in my window. Maybe I can trap him in my house. He must have been looking in for a reason.

I pack up and pretend to leave. I stay out of sight of the village. This is wild rocky land—lots of hiding places. Nobody will know I didn't go anywhere. My backpack is mostly empty. I have pepper. Pepper is hard to get these days so I've saved mine for a weapon. I have a small knife in my boot and a bigger one at my belt. Streams aren't stocked anymore but there's still fish around, though not as many as before. I bring a line and hooks. I'll use those today. I won't go far.

I catch a trout. I have to make a fire the old-fashioned way. No more matches. I always carry a handful of dead sage fibers for tinder. I cook the fish and eat it. After dark and the half-moon comes up, I sneak back to our house as if I was one of those crazies myself.

The door is wide open. There's sand all over the floor.

Couldn't he even shut the door? These days we have sand storms and dust devils more often than we used to. Doesn't whoever it is know that? And that's another reason to move higher up, into the trees where it's less deserty.

I smell him before I see him. I put my knife up my sleeve so it'll drop down into my hand.

I can hear him breathing. Sounds like scared breathing. A man this frightened will be dangerous.

He's huddled in Mother's bedroom down between the bed and the bedside table. All I see is his hat, pulled low so his face is in shadow. I see his bare knees showing through his torn pants. I have a better look at them than his face.

Right away I think my brother wouldn't be in Mother's room, he'd be in his own room. Besides, the room still smells of death and dying. I call, "Clement?" even though I know it can't be him. "Come on out."

He groans.

"Are you sick?" He sounds sick. I suppose that's why he's here in the first place.

I wish I'd lit a lamp first. I was counting on the moonlight, but there isn't much shining in here. It still could be my brother, under all that dirt and wild hair and beard, gone crazy just like everybody else.

"Come out. Come to the main room. I'll light a lamp. I'll fix you food."

"No light."

"Why not? There's only me. And there's no war going on anymore. It's most likely over."

"I pledged to fight until I died."

(I suppose my brother did, too.)

I finger my knife. "I'm going to go light the lamp."

I deliberately turn my back. I go to the main room,

light the lamp with the sparker, keeping my back to the bedroom door. I hear him come in. I turn and get a good look.

Pieced-together hat, long scraggly hair hanging under it. I can't tell if he's a brown man or just weather-beaten, sunburned, and dirty. A full beard with gray in it. Eyes as black as the enemy's always are. Eyebrows just as thick as theirs. He has a broken front tooth. Nowadays that's not unusual. Nobody to fix them. He has a greenish look under his tan and dark circles around his eyes. If he thinks he isn't sick he doesn't know much.

"You *are* the enemy. And you're half-dead already."

There's a chair right beside him, but he sinks sideways to the floor. Ends up flat on our worn linoleum. If he thinks he's still fighting the war, I should kill him now while I have the chance. He looks such a mess and smells so bad I'm almost ready to kill him just for those reasons alone. After Mother died I thought I was finished with disagreeable messes.

"Hide me. Just for tonight. I'll leave in the morning."

"Are you crazy?" I kneel beside him. "You're the one killing people. I should kill you right now."

He's trying to prop himself up against the wall. I don't want to touch him but I grab his shirt front to help him and the rotten cloth rips completely out.

"You stink something awful. And why would I think you won't kill me? You've been killing everybody else."

"I don't have a weapon."

"Strip."

"What?"

"Take those filthy clothes off. I'll burn them. I'll bring you a basin to wash in." (And I'll find out if he has a weapon.)

He hasn't the energy to undress or wash. I hate to touch him but I do it. I'm used to it. Mother was a mess as she was dying. (At the end I sprinkled pine needles all over but it didn't help much.) I thought that was the last of that sort of thing I'd ever have to do. I thought I was free. But, all right, one more thing. I wash him and dress him in my brother's old clothes, and…what then? If I kill him, the town will be grateful.

At least his body is entirely different from Mother's, thin and strong and hairy. It's a nice change. If he wasn't so smelly I'd enjoy it. Well, I do enjoy it.

He's half asleep through it all.

I burn his clothes in our little stove. After I've washed him, I feed him jerky broth with an egg in it, though I keep thinking: Why waste my egg on him? He falls asleep right after he's finished the broth. Slides down the wall flat out again, in what seems more a faint than a sleep.

I decide to shave him and cut his hair. He won't notice. If he'd been more conscious I'd have asked him if he wanted a mustache or a little goatee but I'm glad he isn't. I have fun with different haircuts, different sideburns, smaller and smaller mustaches until there's none. Hair, too. I take off more than I meant to, except what does it matter, he's a dead man.

Not a very handsome man whatever way I fixed his hair and beard, though along the way there were some nicer stages—better than what I ended up with. I finish by shaving him. Also not a good job. I make nicks. Where I shaved his beard, his skin is pale. His forehead, where his hat was, is pale too. There's only a sun-browned strip across his face just below his eyes. I like the maleness of him no matter that he's ugly. I don't mind his broken tooth. We're all in the same boat as to teeth.

I fall asleep at the kitchen table, right in the middle of thinking up ways to kill him. Also thinking about how we've all changed—how, in the olden days, I'd not ever have been thinking things at all like that.

In the morning he seems some better—well enough for me to help him stagger, first to the outhouse, and then into my brother's room. He keeps feeling his face and hair. I stop at the hall mirror and let him take a look. He's shocked. He has a kind of wet cat/plucked chicken look.

I say, "Sorry." I *am* sorry…sorry for anybody who gets their hair cut by me. But he should be glad I haven't slit his throat.

He stares at himself, but then says, "Thank you." And so sincerely that I realize I've made him the best disguise there is. He said, "Hide me," and I did. Nobody will take him for one of those wild men now.

I prop him up on the pillows of my brother's bed and bring him milk and tea. He looks so much better I wonder…. If he's not going to die on his own, I'll have to think what to do with him.

"What's your name?"

He doesn't answer. He could say anything. I'd have believed him and I'd have had something to call him by.

"Tell me a name. I don't care what."

He thinks, then says, "Jal."

"Make it Joe."

I don't trust him. But if he has any sense at all he knows I'm the only one can keep him safe. Though nobody has much sense anymore.

"Everybody got tired of the war a long time ago." I bang my cup down so hard that my tea spills. "Haven't you noticed?"

"I swore to fight to the death."

"I'll bet you don't even know which side is which anymore. If you ever did."

"You're the ones heated up the planet. It wasn't us. It was you and your greed."

I haven't been so aggravated since my brother was around. "It heated up mostly by itself. It's done that before, you know. Besides, all that's over. Our part in it anyway. Killing crazies isn't going to help. You're crazy!" Not the best thing to say to a crazy, but I go on anyway. "All you hermits are crazy. You're nothing but trouble."

He's taking it all in…. Maybe he is. Maybe he just doesn't have the energy to argue.

"I'm going out to get us a rabbit. If you want to keep on making trouble, don't be here when I come back."

I leave. He'll be all alone with my butcher knife and pepper. And I suppose his crossbow isn't far off. I might as well give him a chance to show what he is.

I make the rounds of my traps. They're lower down. I've set them around the town. It's a ghost town. I'm the only one goes down there now and then…usually only on a cool day. Which hardly ever happens. Today it must be well over 110 degrees. Now our whole valley in winter is as if Death Valley in summer.

What I trap down there are rats. We cook those up and call them rabbit, though nobody cares anymore what we call them.

I find two big black ones, big as cats. We like those

better than the small brown kind, lots more meat on them. (Seems as if the rats are getting bigger all the time.) My traps broke their necks. I don't have to worry about killing them. I tie their tails to my belt, then wander the town in hopes of finding something not already scavenged. I find a quarter. I take it though it's worthless. Maybe a Paiute might turn it into jewelry. On purpose I don't climb back up to my house until late afternoon and until I drink all the water I brought.

Before I go in I check around my shed and house for a crossbow and darts, and then beyond, under the bushes, but I don't find them.

He's still there. Asleep. And no weapons that I can see, but I check the kitchen knives. The largest one, big as a machete, is gone. And he might be pretending to be sicker than he is.

Enemy or not, I do like a man in the house. I watch him sleep. He has such long eyelashes. I like the hair on his knuckles. Just looking at his hands makes me think how there's so few men around. Actually only four. His forearms…. Ours don't ever look like that no matter how much we saw and hammer. Even my brother's never looked like that. I like that he already needs a shave again. I even like his bushy eyebrows.

But I have to go clean rats.

When I start rattling around the kitchen section of our main room, he gets up and staggers to the table. Stops at the hall mirror again on the way and studies himself for a long time. As if he forgot what he looked like under all that hair. He sits, then, and watches me make two-rat stew with wild onions and turnips. I thicken it with acorn flour I traded for with the Paiute.

It takes a while for the stew to finish up. I make squaw tea and sit across from him. Being so close and looking into his eyes upsets me. I have to get up and turn my back. I pretend the stew needs stirring. To hide my feelings I say, "Where's your crossbow? And where's my knife? I won't let you have my stew until you tell me." I sound more angry than I meant to.

"Under the bed in the big room. Both of them."

I go check and there they are, and several darts. I bring the bow back to the table. It's a beautiful piece of work. Old scraps of metal and an old screw, salvaged from something, now shiny and oiled. The wood of the bow, carved as if a work of art. All kept up with care. I'll bring it to the town meeting to show I've found the killer and dealt with him. But have I? And they may want a body.

"I'll not shoot anybody. Not now."

"Yeah. But you're still sworn."

"I can fight someplace else."

"Oh yeah."

After we eat I put what's left over into an old bear-proof can, take it to the irrigation ditch, and sink it in wet mud to keep it cool.

I don't know if I should go to bed without barricading my door some way. I wish I still had our dog but Mother and I ate him long ago. He'd be dead by now anyway. It would be nice to have him, though. I'd feel a lot safer. He was a good dog but getting old. We thought we'd better eat him ourselves before somebody else got to him. That was before we were eating rats.

Tired as I am, it takes a while for me to get to sleep. I keep telling myself, if he's going to sneak into my room,

I might as well find out about it. But I put the chair against the door in a way that it'll fall. At least I'll hear if he comes in.

Mainly I can't sleep because, in spite of my better judgment, I'm thinking of keeping the man. Trying to. I like the idea of having him around even though it's scary. I make plans.

It's logical that somebody coming in to our new higher village would come to my house first. Perhaps an outsider with news from the North. And it's logical that I'd take him to a town meeting to tell the news.

What news, though? In the morning (the chair hasn't fallen), we make some up. Carson City is as empty and rat-infested as our town. (It's a good bet it really is.) I remember an airplane (I think it was called the gossamer condor) that flew by the propeller being pumped by a bicycle and doesn't need gas. It can't go far or we'd have seen it down here. Joe can say he's seen it.

He says, "How about an epidemic of a new disease passed on by fleas? It hasn't reached here yet." He says, "How about, way up in Reno, they found a cache of ammunition so they can clean up their old guns and use them again?"

I give him news about Clement to tell people. I'll say that's another reason Joe came to me first—to give me news of my brother. (I think I made up that news because I know my brother's dead. Otherwise I'd not have mentioned anything about him. I'd keep on thinking he's out in our mountains as one of the crazies, but I don't think I ever really believed that. I just hoped.)

Once he takes my hand and squeezes it—says how

grateful he is. I have to get up again, turn my back. I wash our few dishes, slowly. I'm so flustered I hardly know what his hand felt like. Strong and warm. I know that.

Lots of good things happen in those town meetings. We give each other our news. We have all kinds of helping committees. In some ways we take care of each other more than we did before the war. People used to bring in their deer and wild sheep and share the meat around, except there's less and less wild game and more and more mountain lions. They're eating all the game and we're not good at killing lions. I'll bet Joe would be, with his crossbow.

So I bring him to the meeting. Introduce him. They crowd around and ask questions about all their favorite spots, or places where they used to have relatives. He's good at making stuff up. Makes me wonder, was he once an officer? Or did he act?

I admire him more and more, and I can see all the women do, too. He could have any one of us. I'm worried he'll get away from me and I'm the only one knows who he really is. Whoever gets him in the end will have to be careful.

He's looking pretty good, too, horrible haircut and all. My brother's blue farmer shirt sets off his brown skin. It's too large for him, but that's the usual.

The women have been out at the bird nets and had made a big batch of little-bird soup. I was glad they'd made that instead of the other.

There's a Paiute woman who comes to our meetings and reports back to the reservation. She's beautiful—more than beautiful, strange and striking. I should have known.

At his first view of her you can see…both of them stare and then, quickly, stop looking at each other.

Later he sits drinking tea with several women including the Paiute. They all crowd around but I saw him push in so that he was next to her. The tables are small but now nine chairs are wedged in close around the one where he sits. I can't see what's going on, but I do see her shoulder is touching his. And their faces are so close I don't see how they can see anything of each other.

I sneak away and run home. I wish I'd saved his smelly, falling-apart clothes. I wish I'd saved the dirty, tangled hair I cut off, but I burned that, too. I do find the old hat. That helps them to believe me. I bring the crossbow. It also helps that he tries to get away.

They hung Joe up in the depository. I told them not to tell me anything about it. I'd rather not know when we get around to using him.

GINNY SWEETHIPS' FLYING CIRCUS

BY NEAL BARRETT, JR.

Neal Barrett, Jr. was the author of more than fifty novels, including the post-apocalyptic novels *Kelwin*, *Through Darkest America*, *Dawn's Uncertain Light*, and *Prince of Christler-Coke*. He published dozens of short stories, in venues such as *F&SF*, *Galaxy*, *Amazing Stories*, *Omni*, *Asimov's*, and a number of anthologies. His work has been collected in *Slightly Off Center* and *Perpetuity Blues*. He died in 2014.

This story, which was a finalist for both the Hugo and Nebula Awards, introduces readers to Ginny Sweethips and her traveling roadshow that makes its living selling sex, tacos, and dangerous drugs. Her companions are her driver and carnival barker Del, and Possum Dark who lives for the moments when he can spray lead across the land.

So, without further adieu, here she is, gents: Ginny Sweethips. Isn't she all you ever dreamed of?

* * *

Del drove and Ginny sat.

"They're taking their sweet time," Ginny said, "damned if they're not."

"They're itchy," Del said. "Everyone's itchy. Everyone's looking to stay alive."

"Huh!" Ginny showed disgust. "I sure don't care for sittin' out here in the sun. My price is going up by the minute. You wait and see if it doesn't."

"Don't get greedy," Del said.

Ginny curled her toes on the dash. Her legs felt warm in the sun. The stockade was a hundred yards off. Barbed wire looped above the walls. The sign over the gate read:

First Church of the Unleaded God & Ace High Refinery
WELCOME
KEEP OUT

The refinery needed paint. It had likely been silver, but was now dull as pewter and black rust. Ginny leaned out the window and called to Possum Dark.

"What's happening, friend? Those mothers dead in there or what?"

"Thinking," Possum said. "Fixing to make a move. Considering what to do." Possum Dark sat atop the van in a steno chair bolted to the roof. Circling the chair was a swivel-ring mount sporting fine twin-fifties black as grease. Possum had a death-view clean around. Keeping out the sun was a red Cinzano umbrella faded pink. Possum studied the stockade and watched heat distort the flats. He didn't care for the effect. He was suspicious of things less than cut and dried. Apprehensive of illusions of every kind. He scratched his nose and curled his tail around his leg. The gate opened up and men started across the scrub. He teased them in his sights. He prayed they'd do something silly and grand.

Possum counted thirty-seven men. A few carried sidearms, openly or concealed. Possum spotted them all at once. He wasn't too concerned. This seemed like an easygoing bunch, more intent on fun than fracas. Still, there was always the hope that he was wrong.

The men milled about. They wore patched denim and faded shirts. Possum made them nervous. Del countered that; his appearance set them at ease. The men looked at Del, poked each other and grinned. Del was scrawny and bald except for tufts around the ears. The dusty black coat was too big. His neck thrust out of his shirt like a newborn buzzard looking for meat. The men forgot Possum and gathered around, waiting to see what Del would do. Waiting for Del to get around to showing them what they'd come to see. The van was painted turtle-green. Gold Barnum type named the owner, and the selected vices for sale:

Ginny Sweethips' Flying Circus
*** SEX * TACOS * DANGEROUS DRUGS ***

Del puttered about with this and that. He unhitched the wagon from the van and folded out a handy little stage. It didn't take three minutes to set up, but he dragged it out to ten, then ten on top of that. The men started to whistle and clap their hands. Del looked alarmed. They liked that. He stumbled and they laughed.

"Hey, mister, you got a girl in there or not?" a man called out.

"Better be something here besides you," another said.

"Gents," Del said, raising his hands for quiet, "Ginny Sweethips herself will soon appear on this stage, and you'll be more than glad you waited. Your every wish will be fulfilled, I promise you that. I'm bringing beauty to the wastelands, gents. Lust the way you like it, passion unrestrained. Sexual crimes you never dreamed!"

"Cut the talk, mister," a man with peach-pit eyes shouted to Del. "Show us what you got."

Others joined in, stomped their feet and whistled. Del knew he had them. Anger was what he wanted. Frustration and denial. Hatred waiting for sweet release. He waved them off, but they wouldn't stop. He placed one hand on the door of the van—and brought them to silence at once.

The double doors opened. A worn red curtain was revealed, stenciled with hearts and cherubs. Del extended his hand. He seemed to search behind the curtain, one eye closed in concentration. He looked alarmed, groping for something he couldn't find. Uncertain he remembered how to do this trick at all. And then, in a sudden burst of motion, Ginny did a double forward flip, and appeared like glory on the stage.

The men broke into shouts of wild abandon. Ginny led them in a cheer. She was dressed for the occasion. Short white skirt shiny bright, white boots with tassels. White sweater with a big red G sewn on the front.

"Ginny Sweethips, gents," Del announced with a flair, "giving you her own interpretation of Barbara Jean, the Cheerleader Next Door. Innocent as snow, yet a little bit wicked and willing to learn, if Biff the Quarterback will only teach her. Now, what do you say to that?"

They whistled and yelled and stomped. Ginny strutted and switched, doing long-legged kicks that left them gasping with delight. Thirty-seven pairs of eyes showed their needs. Men guessed at hidden parts. Dusted off scenarios of violence and love. Then, as quickly as she'd come, Ginny was gone. Men threatened to storm the stage. Del grinned without concern. The curtain parted and Ginny was back, blond hair replaced with saucy red, costume changed in the blink of an eye. Del introduced Nurse Nora, an angel of mercy weak as soup in the hands of Patient Pete. Moments later, hair black as a raven's throat, she was Schoolteacher Sally, cold as well water, until Steve the Bad Student loosed the fury chained within.

Ginny vanished again. Applause thundered over the flats. Del urged them on, then spread his hands for quiet.

"Did I lie to you gents? Is she all you ever dreamed? Is this the love you've wanted all your life? Could you ask for sweeter limbs, for softer flesh? For whiter teeth, for brighter eyes?"

"Yeah, but is she real?" a man shouted, a man with a broken face sewn up like a sock. "We're religious people here. We don't fuck with no machines."

Others echoed the question with bold shouts and shaking fists.

"Now, I don't blame you, sir, at all," Del said. "I've had a few dolly droids myself. A plastic embrace at best, I'll grant you that. Not for the likes of you, for I can tell you're a man who knows his women. No, sir, Ginny's real as rain, and she's yours in the role of your choice. Seven minutes of bliss. It'll seem like a lifetime, gents, I promise you that. Your goods gladly returned if I'm a liar. And all for only a U.S. gallon of gas!"

Howls and groans at that, as Del expected.

"That's a cheat is what it is! Ain't a woman worth it!"

"Gas is better'n gold, and we work damn hard to get it!"

Del stood his ground. Looked grim and disappointed. "I'd be the last man alive to try to part you from your goods," Del said. "It's not my place to drive a fellow into the arms of sweet content, to make him rest his manly frame on golden thighs. Not if he thinks this lovely girl's not worth the fee, no sir. I don't do business that way and never have."

The men moved closer. Del could smell their discontent. He read sly thoughts above their heads. There was always this moment when it occurred to them there was a way Ginny's delights might be obtained for free.

"Give it some thought, friends," Del said. "A man's got to do what he's got to do. And while you're making up your minds, turn your eyes to the top of the van for a startling and absolutely free display of the slickest bit of marksmanship you're ever likely to see!"

Before Del's words were out of his mouth and on the way, before the men could scarcely comprehend, Ginny appeared again and tossed a dozen china saucers in the air.

Possum Dark moved in a blur. Turned 140 degrees in his bolted steno chair and whipped his guns on target, blasting saucers to dust. Thunder rolled across the flats. Crockery rained on the men below. Possum stood and offered a pink killer grin and a little bow. The men saw six-foot-nine and a quarter inches of happy marsupial fury and awesome speed, of black agate eyes and a snout full of icy varmint teeth. Doubts were swept aside. Fifty-caliber madness wasn't the answer. Fun today was clearly not for free.

"Gentlemen, start your engines," Del smiled. "I'll be right here to take your fee. Enjoy a hot taco while you wait your turn at glory. Have a look at our display of fine pharmaceutical wonders and mind-expanding drugs."

In moments, men were making their way back to the stockade. Soon after that, they returned toting battered tins of gas. Del sniffed each gallon, in case some buffoon thought water would get him by. Each man received a token and took his place. Del sold tacos and dangerous drugs, taking what he could get in trade. Candles and Mason jars, a rusty knife. Half a manual on full-field maintenance for the Chrysler Mark XX Urban Tank. The drugs were different colors but the same: twelve parts oregano, three parts rabbit shit, one part marijuana stems. All this under Possum's watchful eye.

"By God," said the first man out of the van. "She's worth it, I'll tell you that. Have her do the Nurse, you won't regret it!"

"The Schoolteacher's best," said the second man through. "I never seen the like. I don't care if she's real or she ain't."

"What's in these tacos?" a customer asked Del.

"Nobody you know, mister," Del said.

"It's been a long day," Ginny said. "I'm pooped, and that's the truth." She wrinkled up her nose. "First thing we hit a town, you hose 'er out good now, Del. Place smells like a sewer or maybe worse."

Del squinted at the sky and pulled up under the scant shade of mesquite. He stepped out and kicked the tires.

Ginny got down, walked around and stretched.

"It's getting late," Del said. "You want to go on or stop here?"

"You figure those boys might decide to get a rebate on this gas?"

"Hope they do," Possum said from atop the van.

"You're a pisser," Ginny laughed, "I'll say that. Hell, let's keep going. I could use a hot bath and town food. What you figure's up the road?"

"East Bad News," Del said, "if this map's worth anything at all. Ginny, night driving's no good. You don't know what's waiting down the road."

"I know what's on the roof," Ginny said. "Let's do it. I'm itchy all over with bugs and dirt and that tub keeps shinin' in my head. You want me to drive a spell, I sure will."

"Get in," Del grumbled. "Your driving's scarier than anything I'll meet."

Morning arrived in purple shadow and metal tones, copper, silver, and gold. From a distance, East Bad News looked to Ginny like garbage strewn carelessly over the flats. Closer, it looked like larger garbage. Tin shacks and tents and haphazard buildings rehashed from whatever they were before. Cookfires burned, and the locals wandered about and yawned and scratched. Three places offered food. Other places bed and a bath. Something to look forward to, at least. She spotted the sign down at the far end of town.

MORO'S REPAIRS
Armaments * Machinery * Electronic Shit of All Kinds

* * *

"Hold it!" Ginny said. "Pull 'er in right there."

Del looked alarmed. "What for?"

"Don't get excited. There's gear needs tending in back. I just want 'em to take a look."

"Didn't mention it to me," Del said.

Ginny saw the sad and droopy eyes, the tired wisps of hair sticking flat to Del's ears. "Del, there wasn't anything to mention," she said in a kindly tone. "Nothing you can really put your finger on, I mean, okay?"

"Whatever you think," Del said, clearly out of sorts.

Ginny sighed and got out. Barbed wire surrounded the yard behind the shop. The yard was ankle-deep in tangles of rope and copper cable, rusted unidentifiable parts. A battered pickup hugged the wall. Morning heat curled the tin roof of the building. More parts spilled out of the door. Possum made a funny noise, and Ginny saw the Dog step into the light. A Shepherd, maybe six-foot-two. It showed Possum Dark yellow eyes. A man appeared behind the Dog, wiping heavy grease on his pants. Bare to the waist, hair like stuffing out of a chair. Features hard as rock, flint eyes to match. Not bad looking, thought Ginny, if you cleaned him up good.

"Well now," said the man. He glanced at the van, read the legend on the side, took in Ginny from head to toe. "What can I do for you, little lady?"

"I'm not real little and don't guess I'm any lady," Ginny said. "Whatever you're thinking, don't. You open for business or just talk?"

The man grinned. "My name's Moro Gain. Never turn business away if I can help it."

"I need electric stuff."

"We got it. What's the problem?"

"Huh-unh." Ginny shook her head. "First, I gotta ask. You do confidential work or tell everything you know?"

"Secret's my middle name," Moro said. "Might cost a little more, but you got it."

"How much?"

Moro closed one eye. "Now, how do I know that? You got a nuclear device in there, or a broken watch? Drive it on in and we'll take a look." He aimed a greasy finger at Possum Dark. "Leave him outside."

"No way."

"No arms in the shop. That's a rule."

"He isn't carrying. Just the guns you see." Ginny smiled. "You can shake him down if you like. I wouldn't, I don't think."

"He looks imposing, all right."

"I'd say he is."

"What the hell," Moro said, "drive it in."

Dog unlocked the gate. Possum climbed down and followed with oily eyes.

"Go find us a place to stay," Ginny said to Del. "Clean, if you can find it. All the hot water in town. Christ sakes, Del, you still sulking or what?"

"Don't worry about me," Del said. "Don't concern yourself at all."

"Right." She hopped behind the wheel. Moro began kicking the door of his shop. It finally sprang free, wide enough to take the van. The supply wagon rocked along behind. Moro lifted the tarp, eyed the thirty-seven tins of unleaded with great interest.

"You get lousy mileage, or what?" he asked Ginny.

Ginny didn't answer. She stepped out of the van. Light came through broken panes of glass. The skinny windows reminded her of a church. Her eyes got used to shadow, and she saw that that's what it was. Pews sat to the side, piled high with auto parts. A 1997 Olds was jacked up before the altar.

"Nice place you got here," she said.

"It works for me," Moro told her. "Now what kind of trouble you got? Something in the wiring? You said electric stuff."

"I didn't mean the motor. Back here." She led him to the rear and opened the doors.

"God a'Mighty!" Moro said.

"Smells a little raunchy right now. Can't help that till we hose 'er down." Ginny stepped inside, looked back, and saw Moro still on the ground. "You coming up or not?"

"Just thinking."

"About what?" She'd seen him watching her move and didn't really have to ask.

"Well, you know…" Moro shuffled his feet. "How do you figure on paying? For whatever it is I got to do."

"Gas. You take a look. Tell me how many tins. I say yes or no."

"We could work something out."

"We could, huh?"

"Sure." Moro gave her a foolish grin. "Why not?"

Ginny didn't blink. "Mister, what kind of girl do you think I am?"

Moro looked puzzled and intent. "I can read good, lady, believe it or not. I figured you wasn't tacos or dangerous drugs."

"You figured wrong," Ginny said. "Sex is just software to me, and don't you forget it. I haven't got all day to watch you moonin' over my parts. I got to move or stand still.

When I stand still, you look. When I move, you look more. Can't fault you for that, I'm about the prettiest thing you ever saw. Don't let it get in the way of your work."

Moro couldn't think of much to say. He took a breath and stepped into the van. There was a bed bolted flat against the floor. A red cotton spread, a worn satin pillow that said Durango, Colorado, and pictured chipmunks and waterfalls. An end table, a pink-shaded lamp with flamingos on the side. Red curtains on the walls. Ballet prints and a naked Minnie Mouse.

"Somethin' else," Moro said.

"Back here's the problem," Ginny said. She pulled a curtain aside at the front of the van. There was a plywood cabinet, fitted with brass screws. Ginny took a key out of her jeans and opened it up.

Moro stared a minute, then laughed aloud. "Sensory tapes? Well, I'll be a son of a bitch." He took a new look at Ginny, a look Ginny didn't miss. "Haven't seen a rig like this in years. Didn't know there were any still around."

"I've got three tapes," Ginny explained. "A brunette, a redhead, and a blond. Found a whole cache in Ardmore, Oklahoma. Had to look at 'bout three or four hundred to find girls that looked close enough to me. Nearly went nuts 'fore it was over. Anyway, I did it. Spliced 'em down to seven minutes each."

Moro glanced back at the bed. "How do you put 'em under?"

"Little needle comes up out the mattress. Sticks them in the ass lightnin' fast. They're out like that. Seven-minute dose. Headpiece is in the end table there. I get it on and off them real quick. Wires go under the floorboards back here to the rig."

"Jesus," Moro said. "They ever catch you at this, you are cooked, lady."

"That's what Possum's for," Ginny said. "Possum's pretty good at what he does. Now what's that look all about?"

"I wasn't sure right off if you were real."

Ginny laughed aloud. "So what do you think now?"

"I think maybe you are."

"Right," Ginny said. "It's Del who's the droid, not me. Wimp IX Series. Didn't make a whole lot. Not much demand. The customers think it's me, never think to look at him. He's a damn good barker and pretty good at tacos and drugs. A little too sensitive, you ask me. Well, nobody's perfect, so they say."

"The trouble you're having's in the rig?"

"I guess," Ginny said, "beats the hell out of me." She bit her lip and wrinkled her brow. Moro found the gestures most inviting. "Slips a little, I think. Maybe I got a short, huh?"

"Maybe." Moro fiddled with the rig, testing one of the spools with his thumb. "I'll have to get in here and see."

"It's all yours. I'll be wherever it is Del's got me staying."

"Ruby John's," Moro said. "Only place there is with a good roof. I'd like to take you out to dinner."

"Well sure you would."

"You got a real shitty attitude, friend."

"I get a whole lot of practice," Ginny said.

"And I've got a certain amount of pride," Moro told her. "I don't intend to ask you more than three or four times and that's it."

Ginny nodded. Right on the edge of approval. "You've got promise," she said. "Not a whole lot, maybe, but some."

"Does that mean dinner, or not?"

"Means not. Means if I wanted to have dinner with some guy, you'd maybe fit the bill."

Moro's eyes got hot. "Hell with you, lady. I don't need the company that bad."

"Fine." Ginny sniffed the air and walked out. "You have a nice day."

Moro watched her walk. Watched denims mold her legs, studied the hydraulics of her hips. Considered several unlikely acts. Considered cleaning up, searching for proper clothes. Considered finding a bottle and watching the tapes. A plastic embrace at best, or so he'd heard, but a lot less hassle in the end.

Possum Dark watched the van disappear into the shop. He felt uneasy at once. His place was on top. Keeping Ginny from harm. Sending feral prayers for murder to absent genetic gods. His eyes hadn't left Dog since he'd appeared. Primal smells, old fears and needs, assailed his senses. Dog locked the gate and turned around. Didn't come closer, just turned.

"I'm Dog Quick," he said, folding hairy arms. "I don't much care for Possums."

"I don't much care for Dogs," said Possum Dark. Dog seemed to understand. "What did you do before the War?"

"Worked in a theme park. Our Wildlife Heritage. That kind of shit. What about you?"

"Security, what else?" Dog made a face. "Learned a little electrics. Picked up a lot more from Moro Gain. I've done worse." He nodded toward the shop. "You like to shoot people with that thing?"

"Anytime I get the chance."

"You ever play any cards?"

"Some." Possum Dark showed his teeth. "I guess I could handle myself with a Dog."

"For real goods?" Dog returned the grin.

"New deck, unbroken seal, table stakes," Possum said.

Moro showed up at Ruby John's Cot Emporium close to noon. Ginny had a semiprivate stall, covered by a blanket. She'd bathed and braided her hair and cut the legs clean off her jeans. She tugged at Moro's heart.

"It'll be tomorrow morning," Moro said. "Cost you ten gallons of gas."

"Ten gallons," Ginny said. "That's stealin', and you know it."

"Take it or leave it," Moro said. "You got a bad head in that rig. Going to come right off, you don't fix it. You wouldn't like that. Your customers wouldn't like it any at all."

Ginny appeared subdued but not much. "Four gallons. Tops."

"Eight. I got to make the parts myself."

"Five."

"Six," Moro said. "Six and I take you to dinner."

"Five and a half, and I want to be out of this sweatbox at dawn. On the road and gone when the sun starts bakin' your lovely town."

"Damn, you're fun to have around."

Ginny smiled. Sweet and disarming, an unexpected event. "I'm all right. You got to get to know me."

"Just how do I go about that?"

"You don't." The smile turned sober. "I haven't figured that one out."

* * *

It looked like rain to the north. Sunrise was dreary. Muddy, less-than-spectacular yellows and reds. Colors through a window no one had bothered to wash. Moro had the van brought out. He said he'd thrown in a lube and hosed out the back. Five and a half gallons were gone out of the wagon. Ginny had Del count while Moro watched.

"I'm honest," Moro said, "you don't have to do that."

"I know," Ginny said, glancing curiously at Dog, who was looking rather strange. He seemed out of sorts. Sulky and off his feed. Ginny followed his eyes and saw Possum atop the van. Possum showed a wet Possum grin.

"Where you headed now?" Moro asked, wanting to hold her as long as he could.

"South," Ginny said, since she was facing that direction.

"I wouldn't," Moro said. "Not real friendly folks down there."

"I'm not picky. Business is business."

"No, sir," Moro shook his head. "Bad business is what it is. You got the Dry Heaves south and east. Doom City after that. Straight down and you'll hit the Hackers. Might run into Fort Pru, bunch of disgruntled insurance agents out on the flats. Stay clear away from them. Isn't worth whatever you'll make."

"You've been a big help," Ginny said.

Moro gripped her door. "You ever listen to anyone, lady? I'm giving good advice."

"Fine," Ginny said, "I'm 'bout as grateful as I can be."

Moro watched her leave. He was consumed by her appearance. The day seemed to focus in her eyes. Nothing he said pleased her in the least. Still, her disdain was friendly enough. There was no malice at all that he could see.

* * *

There was something about the sound of Doom City she didn't like. Ginny told Del to head south and maybe west. Around noon, a yellow haze appeared on the ragged rim of the world, like someone rolling a cheap dirty rug across the flats.

"Sandstorm," Possum called from the roof. "Right out of the west. I don't like it at all. I think we better turn. Looks like trouble coming fast."

There was nothing Possum said she couldn't see. He had a habit of saying either too little or more than enough. She told him to cover his guns and get inside, that the sand would take his hide and there was nothing out there he needed to kill that wouldn't wait. Possum Dark sulked but climbed down. Hunched in back of the van, he grasped air in the shape of grips and trigger guards. Practiced rage and windage in his head.

"I'll bet I can beat that storm," Del said. "I got this feeling I can do it."

"Beat it where?" Ginny said. "We don't know where we are or what's ahead."

"That's true," Del said. "All the more reason then to get there soon as we can."

Ginny stepped out and viewed the world with disregard. "I got sand in my teeth and in my toes," she complained. "I'll bet that Moro Gain knows right where storms'll likely be. I'll bet that's what happened, all right."

"Seemed like a decent sort to me," Del said.

"That's what I mean," Ginny said. "You can't trust a man like that at all."

The storm had seemed to last a couple of days. Ginny figured maybe an hour. The sky looked bad as cabbage soup. The land looked just the way it had. She couldn't see the difference between sand recently gone or newly arrived. Del got the van going again. Ginny thought about yesterday's bath. East Bad News had its points.

Before they topped the first rise, Possum Dark began to stomp on the roof. "Vehicles to port," he called out. "Sedans and pickup trucks. Flatbeds and semis. Buses of all kinds."

"What are they doing?" Del said.

"Coming right at us, hauling timber."

"Doing what?" Ginny made a face. "Damn it all, Del, will you stop the car? I swear, you're a driving fool."

Del stopped. Ginny climbed up with Possum to watch. The caravan kept a straight line. Cars and trucks weren't exactly hauling timber…but they were. Each carried a section of a wall. Split logs bound together, sharpened at the top. The lead car turned and the others followed. The lead car turned again. In a moment, there was a wooden stockade assembled on the flats, square as if you'd drawn it with a rule. A stockade and a gate. Over the gate a wooden sign:

FORT PRU
Games of Chance & Amusement
Term * Whole Life * Half Life * Death

"I don't like it," said Possum Dark.

"You don't like anything's still alive," Ginny said.

"They've got small arms and they're a nervous-looking bunch."

"They're just horny, Possum. That's the same as nervous, or close enough."

Possum pretended to understand.

"Looks like they're pulled up for the night," she called to Del. "Let's do some business, friend. The overhead don't ever stop."

Five of them came out to the van. They all looked alike. Stringy, darkened by the sun. Bare to the waist except for collars and striped ties. Each carried an attaché case thin as two slices of bread without butter. Two had pistols stuck in their belts. The leader carried a fine-looking sawed-off Remington 12. It hung by a camou guitar strap to his waist. Del didn't like him at all. He had perfect white teeth and a bald head. Eyes the color of jellyfish melting on the beach. He studied the sign on the van and looked at Del.

"You got a whore inside or not?"

Del looked him straight on. "I'm a little displeased at that. It's not the way to talk."

"Hey." The man gave Del a wink. "You don't have to give us the pitch. We're show business folk ourselves."

"Is that right?"

"Wheels of chance and honest cards. Odds I know you'll like. I'm head actuary of this bunch. Name's Fred. That animal up there has a piss-poor attitude, friend. No reason to poke that weapon down my throat. We're friendly people here."

"No reason I can see why Possum'd spray this place with lead and diarrhetics," Del said. "Less you can think of something I can't."

Fred smiled at that. The sun made a big gold ball on his head. "I guess we'll try your girl," he told Del. "'Course we got to see her first. What do you take in trade?"

"Goods as fine as what you're getting in return."

"I've got just the thing." The head actuary winked again. The gesture was starting to irritate Del. Fred nodded, and a friend drew clean white paper from his case. "This here is heavy bond," he told Del, shuffling the edges with his thumb. "Fifty percent linen weave, and we got it by the ream. Won't find anything like it. You can mark on it good or trade it off. Seventh Mercenary Writers came through a week ago. Whole brigade of mounted horse. Near cleaned us out, but we can spare a few reams. We got pencils too. Mirado twos and threes, unsharpened, with erasers on the end. When's the last time you saw that? Why, this stuff's good as gold. We got staples and legal pads. Claim forms, maim forms, forms of every sort. Deals on wheels is what we got. And you got gas under wraps in the wagon behind your van. I can smell it plain from here. Friend, we can sure talk some business with you there. I got seventeen rusty-ass guzzlers runnin' dry."

A gnat-whisker wire sparked hot in Del's head. He could see it in the underwriter's eyes. Gasoline greed was what it was, and he knew these men were bent on more than fleshly pleasure. He knew with androidial dread that when they could, they'd make their play.

"Well now, the gas is not for trade," he said as calmly as he could. "Sex and tacos and dangerous drugs is what we sell."

"No problem," the actuary said. "Why, no problem at all. Just an idea, is all it was. You get that little gal out here and I'll bring in my crew. How's half a ream a man sound to you?"

"Just as fair as it can be," Del said, thinking that half of that would've been fine, knowing dead certain now that Fred intended to take back whatever he gave.

* * *

"That Moro fellow was right," Del said. "These insurance boys are bad news. Best thing we can do is take off and let it go."

"Pooh," said Ginny, "that's just the way men are. They come in mad as foamin' dogs and go away like cats licking cream. That's the nature of the fornicatin' trade. You wait and see. Besides, they won't get funny with Possum Dark."

"You wouldn't pray for rain if you were afire," Del muttered. "Well, I'm not unhitching the gas. I'll set you up a stage over the tarp. You can do your number there."

"Suit yourself," Ginny said, kissing a plastic cheek and scooting him out the door. "Now get on out of here and let me start getting cute."

It seemed to be going well. Cheerleader Barbara Jean awoke forgotten wet dreams, left their mouths as dry as snakes. Set them up for Sally the Teach and Nora Nurse, secret violations of the soul. Maybe Ginny was right, Del decided. Faced with girlie delights, a man's normally shitty outlook disappeared. When he was done, he didn't want to wreck a thing for an hour or maybe two. Didn't care about killing for half a day. Del could only guess at this magic and how it worked. Data was one thing, sweet encounters something else.

He caught Possum's eye and felt secure. Forty-eight men waited their turns. Possum knew the caliber of their arms, the length of every blade. His black twin-fifties blessed them all.

Fred the actuary sidled up and grinned at Del. "We sure ought to talk about gas. That's what we ought to do."

"Look," Del said, "gas isn't for trade, I told you that. Go talk to those boys at the refinery, same as us."

"Tried to. They got no use for office supplies."

"That's not my problem," Del said.

"Maybe it is."

Del didn't miss the razor tones. "You got something to say, just say it."

"Half of your gas. We pay our way with the girl and don't give you any trouble."

"You forget about him?"

Fred studied Possum Dark. "I can afford losses better than you. Listen, I know what you are, friend. I know you're not a man. Had a CPA droid just like you 'fore the War."

"Maybe we can talk," Del said, trying to figure what to do.

"Say now, that's what I like to hear."

Ginny's fourth customer staggered out, wild-eyed and white around the gills. "Goddamn, try the Nurse," he bawled to the others. "Never had nothin' like it in my life!"

"Next," Del said, and started stacking bond paper. "Lust is the name of the game, gents, what did I tell you now?"

"The girl plastic, too?" Fred asked.

"Real as you," Del said. "We make some kind of deal, how do I know you'll keep your word?"

"Jesus," Fred said, "what do you think I am? You got my Life Underwriter's Oath!"

The next customer exploded through the curtain, tripped and fell on his face. Picked himself up and shook his head. He looked damaged, bleeding around the eyes.

"She's a tiger," Del announced, wondering what the hell was going on. "'Scuse me a minute," he told Fred, and slipped inside the van. "Just what are you doing in here?" he asked Ginny. "Those boys look like they been through a thrasher."

"Beats me," Ginny said, halfway between Nora and Barbara Jean. "Last old boy jerked around like a snake having a fit. Started pulling out his hair. Somethin' isn't right here, Del. It's gotta be the tapes. I figure that Moro fellow's a cheat."

"We got trouble inside and out," Del told her. "The head of this bunch wants our gas."

"Well, he sure can't have it, by God."

"Ginny, the man's got bug-spit eyes. Says he'll take his chances with Possum. We better clear out while we can."

"Huh-unh." Ginny shook her head. "That'll rile 'em for sure. Give me a minute or two. We've done a bunch of Noras and a Sally. I'll switch them all to Barbara Jean and see."

Del slipped back outside. It seemed a dubious answer at best.

"That's some woman," said Fred.

"She's something else today. Your insurance boys have got her fired."

Fred grinned at that. "Guess I better give her a try."

"I wouldn't," Del said.

"Why not?"

"Let her calm down some. Might be more than you want to handle."

He knew at once this wasn't the thing to say. Fred turned the color of ketchup pie. "Why, you plastic piece of shit! I can handle any woman born...or put together out of a kit."

"Suit yourself," Del said, feeling the day going down the drain. "No charge at all."

"Damn right there's not." Fred jerked the next man out of line. "Get ready in there, little lady. I am going to handle all your policy needs!"

The men cheered. Possum Dark, who understood at least three-fifths of the trouble down below, shot Del a questioning look.

"Got any of those tacos?" someone asked.

"Not likely," Del said.

Del considered turning himself off. Android suicide seemed the answer. But in less than three minutes, unnatural howls began to come from the van. The howls turned to shrieks. Life underwriters went rigid. Then Fred emerged, shattered. He looked like a man who'd kicked a bear with boils. His joints appeared to bend the wrong way. He looked whomper-eyed at Del, dazed and out-of-synch. Everything happened then in seconds thin as wire. Del saw Fred find him, saw the oil-spill eyes catch him clean. Saw the sawed-off barrels match the eyes so fast even electric feet couldn't snatch him out of the way in time. Del's arm exploded. He let it go and ran for the van. Possum couldn't help. The actuary was below and too close. The twin-fifties opened up. Underwriters fled. Possum stitched the sand and sent them flying ragged and dead.

Del reached the driver's seat as lead peppered the van. He felt slightly silly. Sitting there with one arm, one hand on the wheel.

"Move over," Ginny said, "that isn't going to work."

"I guess not."

Ginny sent them lurching through the scrub. "Never saw anything like it in my life," she said aloud. "Turned that poor fella on, he started twisting out of his socks, bones snapping like sticks. Damndest orgasm I ever saw."

"Something's not working just right."

"Well, I can see that, Del. Jesus, what's that!" Ginny twisted the wheel as a large part of the desert rose straight up in the air. Smoking sand rained down on the van.

"Rockets," Del said grimly. "That's the reason they figured that crazy-fingered Possum was a snap. Watch where you're going, girl!"

Two fiery pillars exploded ahead. Del leaned out the window and looked back. Half of Fort Pru's wall was in pursuit. Possum sprayed everything in sight, but he couldn't spot where the rockets were coming from. Underwriter assault cars split up, came at them from every side.

"Trying to flank us," Del said. A rocket burst to the right. "Ginny, I'm not real sure what to do."

"How's the stub?"

"Slight electric tingle. Like a doorbell half a mile away. Ginny, they get us in a circle, we're in very deep shit."

"They hit that gas, we won't have to worry about a thing. Oh Lord, now why did I think of that?"

Possum hit a semi clean on. It came to a stop and died, fell over like a bug. Del could see that being a truck and a wall all at once had its problems, balance being one.

"Head right at them," he told Ginny, "then veer off sharp. They can't turn quick going fast."

"Del!"

Bullets rattled the van. Something heavy made a noise. The van skewed to a halt.

Ginny took her hands off the wheel and looked grim. "It appears they got the tires. Del, we're flat dead is what we are. Let's get out of this thing."

And do what? Del wondered. Bearings seemed to roll about in his head. He sensed a malfunction on the way.

The Fort Pru vehicles shrieked to a stop. Crazed life agents piled out and came at them over the flats, firing small arms and hurling stones. A rocket burst nearby.

Possum's guns suddenly stopped. Ginny grimaced in disgust. "Don't you tell me we're out of ammo, Possum Dark. That stuff's plenty hard to get."

Possum started to speak. Del waved his good arm to the north. "Hey now, would you look at that!"

Suddenly there was confusion in the underwriters' ranks. A vaguely familiar pickup had appeared on the rise. The driver weaved through traffic, hurling grenades. They exploded in clusters, bright pink bouquets. He spotted the man with the rocket, lying flat atop a bus. Grenades stopped him cold. Underwriters abandoned the field and ran. Ginny saw a fairly peculiar sight. Six black Harleys had joined the truck. Chow Dogs with Uzis snaked in and out of the ranks, motors snarling and spewing horsetails of sand high in the air. They showed no mercy at all, picking off stragglers as they ran. A few underwriters made it to cover. In a moment, it was over. Fort Pru fled in sectional disarray.

"Well, if that wasn't just in the nick of time," Del said.

"I hate Chow Dogs," Possum said. "They got black tongues, and that's a fact."

"I hope you folks are all right," Moro said. "Well now, friend, looks as if you've thrown an arm."

"Nothing real serious," Del said.

"I'm grateful," Ginny said. "Guess I got to tell you that."

Moro was taken by her penetrating charm, her thankless manner. The fetching smudge of grease on her knee. He thought she was cute as a pup.

"I felt it was something I had to do. Circumstances being what they are."

"And just what circumstances are that?" Ginny asked.

"That pesky Shepherd Dog's sorta responsible for any trouble you might've had. Got a little pissed when that Possum cleaned him out. Five-card stud, I think it was. 'Course there might have been marking and crimping of cards, I couldn't say."

Ginny blew hair out of her eyes. "Mister, far as I can see, you're not making a lot of sense."

"I'm real embarrassed about this. That Dog got mad and kinda screwed up your gear."

"You let a Dog repair my stuff?" Ginny said.

"Perfectly good technician. Taught him mostly myself. Okay if you don't get his dander up. Those Shepherds are inbred, so I hear. What he did was set your tapes in a loop and speed 'em up. Customer'd get, say, twenty-six times his money's worth. Works out to a Mach seven fuck. Could cause bodily harm."

"Lord, I ought to shoot you in the foot," Ginny said.

"Look," Moro said, "I stand behind my work, and I got here quick as I could. Brought friends along to help, and I'm eating the cost of that."

"Damn right," Ginny said. The Chow Dogs sat their Harleys a ways off and glared at Possum. Possum Dark glared back. He secretly admired their leather gear, the Purina crests sewn on the backs.

"I'll be adding up costs," Ginny said. "I'm expecting full repairs."

"You'll get it. Of course you'll have to spend some time in Bad News. Might take a little while."

She caught his look and had to laugh. "You're a

stubborn son of a bitch, I'll give you that. What'd you do with that Dog?"

"You want taco meat, I'll make you a deal."

"Yuck. I guess I'll pass."

Del began to weave about in roughly trapezoidal squares. Smoke started to curl out of his stub.

"For Christ's sake, Possum, sit on him or something," Ginny said.

"I can fix that," Moro told her.

"You've about fixed enough, seems to me."

"We're going to get along fine. You wait and see."

"You think so?" Ginny looked alarmed. "I better not get used to having you around."

"It could happen."

"It could just as easy not."

"I'll see about changing that tire," Moro said. "We ought to get Del out of the sun. You think about finding something nice to wear to dinner. East Bad News is kinda picky. We got a lot of pride around here…"

THE END OF THE WORLD
AS WE KNOW IT

BY DALE BAILEY

Dale Bailey is the author of three novels, *The Fallen*, *House of Bones*, and *Sleeping Policemen* (with Jack Slay, Jr.). His short fiction, collected in *The Resurrection Man's Legacy and Other Stories*, has been a three-time finalist for the International Horror Guild Award, a two-time finalist for the Nebula Award, and a finalist for the Shirley Jackson Award and the Bram Stoker Award. His International Horror Guild Award-winning novelette "Death and Suffrage" was adapted for film by director Joe Dante as part of Showtime Television's anthology series, *Masters of Horror*. A new collection, *The End of the End of Everything: Stories*, will be out in 2015.

This story, which was a finalist for the Nebula Award, grew out of Bailey's attempt to understand our rather morbid fascination with the genre and the prospect of our own extinction. "The End of the World as We Know It" is about the lone survivor of an apocalypse attempting to grapple with the emotional dimension of his loss. But more than that, it's an end-of-the-world story about how end-of-the-world stories actually work.

One thing Bailey realized in writing the story is that the world is ending for someone every minute of every day. He says, "We don't need the destruction of entire cities to know what it's like to survive a catastrophe. Whenever we lose someone we love deeply we experience the end of the world as we know it. The central idea of the story is not merely that the apocalypse is coming, but that it's coming for you. And there's nothing you can do to avoid it."

Between 1347 and 1450 AD, bubonic plague overran Europe, killing some 75 million people. The plague, dubbed the Black Death because of the black pustules that erupted on the skin of the afflicted, was caused by a bacterium now known as *Yersinia pestis*. The Europeans of the day, lacking access to microscopes or knowledge of disease vectors, attributed their misfortune to an angry God. Flagellants roamed the land, hoping to appease His wrath. "They died by the hundreds, both day and night," Agnolo di Tura tells us. "I buried my five children with my own hands . . . so many died that all believed it was the end of the world."

Today, the population of Europe is about 729 million.

Evenings, Wyndham likes to sit on the porch, drinking. He likes gin, but he'll drink anything. He's not particular. Lately, he's been watching it get dark—really *watching* it,

I mean, not just sitting there—and so far he's concluded that the cliché is wrong. Night doesn't fall. It's more complex than that.

Not that he's entirely confident in the accuracy of his observations.

It's high summer just now, and Wyndham often begins drinking at two or three, so by the time the sun sets, around nine, he's usually pretty drunk. Still, it seems to him that, if anything, night *rises*, gathering first in inky pools under the trees, as if it has leached up from underground reservoirs, and then spreading, out toward the borders of the yard and up toward the yet-lighted sky. It's only toward the end that anything falls—the blackness of deep space, he supposes, unscrolling from high above the earth. The two planes of darkness meet somewhere in the middle, and that's night for you.

That's his current theory, anyway.

It isn't his porch, incidentally, but then it isn't his gin either—except in the sense that, in so far as Wyndham can tell anyway, *everything* now belongs to him.

End-of-the-world stories usually come in one of two varieties.

In the first, the world ends with a natural disaster, either unprecedented or on an unprecedented scale. Floods lead all other contenders—God himself, we're told, is fond of that one—though plagues have their advocates. A renewed ice age is also popular. Ditto drought.

In the second variety, irresponsible human beings bring it on themselves. Mad scientists and corrupt bureaucrats, usually. An exchange of ICBMs is the typical route, although the scenario has dated in the present geo-political environment.

Feel free to mix and match:

Genetically engineered flu virus, anyone? Melting polar ice caps?

On the day the world ended, Wyndham didn't even realize it *was* the end of the world—not right away, anyway. For him, at that point in his life, pretty much *every* day seemed like the end of the world. This was not a consequence of a chemical imbalance, either. It was a consequence of working for UPS, where, on the day the world ended Wyndham had been employed for sixteen years, first as a loader, then in sorting, and finally in the coveted position of driver, the brown uniform and everything. By this time the company had gone public and he also owned some shares. The money was good— very good, in fact. Not only that, he liked his job.

Still, the beginning of every goddamn day started off feeling like a cataclysm. *You* try getting up at 4:00 AM every morning and see how you feel.

This was his routine:

At 4:00 AM, the alarm went off—an old-fashioned alarm, he wound it up every night. (He couldn't tolerate the radio before he drank his coffee.) He always turned it off right away, not wanting to wake his wife. He showered in the spare bathroom (again, not wanting to wake his wife; her name was Ann), poured coffee into his thermos, and ate something he probably shouldn't—a bagel, a Pop Tart—while he stood over the sink. By then, it would be 4:20, 4:25 if he was running late.

Then he would do something paradoxical: He would go back to his bedroom and wake up the wife he'd spent the last twenty minutes trying not to disturb.

"Have a good day," Wyndham always said.

His wife always did the same thing, too. She would screw her face into her pillow and smile. "Ummm," she would say, and it was usually such a cozy, loving, early-morning cuddling kind of "ummm" that it almost made getting up at 4 in the goddamn morning worth it.

Wyndham heard about the World Trade Center—*not* the end of the world, though to Wyndham it sure as hell felt that way—from one of his customers.

The customer—her name was Monica—was one of Wyndham's regulars: a Home Shopping Network fiend, this woman. She was big, too. The kind of woman of whom people say "She has a nice personality" or "She has such a pretty face." She did have a nice personality, too—at least Wyndham thought she did. So he was concerned when she opened the door in tears.

"What's wrong?" he said.

Monica shook her head, at a loss for words. She waved him inside. Wyndham, in violation of about fifty UPS regulations, stepped in after her. The house smelled of sausage and floral air freshener. There was Home Shopping Network shit everywhere. I mean, *everywhere*.

Wyndham hardly noticed.

His gaze was fixed on the television. It was showing an airliner flying into the World Trade Center. He stood there and watched it from three or four different angles before he noticed the Home Shopping Network logo in the lower right-hand corner of the screen.

That was when he concluded that it must be the end of the world. He couldn't imagine the Home Shopping

Network preempting regularly scheduled programming for anything less.

The Muslim extremists who flew airplanes into the World Trade Center, into the Pentagon, and into the unyielding earth of an otherwise unremarkable field in Pennsylvania, were secure, we are told, in the knowledge of their imminent translation into paradise.

There were nineteen of them.

Every one of them had a name.

Wyndham's wife was something of a reader. She liked to read in bed. Before she went to sleep she always marked her spot using a bookmark Wyndham had given her for her birthday one year: It was a cardboard bookmark with a yarn ribbon at the top, and a picture of a rainbow arching high over white-capped mountains. *Smile,* the bookmark said. *God loves you.*

Wyndham wasn't much of a reader, but if he'd picked up his wife's book the day the world ended he would have found the first few pages interesting. In the opening chapter, God raptures all true Christians to Heaven. This includes true Christians who are driving cars and trains and airplanes, resulting in uncounted lost lives as well as significant damages to personal property. If Wyndham *had* read the book, he'd have thought of a bumper sticker he sometimes saw from high in his UPS truck. *Warning,* the bumper sticker read, *In case of Rapture, this car will be unmanned.* Whenever he saw that bumper sticker, Wyndham imagined cars crashing, planes falling from the sky, patients abandoned on the operating table— pretty much the scenario of his wife's book, in fact.

Wyndham went to church every Sunday, but he couldn't help wondering what would happen to the untold millions of people who *weren't* true Christians— whether by choice or by the geographical fluke of having been born in some place like Indonesia. What if they were crossing the street in front of one of those cars, he wondered, or watering lawns those planes would soon plow into?

But I was saying:

On the day the world ended Wyndham didn't understand right away what had happened. His alarm clock went off the way it always did and he went through his normal routine. Shower in the spare bath, coffee in the thermos, breakfast over the sink (a chocolate donut, this time, and gone a little stale). Then he went back to the bedroom to say good-bye to his wife.

"Have a good day," he said, as he always said, and, leaning over, he shook her a little: not enough to really wake her, just enough to get her stirring. In sixteen years of performing this ritual, minus federal holidays and two weeks of paid vacation in the summer, Wyndham had pretty much mastered it. He could cause her to stir without quite waking her up just about every time.

So to say he was surprised when his wife didn't screw her face into her pillow and smile is something of an understatement. He was shocked, actually. And there was an additional consideration: She hadn't said "Ummm," either. Not the usual luxurious, warm-morning-bed kind of "ummm," and not the infrequent but still familiar stuffy, I-have-a-cold-and-my-head-aches kind of "ummm," either.

No "ummm" at all.

The air-conditioning cycled off. For the first time Wyndham noticed a strange smell—a faint, organic funk, like spoiled milk, or unwashed feet.

Standing there in the dark, Wyndham began to have a very bad feeling. It was a different kind of bad feeling than the one he'd had in Monica's living room watching airliners plunge again and again into the World Trade Center. That had been a powerful but largely impersonal bad feeling—I say "largely impersonal" because Wyndham had a third cousin who worked at Cantor Fitzgerald. (The cousin's name was Chris; Wyndham had to look it up in his address book every year when he sent out cards celebrating the birth of his personal savior.) The bad feeling he began to have when his wife failed to say "ummm," on the other hand, was powerful and *personal*.

Concerned, Wyndham reached down and touched his wife's face. It was like touching a woman made of wax, lifeless and cool, and it was at that moment—that moment precisely—that Wyndham realized the world had come to an end.

Everything after that was just details.

Beyond the mad scientists and corrupt bureaucrats, characters in end-of-the-world stories typically come in one of three varieties.

The first is the rugged individualist. You know the type: self-reliant, iconoclastic loners who know how to use firearms and deliver babies. By story's end, they're well on their way to Re-Establishing Western Civilization—though they're usually smart enough not to return to the Bad Old Ways.

The second variety is the post-apocalyptic bandit. These characters often come in gangs, and they face off against the rugged survivor types. If you happen to prefer cinematic incarnations of the end-of-the-world tale, you can usually recognize them by their penchant for bondage gear, punked-out haircuts, and customized vehicles. Unlike the rugged survivors, the post-apocalyptic bandits embrace the Bad Old Ways—though they're not displeased by the expanded opportunities to rape and pillage.

The third type of character—also pretty common, though a good deal less so than the other two—is the world-weary sophisticate. Like Wyndham, such characters drink too much; unlike Wyndham, they suffer badly from *ennui*. Wyndham suffers too, of course, but whatever he suffers from, you can bet it's not *ennui*.

We were discussing details, though:

Wyndham did the things people do when they discover a loved one dead. He picked up the phone and dialed 9-1-1. There seemed to be something wrong with the line, however; no one picked up on the other end. Wyndham took a deep breath, went into the kitchen, and tried the extension. Once again he had no success.

The reason, of course, was that, this being the end of the world, all the people who were supposed to answer the phones were dead. Imagine them being swept away by a tidal wave if that helps—which is exactly what happened to more than 3000 people during a storm in Pakistan in 1960. (Not that this is *literally* what happened to the operators who would have taken Wyndham's 9-1-1 call, you understand; but more about what *really* happened to them later—the important thing is that one moment they had been alive; the next they were dead. Like Wyndham's wife.)

Wyndham gave up on the phone.

He went back into the bedroom. He performed a fumbling version of mouth-to-mouth resuscitation on his wife for fifteen minutes or so, and then he gave that up, too. He walked into his daughter's bedroom (she was twelve and her name was Ellen). He found her lying on her back, her mouth slightly agape. He reached down to shake her—he was going to tell her that something terrible had happened; that her mother had died—but he found that something terrible had happened to her as well. The same terrible thing, in fact.

Wyndham panicked.

He raced outside, where the first hint of red had begun to bleed up over the horizon. His neighbor's automatic irrigation system was on, the heads whickering in the silence, and as he sprinted across the lawn, Wyndham felt the spray, like a cool hand against his face. Then, chilled, he was standing on his neighbor's stoop. Hammering the door with both fists. Screaming.

After a time—he didn't know how long—a dreadful calm settled over him. There was no sound but the sound of the sprinklers, throwing glittering arcs of spray into the halo of the street light on the corner.

He had a vision, then. It was as close as he had ever come to a moment of genuine prescience. In the vision, he saw the suburban houses stretching away in silence before him. He saw the silent bedrooms. In them, curled beneath the sheets, he saw a legion of sleepers, also silent, who would never again wake up.

Wyndham swallowed.

Then he did something he could not have imagined doing even twenty minutes ago. He bent over, fished the key from its hiding place between the bricks, and let himself inside his neighbor's house.

The neighbor's cat slipped past him, mewing querulously. Wyndham had already reached down to retrieve it when he noticed the smell—that unpleasant, faintly organic funk. Not spoiled milk, either. And not feet. Something worse: soiled diapers, or a clogged toilet.

Wyndham straightened, the cat forgotten.

"Herm?" he called. "Robin?"

No answer.

Inside, Wyndham picked up the phone, and dialed 9-1-1. He listened to it ring for a long time; then, without bothering to turn it off, Wyndham dropped the phone to the floor. He made his way through the silent house, snapping on lights. At the door to the master bedroom, he hesitated. The odor—it was unmistakable now, a mingled stench of urine and feces, of all the body's muscles relaxing at once—was stronger here. When he spoke again, whispering really—

"Herm? Robin?"

—he no longer expected an answer.

Wyndham turned on the light. Robin and Herm were shapes in the bed, unmoving. Stepping closer, Wyndham stared down at them. A fleeting series of images cascaded through his mind, images of Herm and Robin working the grill at the neighborhood block party or puttering in their vegetable garden. They'd had a knack for tomatoes, Robin and Herm. Wyndham's wife had always loved their tomatoes.

Something caught in Wyndham's throat.

He went away for a while then.

The world just grayed out on him.

When he came back, Wyndham found himself in the living room, standing in front of Robin and Herm's television. He turned it on and cycled through the channels, but there was nothing on. Literally nothing. Snow, that's all. Seventy-five channels of snow. The end of the world had always been televised in Wyndham's experience. The fact that it wasn't being televised now suggested that it really *was* the end of the world.

This is not to suggest that television validates human experience—of the end of the world or indeed of anything else, for that matter.

You could ask the people of Pompeii, if most of them hadn't died in a volcano eruption in 79 AD, nearly two millennia before television. When Vesuvius erupted, sending lava thundering down the mountainside at four miles a minute, some 16,000 people perished. By some freakish geological quirk, some of them—their shells, anyway—were preserved, frozen inside casts of volcanic ash. Their arms outstretched in pleas for mercy, their faces frozen in horror.

For a fee, you can visit them today.

Here's one of my favorite end-of-the-world scenarios by the way:

Carnivorous plants.

Wyndham got in his car and went looking for assistance—a functioning telephone or television, a helpful passer-by. He found instead more non-functioning telephones and televisions. And, of course, more non-functioning people: lots of those, though he had to look harder for them than you might have expected. They weren't scattered in the streets, or dead at the wheels of their cars in a massive traffic jam—though Wyndham supposed that might have been the case somewhere in Europe, where the catastrophe—whatever it was—had fallen square in the middle of the morning rush.

Here, however, it seemed to have caught most folks at home in bed; as a result, the roads were more than usually passable.

At a loss—numb, really—Wyndham drove to work. He might have been in shock by then. He'd gotten accustomed to the smell, anyway, and the corpses of the night shift—men and women he'd known for sixteen years, in some cases—didn't shake him as much. What *did* shake him was the sight of all the packages in the sorting area: He was struck suddenly by the fact that none of them would ever be delivered. So Wyndham loaded his truck and went out on his route. He wasn't sure why he did it—maybe because he'd rented a movie once in which a post-apocalyptic drifter scavenges a US Postal uniform and manages to Re-Establish Western Civilization (but not the Bad Old Ways) by assuming the postman's appointed rounds. The futility of Wyndham's own efforts quickly became evident, however.

He gave it up when he found that even Monica—or, as he more often thought of her, the Home Shopping Network Lady—was no longer in the business of receiving packages. Wyndham found her face down on the kitchen floor, clutching a shattered coffee mug in one hand. In death she had neither a pretty face nor a nice personality. She did have that same ripe unpleasant odor, however. In spite of it, Wyndham stood looking down at her for the longest time. He couldn't seem to look away.

When he finally *did* look away, Wyndham went back to the living room where he had once watched nearly 3000 people die, and opened her package himself. When it came to UPS rules, the Home Shopping Network Lady's living room was turning out to be something of a post-apocalyptic zone in its own right.

Wyndham tore the mailing tape off and dropped it on the floor. He opened the box. Inside, wrapped safely in three layers of bubble wrap, he found a porcelain statue of Elvis Presley.

Elvis Presley, the King of Rock 'n' Roll, died August 16, 1977, while sitting on the toilet. An autopsy revealed that he had ingested an impressive cocktail of prescription drugs—including codeine, ethinamate, methaqualone, and various barbiturates. Doctors also found trace elements of Valium, Demerol, and other pharmaceuticals in his veins.

For a time, Wyndham comforted himself with the illusion that the end of the world had been a local phenomenon. He sat in his truck outside the Home Shopping Network Lady's house and awaited rescue—the sound of sirens or approaching choppers, whatever. He fell asleep cradling the porcelain statue of Elvis. He woke up at dawn, stiff from sleeping in the truck, to find a stray dog nosing around outside.

Clearly rescue would not be forthcoming.

Wyndham chased off the dog and placed Elvis gently on the sidewalk. Then he drove off, heading out of the city. Periodically, he stopped, each time confirming what he had already known the minute he touched his dead wife's face: The end of the world was upon him. He found nothing but non-functioning telephones, non-functioning televisions, and non-functioning people. Along the way he listened to a lot of non-functioning radio stations.

You, like Wyndham, may be curious about the catastrophe that has befallen everyone in the world around him. You may even be wondering why Wyndham has survived.

End-of-the-world tales typically make a big deal about such things, but Wyndham's curiosity will never be satisfied. Unfortunately, neither will yours.

Shit happens.

It's the end of the world after all.

The dinosaurs never discovered what caused *their* extinction, either.

At this writing, however, most scientists agree that the dinosaurs met their fate when an asteroid nine miles wide plowed into the Earth just south of the Yucatan Peninsula, triggering gigantic tsunamis, hurricane-force winds, worldwide forest fires, and a flurry of volcanic activity. The crater is still there—it's 120 miles wide and more than a mile deep—but the dinosaurs, along with 75% of the other species then alive, are gone. Many of them died in the impact, vaporized in the explosion. Those that survived the initial cataclysm would have perished soon after as acid rain poisoned the world's water and dust obscured the sun, plunging the planet into a years-long winter.

For what it's worth, this impact was merely the most dramatic in a long series of mass extinctions; they occur in the fossil record at roughly 30-million-year intervals. Some scientists have linked these intervals to the solar system's periodic journey through the galactic plane, which dislodges millions of comets from the Oort cloud beyond Pluto, raining them down on Earth. This theory, still contested, is called the Shiva Hypothesis in honor of the Hindu god of destruction.

The inhabitants of Lisbon would have appreciated the allusion on November 1, 1755, when the city was struck by an earthquake measuring 8.5 on the Richter Scale. The tremor leveled more than 12,000 homes and ignited a fire that burned for six days.

More than 60,000 people perished.

This event inspired Voltaire to write *Candide*, in which Dr. Pangloss advises us that this is the best of all possible worlds.

Wyndham could have filled the gas tank in his truck. There were gas stations at just about every exit along the highway, and *they* seemed to be functioning well enough. He didn't bother, though.

When the truck ran out of gas, he just pulled to the side of the road, hopped down, and struck off across the fields. When it started getting dark—this was before he had launched himself on the study of just how it is night falls—he took shelter in the nearest house.

It was a nice place, a two-story brick house set well

back from the country road he was by then walking on. It had some big trees in the front yard. In the back, a shaded lawn sloped down to the kind of woods you see in movies, but not often in real life: enormous, old trees with generous, leaf-carpeted avenues. It was the kind of place his wife would have loved, and he regretted having to break a window to get inside. But there it was: It was the end of the world and he had to have a place to sleep. What else could he do?

Wyndham hadn't planned to stay there, but when he woke up the next morning he couldn't think of anywhere to go. He found two non-functional old people in one upstairs bedroom and he tried to do for them what he had not been able to do for his wife and daughter: Using a spade from the garage, he started digging a grave in the front yard. After an hour or so, his hands began to blister and crack. His muscles—soft from sitting behind the wheel of a UPS truck for all those years—rebelled.

He rested for a while, and then he loaded the old people into the car he found parked in the garage—a slate-blue Volvo station wagon with 37,312 miles on the odometer. He drove them a mile or two down the road, pulled over, and laid them out, side-by-side in a grove of beech trees. He tried to say some words over them before he left—his wife would have wanted him to—but he couldn't think of anything appropriate so he finally gave it up and went back to the house.

It wouldn't have made much difference: Though Wyndham didn't know it, the old people were lapsed Jews. According to the faith Wyndham shared with his wife, they were doomed to burn in hell for all eternity anyway. Both of them were first-generation immigrants; most of their families had already been burned up in ovens at Dachau and Buchenwald.

Burning wouldn't have been anything new for them.

Speaking of fires, the Triangle Shirt Waist Factory in New York City burned on March 25, 1911. One hundred and forty-six people died. Many of them might have survived, but the factory's owners had locked the exits to prevent theft.

Rome burned, too. It is said that Nero fiddled.

Back at the house, Wyndham washed up and made himself a drink from the liquor cabinet he found in the kitchen. He'd never been much of a drinker before the world ended, but he didn't see any reason not to give it a try now. His experiment proved such a success that he began sitting out on the porch nights, drinking gin and watching the sky. One night he thought he saw a plane, lights blinking as it arced high overhead. Later, sober, he concluded that it must have been a satellite, still whipping around the planet, beaming down telemetry to empty listening stations and abandoned command posts.

A day or two later the power went out. And a few days after that, Wyndham ran out of liquor. Using the Volvo, he set off in search of a town. Characters in end-of-the-world stories commonly drive vehicles of two types: The jaded sophisticates tend to drive souped-up sports cars, often racing them along the Australian coast line because what else do they have to live for; everyone else drives rugged SUVs. Since the 1991 Persian Gulf War—in which some 23,000 people died, most of them Iraqi conscripts killed by American smart bombs—military-style Humvees have been especially coveted. Wyndham, however, found the Volvo entirely adequate to his needs.

No one shot at him.

He was not assaulted by a roving pack of feral dogs.

He found a town after only fifteen minutes on the road. He didn't see any evidence of looting. Everybody was too dead to loot; that's the way it is at the end of the world.

On the way, Wyndham passed a sporting goods store where he did not stop to stock up on weapons or survival equipment. He passed numerous abandoned vehicles, but he did not stop to siphon off some gas. He *did* stop at the liquor store, where he smashed a window with a rock and helped himself to several cases of gin, whiskey, and vodka. He also stopped at the grocery store, where he found the reeking bodies of the night crew sprawled out beside carts of supplies that would never make it onto the shelves. Holding a handkerchief over his nose, Wyndham loaded up on tonic water and a variety of other mixers. He also got some canned goods, though he didn't feel any imperative to stock up beyond his immediate needs. He ignored the bottled water.

In the book section, he *did* pick up a bartender's guide.

Some end-of-the-world stories present us with two post-apocalypse survivors, one male and one female. These two survivors take it upon themselves to Re-Populate the Earth, part of their larger effort to Re-Establish Western Civilization without the Bad Old Ways. Their names are always artfully withheld until the end of the story, at which point they are invariably revealed to be Adam and Eve.

The truth is, almost all end-of-the-world stories are at some level Adam-and-Eve stories. That may be why they enjoy such popularity. In the interests of total disclosure, I will admit that in fallow periods of my own sexual life—and, alas, these periods have been more frequent than I'd care to admit—I've often found Adam-and-Eve post-holocaust fantasies strangely comforting. Being the only man alive significantly reduces the potential for rejection in my view. And it cuts performance anxiety practically to nothing.

There's a woman in this story, too.
Don't get your hopes up.

By this time, Wyndham has been living in the brick house for almost two weeks. He sleeps in the old couple's bedroom, and he sleeps pretty well, but maybe that's the gin. Some mornings he wakes up disoriented, wondering where his wife is and how he came to be in a strange place. Other mornings he wakes up feeling like he dreamed everything else and this has always been his bedroom.

One day, though, he wakes up early, to gray pre-dawn light. Someone is moving around downstairs. Wyndham's curious, but he's not afraid. He doesn't wish he'd stopped at the sporting goods store and gotten a gun. Wyndham has never shot a gun in his life. If he did shoot someone— even a post-apocalyptic punk with cannibalism on his mind—he'd probably have a breakdown.

Wyndham doesn't try to disguise his presence as he goes downstairs. There's a woman in the living room. She's not bad looking, this woman—blonde in a washed-out kind of way, trim, and young, twenty-five, thirty at the most. She doesn't look extremely clean, and she doesn't smell much better, but hygiene hasn't been uppermost on Wyndham's mind lately, either. Who is he to judge?

"I was looking for a place to sleep," the woman says.

"There's a spare bedroom upstairs," Wyndham tells her.

The next morning—it's really almost noon, but Wyndham has gotten into the habit of sleeping late—they eat breakfast together: a Pop Tart for the woman, a bowl of dry Cheerios for Wyndham.

They compare notes, but we don't need to get into that. It's the end of the world and the woman doesn't know how it happened any more than Wyndham does or you do or anybody ever does. She does most of the talking, though. Wyndham's never been much of a talker, even at the best of times.

He doesn't ask her to stay. He doesn't ask her to leave.

He doesn't ask her much of anything.

That's how it goes all day.

Sometimes the whole sex thing *causes* the end of the world.

In fact, if you'll permit me to reference Adam and Eve just one more time, sex and death have been connected to the end of the world ever since—well, the beginning of the world. Eve, despite warnings to the contrary, eats of the fruit of the Tree of Knowledge of Good and Evil and realizes she's naked—that is, a sexual being. Then she introduces Adam to the idea by giving him a bite of the fruit.

God punishes Adam and Eve for their transgression by kicking them out of Paradise and introducing death into the world. And there you have it: the first apocalypse, *eros* and *thanatos* all tied up in one neat little bundle, and it's all Eve's fault.

No wonder feminists don't like that story. It's a pretty corrosive view of female sexuality when you think about it.

Coincidentally, perhaps, one of my favorite end-of-the-world stories involves some astronauts who fall into a time warp; when they get out they learn that all the men are dead. The women have done pretty well for themselves in the meantime. They no longer need men to reproduce and they've set up a society that seems to work okay without men—better in fact than our messy two-sex societies ever have.

But do the men stay out of it?

They do not. They're men, after all, and they're driven by their need for sexual dominance. It's genetically encoded so to speak, and it's not long before they're trying to turn this Eden into another fallen world. It's sex that does it, violent male sex—rape, actually. In other words, sex that's more about the violence than the sex.

And certainly nothing to do with love.

Which, when you think about it, is a pretty corrosive view of male sexuality.

The more things change the more they stay the same, I guess.

Wyndham, though.

Wyndham heads out on the porch around three. He's got some tonic. He's got some gin. It's what he does now. He doesn't know where the woman is, doesn't have strong feelings on the issue either way.

He's been sitting there for hours when she joins him.

Wyndham doesn't know what time it is, but the air has that hazy underwater quality that comes around twilight. Darkness is starting to pool under the trees, the crickets are tuning up, and it's so peaceful that for a moment Wyndham can almost forget that it's the end of the world.

Then the screen door claps shut behind the woman. Wyndham can tell right away that she's done something to herself, though he couldn't tell you for sure what it is: that magic women do, he guesses. His wife used to do it, too. She always looked good to him, but sometimes she looked just flat-out amazing. Some powder, a little blush. Lipstick. You know.

And he appreciates the effort. He does. He's flattered even. She's an attractive woman. Intelligent, too.

The truth is, though, he's just not interested.

She sits beside him, and all the time she's talking. And though she doesn't say it in so many words, what she's talking about is Re-Populating the World and Re-Establishing Western Civilization. She's talking about Duty. She's talking about it because that's what you're supposed to talk about at times like this. But underneath that is sex. And underneath that, way down, is loneliness—and he has some sympathy for that, Wyndham does. After a while, she touches Wyndham, but he's got nothing. He might as well be dead down there.

"What's wrong with you?" she says.

Wyndham doesn't know how to answer her. He doesn't know how to tell her that the end of the world isn't about any of that stuff. The end of the world is about something else, he doesn't have a word for it.

* * *

So, anyway, Wyndham's wife.

She has another book on her night stand, too. She doesn't read it every night, only on Sundays. But the week before the end of the world the story she was reading was the story of Job.

You know the story, right?

It goes like this: God and Satan—the Adversary, anyway; that's probably the better translation—make a wager. They want to see just how much shit God's most faithful servant will eat before he renounces his faith. The servant's name is Job. So they make the wager, and God starts feeding Job shit. Takes his riches, takes his cattle, takes his health. Deprives him of his friends. On and on. Finally—and this is the part that always got to Wyndham—God takes Job's children.

Let me clarify: In this context "takes" should be read as "kills."

You with me on this? Like Krakatoa, a volcanic island that used to exist between Java and Sumatra. On August 27, 1883, Krakatoa exploded, spewing ash fifty miles into the sky and vomiting up five cubic miles of rock. The concussion was heard 3000 miles away. It created tsunamis towering 120 feet in the air. Imagine all that water crashing down on the flimsy villages that lined the shores of Java and Sumatra.

Thirty thousand people died.

Every single one of them had a name.

Job's kids. Dead. Just like 30,000 nameless Javanese.

As for Job? He keeps shoveling down the shit. He will not renounce God. He keeps the faith. And he's rewarded: God gives him back his riches, his cattle. God restores his health, and sends him friends. God replaces his kids.

Pay attention: Word choice is important in an end-of-the-world story.

I said "replaces," not "restores."

The other kids? They stay dead, gone, non-functioning, erased forever from the Earth, just like the dinosaurs and the 12 million undesirables incinerated by the Nazis and the 500,000 slaughtered in Rwanda and the 1.7 million murdered in Cambodia and the 60 million immolated in the Middle Passage.

That merry prankster God.

That jokester.

That's what the end of the world is about, Wyndham wants to say. The rest is just details.

By this point the woman (You want her to have a name? She deserves one, don't you think?) has started to weep softly. Wyndham gets to his feet and goes into the dark kitchen for another glass. Then he comes back out to the porch and makes a gin and tonic. He sits beside her and presses the cool glass upon her. It's all he knows to do.

"Here," he says. "Drink this. It'll help."

A SONG BEFORE SUNSET

BY DAVID GRIGG

David Grigg is the author of just a handful of stories, which were published between 1976 and 1985. This story, the first he ever had accepted for publication, first appeared in the anthology *Beyond Tomorrow*, which saw him sharing a table of contents with no less than six SFWA Grand Masters. In 2004, it was performed as an audiobook by Alex Wilson of Telltale Weekly (www. telltaleweekly.org), and is included in Grigg's story collection, *Islands*. Grigg has been nominated for the Australian Ditmar Awards several times, once in the short fiction category, twice as a fan writer, and once for editing the fanzine *The Fanarchist*.

Grigg says that the seed of the story was a line in Chekhov's "Three Sisters" where Tuzenbach says (of one of the sisters), "Fancy being able to play so exquisitely, and yet having nobody, nobody at all to appreciate it!" It was this sad irony of wasted talent that started Grigg thinking about how the very talented might cope—or not cope—once our civilization was no more. If, as Grigg says, culture is an epiphenomenon of civilization, without civilization, would culture be entirely irrelevant?

It took him three weeks to find the sledgehammer. He was hunting rats among the broken concrete and rusted metal of an ancient supermarket. The sun was beginning to descend over the jagged horizons of the city, casting shadows like giant gravestones onto the nearer buildings. An edge of blackness had begun to creep across the rubble that was all that remained of the store.

He picked his way carefully from one piece of concrete to another, skirting the twisted metal, looking for a hole or a cover that might make a suitable nest for a brood of rats, here and there using his stick to turn over a loose chunk in the vain hope of finding a can of food undiscovered after years of looting. At his waist hung three large rats, their heads squashed and bloody from his stick. Rats were still fat and slow enough these days to be caught by surprise with a blow to the head, which was fortunate, for his eye and his skill with the slingshot he carried were not as they had once been. He rested a while, sniffing at the cold wind. There would be a frost tonight, and his bones knew fear of the cold. He was getting old.

He was sixty-five, and the years had starved him. The flesh of his youth had loosened and sagged, leaving his frame thinly draped and his eyes staring from his bony head like some curious troll.

He was sixty-five, and his hair, gray many years ago, now raised a white halo about his leather-colored face.

That he had survived so long was a wonder to him, for his earlier years had not prepared him for this present world. But somehow he had learned to fight and kill and run and all else that had been necessary in the long years since the city had died.

The days now, however, were not so foul and desperate as they had once been. Now it was seldom that he feared he would starve to death. But in the bad days, like many others, he had eaten human flesh.

His name was Parnell and he had gone on living. The sun was sinking fast, and he turned about to go back before the dark could overtake him. It was as he turned that he caught the dull shine of metal in the corner of his eye. He peered more closely, put out his hand and heaved a sledgehammer up from the rubble. He swung its mass experimentally, weighed it in his hands, and felt its movement. After a moment he was forced to put it down again, as his arms began to tremble with unaccustomed strain. But no matter: given enough time, he knew this was the tool to realize the hope he had been hugging to himself for three weeks. He tied the hammer awkwardly to his belt and began to hurry home, fleeing the shadow of the city.

It was almost dark when he reached his home, a weather-stained stone house hedged around with the tangled jungle of an overgrown garden. Inside, he carefully lit each of the smoky candles in the living room, calling up a cancerous light that spread relentlessly into the corners. His door was locked and barred, and at last he sat in peace before the woodwormed piano in the main room. He sighed a little as his fingers tapped at the yellowed and splitting keys, and felt an accustomed sorrow as the fractured notes ascended. This piano had perhaps been a good learner's instrument in its day, but time had not been kind to it. Even if he had not feared attracting the attention of the dwellers in the dark outside, the effort of playing was more agony than pleasure.

Music had once been his life. Now his greatest aim was only to quiet the rumbling of his belly. Then he remembered—his eyes drifted to the hammer he had found in the rubble that day—and his hope came alive again, as it had weeks ago.

But there was no time to daydream, no time for hoping. There was time before he slept only to clean and skin the rats he had caught. Tomorrow he was to go trading with the Tumbledown Woman.

The Tumbledown Woman and her mate lived in the midst of a hundred decrepit trams in an old depot. Why they chose to live there was a puzzle none who traded with her had ever managed to solve. Here she stayed, and here she traded. Her store counter was a solitary tram left on the rails a few meters outside the depot, its paint peeling away but still bearing pathetic advertisements of a lost age. While the outside of the tram offered far-away holidays and better deodorants, the Tumbledown Woman inside traded garbage as the luxuries of a world which had died. Inside, arrayed along the wooden seats or hung from the ceiling were tin cans with makeshift hand-grips, greasy home-made candles, racks of suspect vegetables grown no one knew where, rows of dead rats, cats, rabbits and the occasional dog, plastic spoons, bottles, coats of ratskin and all sorts of items salvaged from the debris of oft-looted shops.

The Tumbledown Woman was old, and she was black, and she was ugly, and she cackled when she saw

Parnell approaching slowly in the chill morning. She had survived better than many men through the crisis, by being more ruthless and more cruel than they had ever managed to be to her in the years before. She rubbed her hands together with a dry, dry sound, and greeted Parnell with a faded leer.

"Two rats, Tumbledown Woman, fresh killed yesterday," he opened without hesitation.

"I give you something good for them, Mr. Piano Player," she said.

"Then that will be the first time ever. What?"

"A genuine diamond ring, twenty-four-carat gold, see!" And she held the flashing gem to the sun.

Parnell didn't bother to smile at her taunt. "Give me food, and be done with your mocking."

She sneered, and offered him a cabbage and two carrots. Nodding, he handed her the skinned corpses, lodged the food in his bag, and turned to go. But he was carrying the sledgehammer at his side, and she stopped him with a yell. "Hey, piano player man, that hammer! I give you good fur coat for it! Genuine rabbit!"

He turned and saw that she was not mocking him this time. "When I've finished with it, maybe. Then we'll see."

His reply seemed to make her pleased, for she grinned and yelled again: "Hey, piano man, you hear the news about Ol' Man Edmonds? Them Vandalmen come an' kill him, burn down that book place Ol' Man Edmonds live in!"

Parnell gasped in shock. "The Library? They burnt the Library down?"

"That's right!"

"My God!" He stood, silent and bewildered for a long

minute as the Tumbledown Woman grinned at him. Then, unable to speak further in his anger, he clamped his hands together in bitter frustration and walked off.

The sledgehammer was an awkward thing to carry. Slipped into his belt with the metal head at his waist, the wooden handle beat at his legs as he walked. If he carried it in his arms, his muscles protested after no more than a few minutes, and he was forced to rest. He was getting old, and he knew it. The slide to death was beginning to steepen and he was not, he thought, very far from its end.

In slow, weary stages he walked the distance into the heart of the corpse that was the city: Long ago its pulse had stopped. He walked past the rusty hulks of cars and along the dust-filled tram-tracks, through streets of shattered buildings standing in rows like jagged reefs. Long ago the lungs of the city had expired their last breath; the tall chimneys were fallen, casting scattered bricks across the road before him.

He came at last to the center and faced again the strongly barred and sealed doors of the old City Hall, half buried in the rubble of its long-crumbled entranceway. Even if he had been able to break open the bars of the door, he would have needed to clear away the rubble to allow the doors to open. Such was beyond him.

But at the side of the building, the skeleton of a truck lay crazily against the wall, mounted on the pavement and nuzzled face to face with a tree that now made a leafy wilderness of the cab.

Parnell climbed onto the truck and carefully ascended until he perched with little comfort on a branch of the tree, close to a barred window. Three weeks ago he had cleaned away the grime on the glass to see the dusty corridors inside. On the far wall of the corridor was a direction sign, faded and yellowed, but still bearing the words: CONCERT HALL.

Once again, looking at that dim sign, he was filled to overflowing with memories of concerts he had given. His hands followed a memory of their own on the keys, the music spiraled and, after, the almost invisible audience in the darkened hall applauded again and again…

His memories vanished as he swung the sledgehammer from his shoulder, jarring it into the bars of the window. Dust showered and cement crumbled. The task looked easier than he had at first thought, which was fortunate, for the one stroke had weakened him terribly. He swung again, and the bars moved and bent. Somehow, he found the strength for another swing, and the bars buckled and came loose and smashed through the glass into the corridor beyond.

Triumph came to him in a cloud of weakness, leaving him gasping and his arms weak and trembling. He sat for a long moment on the branch, gaining strength and hope to venture within.

At last he swung his legs over the edge and dropped onto the corridor floor. Glass crackled. He reached into his bag and brought out a small candle and some precious matches. The box of usable matches had cost him ten ratskins at the Tumbledown Woman's tram two weeks ago. He lit the candle and yellow light flooded into the dusty corridor.

He walked along it, making footprints in the virgin dust. A memory floated back to him of telecasts of moon explorers, placing footprint after footprint in age-old lunar dust, and he smiled a grim smile.

Eventually he came to a set of double doors, barred and padlocked. Here he was forced to rest again before he could smash the lock with his hammer, and step into the space-like blackness beyond.

After his eyes had adjusted to the light of the candle, dimmed by the open space, he saw row upon row of once plush seats. Somewhere a rat scurried, and above he could hear the soft rustle and squeaks of what might be a brood of bats on the high ceiling.

The aisle stretched before him, sloping slightly downwards. Parnell walked forward slowly, kicking up dust. In the dark immensity of the hall, his candle was just a spark, illuminating only a tight circle around him and filtering through puffs of dust stirred by his passage.

On the stage, metal gleamed back images of the candleflame from scattered corners. Around him were the music stands and music sheets of a full orchestra, filmed with years of dust. Here was a half-opened instrument case, and in it the still-shining brass of a French horn, abandoned by some long-gone performer in forgotten haste. And shrouded in white, topped by a tarnished candelabra, stood the grand piano.

Parnell's heart began a heavier, more rapid beat as he brushed dust from the sheet covering the piano. With an anxious hand he lit the candelabra with his own meager candle, and lifted it high as the light swelled across the stage. He could see other instruments now, long lost by their players: here a violin, there an oboe, cast aside by a time that had made their possession unimportant.

Placing the light on the floor, he carefully eased the sheet from the piano. Yellow light danced on the black surface of polished wood and sparkled in the brass.

For a long, long time his aged hands could do no more than caress the instrument with a growing affection. Finally, he sat on the piano stool, realizing perhaps for the first time how tired he was. The key, he saw with relief, was still in the lock. No doubt he could have forced it, but it would have broken his heart to have damaged that perfect form.

Turning the key in the lock, he lifted the cover and ran his hand softly over the white and black of the piano keys. He sat back, and with a self-consciously wry gesture, flipped his ragged coat away from his seat and turned to face the hall.

A full house tonight, Mr. Parnell. All of London queues to hear you. The radio stations are paying fortunes to broadcast your concert. The audience is quiet, expectant. Can you hear them breathe, out there? Not a cough, not a sneeze, not a mutter as they wait, hushed, to hear the first notes drop from your fingertips. The music trembles in your hands, waiting to begin—now!

Discords shattered the empty hall, and the bats, disturbed, flew in a twittering crowd above the deserted, rotting seats. Parnell let out his breath in a painful sigh.

The instrument would have to be painstakingly retuned, note by note. His goal had yet to be reached. But now, at last, he could reach out and touch it. Now, one by one, he began to realize the difficulties that remained. He felt his hunger and saw the candles burning fast. He could probably find pitch pipes in the hall, but he would need some kind of tool to tighten the strings of the piano. And he would have to support himself somehow while he spent his time in here and was unable to hunt or forage. He would have to go back to the Tumbledown

Woman, and see what she would offer him in trade for the sledgehammer. It was no fur coat he would be getting, he knew.

Outside again, he opened his bag and took out the food he had brought with him. He sat on the truck eating pieces of roasted rat and raw cabbage, pondering whether there was some way he could net and kill some of the brood of bats within the hall. No doubt they would make curious eating, and perhaps their leathery wings might have a use. But all these schemes were impractical, and he dismissed them.

In the distance, over the broken buildings, a thin trail of black smoke was rising leisurely toward the sky. The day had become bright and cloudless, and the smoke was a smear against the blue. Puzzled, Parnell wondered what was burning. The trail was too contained to be a forest fire. Unless some building had spontaneously ignited, after all these years, it had to be the work of men. Unable to arrive at any more satisfactory a conclusion, he turned away, thrusting the question from his mind.

After bundling away the remnants of the food, he loosely replaced the bars of the window to make his entry less obvious to any passing wanderer. Heaving up the sledgehammer, he began the long walk away from his heart's desire.

The Tumbledown Woman had turned sour in the late afternoon, like a fat black toad basking in the last rays of the sun. She sat on the running-board of the tram; greeted Parnell with little enthusiasm. Her withered husband now sat atop the tram and glared menacingly at the horizon, an ancient shotgun beneath his arm, ignoring his wife and Parnell equally.

Parnell sat and bickered with the woman for nearly an hour.

She would still offer him the fur coat, but he wanted an adjustable wrench, candles, matches, and food in exchange for the sledgehammer, and these were expensive items. In the end, Parnell gave in and accepted her final offer, which was everything he wanted except the food.

The Tumbledown Woman hung the sledgehammer in a prominent position within the tram and gave him the items he wanted. She turned and looked at him with a bitter eye. "You crazy, piano player man, you know that?"

Parnell, leaning wearily in the doorway of the tram, cradling his candles, was moved to agree with her. "I suppose you're right."

"Sure I'm right!" she answered, nodding her head vigorously. "You a crazy coot."

"Must be crazy to come and trade with you," he said, but the woman just glared at him. Then he remembered: "There was a lot of smoke in the south this morning. Do you know what it was?"

The Tumbledown Woman grinned and winked at him. "Sure I know. Didn' I tell you this morning about them Vandalmen? Them Vandalmen coming all over this town now. Last week burn down Ol' Man Edmonds and his books. Now it's that picture place. Sure crazy, them Vandalmen." And she puttered around the tram, arranging and rearranging her goods.

Parnell's heart sank a little more. "The Art Gallery?"

"'Yeah, that's what I hear. Limpin' Jack, he been south this morning, he told me. Them Vandalmen don't like them books or them pictures, no way."

Parnell's anger warmed within him, only to turn into

bitter frustration for the lack of an object. Most of the things he treasured had been destroyed during the crisis. Now those that were left were going the same way, in senseless destruction.

"What do they do it for?" he protested, sitting down in an empty seat to stop himself shaking. "What point is there in what they do?"

"Who cares?" said the woman. "Can't eat them books, can't keep warm in them pictures. Them Vandalmen crazy to burn them, sure, but who cares?"

"All right," said Parnell, "all right." The answers he felt within him would mean nothing to the Tumbledown Woman. All he could do was smother his loss and sorrow, hide it away. He clenched his jaws and wearily picked up his trades, placed them in his bag and stepped out of the tram. The Tumbledown Woman watched him go with a tired disgust. Her husband sat above, glaring, glaring, at the darkening horizon, his gun beneath his arm.

Parnell spent the morning of the next day hunting rats again in the rows of time-shattered houses that still stood in uniform lines to the west of the city. After a few hours of vain search he was lucky and found a rabbit warren riddling the soft earth in an overgrown and enclosed back yard. He caught two surprised rabbits before the others ran for safety. He spent the rest of the morning cleaning and roasting the rabbits and salting their skins. In the afternoon he was again within the dark hall, beginning the long task of tuning each string of the piano to a perfect pitch. Had he been a professional tuner, he would have been able to proceed with greater speed, but he was forced to go at a frustrating creep, making trial-and-error decisions as he listened to each string, hearing it in relation to the others he had tuned, listening to the pitch pipes, then tightening the string again with his rusty wrench.

He measured time by the rate at which the smoky candles burned, and left again before darkness fell.

Days passed in this way, until he could hardly trust his hearing and had to leave off for hours at a time before he could resume.

Every time he emerged from the hall to eat or to let his eyes and ears repair, there was smoke somewhere on the horizon. There came a day when he was finished; when he had tested the piano with scales and simple exercises and was sure the tuning was perfect. He knew then that he was afraid to begin, afraid to sit down and play a real piece of music on the piano. His hands still remembered his favorite pieces but there was a hollow fear in his heart that he would fumble and distort the music in some way. He had kept his hands strong, and his fingers limber by fighting the aged monster of a piano in his house for all these years, but he could not tell whether or not he still retained his skill. It had been a long time.

Parnell made his way outside the hall and sat, despondent and trembling, on the rusty, overgrown truck. It was early afternoon and, for the first time in days, there was no smoke to be seen in the sky. He ate the last of the rabbit and realized he would have to go hunting the following day. He laughed at himself for an old fool, gulped water from his bottle, lit his candle, and hurried back inside the hall, trailed by clouds of dust.

On the stage he had cleared the music stands to one side, leaving the grand piano alone and uncluttered. Now he dusted the polished surface one more time, buffed the brass lettering, raised the lid, lit the candelabra, and sat before the keyboard. The bats twittered tumultuous applause. He bowed his head slightly toward the moth-eaten velvet of the empty seats, and began to play.

He began with a Beethoven Piano Sonata, Opus 109. It flowed; it swelled; it poured from the strings of that magnificent piano as his hands moved and fell, remembering what his brain was unsure of. And he knew, listening, that he had not lost his skill, that somehow it had been kept somewhere safe within him, sleeping through the years of torment. He wove a web of music, cast motion and light and harmony into the darkness, wrapped himself within its sound, and played on. And as he played, he wept.

The piece ended; he began another. And another. Beethoven, Mozart and Chopin were resurrected. The music expanded through the hours, a torrent of joy, of sorrow, and of yearning. He was blind and insensate and deaf to all but his music, insulated from the outside world by the castle of sound he was building around himself.

At last Parnell stopped, his hands throbbing and aching, and raised his eyes above the level of the piano.

Standing before him was a Vandal. In his arms he cradled the sledgehammer Parnell had traded to the Tumbledown Woman. There was blood on its head.

The Vandal stood and regarded him contemptuously, all the time stroking, stroking, the shaft of the hammer he carried. He was dressed in roughly cured leather and rusted metal. Around his neck he wore a dozen metal necklaces and chains that dangled on his bare and hairy chest—crosses and swastikas, peace symbols and fishes—

clinking gently against each other. He was dirty, his hair was greasy and awry, and on his forehead was burned a V-shaped scar. He stank.

Parnell was unable to speak. Fear had made stone of him and his heart flopped around inside him like a grounded fish.

The Vandal uttered a hoarse giggle, enjoying the shock on Parnell's face. "Hey, old man, you play real pretty! Tell me now, Music Man, how well do you sing?"

Parnell's voice was a rustle in his throat: "I can't."

The Vandal shook his head in mock sorrow. "That's too bad, Music Man. But I tell you, you're gonna sing real good when I'm finished with you. Real good and loud." He shifted the sledgehammer to bring out a long knife. It cast fiery gleams about the stage as its edge caught the candlelight.

Parnell felt as though he was about to be sick but, insanely, his old anger grew in him even in the face of his fear. "Why?" he asked, his voice trembling. "Why do you want to kill me? What harm am I doing you?"

The eyes of the Vandal narrowed in concentration and fierce humor. "Why? Why not?" And the knife flashed yellow at Parnell's eyes.

"All that you do… destroying all the beautiful things, the books, the pictures…" Parnell was becoming excited in spite of his fear: "Those things are all we have left of our heritage, our culture; of civilization, of Man's greatness, don't you see? You're no more than barbarians, killing and burning…" He stopped as the Vandal waved the knife toward him, his face losing its mirth.

"You're pretty with your music and pretty with your words, but you talk a lot of shit. You know what your pretty culture gave us? Gave us dirt and fighting and eating each other, man. You're nice and old, pretty man; you were old when the murdering and the hunger started. Me and mine, we were just kids then. You know how it was for us? We had to run and hide so as not to be food for grown-ups; we had to eat dirt and scum to live, man. That's what your pretty heritage was for us, pretty man, so don't bullshit me about how great Man was, cause he ain't."

The Vandal was leaning over Parnell, breathing his foul breath hard into the old man's face. Parnell grew silent as the Vandal drew back and glared. "And you sitting here in the dark playing that nice music—all you wish is that it was back the way it was! Well, me and mine are making sure that it ain't never back that way again. Now you tell me, man, what good did that music, that culture, ever do, hey?"

Parnell's thoughts were tumbling. At last he said simply: "It gave people pleasure, that's all."

The Vandal regained his sneer. "Okay, Music Man, killing you is gonna give me lots of pleasure. But first, man, it's gonna give me real kicks to smash up this pretty music thing in front of you just so you can enjoy it too. How about that?" And, turning, the Vandal hefted the sledgehammer and raised it high above the strings of the grand piano.

Something snapped within Parnell.

He leapt up and grasped at the Vandal's arms. Surprised, he let the hammer drop. Parnell clawed at his face. The Vandal swung out a hairy fist, catching Parnell a jarring blow on the jaw and almost striking him to the ground, but Parnell's hands were about the Vandal's throat. Parnell's hands were the only part of him that was not weak and trembling—hands made iron-firm by decades of exercise on the keyboard—and his thumbs were digging into the Vandal's windpipe. The youth began to choke, and tried vainly to tear Parnell's hands away, but the gnarled fingers were locked in a murderous grip; they tightened with hysterical energy. For a seemingly endless moment the two hung together in a bizarre embrace. Then the Vandal crumpled to the stage, with Parnell on top of him, throttling the life from him, until the Vandal was dead.

Parnell let out a choking cry and retched violently over the edge of the stage. He crouched on his knees for some time, transformed by reaction and horror into a mindless animal. Eventually he turned around and stared with strange emotion at the body of the Vandal. Outside the hall, very faintly, he could hear the yells and shouts of the rest of the pack of new barbarians as they burned and looted. Inside, there was only the quiet of death and the soft twittering of the bats.

He crawled toward the piano where the sledgehammer lay. He stood, using the hammer as a prop for his trembling legs, then took it into his arms.

With one anguished swing, he brought the sledgehammer crashing down into the piano strings.

The shock jarred his whole body. The strings snapped with violent twangs and wood splintered, filling the air with jagged sound. The candelabra, toppling, plunged to the floor and went out, spilling darkness throughout the hall.

The silence seemed to last for a long time.

EPISODE SEVEN: LAST STAND AGAINST THE PACK IN THE KINGDOM OF THE PURPLE FLOWERS
BY JOHN LANGAN

John Langan is the author of the novel *House of Windows* and of many short stories, most of which have been collected in two volumes: *Mr. Gaunt and Other Uneasy Encounters* and *The Wide Carnivorous Sky and Other Monstrous Geographies*. His short fiction has appeared in *The Magazine of Fantasy & Science Fiction* and *Lightspeed*, and in anthologies such as *Fearful Symmetries*, *Blood and Other Cravings*, *By Blood We Live*, *The Living Dead*, and *Ghosts by Gaslight*. With Paul Tremblay, he co-edited the anthology, *Creatures: Thirty Years of Monsters*. He teaches courses in creative writing and gothic fiction at SUNY New Paltz, and lives in upstate New York with his family.

"Episode Seven" is a reinvention of a story Langan wrote in his early twenties. This current version was influenced by another story in this volume: "The End of the World as We Know It" by Dale Bailey. "Dale's story is a great revision of the classic, mid-century post-apocalypse story," Langan says. "I admired what he'd achieved, but I also felt a bit of rivalry, a desire to show that not everyone would roll over and go gently into that good night."

"There's a whole lot of hate left on this world, Spiderman."
—Samuel R. Delany, *The Einstein Intersection*

"Come On Down, Make the Stand."
—The Alarm, "The Stand"

"He was not assaulted by a roving pack of feral dogs."
—Dale Bailey, "The End of the World As We Know It"

After three days and nights on the run—

—during which they slept in thirty-, sixty-, and ninety-minute snatches, in the backs of large cars and SUVs, in a hotel lobby, in a sporting goods store at one end of a mall—

—they managed to pull ahead of the Pack—

—who had been too close from the start and drawn closer than that, despite Wayne's traps, all of which were clever and a few ingenious and the least of which thinned the Pack by two or three; until Wayne succeeded in luring them onto the walkway between the foodcourt and the mall's front entrance, where he detonated something that not only dropped the floor out from beneath the Pack, but brought the roof down, too, raining shards of glass like so many economy-sized guillotines—Jackie had wanted to stay and finish the survivors, but Wayne had declared it was still too dangerous and hauled her out the door—

—**cross the Bridge**—

—too congested with cars for them to take the Jeep Cherokee Wayne had navigated up the surprisingly empty stretch of Route 9 between the mall and the Mid-Hudson Bridge, which had made them debate the pros and cons of continuing north along this side of the Hudson until they reached the next bridge, which might be clear or might not (for once, Wayne couldn't make up his mind), until Jackie insisted they might as well cross here as cross anywhere: there would be plenty of cars on the other side, and if they didn't do something, they were going to squander their lead and face the Pack on *their* terms (which, aside from that first, terrible introduction, they'd succeeded in avoiding)—so they abandoned the Jeep, shouldered the backpacks, heavy as ever (so much for having rested), and (the Bridge shifting underfoot in the wind that hummed through its cables like a choir warming up) wound their way through a labyrinth of vehicles jammed, it seemed, into every possible configuration, their interiors choked with the oversized, thick-stemmed purple flowers Jackie and Wayne had found inside the vast majority of vehicles they'd encountered thus far, wound around steering wheels, gearshifts, and pedals (the windows talced with violet pollen), which made operating the cars a problem they had neither tools nor time to solve—there was a pickup whose cab was empty, but it was boxed against

the railing by a trio of smaller cars, as if they'd brought
it to bay there—

—set up camp on the other shore—

—on a
ledge overlooking the spot where the Bridge slotted into
the steep hills on the western shore of the Hudson—
Wayne had noticed the shelf of rock as they followed the
road up and to the right, past another cluster of cars full
of purple flowers, pointing it out to Jackie—when they
reached a place where the ledge was accessible from
the road, up a steep path blocked by a gate Wayne was
certain he could open, he had steered them towards it
(even though Jackie's legs trembled at the prospect of
more and harder climbing), urging her on, murmuring
encouragements, praise, until they had gained the top of
the path and Wayne had sprung the lock on the gate, let
them through, and snapped the lock closed again behind
them—Jackie had followed him as he picked his way
across the rocks littering the shelf; no more than fifteen
feet at its widest, she guesstimated; the Bridge returning
to view, and then Wayne had held up his hand as if he
were some kind of native guide signaling the rest of the
safari and said that this would do—

**—and were preparing
an ambush—**

—Wayne starting back along the ledge almost
as soon as they'd shucked their backpacks, taking with
him only the bulky black canvas bag that Jackie thought
of sometimes as his bag of tricks and sometimes as his
utility belt, and one of the pistols, leaving the other guns
with her: the rifle whose name she couldn't remember
but which Wayne had been very excited to find in the

sporting goods store, and the two remaining pistols, one of which had come from Wayne's father's safe, the other from an empty police cruiser—"You don't have to cover me," he'd said, "but pay attention," and she had, sitting with her bag propped against the backpacks, the rifle resting against the dome of her belly, as Wayne retraced their route down the hill to the Bridge and then out onto it, to set up some trap that had occurred to him, maybe two if there were time, till he was lost to view, obscured by the lean of the hill opposite her.

Jackie—

—Jacqueline Marie DiSalvo: twenty years old; five foot six, tall as her (most likely dead) father; she didn't know how many pounds anymore, since stepping on scales hadn't been at the top of her list of priorities for some time, now; her hair dark brown, long enough not to look short; her eyes brown, as well; her features carefully proportioned, (once, her [dead] father had described them to her as prim, which she hadn't been sure how to take); her skin less tanned than she would have expected, considering all the time they'd spent outdoors this past month: much of it at night, true, and there had been almost a solid week of rain in the middle of it, but still; wearing an extra-large men's white cotton t-shirt, gray sweatpants, white cotton athletic socks, and knock-off Birkenstocks that were comfortable but growing too tight: again, shoe shopping not a priority when you were running (or waddling, in her case) for your life—five weeks ago, she had been thirty-five days less pregnant, six and a half instead of nearly eight months "along" (her [most likely dead] doctor's favorite euphemism for pregnancy, as if carrying a child were an exotic vacation):

a difference that meant, practically speaking, a smaller stomach, smaller breasts, smaller everything; smaller her, who didn't tire quite so quickly; who didn't feel so out of breath all the time; who didn't sleep well but better than lately, when comfort had taken the last train out; who didn't need to stop to pee all the time, while Wayne stood guard, his gun out, his eyes sweeping whatever landscape they were in for the inevitable (re)appearance of the Pack—

—sat waiting for Wayne—

—Wayne Anthony Miller: twenty years old, two days younger than Jackie, in fact: she born on the third of July, he the fifth; six foot three; maybe one hundred and seventy pounds, not yet grown out of adolescent gangliness (his [most likely dead] mother's term, which he'd overheard her use at a New Year's party and which he'd confessed to Jackie left him feeling betrayed in some fundamental way); his hands and feet large, hung from long, skinny arms and legs that attached to a long, skinny torso; his hair grown long, a light brown that had been blond until his teens, framing a broad, square face with a small nose, narrow eyes, and generous mouth; he was wearing the same pair of jeans that had seen him through the last month, and which were little worse for wear (what an ad campaign: "Levi's: We'll Get You Through the End of Civilization: Rated Number One in Post-Apocalyptic Scenarios"), with a red plaid shirt open over a gray t-shirt emblazoned with Batman's black bat emblem, and Doc Marten's—five weeks ago, he had been working at the Barnes and Noble just south of the Bridge on the other side of the river and spending more of each paycheck than he should have at the comic book store in the plaza, there; his Associates Degree in Liberal Arts from Dutchess County Community College completed the previous semester; his future, which revolved around dreams of writing one of the Batman titles, still, as he liked to put it, a work-in-progress (this back when the future had extended further forward than the next twelve hours, and been somewhat more complex, yet also somewhat simpler, than trying to locate food and defensible shelter).

The sun was hot—

—roasting was a better word for it; although there was a substantial breeze blowing up from the river—Jackie supposed that the exposed rock around her, a grayish, sharp stuff that she should have been able to name but whose identity apparently lay in that part of her memory marked "No Longer Useful," amplified the heat, which wasn't completely oppressive (soon, it would be, she would be panting like a dog with it, most likely feel the urge to strip down to her underwear, but for the moment it radiated through her pleasantly).

Later—

—the better part of two hours; what had he been doing out there?—

—Wayne returned—

—waving to her as he walked off the Bridge; she waved back—

—long enough to pick up some rope—

—digging it out of his backpack, a hefty coil that looked like something a mountain climber might use and that he had been happy to find in a hardware store two weeks ago, which Jackie hadn't understood, since the rope looked pretty heavy and she didn't see the point in either of them taking on any more weight than was absolutely necessary—already, Wayne was carrying more than his fair share to compensate for her; she didn't want him exhausting himself because of an inability to pass on everything that might prove useful someday—she hadn't said anything out loud, though, and the addition of the rope seemed to have made no significant difference to him—

—and return to the Bridge—

—where he strung the rope across the road, running it back and forth and back and forth between a pair of the Bridge's support cables, weaving a kind of improvised web that Jackie thought would slow down the weakest members of the Pack for about half a second, and that the leader and its (hers? his?) companions would be through in no time at all.

When he was done with his final trap—

—which didn't look any more impressive once it was finished than it had when Jackie had realized what it was; although there was more of it than she had expected, a dozen, maybe fifteen strands that Wayne had layered according to a design she couldn't discern, so that some strands ran a foot or more behind the others—she hadn't exactly dozed while he'd constructed it: she'd kept her eyes open throughout the process, but her mind had wandered, as it had so often in the last day and a half, to the baby, which had gone from what she referred to as its daily calisthenics to complete stillness, not moving at all that she could feel (and, at this stage, she could feel a lot) for roughly thirty-six hours, now, which might have been entirely normal for all she knew: there was a rather dramatic lack of obstetricians in these parts (ha ha) and while Wayne knew a surprising amount about all sorts of things, his expertise tended towards the ultraviolent and not so much the whole miracle-of-life end of the spectrum—the best he could do was hear her concerns, shrug, and tell her not to worry about it, advice she'd already given herself and that was growing impossible to follow—she could feel panic gathering inside her, coalescing into a storm that would wash her away in a torrent of tears and screaming, because the child inside her was dead, she was carrying a dead baby—all right, to be honest, her mind hadn't wandered so much as gone directly to her anxiety and watched it growing—the point was, she wasn't sure if Wayne had rigged his web with any of the explosives (proper and improvised) that stuffed his bag of tricks, or if he had other plans for his oversized Cat's Cradle—

—he came back—

—and a good thing, too, because the sun had dipped behind the hill to her back, and though the sky overhead was still blue, it was that darker blue that would spend the next couple of hours shading steadily darker, into that indigo that a month of looking up at the night sky had shown her was the actual color against which the stars shone, and while the Pack had more than proved their ability to appear at any time of day, there was no doubting they preferred to move after the sun was down, and although Jackie had trained with the pistols, had opened up on one of the Pack at terrifyingly close range (it had scampered off, unhurt), she'd had a single lesson with the rifle (whose name was on the tip of her mind) with it unloaded, and had no faith in her ability to get off more than a single shot, if that, which was not saying anything about her ability to kill or even hit her target, so when Wayne tied the final knot in his rope barrier and started up the road, relief suffused her—

—and built a fire—

—using wood he collected from the trees along the path up to the ledge, a heavy armload that he arranged into a larger fire than she would have thought wise, an almost inexplicable lapse of Wayne's part—unless he wanted to be visible; if so, it was a new strategy for him: his previous traps had depended on misdirection, on leading the Pack into thinking the two of them were someplace they were safely away from, which had become increasingly difficult as the Pack adapted to Wayne's tactics—frankly, Jackie had been shocked that the mall trap had succeeded as well as it had, because it had been so obvious, as obvious as any of his early efforts, so much so that the Pack must have assumed (if you could apply such a word to them; though they evidently had some process of cognition) it couldn't possibly be a set-up, and so had walked right into the middle of it—strictly speaking, there was no need for a fire, not yet, heat poured up from the ledge and would do so well into the night, while the Bridge's lights, a row of flame-shaped bulbs tracing the arc of each of the suspension cables, had blinked on as the daylight ebbed (one of those intermittent events that indexed the random status of what she already was referring to herself as the Old World's machineries), their bright glow traversing the spectrum from blue to red and back down to blue again, their light sufficient for Jackie to read her battered copy of *What to Expect When You're Expecting* if she wanted to (she didn't; she felt vaguely guilty about it, but she was too tired [and—tell the truth—afraid of what the book might tell her about the baby's stillness])—when you came right down to it, the fire was a beacon and a goad, Wayne's way of thumbing his nose at whatever members of the Pack might have survived the mall and guiding them across the Bridge—as she reclined against her backpack and accepted the peanut butter bagel Wayne passed her, Jackie thought, *This really is it, our last stand; after four weeks, we're making our stand.*

They ate dinner in silence—

—the way they did practically everything in silence, the last week or so— formerly, Wayne had been a talker of epic proportions, the kind of person you don't start a conversation with unless you've got, say, three days to spare, which Jackie had found mostly charming, because a lot of what he had to say was funny and interesting, and if she rolled her eyes, it was only when he started talking about whatever comic book he was currently infatuated with, which he could and would do in microscopic, mind-numbing detail—comics never had interested her, the secret exploits of men playing dress-up in what was essentially a consequence-free arena just hadn't appealed; although the length and depth of description and analysis Wayne lavished on them prompted her to second-guess herself once in a while; now, she wished she had read some of the titles Wayne had rhapsodized about (*The Dark Knight Returns* and *Batman: Year One* [but not *The Dark Knight Strikes Again*, that was so much overpriced crap] and *The*

Sandman and *Johnny the Homicidal Maniac* [whose title she wished she found funnier]) or at least paid better attention to his lectures on them, because they might have helped her understand what had happened to Wayne in the last month, since the bottom had dropped out of the world, the least manifestation of which was the drying up of the torrent of words that poured from his mouth, and the most dramatic example of which was...was crazy—

—then cleaned the guns—

—one at a time, Wayne stripping each of the pistols in turn while Jackie trained the rifle on the rope barrier, then the rifle as Jackie aimed the policeman's automatic—she could have broken each of the weapons down, cleaned and greased them, herself: Wayne had insisted she learn in case anything happened to him (which was a joke: did he really imagine that, at this stage, big and awkward as she was, she'd get anywhere without him? it was almost funny: the hugely pregnant woman, a smoking gun in either hand, fighting off the Pack), but the thick smell of the grease nauseated her, so she stood (reclined, actually) guard and let Wayne do things the way he not-so-secretly wanted to—

—and

settled down for the night—

—to wait and sleep, him taking the first watch, her the second—after she'd unrolled her sleeping bag and used her feet to push off her sandals, she looked at Wayne, sitting on the other side of the fire (to which he'd added even more wood, keeping it hot and bright), and asked, "When will they be here?" to which Wayne answered, "Hard to tell. If we're lucky, late morning, early afternoon," which surprised her: ambush or not, last stand or not, she would have expected that, if the Pack hadn't put in an appearance by first light, maybe a little later, the two of them would abandon their position, which, for all its advantages in terms of height ("Control the high ground": how often had Wayne repeated that?) was a dead-end: if the Pack made it through whatever Wayne had prepared for them on the Bridge, not to mention his improvised web, and surged up the road till they reached the path to the ledge, she and Wayne would be trapped (violating another of his mantras, "Always have a way out"); better, she thought, to keep their options open and retreat, trust Wayne's ingenuity to thin the Pack further—all of which she said to him, and none of which made a difference: "This is our best chance," he said, and while she argued, appealing to her mantra, "He who fights and runs away, lives to fight another day," Wayne was unmovable, and anyway her eyelids were sliding down, so she abandoned her argument until daylight and slid into her sleeping bag.

Jackie's sleep was light, troubled—

—because sleeping soundly was impossible at this stage of pregnancy; not on a rock shelf in a sleeping bag, at least; and because her dreams were vivid and disturbing; no surprise, so *What to Expect* assured her: pregnant women were subject to all kinds of anxiety dreams, a tendency compounded on her part by the last month's events, the long struggle to keep on the move and ahead of the Pack, which had given her unconscious a whole new vocabulary of unease and terror—

* * *

[—she was on that stretch of Route 9 where all the cars; two, three dozen; had come to a halt pretty much simultaneously, with the exception of a black SUV that had crumpled the trunk of the red sedan in front of it— she and Wayne peering through the cars' windows at their interiors, every one crowded by purple flowers, anywhere from one to four per vehicle, stalks thick and twisting as snakes, blossoms the size of sunflowers, a kind of plant she'd never seen, and while she was no expert, botany was a hobby—each flower an accumulation of overlapping petals, vaguely roselike except that each petal was four to six inches long, edges ragged, almost serrated, and a uniform eggplant hue; the flowers' centers obscured by clusters of closed petals that suggested mouths pursed for a kiss, an effect she found sufficiently unsettling to drop her eyes to the stems, parsley-green, woody, covered in coarse hairs, fan-shaped leaves tiny, almost vestigial— Jackie had studied the plants, looped around steering wheels, gearshifts, headrests, door handles, pedals, one another, through windows dusted with violet pollen, each car a separate terrarium, thinking that none of this made any sense: there was no way for this size of plant to survive in this kind of environment, deprived, as far as she could see, of food and water—before Wayne could stop her, she had grabbed the door handle of the car she was standing next to so she could open it and take a cutting from the flower whose blossom pressed against the window like a child's face peering out; but the stem held the door closed with surprising force, so that the best she could manage was opening the door a crack, not enough to reach the plant, just sufficient for a small cloud of pollen to puff out—then Wayne was there, pulling her back from the car onto the shoulder, though not before she'd inhaled some of the pollen, filling her nose with the astringent smell of lavender, which lingered for the rest of the day despite the fit of violent sneezing it precipitated—she had been annoyed at Wayne, not only for being so patronizing, but for reminding her that there wasn't much point in her taking a cutting—what was she going to do with it? she could put it under a microscope if they could find one, and then what? she was a college junior majoring in Biology and minoring in Psych: about the best she'd be able to do if she could study a slide of a purple flower would be to identify it as a plant—it wasn't as if she'd be able to offer any insight into their situation—she had stalked away from him as best she could, and answered his regular questions of how she was feeling with the same monosyllable, "Fine," which was pretty much true, except for the lavender smell (but that night she'd had dreams in which she was driving and her skin, which was incredibly itchy, so much so that she was finding it difficult to concentrate on the road, began to crumble beneath her fingertips, becoming powdery, dusty, and suddenly all of her was on the verge of coming apart—for a moment, she was aware of her entire body drying, loosening, streams of dust pouring from her hands, her chin, her fingers raining down over the steering wheel, her body dissolving against the seat, her feet reducing to powder in her shoes—she had time for the panicked thought that she couldn't breathe, then that didn't matter anymore, and she collapsed—and woke with heart pounding, the baby kicking in response to her excitement, but that was fine, fine, because it meant she was still here, still in her body—for a good half hour, she ran her hands back and forth over her skin, reassuring herself with every pimple, every blemish, every strand of unwashed hair, that she was whole, not coming apart—Wayne must have noticed, but he remained silent, and another week would elapse before Jackie had gained sufficient distance from the dream and its sensations to narrate it to him—but, to her surprise, he didn't have an interpretation ready, just grunted and didn't refer to it again)]—

[—that dream sliding into one in which she was in her parents' den with Glenn, who was drunk again… still: he'd brought the bottle of gin and the bottle of tonic out beside the couch so he wouldn't have to travel so far to refill his glass, along with a bucket of ice from which he scooped half-melted cubes to deposit in his drink when it became too warm—the end of the world, or something close, and he'd spent pretty much all of it submerged in alcohol, because who was going to tell him not to? her parents hadn't returned from the trip to Shop Rite that shouldn't have taken them more than two hours, three at most, and that they'd left for twenty-two, no, twenty-four hours before, kissing her and ignoring Glenn (as they had ever since they'd learned the news of her pregnancy), promising to be back soon, a promise something had prevented them from keeping, which had her nervous but not as upset as she should have been; she wasn't done thinking they might yet appear, despite what the t.v. had shown before the channels started blinking off, whatever horror they'd been covering replaced by the tranquility of an electric blue screen—when Jackie climbed the stairs to the living room and looked out its picture window, all she saw was their slice of neighborhood, the same as ever: no fires, no riots, no people dying from whatever it was was boiling the flesh off their bones (which had spread faster than the pundits' ability to hypothesize explanations for it: a new strain of bird flu had given way to a bioweapon; some kind of mutated smallpox; which was more plausible, given its unbelievable virulence; but if so, whoever had released it had miscalculated, because it had taken the planet in its grip in all of three days—terrorism had been supplemented by other, more fanciful explanations: rampant nanotech, set free during the mishap at that plant in Albany the week before; an alien virus, imported by one of the meteors that had streaked across the sky a few nights ago; and, of course, the Wrath of God, and never mind that global events bore little to no resemblance to what was described in the *Book of Revelation*: the preachers who insisted on this answer had been so practiced at adapting Biblical texts to their own ends it was no surprise they should be able to do the same in this case) (and what about those other pictures she and Glenn had seen, almost lost in the rush of things falling apart? that couldn't have been the shadow of something walking falling across that building in Chicago, could it? the thought was absurd: it would have had to be impossibly tall—but what had collided with Air Force One? those hadn't been wings, had they? equally ridiculous: you couldn't have a bird that size)—she gazed out the window and saw movement, a car speeding up the road—for a second, she was sure it was her parents, back from their trip at last, then she realized it wasn't their Subaru but a smaller car, a white Geo Metro, Wayne's car, which none of them ever stopped teasing him about, its engine straining as it raced along, and as she watched it, she was aware of something hovering over her, some badness preparing to fall on her and take her into its jagged gullet, and there was the opportunity for her to think, *Stay away, keep driving*, before, tires screaming, Wayne turned the car into her driveway, fishtailing half-onto the lawn, spraying chunks of dirt and grass—leaving the car running, he fell out of it and sprinted to the front door, hammering on it with both hands, shouting her name from a throat already worn hoarse—she remained where she was, hoping Wayne would race back to his undersized car and take away whatever catastrophe attended him, until she heard Glenn's slurred insistence that he was coming, for Christ's sake, keep your shirt on, so she crossed to the door, which Wayne had not stopped pounding on, fully intending to tell him to leave, whatever it was, it wasn't their problem (amazing to think that she could so completely turn her back on Wayne, whom she'd described as her best guy friend; after Glenn, of course; for years), but the instant she turned the lock, the door leapt open and Wayne was inside the house, shouting that she had to leave, now, there was no time—Jackie registered his smell, first, a heavy blend of copper and alkali: blood and fear, she realized as she took in his clothes, plastered and clotted with blood and other things (was that a piece of bone? that pink clump—)—This was already bad, and finally his words resolved themselves into sense and she placed her hand on his arm, wincing at the blood still fresh to the touch (what had happened to him?), telling him to relax, calm down, it was all right; but none of her reassurances reached him, he kept insisting they had to go and grabbed her by the arm, which was when Glenn found the top of the stairs and who knew what he saw? the guy he'd never stopped worrying about, the source of his anxieties about their relationship, come to carry Jackie away at last—she should have anticipated what came next, but despite his macho posturing, Glenn always had seemed to her fundamentally gentle, peaceful; still, there was nothing like a quart of gin-and-tonic to put you in touch with your inner linebacker, which he proved by barreling across the room, catching Wayne around the middle, and slamming him into the wall with sufficient force to drop them both to the floor—Wayne kept hold of Jackie as long as he could, tumbling her backwards onto the couch—now Glenn was covered in gore, too, and raising his fist to pummel Wayne, who managed to wedge a leg between the two of them and kick Glenn off him, almost to the top of the stairs—Jackie, her hands pressed over her stomach, was shouting for the two of them to stop it, this was ridiculous, but Wayne hadn't liked Glenn any more than Glenn had him; jealous, she knew, although she'd done her best to ignore the reasons fueling that jealousy—the two of them rushed together and went down in a tangle of arms and legs, grunting and cursing each other, and Jackie thought, *Great: watch Mom and Dad come home, now*—then the picture window exploded inwards and a massive, snarling shape was standing in the living room, shaking glass off itself the way a dog might shake off water—she screamed, feet kicking her away from it, right up onto the couch—there was an instant for her to register the sheer size of the thing, its bulk: it had to stand four feet at the shoulder, with a hump that arched its back another foot over that, its head big as a Thanksgiving turkey, its feet the size of diner plates; and to think simultaneously, *What's a hyena doing in upstate New York?* and *This is no hyena*—before it pounced on Glenn, who had paused, arm upraised, when the window blew in—the thing caught his extended arm in its blunt jaws and tore it off at the shoulder: the crack and snap of bone and rip of sinew combining with the jet of blood and the scream from Glenn's throat and the growl from the thing's, a bass roar with the shriek of a violin on top of it—the thing held Glenn's arm dangling from its mouth like a puppy with a chew toy, then tossed the arm to one side with a flick of its head and lunged at him, while Wayne scrambled out of the way, his face blank with terror, and Jackie joined her scream to Glenn's as the thing bulled him back against the wall and seized his head between its teeth, his voice climbing registers she wouldn't have thought possible, surely his vocal cords would have to give out—she didn't know how much more she could bear—the thing brought its jaws together; there was a pop and crunch like an egg surrendering to the pressure of a hand; and Glenn's scream stopped; although Jackie's continued, pouring out her horror at what she was watching at the top of her lungs—even when Wayne found his feet, stumbled across the living room to her, right past where the thing was busy feeding, almost slipped on a large piece of glass, took her hand, and started pulling her to the front door, which was still open, only to stop as a new sound flooded the air, a high-pitched cacophony like an orchestra out of tune, and dark shapes (who knew how many? twenty? thirty? more?) galloped up the road, almost to the end of her driveway—Wayne's hand trembled in hers as if he were being electrocuted; later, she would understand that his mind had been on

the point of breaking, some fundamental motor about to
snap its belt and seize up—she was taking in breath for
another scream, because it was hard to take in enough
air for a long scream when you were six and a half months
pregnant (courtesy of a bottle of Jack Daniel's and the
love of her life, who had just ended his life at the teeth of,
of—), when Wayne's hand stilled; she glanced at his face,
and what she saw reflected there, a change from vacant-
eyed terror to something else, stopped her voice—"Come
on," he said, pulling her away from the front door, across
the living room (the thing growling and snapping at them,
and, *Oh My God Glenn*), into the kitchen and the cellar
door, down the stairs and across the cellar to the oil tank,
with a stop at her father's workbench to grab a rag and
the box of long wooden matches Dad had had on his
workbench for as long as she could remember—overhead,
the floor thumped and creaked, more of the things
springing into the house—Wayne consulted the gauge
on top of the oil tank, and began unscrewing it—the gauge
turned once, twice, then stuck—he ran back to the
workbench for a wrench while above, the things whined
and growled, their claws skittering on the hardwood
floor—*Glenn*, she thought, *They're fighting over him, over
what's left of him*—Wayne had the gauge off; a thick,
petroleum odor filled her nostrils; and was dipping the
rag into the tank, first one half, then the other—he left
the rag hanging out of the tank and slid open the box of
matches—"Go to the outside doors and open them," he
said, selecting three matches, "but not all the way, just
enough to scope out the situation in the backyard"; she
did as he instructed, unlatching and shouldering up the
metal doors that led out of the cellar—the arc of yard she

could see was green and tranquil—"Good," Wayne said, "when I say 'Now,' throw open the doors and run for your neighbors' house, the yellow one," and before she could ask him how he expected someone six and a half months pregnant to do anything that might remotely resemble running, he was scraping the first match along the side of the box—it popped into flame, and without pause he touched it to the end of the rag—a tongue of fire licked the rag, and she was ten feet across the yard before Wayne shouted, "Now!" behind her, her belly and breasts swinging heavily, painfully; her legs protesting, threatening to cramp, already; her lungs burning; not looking back, because she didn't want to see the thing that killed her; she just prayed it would do so quickly; and Wayne was beside her, slowing his frantic pace to match hers, and they were at the edge of the yard when the oil tank blew, gutting the house in a yellow-orange BOOM that sent wood and glass spinning across the yard and triggered the gas tank beneath the window and, from the sound of it, Wayne's car—she could feel the heat from where she was, see the carcasses of she couldn't tell how many of the things sprawled around the house's wreckage—"Glenn," she said, but Wayne was urging her on—]—

   —once, she woke, saw Wayne sitting at the fire, and went back to sleep—

                  —and more dreams—[—they were inside the walk-in urgent-care building on Route 9, which Jackie had insisted they stop at for medical supplies and because they needed to attend to the slash zigzagging up Wayne's forearm, which she'd bound to the best of her ability but was worried was becoming septic: the skin around the black scab was yellow going to green, and the wound gave off a sweet smell that made her want to gag—at the very least, she wanted to locate a blister-pack of Zithromax for him; at most, if she could locate proper tools, debride it (the advantage of having [had] a nurse mother who was a frustrated doctor)—Wayne protested that he was fine, but went ahead of her through the building, a gun held in either hand, arms outstretched—Jackie had not yet decided she should be carrying a firearm, too, so she held the oversized flashlight they'd taken from her neighbors' house like a club; there was sufficient light in the corridors for her not to waste the batteries: although the fluorescent lights overhead were dark, the ceiling opened into skylights at regular intervals, which leaked in enough of the gray, rainy day outside to permit her and Wayne their search—she wasn't sure what, if anything, they would encounter in the urgent care's dim interior—she was reasonably certain they had gained sufficient ground on what she had started referring to as the Pack (following Wayne's lead; the name no doubt a comic book reference she wasn't plugged into) for them not to have to worry about coming face-to-snout with one of its snarling constituents—one or more of the strange purple flowers seemed more likely: almost all the cars they'd seen on their trek up Route 9 had been full of the plants; although that was the only place they'd seen them: the various stores they'd entered for food, clothing, and assorted other supplies had been empty (she'd thought she had caught movement from the corners of her eyes, but when she'd looked, there had been nothing—most likely, her nerves tricking her)—despite which, Wayne refused to abandon caution, leaping through every open door with both guns pointed ahead, then sweeping them to either side as he glanced around the room, before calling, "Clear," to Jackie, who found his performance amusing in a way she knew she shouldn't have; caution was warranted, and Wayne had proven his ability a number of times, from turning her house into a bomb, which had reduced the Pack's ranks by at minimum a half, maybe sixty percent, to the previous day, when he'd lured one of the Pack's outriders into the walk-in freezer at a McDonald's and trapped it there—it was just, there was an element of the performative to Wayne's actions, as if he were seeing himself doing whatever he was doing in the panels of a comic, illustrated by one of his favorite artists—the last week and a half's events had damaged Wayne in ways you didn't need a degree in Psych to notice (although you would need a post-doc to plumb their depths)—she might be overreacting to the changes he'd displayed in his behavior: a ruthless, fiendishly inventive violence directed principally at their pursuers; or she might be misreading his response to the extremity of the past eleven days, but she was uncomfortably certain Wayne had developed a split in his personality, possibly a rough reorganization of his psyche that allowed him access to areas of his self previously road-blocked by norms of upbringing, society, and religion, possibly an entirely separate identity—it was as if he were living out one of the scenarios he'd read about for years, which might be the reason for her impression that, unimaginable psychic trauma and continuing horror and anxiety aside, on some level, Wayne was enjoying this, the world reshuffled into an arrangement he could deal with more competently and confidently than his previous existence of minimum-wage labor and career stagnation, each day's priorities food, sleep, and movement—in the second exam room they entered, they found a locked cabinet that Wayne broke open; it was stacked with blister packs and bottles of antibiotics and other medications, which Jackie swept into the plastic shopping bag she'd taken from the Stop-N-Shop in great handfuls—in the third room, they found a steel box like an oversized pencil case that was full of scalpels, probes, and tweezers, as well as a dozen bottles of saline and an assortment of gauze bandages and rolls of surgical tape—"Jackpot," she said, (which had been her [dead] father's nickname for her until she'd turned twelve and refused to answer to it anymore; wiping her eyes, she choked down nostalgia)—she positioned Wayne with his arm on the edge of the room's sink, for the blood, and had him hold the flashlight with his free hand—he wasn't happy about having to put down the guns, but in the absence of any better source of light (there was no skylight in this room) there was no other option; he settled for balancing the pistols on the opposite side of the sink and instructing her to duck if anything came through the door, which she assured him would not be a problem—she rinsed the scab on his arm with saline, to moisten and loosen it, and went to work with the scalpel and probe, flaking away the crusted blood, easing the scalpel under more stubborn patches and levering them off, Wayne gasping as they tore away; once the wound was exposed, she used half a bottle of saline to irrigate it, washing out assorted pieces of debris in the process, and had Wayne bring the flashlight in close, so that she could study the cut, testing it as gently as she could with the probe, which made the light quiver, abandoning the probe for a pair of needling tweezers she used to pop a pocket of pus and lift a piece of something out of it (which she thought was a fragment of one of the Pack's teeth, and which she would have loved the chance to examine in greater detail, but which she didn't mention to Wayne, since he'd only remind her that she was a Biology student, not a world-renowned scientist who might be able to learn something helpful from the sample), after which she rinsed the pus out, surveyed the arm one more time, was satisfied, squeezed a heavy stream of antibiotic cream over the wound, and began bandaging it—Jackie had done her best not to look at Wayne's face as she was working, not wanting her focus to be compromised by the pain she knew she'd find twisting its features, but with his arm cleaned and tended to the best of her ability, not to mention enough drugs to knock out any lingering infection, she relaxed and glanced at him, smiling—to leap back with a shriek at what she saw: Wayne's face gone from the mouth up, shrouded in heavy oily blackness, as if someone had dumped a can of black paint over his head; except that, instead of running down his skin, this was staying in place—Jackie backpedaled out of the room, into the hall, colliding with one of the walls, Wayne following, saying, "What? What is it?" pointing the flashlight at her, then up and down the hall, then back to her, the glare dazzling, reducing him to a silhouette; despite which, she could see something behind and above him, a cloud of blackness, billowing out like a cape or a pair of wings—she held one hand over her stomach, the other over her eyes as Wayne finally lowered the flashlight beam to the ground, still asking what it was, what was wrong, and when she risked a look at his face, it was clear of whatever she'd witnessed (if it had been there to begin with), nor was there anything behind him—she dropped her hands, waving his continuing questions away with, "Sorry—I just freaked out," a response she knew didn't satisfy him but that he was willing to let stand in the interest of maintaining their lead on the Pack—so far as she could tell, he didn't suspect she'd seen what she had—whatever it was—].

In the early morning—

—three thirty—

—Wayne woke her for the second watch—

—which Jackie spent sitting close to the fire, died to a heap of embers, wrapped in her sleeping bag, because the night had turned colder than she'd expected, colder than any recently (forecast of an early winter?), the rifle whose name she had meant to ask Wayne, to satisfy her curiosity, on the ground beside her; although every fifteen minutes or so she'd pick it up and sweep the end of the Bridge with the telescopic sight, Wayne's rope trap jumping into focus, but all she saw were the couple of cars beyond the trap on the Bridge, whose lights continued their climb up and down the spectrum, blue to red to blue again—she checked Wayne, too: asleep, so far as she could tell, in his sleeping bag—her dreaming still clinging to her, Jackie found herself, not for the first time, trying to imagine what had happened to him, speculating on the tectonic shifts in his psychic geography—he had refused to narrate what had taken place before he fled to her house, whose blood and gore had been spattered over him, but she knew that his mother stayed at home, and chances were good that his father and younger sister would have been there with her; since he wouldn't answer her questions about any of them, it seemed likely that they were dead, that the Pack had burst in on Wayne and his family and torn them to pieces in front of him—which begged the question, *How had he escaped?* (not to mention, *Where had the Pack come from in the first place?*)—she suspected the answer was some variety of chance, dumb luck: maybe the Pack had come in through the back of Wayne's house, allowing him to run out the front door; maybe he'd fallen down the basement stairs and been able to sneak out the garage; it was possible his father or mother had created a diversion, sacrificed themselves to allow him to reach his car—that kind of trauma, combined with another close brush with the Pack in the form of the one that had killed Glenn, must have inaugurated some compensatory process, jury-rigged the freshly fractured fragments of his mind into an arrangement that would let him survive; and yes, she was aware that she was describing the ur-plot of any number of super-heroes' origins, the grievous psychic wound that gives rise to the costumed alter-ego, both answer to and continuing symptom of the trauma, but perhaps Wayne had reached for that template to keep what was left of his consciousness from flying off in all directions—how she wished she'd taken that class in Abnormal Psych this past semester, instead of putting it off for a future that hadn't come; although, would anything she would have covered in an undergraduate class have equipped her for this? and, more to the point, what was she looking for? to understand Wayne, or to try to cure him, which would consist of what, exactly?

returning him to the calm, talkative guy she'd known half a million years ago?—could she afford that? would that Wayne be able to help keep her and her baby safe the way this Wayne (whom she thought of sometimes as Batman and sometimes as the Shadow; although she mentioned neither name to him), who apparently remembered every trick and trap he'd read in *Soldier of Fortune* and the *Getting Even* books, had proven he could?—the question was rhetorical; though how much safer was she with someone whose personality continued to drift in darker directions (or whose secondary personality seemed to be subsuming his first)? someone who; what was the right word? possessed? was possessed by? whatever the oily shadow that had masked his face, stretched behind him like a cloak, was, because however much she'd done her best to convince herself that she'd undergone some variety of hallucination, she knew that wasn't the case: she had seen what she'd seen, which she thought might have been drawn out from wherever it hid by his pain, by the stress of having to hold the flashlight on the wound Jackie had reopened and picked through—in the two and a half weeks since, she'd kept on the lookout for it, but the closest she'd come to seeing it again had been last week, when she'd awakened from yet another dream of Glenn's dying scream to see Wayne leaning against the wall opposite her, an enormous shadow sprawling behind him—she'd sat up, heart jolting, only to discover it was a trick of the light (she thought)—so far, Wayne hadn't shown the slightest sign that he knew that she knew; although, how could she be sure? and she wondered if he were even aware of the darkness shadowing him—it was funny: you would have thought that here, now, in the country of fundamental things, she would have been able to turn to Wayne and ask him what was going on, and he would be able to answer her as directly, but no, she couldn't risk alienating him, making him feel she'd discovered a secret he wished to keep concealed, because what would she do if he abandoned her?—it was like when she'd learned definitely that she was pregnant, a pale blue plus confirming what her stomach had been telling her for weeks: you would have expected the gravity of the situation to have compelled her and Glenn, her and her parents, to talk about what mattered, but the opposite had been the case: Glenn hadn't been able to bring himself to say anything, as if he were afraid that putting words to their situation would be an irretrievable admission on his part, and so had retreated behind vague assurances and trying to have sex even more, since there was no point in worrying about protection now, which she had gone along with, even if they were in his car in the parking lot of the community college, because at least it was contact—as for her parents, they had refused to follow their initial expressions of dismay and (reluctant) support with anything—ironically, it had been Glenn's father, who had gone up one side of them and down the other, leaving the two of them in tears before ordering them the hell out of his house, and who had called at least once a week demanding to know what was going on, who seemed, in retrospect, the most honest of them all, the best able to express his feelings—no, the pressure of events didn't make conversation any easier; if anything, it made significant communication almost exponentially more impossible—all Jackie could say with any surety was that Wayne's shadow was connected to everything else, to the plague(s), the purple flowers, the Pack (which, to answer that other begged question, she had no explanation for: what they were, let alone where they'd come from; how they'd arrived in upstate New York pretty much overnight—in too many ways to count, they didn't make sense; she had watched enough specials on *Nature* and *Nova* to know that predators this size and activity would require an enormous amount of food, which, as far as she could tell, was not available: she and Wayne had encountered only a handful of bodies in their travels [everyone else, she assumed, consumed by the virus she'd seen melting people's faces on CNN, which must have continued its work right down to the bones; although that was another problem], hardly enough to sustain even the Pack's reduced numbers, and they certainly didn't appear to have much interest in vegetation; though it was possible, she supposed—nor was there much sense in them pursuing her and Wayne for as long as they had: neither of them would make much of a meal for the Pack, and surely the animals[?] should have learned to associate following them with pain and death—it was like being caught in one of those z-grade science fiction movies where spectacle and suspense trumped logic and consistency: *Last Stand Against the Pack* or somesuch), all of them pieces to a jigsaw they'd lost the box to— during the second to last day of the week of rain, when the sky had delivered itself with such force it had been impossible to see anything out of the windows of the house they'd sought shelter in (whose driveway was occupied by a minivan filled with the largest example of the purple flowers they'd encountered yet), and the roof had creaked ominously with each gust of the wind, she and Wayne had diverted themselves by inventing explanations for what had befallen the world, the more fanciful, the better: God had decided that the apocalypse proposed in *Revelation* wasn't sufficiently *au courant*, and so had pillaged paperback thrillers for something with more panache; monsters had broken through from the other side of the mirror, Alice's Looking-Glass Land on acid; this world had intersected some other dimension, another Earth or even series of Earths, each of them radically different, and everything had become tangled (Wayne had coined the term "quantum rupture" for this scenario); the collective unconscious, the *Spiritus Mundi*, had burst, disgorging nightmares by the score—at one point, excited by what had felt like the resurgence of the old Wayne, the one with whom she could talk about anything, Jackie had tried to verbalize the feeling that had refused to abandon her since the catastrophes had begun: that somehow all of this was contingent, none of the changes that had contorted the world permanent, not yet—the best she could manage to explain the sensation was to compare it to the way she'd felt after her best girlfriend, Elaine Brown, had been killed by a drunk driver on her way home from her job at Dunkin' Donuts the year before: for about a day after her parents had sat her down at the kitchen table to tell her, Jackie had been absolutely convinced that Elaine's death was not yet set in stone, that there was some way for her to change things, if only she could figure out what it was—she'd been in shock, yes, but it was as if that blow to her system had brought her temporarily closer to the machinery of the world, allowed her to feel the peeling away of this course of events from other possibilities—the sensation she had now was different mostly in terms of magnitude and duration: when Elaine had been killed, it had been like standing next to a small motor, a motorcycle, say, for twenty-four hours or so; this was like standing beside railroad tracks while a three-engine freight train rumbled past, night and day, for weeks—Wayne had named the feeling "quantum divergence," (an awful lot of quanta flying around that day), which sounded impressive but didn't really mean what he wanted it to—it was, Jackie said, like being able to feel the Fates changing the weave of the world—whatever name you gave her awareness, whether it was anything more than a peculiar effect of profound shock, a milder version of the transformations that were altering Wayne (for all she knew, it was a well-documented response to trauma), the problem with her conviction of the freight train of events rattling away from alternate scenarios was its utter uselessness: after all, what could she do about it? it wasn't as if she had the ability to reverse events, to cause the Fates to loosen what they'd woven and start again (though secretly she wondered if, somewhere, there might be a door that would open back to the world she'd known)—his attempt at naming it aside, Wayne hadn't known what to say to her sensation, and the conversation had moved on to other topics, to the baby, and how much longer till Jackie was due, and what were they going to do when she was ready to give birth?—at the time, she'd hoped they'd be able to use the facilities at Vassar Hospital, at which, at the rate they were going, she projected they'd arrive around the time the baby was about to come, and if the Pack had been defeated, killed by then, there would be no reason they couldn't set up camp in it; there was a lot to be said for staying in a hospital—but they had fled up Route 9 faster than she'd anticipated; the Pack had proven more wily and ever-more-difficult to kill, and now they would have to try one of the hospitals in Kingston (if there were any point to it; if the baby were still alive; if her body didn't go into labor before then and deliver a stillborn child)—*Enough*, she thought, one hand rubbing her stomach in broad circles, as if it were a lamp and she summoning the genie; *Be all right*, she told the baby, *be all right*—funny, how much you could want something that intimidated the hell out of you, that you hadn't wanted in the first place but had felt powerless to refuse (thank you, twelve years of Catholic school), that had wrenched the wheel from your hands and turned your life onto an unexpected, unpaved road; talk about quantum divergence—she remembered the first time she'd felt the baby move, the first time she'd been sure, a flutter that had simultaneously freaked her out and thrilled her, and which had grown into kicks and jabs and using her bladder as a personal trampoline—the emotion that had grown up in response to her pregnancy had been different than what she'd expected: there had been none of the treacly sentimentality she'd been sure would ooze through her; instead, what had sprouted in her had been more basic, primitive, even, a deep connection to the child pushing out her belly, as if she could feel the umbilicus tying them together—the emotion had been supplemented by others: anxiety, mostly, and teary pathos, and occasionally profound contentment, as solid and heavy as a stone—*Be all right*, she told the baby, *be all right*.

Just before dawn—

—the sky filling with light, indigo paling to dark blue, the faintest stars fading out—

—**t h e Pack came**—

—their arrival heralded by the blat of a car alarm, which, she realized, Wayne must have rigged for exactly this purpose—in an instant, she had hefted the rifle to her cheek and one of the Pack leapt into focus; she moved the gun back and forth and saw two behind that one, and one more bringing up the rear, the four of them about ten feet behind the rope barrier, making their way slowly, placing each plate-sized foot with care, stopping to sniff the road in front of them, pausing to study the Bridge's support cables—there was enough time for Jackie to verify her initial count a second, a third time, and once she was certain that the four things she saw were the Pack, that was it, there were no others padding along behind them, her heart lifted with a fierce joy and she thought, *Four, there are four of them; we can do this; Wayne was right; we can be free of them, finally*—they were in rough shape, these four; it looked as if they'd pulled themselves from the wreckage of the trap at the mall: their hides were decorated with cuts, slashes, burns; patches of hair had been torn and scraped away; flaps of skin hung down like streamers; the one she'd focused on first appeared to have something wrong with its left eye, which was crusted with dark blood, while the one bringing up the rear was trailing its left back leg behind it—that they had survived made them the fittest, yes, thank you, Mr. Darwin, but watching their cautious advance, Jackie was reminded of her grandmother's dog, a poodle that had been old when she was a child and had grown steadily more gray, more infirm, more trembling and tentative each year, and if her heart wasn't moved to pity; the last four weeks had insured the impossibility of that; the association tempered her joy—*It's time to end this*, she thought, and turned to wake Wayne, who was (of course) already up and jamming pistols into his jeans, slipping the strap of his bag-of-tricks over his head, his face still—he crouched beside her, holding a third pistol out to her: "In case one of them makes it past me," he said as she took it, checked the safety, and set it on the rock beside her—he reached for her backpack, dragged it around for her to lean on: "Take the one to the rear," he said, "and any others that try to escape," and before she could answer, he was running away from her, heading back along the ledge—holding the rifle aloft with her right hand, Jackie eased herself up and down, until she was lying against the backpack, then brought the rifle into position, fitting the stock against her shoulder, anchoring it against the meat to take the kick, which Wayne had assured her wasn't that bad—she looked through the sight and there were the Pack, stopped in their tracks, their hackles raised; she could hear them, a deep bass note like a viol whose strings were frayed out of true, and she curled her finger around the trigger, ready for them to panic and flee, reminding herself to squeeze, not pull, and wondering if she would be able to hit, let alone stop, any of them—Wayne was running down the road toward the Bridge, his hands empty, and when the Pack saw him, the note they were holding rose to a ragged shriek, drowning out whatever Wayne was shouting at them; taunting them, no doubt, urging them on (and a part of her wondered why that should work, why animals would respond to insult, and she wondered if they weren't animals, but wasn't sure what such a question implied, because she couldn't imagine machines being bothered by Wayne's provocations, which left what? people? which was ridiculous).

It was over quickly—

—or so Jackie would think afterwards—while everything was taking place, it seemed to occur with agonizing slowness, almost a series of tableaux that shifted with each change in the Bridge's lights:

violet, and Wayne was in mid-run, his mouth open, his hands out to either side of him, the leader of the Pack's jaws tightening into a snarl that was strangely close to a grin, the others stepping forward;

blue, and Wayne was stopped, no more than twenty feet from the rope barrier, which, seen against the Pack drawing closer to it, seemed fanciful, a child's approximation of a more substantial arrangement;

green, and the leader was crouching to jump, Wayne's hands were still empty, the rear member of the Pack had ceased moving forward and appeared to be considering retreat; Jackie had its shortened head in the crosshairs;

yellow, and the leader was in the air, Wayne's hands were full of the pistols he was pointing not at the thing hanging suspended before him, but the pair behind it; the rearguard had turned to bolt, jerking its head out of the target, showing Jackie its neck;

orange, and the leader had struck the web and been caught in it, the ropes sagging but holding it up; the ends of Wayne's pistols were flaring white as he emptied them into the middle two members of the Pack, which lurched forward even as he blew their heads to pieces; the remaining thing was in the process of swinging itself around to flee, exposing the back of its head to Jackie's aim and she squeezed the trigger, the rifle flashing and cracking and slamming back into her shoulder, almost tearing itself out of her hands;

red, and she was struggling the sight back to her face, trying to find the last member of the Pack before it was too far away, hoping for one more shot, maybe she could wound it, cripple it and Wayne could finish it, but she couldn't see it, it was gone, and she swept the sight back and forth and there it was, its legs splayed out, the front of its head gone, shattered, and for a moment she was so happy she wanted to shout out loud, and then she thought of Wayne and searched for him, her finger hovering over the trigger;

orange, again, and she saw that Wayne had abandoned the pistols, cast them to either side, and was walking towards the last member of the Pack, which had not succeeded in disentangling itself from Wayne's rope trap and which twisted and writhed, biting the air in its frustration; she thought, *What the hell?* and aimed for the thing's chest; but

yellow, and something was wrong, the sight was dark; she drew back from it, blinked, and looked through it, again;

green, and she saw that Wayne was wearing a cape, that he was trailed by a length of blackness that billowed behind and to either side of him, across which the green light rippled and shimmered;

blue, and Wayne was standing in front of the thing, his head covered by the same blackness, except for his mouth, which was saying something to the thing that scrambled to get at him, and Jackie should have been able to read his lips; she had always been good at that; but she couldn't believe what she was seeing;

violet, and Wayne had reached out arms coated in black, seized the last member of the Pack's jaws, and torn its head apart, the thing convulsing as blood as dark as whatever it was enshrouded Wayne geysered from its neck—without thinking, Jackie centered the crosshairs on Wayne's chest, on the darkness that she could swear was undulating across it, that, God help her, was twitching towards the blood misting the air, and time became a room she could walk around in, sorting out the multitude of voices screaming in her head: one of them shouting, "What the fuck!" and another, "What are you doing?" and a third, "How are you going to survive without him?" a fourth, "You owe him," and a fifth, "What *is* he?"—her finger light on the trigger; if she were going to do this, it had to be now; in another second, Wayne would notice what she was doing—then the lights went out on the Bridge, plunging her view into shadow, and the baby chose that moment to kick, hard, a blow that made her say, "Oof!" and release the trigger, and then whatever Wayne had set up on the Bridge detonated in a burst of light and sound, a brilliant white CRUMP that had her ducking behind the backpack, hands over her head, the rifle dropped, forgotten—the air around her convulsed with the force of it; the rock behind her shuddered as the surface of the Bridge fell away to the river below, support wires snapping like overtightened guitar strings, shreds of metal, shards of pavement, a steering wheel raining around her as the Bridge groaned—Jackie risked a glance and saw it sagging inwards, its back broken, the forces it had balanced unleashed upon it—the suspension cables trembled, the towers leaned towards each other and she was sure the entire structure was going to twist itself asunder—the baby kicked again, a one-two combination, and she took what shelter she could behind the backpack, while the ledge continued to vibrate and the moan of thousands of tons of metal protesting its end echoed off the hills above her, making the baby squirm, and she covered her stomach with her hands, curling around it as best she could, saying it was all right, everything was all right—

    —and after, Jackie set out north—

                        —past another trio of cars offering their floral inhabitants the same view day in, day out—she was accompanied by Wayne, who had reappeared while the Bridge was not done complaining (though it didn't fall: its towers canted crazily; its cables were too taut at the ends and too slack in the middle; and there was no way it was passable; but it still joined one shore to the other), and who was free of his black, what would you call it? costume?—she settled for accompaniment, awkward but accurate—in response to her question, he answered that yes, that was the end of them, but they had better get a move on: Kingston was a long way off, and who knew what this side of the Hudson would be like?—If he knew that Jackie had held him in her sights, cradling his life as she cradled the life of the baby who hadn't stopped reminding her of its presence these last hours, (which meant that [maybe] she could relax about it), or if he suspected the questions that balanced at the very limit of her tongue, threatening to burst forth with the slightest provocation, or if he guessed that she walked with one hand jammed into the sweatjacket she'd tugged on because she'd hidden the third pistol there, telling him it must have been carried off the ledge by the force of the explosion, Wayne gave no sign of it.

By nightfall, they had traveled far.

ABOUT THE EDITOR

JOHN JOSEPH ADAMS is the series editor of *Best American Science Fiction & Fantasy*, published by Houghton Mifflin Harcourt. He is also the bestselling editor of many other anthologies, such as *The Mad Scientist's Guide to World Domination*, *Armored*, *Brave New Worlds*, and *The Living Dead*. Recent and forthcoming projects include: *Help Fund My Robot Army!!! & Other Improbable Crowdfunding Projects*, *Robot Uprisings*, *Dead Man's Hand*, *Operation Arcana*, *Wastelands 2*, and *The Apocalypse Triptych: The End is Nigh*, *The End is Now*, and *The End Has Come*. Called "the reigning king of the anthology world" by Barnes & Noble, John is a winner of the Hugo Award (for which he has been nominated eight times) and is a six-time World Fantasy Award finalist. John is also the editor and publisher of the digital magazines *Lightspeed* and *Nightmare*, and is a producer for *Wired's* The Geek's Guide to the Galaxy podcast. Find him on Twitter @johnjosephadams and at johnjosephadams.com.